continued . . .

TITLES BY FAITH HUNTER

The Jane Yellowrock Novels

Skinwalker
Blood Cross
Mercy Blade
Cat Tales
(a short-story compilation)
Raven Cursed
Have Stakes Will Travel
(a short-story compilation)
Death's Rival
The Jane Yellowrock World Companion
Blood Trade
Black Water
Black Arts
Broken Soul
Dark Heir
Blood in Her Veins
(a short-story compilation)
Shadow Rites
Cold Reign
Dark Queen

The Soulwood Novels

Blood of the Earth
Curse on the Land
Flame in the Dark

The Rogue Mage Novels

Bloodrings
Seraphs
Host

DARK QUEEN

A Jane Yellowrock Novel

Faith Hunter

ACE
New York

ACE
Published by Berkley
An imprint of Penguin Random House LLC
375 Hudson Street, New York, New York 10014

ISBN: 9781101991428

First Edition: May 2018

Printed in the United States of America
1   3   5   7   9   10   8   6   4   2

Cover art by Cliff Nielsen/Shannon Associates
Cover design by Katie Anderson

To Jessica Wade, at ACE/Penguin Random House,
with all my thanks.

ACKNOWLEDGMENTS

The HUBS. For EVERYTHING.

Teri Lee, Timeline and Continuity Editor Extraordinaire, for the tight reins and careful details. All the changes . . .

Norman Froscher for the wine suggestions.

Margot Dachuna for the French.

Mindy "Mud" Mymudes, Beta Reader and PR.

Donald Kirby, daddy to a fierce Monster, Druid or witch, writer and gay man, who was my sensitivity reader and beta'd all the scenes with werewolves, queens, and LGBT.

Let's Talk Promotions at ltpromos.com, for managing my blog tours and the Beast Claws fan club.

Lee Williams Watts for being the best travel companion and PA a girl can have!

Beast Claws! Best Street Team Evah!

Carol Malcolm for the timeline update.

Sheila Moody for the really good copy edit. Best one in ages!

Melissa Gilbert for the character history! 330 pages and still growing!

Mike Pruette at celticleatherworks.com for all the fabo merch!

Lucienne Diver of The Knight Agency, as always, for guiding my career, being a font of wisdom when I need advice, and for applying your agile and splendid mind to my writing and my social presence.

Cliff Nielsen . . . for all the work and talent that goes into the covers.

Poet and writer Sarah Speith for giving me Jane's medicine bag. It is still perfect!

As always, a huge thank-you to Jessica Wade of Penguin Random House. Without you there would be no book at all!

CHAPTER 1

I Killed the Only *U'tlun'ta* in NOLA

I had been in my bed for all of one hour, and though the scent of Bruiser from the sheets and from his boxing gloves tied to my bedpost usually filled my head with calm, today his personal aromatherapy wasn't working. I had rolled over half a dozen times trying to find a comfortable spot. Now the covers were twisted around me, my hair was tangled in a knotted mess, trapping me, and I was ready to explode. I resorted to punching my pillows in growing irritation, not that it helped. "I should give up and find something else to punch. Someone else to punch," I muttered, thinking of Leo Pellissier, the Master of the City of New Orleans.

My attitude was so bad that my Beast retreated into the deeps of my mind to get away, her paws padding in a jog. "Coward," I snarled at her. Being two-souled wasn't easy for either of us.

A soft knock sounded at the front door. *Tap, tap, tap, tap. Tap, tap, tap, tap.* The first tap in each repetition more forceful than the others, but barely loud enough to hear through the closed bedroom door. Maybe a preacher. Or a steak salesman. Beast stopped and looked back at me. Excitement zinged through her. *Man who sells meat? Cow at door?*

I chuckled internally. *Could be,* I thought back at her. *Or a proselytizing vacuum cleaner salesman.* Did vac salesmen even exist now?

Is vacuum good to eat? Or salesman? Both? she added hopefully.

The knocking came again, a bit louder. *Tap, tap, tap, tap. Tap, tap, tap, tap.* It was a rhythm that Aggie One Feather, my Cherokee Elder, might have drummed. My partner and soon-to-be adopted brother Eli hadn't answered the door, and I could hear shower water upstairs. I grinned and I was pretty sure I was showing teeth. Lots of teeth. I wondered if they were all mine, but I didn't really care. I was sleep deprived and ornery and if this was some vamp's minions calling to cause trouble about the arrangements for the upcoming Sangre Duello, that might actually make my day. I could use a good fight. A blood challenge to the death between Leo and the European emperor and all their pals would surely provide that, but until then, I had the knocking visitor.

I threw off the covers and twisted my long black hair back in a knot. In the black yoga pants and black T-shirt, I looked like a ticked-off ninja. I picked up a fourteen-inch-long vamp-killer I kept on the nightstand and tore open the bedroom door. The knob slammed into the wall behind as I reached the foyer. Eli stopped on the stairs behind me, shower-wet, a weapon at his side. My partner in protect mode. I shared my grin at him and his brows lifted, an infinitesimal gesture that meant loads for the former (and forever) Army Ranger. I didn't bother to try to figure out loads of what. I peeked out the front, through the tiny slice of clear glass in the layers of bullet-resistant and stained glass window.

On the other side of the door stood a man, facing the street. He was tall, lean, maybe six feet three. Straight black hair hung long, down his back to his hips. Golden skin showed at his clean-shaven jaw, which looked tight with frustration. He was wearing black slacks and black blazer jacket. A white dress shirt collar showed from this angle and he was wearing polished leather cap-toe oxford shoes, what my boss, the Master of the City and walking, talking fashion plate, called a Balmoral. Imported shoes.

It griped my goat that I knew all that. Just another useless thing I had learned hanging around vamps. Another way they had changed me and my life. My irritation flamed.

I yanked open the door. The air swept his scent in. It was vaguely floral. A scent that teased at the back of my mind. *Tsalagi*. Cherokee scent. Beast surged into the forefront of my brain, landing crouched on silent paws. The man turned.

He had yellow eyes.

Beast thought, *Littermate*.

What? I said to her.

"Hello, *e-igido. Dalonige' i Digadoli*," the man said, his expression soft but intent. *"Nuwhtohiyada gotlvdi."*

How did he know my Cherokee name? I knew those last words: Make peace with me.

The air swirled inside and back out. The man's nostrils widened as he took a breath. Taking in my scent. His face changed—fear, horror, revulsion, dread. *"U'tlun'ta,"* he whispered, the word meaning liver-eater, black-magic skinwalker. Evil. Faster than I could follow, he drew a weapon, centered it on my chest.

Inside me Beast tore through, doing . . . something.

In a single instant, the man fired.

Beast screamed.

Time stood still.

The round exiting the weapon was stopped an inch from the barrel. The killer was frozen. Everything was frozen except me. Beast had bubbled time, taking me outside of normal space/time/relativity physics. She had saved my life. Again. "Thanks," I muttered aloud to her.

She snorted, a half chuff, half growl, staring through my eyes at the man, even as the headache/bellyache/muscle aches hit. It was like a tiny bomb going off behind my left eye combined with a case of the flu, and if the two most recent time-bubbling experiences were an indication, it would only get worse. For now, I was okay-ish. Not perfect. Not totally okay. But able to function.

The stranger was firing one of the new Glock GDP-20s, a military-issued police service weapon. I looked closely to see a hollow-point round. Somehow, being shot at calmed my anger. Using my vamp-killer and muscle power, Beast knocked the round down, changing its trajectory to impact the floor molding. The sound of silver-plated vamp-killer blade hitting lead was a dull tang in the Gray Between. The wood stood the best chance of stopping the round and the hole could be filled with wood filler and painted over. Eli was good at that kinda stuff.

I stepped into the man's reach and, still using the blade, lifted his notched lapel to reveal a pocket beneath, heavy with a case about the size of a pack of playing cards. Without touching his body, I pulled out the case and opened it to reveal a badge.

"Well. That figures," I muttered, maybe talking to God, maybe talking to whatever evil spirit had cursed me. "Like I needed the candy sprinkles of a gun-happy cop dumped over my blood duel ice-cream cone." The badge was a PsyLED shield, issued to the Psychometric Law Enforcement Division of Homeland Security, the cops that police paranormals. Like me. But I'd think not even PsyLED would send someone to kill me at my own front door. In the middle of the day. With tourists walking across the street. Maybe the badge was a fake? I looked at the guy. He didn't look like a killer. There was nothing forgettable about him and most assassins worked to be average and unmemorable. His clothing was well-tailored but more Brooks Brothers and Men's Wearhouse than Armani. His eyes were wide. Terrified. And he was firing one-handed, his left still rising for a standard two-hand grip. Panic-shot.

Not good ambush hunter, Beast said.

Right. This had been surprised, messy, not well planned. I went back over what had just happened. An assassin or a PsyLED cop came to my door. A Cherokee, one with yellow eyes, who spoke at least some Tsalagi, knew my full Cherokee name, and asked me to make peace. Then freaked out over my scent, called me a nasty name, and shot me. Yeah, that covered it. I leaned in closer and searched his irises for the telltale shimmer of amber contact lenses. There was nothing. A frisson of shock lanced through me and I shoved down on it.

Yellow eyes. Floral scent. Beast calling him littermate. What did Beast mean? My breath was still coming fast. Getting shot at will do that to a girl. I shoved down on my reaction and slipped out of the assassin's reach without touching him. Last thing I needed was to drag a killer inside a time bubble with me.

Beast said nothing, but I felt faint tremors running through her.

My belly wrenched, a sick, snaking pain, as if my guts were knotting, a reaction to bubbling time.

I stood barefooted in the entry and studied him. The man was handsome. Golden skinned, lightly tanned even in winter. Fine lines at the corners of his eyes. Maybe twenty-five, showing age from spending time in the sun. Or older if he had a good beauty regimen. I sniffed again. Definitely floral, very delicate and faint. Aftershave? Traces of a woman's perfume? I studied his jaw. Not shaved. But the clean, hairless jaw of some tribal males. The electric shock trying to flood me intensified. My whole body was aching.

I looked up the stairs. Eli, wearing only damp workout shorts, had a steady aim on the man, just over where my shoulder would have been. He had already fired, the round in midair. My bro had fast reflexes after drinking vamp blood for healing. His round would enter the man's right eye, killing him instantly.

A man had come to my door and tried to kill me. I should let Eli do his job. Except . . . A cop, maybe even a real cop with real badge. Yellow eyes. Floral scent.

Skinwalker, Beast thought at me again. Demanding.

My shock settled. Just having the word spoken between us helped. "Yeah."

I climbed the stairs to Eli. I needed to talk to him before I did anything. I needed my partner's tactical and strategic experience. Mostly I just needed Eli Younger to

help me get . . . steady. To help me think. My belly seemed
a bit better, but the headache was getting worse and rational thinking wasn't easy. I knocked Eli's round down too,
until it now aimed at the floor. I stood in front of Eli, not
certain what to do. Eli would say I should pull him into
the time bubble with me. It was the most satisfactory tactic in this battle situation. But spending time in no-time
did bad things to genetic structures.

My own was a scrambled mess that might lead to death
someday from a brain tumor, a brain aneurysm, a stroke, or
maybe bleeding out through my damaged digestive tract.
The nausea and headaches were getting much worse much
faster, and after today, I had no doubt that they were part
of bending/bubbling time. Not that a doctor could tell me
what might happen to a skinwalker with damaged genes.
Until this minute I'd thought I was the only skinwalker
alive. I'd killed the only other one I had met in the last
hundred seventy years. He had been *u'tlun'ta*, killing and
eating and replacing people with his own shape-shifting
abilities. Black magic even worse than what I had done
when I killed Beast and pulled her soul inside with me.

Beast thought, *Prey is at watering hole. Attack or hide.*

It was the thought concept of a predator cat, a *Puma
concolor*, making me decide.

Bad use of Jane's minutes, she added, though Beast
had little concept of time except now, soon, later, before,
hungry, seasons, and moon cycles. Animals didn't follow
time as humans did.

Choose, she demanded. *Head hurts.*

I gripped Eli's right arm, pulling him into the time bubble. He stumbled and I caught him, shoving his weapon up
and away. "Jane?" he said, almost startled at the time
change. Almost but not quite. It was hard to startle one of
Uncle Sam's best, especially as he had been in the Gray
Between with me before. He looked at the unwelcome visitor. "Who?"

"Don't know. Wearing a PsyLED badge." I held up the
badge as proof. "Using the new Glock issued to PsyLED.
He speaks some of the language of The People. He called
me by my Cherokee name. And then called me *u'tlun'ta*."

"He smell like you?"

"No. Floral." My own scent was a challenge to most vampires, until the team leader accepted me. Then that one's underlings fell into line and accepted me too. But oral history, things people had told me about a skinwalker who had lived in New Orleans a century and more ago, hinted that at least one other skinwalker had smelled like flowers. At some point soon, I had to track down the vamp who had owned her and ask questions. In my copious free time. Right.

Eli frowned. He checked the altered trajectory of his round, patted my hand, telling me to not let go, which would drop him into normal time. He lifted a thigh rig from the floor and strapped it onto his shower-damp body and seated his weapon in its Kydex holster. He looked me over, seeing too much. "Your head?"

"Bearable."

Eli grunted. With one free hand, he gripped my arm, making sure we didn't separate. Together we pattered down the steps, back to the killer. "We still don't know if all skinwalkers can bubble time or if it's unique," he said, "part of you and Beast. We need to make sure he doesn't learn that you have that skill."

"It's on video footage at HQ," I said.

"Yeah. But that's in a time and place where witch magic could be playing tricks. Discussing that with cops is a battle for tomorrow. We play it by ear, wronged, in danger, and innocent." Eli looked the visitor over as if he was a piece of terrain to be taken from the enemy, staring into the yellow eyes, as if looking for contacts. Eli frowned. "Too bad I can't get his weapon away without pulling him into time with us. Let me get to the left side of the doorframe, weapon drawn, ready to fire. You get into your previous position, and let me go. Then you take the guy out. I'll take care that the weapon doesn't fire again."

"Okay. Modified kata guruma?" Kata guruma was a dramatic, vicious martial takedown.

"Okay by me. Use his hair. Grab his dumplings and give 'em a twist as you slam him down, but toss him inside. We got gawkers." He meant the tourists on the sidewalk across the street. "I'll have his weapon long before he hits."

I shrugged and put the vamp-killer and the PsyLED badge on the floor, out of the way, then stepped into position, my foot touching Eli's to keep him in my time bubble, my body and hands almost touching the stranger. Eli positioned his hands just above and beneath the killer's gun hand. "Now," I said to my partner. Eli moved his foot. Instantly I was alone in the Gray Between. My head spun and spiked with pain. I took a breath to keep from throwing up and blew it out. And dropped the Gray Between. Drew on Beast speed.

The overlapping gunshots sounded, blasting the silence away as I seized the lustrous, slick black hair instead of the back of his neck. Reached between his legs and seized his testicles in a crushing grip. Lifted high, as I pulled his head down low to my right side. And slammed him inside the house and into the foyer floor. Not a textbook move but good enough. All in one faster-than-human motion.

The house shook. The man made a breathless, squealing, squeaking sound. Eli was standing over him, holding the attacker's weapon and his own, both pointing at the man. Maybe a whole second had passed. He lay on the floor, his hands between his legs. Squeaking still. His golden-skinned face pale as death. His eyes rolled up.

"I will not"—I hesitated—"*nuwhtohiyada gotlvdi*. I don't make peace with assassins." I kicked his foot out of the way and closed the door on the startled cries of the onlookers and the winter air. Winter in New Orleans meant the high sixties, but still. It was the ecologically appropriate thing to do.

"I missed it. What happened?" Eli's younger brother, Alex, asked, running in from the living room. He hadn't answered the door. Probably playing some kind of video game and couldn't be bothered.

"Jane happened," Eli said, his dark skin picking up the lights through the layers of stained glass and bulletproof glass.

The man on the floor groaned. Eli patted him down

and removed a weapon from a leather ankle holster. From a small pocket built in the holster, he also pulled a tooth and held it out to me. The canine tooth was curved and sharp, nearly two inches in length. A big-cat tooth, longer and slightly more narrow at the root end than a *Puma concolor* tooth, though curved, like all Western Hemisphere big-cats. Whatever species, it was additional evidence that the man was a skinwalker. He carried the genetic material of his favorite animal to shift into in case of injury or near death. He might feel like he was dying, but he'd live. I curled my fist around the tooth. Ignored the bass drum pounding and the ice picks stabbing inside my head. Ignored the desire to hurl my cookies.

Alex brought up kitchen chairs. We all three sat in a small ring around the downed man and watched, as if he was a one-man play. Alex passed around ice-cold bottled Cokes—my favorite way to drink Coke now—and a bag of potato chips. I smothered a laugh at the picture we must have made. I chewed, watching. The man's color wasn't getting any better. "How long does it take to get over a testicle twisting?"

"With your grip?" Eli asked casually. "Days?"

Alex made a sound that was mostly "gack" and crossed his legs, suddenly pale even despite his mixed-race heritage.

"Three minutes till he can breathe?" Eli guessed. He reached out and took my wrist, guesstimating my pulse, still saying nothing in front of the outsider about my headache and nausea.

"Better cuff him," Alex advised. "As entertaining as this is, we got work to do."

"True," I said. "And I'm in my jammies."

"You went to the door in your PJs? Shame on you," Alex said.

"I know, right? I should comb my hair. Dress. Maybe even makeup. For company, you know."

"Girly stuff," Eli said at my makeup comment. Frowning, he dropped my wrist. "You get any sleep?" he asked, but really asking about my sickness.

"Not a lick." I touched my head and winced. "Of course,

now that I've exercised a little, I'm sleepy. And we have uninvited company and I can't go back to bed."

"Always the way," Eli said.

"Dude showed up unannounced, and tried to kill you. Double case of the rudes," Alex said.

The man on the floor gurgled.

"Ice pack?" I suggested.

"Nah. Let him suffer," Eli said. He bent forward and rested his elbows on his knees, hands together under his chin, watching the man's ribs try to work. Casually, he added, "He's turning blue."

"I see that," I said.

"You people are sadistic. I'm going back to my game."

"Shooting and dismembering nonhumans on video? Sadistic, much?" Eli asked, his words sorta mushy, due to his chin on fists.

"Totally not the same," Alex said, shaking his head, the long, tight curls around his face swinging. "Alien bugs. Exoskeletons. Antennae. Multiple legs. Green goo instead of blood." The curls stopped swaying. They were tangled, hanging in spirals like a shaggy mop. He needed a haircut. And a shave. Alex had a lot of whiskers on his dark-skinned chin.

I blinked, surprised. His masculine chin. His eyes were deep-set over sharp cheekbones. His shoulders were broad and his arms were well-defined under his T-shirt. Holy crap. He had been doing chores and helping to cook and clean up without being asked for months. Taking showers regularly. Joining us in weightlifting, martial art practice, and sparring workouts, and he had been to the shooting range several dozen times. Alex was . . . adulting. Stinky had grown up into a very nice-looking man.

"What?" he demanded when he caught me gawking, jutting out his chin, peeved. His tone was the one a teenager makes to meddlesome parents. He squinted his eyes and frowned, short-tempered and petulant. A child still.

"Never mind. Just a bad dream. Go back to your game." Alex stomped off.

"Kid's growing up," Eli said without looking up, reading my mind. "It's disconcerting."

"Yeah. It is." I picked up my vamp-killer and went to my room, setting the blade on the bedside table beside the nine-mil and bringing back my cuffs. "You cuff him. I'll sit on him in case he's faking."

"No way he's faking. Men do not turn that color from anything else. You cuff him."

I shrugged, bent over the man on the floor, grabbed his arm, and whipped him facedown. Stepped on his spine. Yanked up his arms. Cuffed him. He made a sound that let me know he had managed a breath. "He'll live. If he's a skinwalker he'll heal even if he has to shift. And I'm not feeling really chatty right now with a guy who tried to kill me."

The shooter was lying on the very dusty foyer floor, the dust well scuffed around him, smeared all over his nice pants and jacket. We had a renovation going, opening the attic into a third floor, and the dust had quickly become ubiquitous. Even Eli's super-neat streak couldn't keep up with it.

Eli said, "He had a big-cat tooth amulet. Like yours."

"Yeah. He did." I wore my tooth fetish on a gold chain around my neck, with the gold nugget that tied me metaphysically to the time and place I'd shifted for the first time as an adult. Most days, I hardly noticed the necklace; it was part of me. I also owned several fetish necklaces with the bones and teeth of other predators I might need to change into, and I'd added a few creatures to my collection recently. I had the ability to shift into prey animals of a similar mass, but Beast hated it when I did that. She was a carnivore and preferred to never be a prey animal. She was also grumpy and callously passive-aggressive. I tried to keep her happy.

I closed my door on Eli and the stranger and tossed my black jammies on the bed. I took a half dozen antacid tablets, four aspirin, and two Tylenol. Meds don't work on me like they do on humans, but at this point I was willing to try anything. I dressed in jeans and layered tees and stomped into an old, scuffed pair of Lucchese boots. They had started out a gorgeous green, but I hadn't made a habit of cleaning and caring for the leather, and the damp Louisiana air had left them sorta moldy on the outside. I wiped them down with a rag to reveal the color of the leather, which had weathered to a greenish charcoal. They looked like something I'd wear to a barn to muck out stalls. I really needed to pay them some attention. I combed and braided my hair and slashed lipstick on my mouth. Looked at myself in the mirror. Black hair. Amber eyes. Golden-copper skin.

The man had hair the same length and color as mine. I ran my hand down my braid. Same texture. He was Tsalagi. He was skinwalker.

I was no longer alone in the world.

Hope billowed up from some forgotten crevice deep inside me.

But like the last one I found, this skinwalker had tried to kill me too. I shoved down the useless traitor of hope and capped off the fissure. I would not waste emotion on the possibility of finding a skinwalker who didn't want to kill me. Hope was a lie.

Sometimes life sucked.

I dropped my braid and left my room. In the foyer, the chairs were gone. So was the man. Eli was carrying the stranger to the kitchen, a handful of long hair and the cuffs in his right hand, the man's belt in his left. The fancy shoes were getting scuffed as they dragged, and by his breathing, it was clear the carry position wasn't helping his cojones. The stranger had to weigh two hundred pounds, but Eli carried him as if he weighed forty. Eli swung him up and into a chair like a bale of hay and the guy landed with a thump. On his butt, but probably banging his damaged cojones on the wood seat. The man groaned.

"Been there, bub. Hurts like a mother," Eli muttered, recuffing the man's hands in front. "I'm making coffee and tea. You act like a normal polite human and I'll let you have some. And some aspirin. You act stupid and I'll let my sister at you again. Understand?"

The man didn't reply, but I swelled up with happiness. Eli had called me his sister, and neither the Cherokee adoption procedures nor the vamp ones had even started.

Alex, apparently over his pique, grunted behind me

and said, "My bro's getting all lovey-dovey in his old age."
I felt something deflate inside me, until he added, "Offering a coffee to a killer. So sweet."

"I didn't offer him the best espresso, just some coffee.
Standard American. Or one of Jane's cheaper teas."

I let the smile that had started at the use of the word
sister spread. This was way better than hope. This was
real. The thought of family settled me.

I heard a horn beep outside. Eli tossed the man's
badge, his wallet, his key fob, and a pack of gum on the
table. "PsyLED ID or a very good fake. Key beeped to a
government vehicle with government plates down the
street. Appears he drove here alone, but Alex's systems
are keeping watch on the exterior cams for a partner."

The man lifted his head. His eyes were squinted in pain,
but his breathing was slow and regulated as he tried to work
through the misery. Skinwalker healing was way better
than human. His color was returning. But he didn't talk.

I said, "While my brother makes us all something civilized to drink, I can duct tape your legs to the chair or
you can give me your word of honor that you'll be good."

The stranger sat up straighter and tossed his tangled
hair back. "Brother?" His voice was graveled with pain.
"Not by blood. Mixed race black and maybe Choctaw.
Not *Chelokay*." *Chelokay* was another way of saying
Tsaligi—Cherokee in the speech of The People. That was
intended as an insult, delivered without looking at Eli. Ignoring another warrior was an additional insult. "You're
u'tlun'ta," he said to me, pronouncing the word a little different from my own *hut-luna*, though close enough. It was
insult number three. On top of trying to kill me. Dude
was not the brightest bulb in the chandelier, obviously
being deliberately bad mannered to see if I'd go *u'tlun'ta*
on his ass. "But you didn't try to kill me," he said as if
thinking things through. "Why? Since I fired at you. And
how did you not get shot? There is no way I could have
missed."

He had not answered my question, instead muddying
the emotional waters with insults and turning the table
with his own questions. Basic reverse interrogation tactic.

Law enforcement tactic. I decided to roll with it for now. "You always shoot unarmed women and ask questions later?"

He looked away at that one. Shoulders tensing in shock. As if just remembering that part.

"In front of witnesses? There were people on the side-walk." My tone called him stupid.

His lips were firm and tight. I realized that he didn't know why he'd tried to kill me. He had reacted on instinct when he smelled me, just like vamps did. Interesting. Last time that happened I nearly had to kill a vamp in Sedona. Time before that I had to threaten Katie and then hurt Leo. "You ever met an *u'tlun'ta*? They smell like rotted meat."

His eyes widened in surprise.

Clearly I had hit the nail, and he had never met a liver-eater. I pointed to my chest. "I don't. I smell like preda-tor. Not pretty flowers like you. Not like dead meat. And I killed the only *u'tlun'ta* in NOLA."

"I saw the footage," he said, no inflection to tell me what he thought about me killing a massive half-human, half–sabertooth lion.

"Uh-huh." I had still shots. The video was Leo Pellis-sier's private in-house security footage. No way should this man have been able to get it. Yet his offhand reply told me he had really seen it. Not good.

Eli placed a mug in front of me. It was really a soup mug, white, with a picture of Santa Claus on it, the dia-logue bubble saying, "Jane Takes Care of My Naughty List." Below that was the body of a dead vampire, staked and his head removed.

The stranger's eyes took in the mug. "Cup's a little out of date, isn't it? You work for the Mithrans now."

I still killed vamps who got out of line. A lot of vamps. Either his intel was bad or he was being a pain in the butt. I was going for door number two, so I said nothing. Eli placed a tub of Cool Whip on the table and I used the soup spoon to dig out a glob of the white frothy stuff and place it on top of the tea. I added a similar amount of sugar from the restaurant-style pour-decanter and stirred.

Eli sat down and placed a cup at his side. Another one with a straw in it went in front of the killer.

"You don't think I'm going to drink that. It could be poisoned."

Despite the stabbing headache, which had developed razor edges cutting its way out of the left part of my head and into the middle of my brain, I chuckled softly. Eli gave me a twitch of a smile. We actually had a mug with the words YOU'VE JUST BEEN POISONED in the bottom, so you saw it only after you finished the drink. It was cute.

Eli pulled out a chair and turned it around, sitting, straddling it. He took his own weapon in one hand and his mug in the other and sipped. "We don't poison. We shoot, stab, cut, slice and dice, eviscerate, disembowel, and decapitate. Sometimes shoot and blow up our enemies. We've been known to bury our dead in the swamp. But we don't poison. Poison is wussy."

I laughed aloud and drank a gulp of the tea. It was a really good Bombay chai with fresh ginger, strong, and the caffeine might help the headache a bit. The nausea receded. "Now that we've laid out the consequences of trying to get feisty again," I said, "talk."

The stranger looked at me. His squint was less and his color was almost normal. He leaned in and sipped the coffee through the straw. "If it's poisoned, it's good poison," he said.

I thought about the muscle power of a skinwalker at full strength, and any weak link on the cuffs. "He's just about healed enough to get free. He'll be fast. And though you've had the hand of Uncle Sam in your training, he could be decades old. He'll have experience in multiple martial art forms."

"I've sparred with you, Babe. He's going no place fast, not without a hole in him and leaking a blood trail." Eli sipped, slouched, seeming relaxed, gun pointed at our violent visitor. "What she said. Talk."

The man ignored my partner, which showed stupidity on his part, as he studied me. "Not *u'tlun'ta*? So why do you smell of predator?"

"Talk," I said, so softly he would have missed it had he been human. "Now."

His eyes tightened in surprise. For sure he had golden eyes, not black, not eyes of The People, but eyes of a skin-walker. My heart ached. If he was a trap, he was a good one. "I had a speech all prepared," he said, a swift hint of humor appearing in those golden eyes, "and despite the unfortunate way we have made our acquaintance, I would like to speak the words."

I nodded. He leaned and sucked up coffee through his straw. Eli sipped. I gulped. Headache eased some more.

The man sat back and tossed a lost strand of hair from his face. It wasn't a feminine gesture. It stirred a memory in me, one that was tied to the Tsalagi and to my past. A memory of my true youth, before my grandmother had forced me into the shape of the bobcat and cast me into the snow to live or die. That had been on the Trail of Tears. *Nunna Daul Tsuny*. But the memory was from before that. Just the vision of a man's long hair being tossed back against a sunset sky.

Then the vision of golden hands braiding that hair before a crackling fire, the strands picking up the light of the comforting flames. My father's hair. My mother's hands. *Edoda* had let no one touch his hair but her. Braiding hair was a spiritual exercise for the Tsalagi, a sharing of power and energy. I had forgotten that. I had let lots of people braid my hair.

The visitor spoke, shattering the memory. "Few people outside of my family know this, and no one in PsyLED except my mentor, who keeps secrets of her own. It isn't in my PsyLED personnel folder. It isn't in my records. I'm sharing this with you so you will know I mean it when I say I come to make peace with you. I speak the truth."

As he talked, the cadence of his speech had changed, the rhythm altering. It was the unconscious linguistic dance of a speaker of The People speaking English.

"I am Cherokee skinwalker," he said. "I was named at birth *Nvdayeli Tlivdatsi* of Ani Gilogi, or Nantahala Panther of the Panther Clan. But the name was a thing of sadness, as the Nantahala River was only a memory, lost to our people since the *yunega* forced the tribal peoples away from their lands to the territories. And since the panthers had been hunted to extinction. It was a name of failure, of loss, a name I hated."

His eyes were holding mine, trying to read me, trying to tell me something, but I had no idea what. He shifted and his cuffs clinked softly as he rearranged his position. Eli's weapon followed, as if anticipating the movement.

"When I grew up, I took the name Ayatas Nvgitsvle, or One Who Dreams of Fire Wind, for the raging fires I saw in my dreams." His lips were chiseled, sharply defined, the tissue dry and smooth, and they moved in familiar ways when he spoke the Cherokee words of his name. The syllables were murmured, just as they ought to be. "I left home, from the Indian Territory, west of the Mississippi, and out to the Wild West, where I stayed for some years."

My eyes flew to the man's at the words *Indian Territory* and *Wild West*. Eli centered his weapon on the man's chest in a two-handed grip. I didn't have to ask if there was a round in the chamber. The use of the words suggested that the man was far older than expected. Maybe nearly as old as I was and I'd been around some one hundred seventy years, not that I remembered much about the first hundred fifty. He had called me *e-igido*. That felt important, though I couldn't say why, the word prying at my mind.

I sipped my tea, but I no longer tasted it. Wild West. Terms of an older man. Manners of an older man. Eyes of an older man, one who had seen too much, lost too much. Ayatas was old. Hope spiraled up again, signaling a desire I had forgotten I ever had. Hope, traitorous and volatile, insubstantial as smoke and as difficult to grasp. Hope was a well-baited trap.

"Let him talk," I said softly. I slurped again, positioned the tea a little to my side, pushed it away, and leaned in. I had his scent now. I had it when he was calm, had it fearful and angry and full of fight-or-flight pheromones, had him pained. If he lied, I'd detect it in his scent. If my head didn't explode, that is. "Go on."

"I am Senior Special Agent Ayatas FireWind of PsyLED, in charge of the states east of the Mississippi.

My up-line boss is the newly appointed assistant director in charge of all paranormal investigations. Soul. No last name. You know her."

I nodded, a single drop of my chin in the tribal way. "How are you classified species-wise with PsyLED?"

PsyLED had once been a human-only law enforcement organization created to deal with paranormal creatures who attacked humans or broke human laws. In the last few years, when it became apparent that humans without heavy artillery were no match for paras, the agency had begun to draw on the paranormal community for agents, whom it classified according to species and gift. They might not know he was skinwalker, but they could read his magical energies with a device called a psy-meter. I knew because I'd been read by the device. There was no hiding paranormal abilities, not anymore.

"You're well versed in PsyLED internal policies," he said. When I didn't reply, he added, "I am an unclassified, noncontagious, non-moon-called shape-shifter. No mention of a Cherokee skinwalker in my dossier."

Skinwalkers weren't unknown in the mythos. That had to be willful blindness or the influence of someone in high places. "Go on."

"I had heard of the woman who killed a sabertooth lion. Had heard rumors of the woman who changed shape into a mountain lion in the car of the Master of the City of New Orleans. I had heard she claimed to be Chelokay. Yet had yellow eyes."

I nodded, breathing slowly through nose and mouth, letting his scent trace over my tongue. As well as I could tell on such short acquaintance, he was speaking the truth. And Soul had been present when I shifted. So Soul was a likely source of his intel. Had she sent him to me? And if so, why not an official meet-and-greet? Why the personal ambush, followed by a weapon-based one? Had Soul expected this? Allowed it to happen?

"The woman's name was Jane Yellowrock. My research took time to compile, but once it was together, it all suggested she was like me. Skinwalker."

He seemed to be waiting for me to respond, but I said nothing.

"I have lived in Colorado, New Mexico, Arizona, and Wyoming for decades, in law enforcement, as a teacher, a lawyer." He frowned slightly. "I joined PsyLED ten years ago, and . . ." He shrugged, a very Cherokee gesture, lifting the shoulder blades in back, tilting the head, eyebrows quirking just a bit. "They discovered I was a para. They kept me on. And then there was the evidence of you on YouTube. A video of you walking from a cave, injured, your eyes glowing."

I knew the video he was talking about and gave him the same shrug back. I wasn't ready to show interest or ask questions. Not yet. Because I knew way more than this guy seemed to think I knew.

"I made changes and requested this PsyLED territory. Was assigned to New Orleans when the European Mithran emperor showed up offshore. I came here today to make peace with Jane Yellowrock, should she turn out to be who I thought she might be. Soul told me—several times—that she knew you and offered to introduce us, but I thought . . . I hoped . . . it might be a highly personal meeting and wanted it to be private."

Soul had wanted us to meet. Soul, who knew what I was. Soul, who, despite our sorta friendship, might have had a stronger tie to this man than to me, and let him decide how and when to proceed with an intro.

The frisson of energies that had begun when I first saw the man swept through me again and unexpected tears gathered in my eyes. I blinked them away. He was skinwalker. He was of The People. He had come to make peace with me. This was the first time this had ever happened to me. The first time any one of The People had ever come to me. Had ever wanted to come to me.

Yet, the same words that seemed to offer kinship and tribal welcome made my heart tumble with disappointment, and I struggled to understand why.

"You had an unusual history," he continued before I could speak. "I wanted to meet you. And if things went well, ask you to take me when I presented papers and letters to Leonard Pellissier, letters of introduction."

That, I thought. That was what was wrong with this entire scenario. Ayatas wanted info and maybe the opportunity to be present at the fight to the death between the Master of the City, Leo Pellissier, and the European vampire emperor, Titus Flavius Vespasianus. And he wanted me to give it to him.

"So you show up here, planning to give PsyLED a finger on the pulse of the upcoming Sangre Duello," Eli said. It was his battle voice, soft, unforgiving, ready to kill. He was angry that the man had intended to forge and then use a personal relationship with me to get to Leo. Using me. Why not ask Rick to do this? My ex had his fingers in every pie there was.

"Yes. I . . . I reacted badly to your scent. I shot you. At you. I don't know why I shot at you or why I missed." He closed his eyes, his scent smelling of shock and fear, strong and harsh on the air. He had shot at someone while technically on the job, revealing an unexpected lack of control. Professional suicide. That seemed to be sinking in. Ayatas went on. "I put too many of my hopes in this one small basket, in this one meeting. I ruined it and I can't even explain to you why, except that your scent triggered something in me. I thought you were black magic. The thing our kind fears most. I am sorry, *e-igido*."

"What's *eigido*?" Eli asked, mangling the word.

The tears I was trying to blink away spilled over and dashed down my cheeks.

I remembered the word as he spoke. The word in his first line when he still stood uninjured at the door.

"*E-igido*," I whispered, finally placing the term. "*E-igido* means 'my sister.'" I was an only child. My father died when I was five years old, killed by white men in front of me. He might smell of truth, but this man lied. For reasons I couldn't explain, that final lie cut deep.

CHAPTER 2

Lots of Bloody Bubbles

The man claiming to be my brother was no longer in the room with us, though to be fair, with skinwalker hearing he probably could hear us chatting.

Littermate, Beast thought at me. I ignored her. It was impossible.

"He knows just enough to have done his research," Alex said. "Most everything he said is either on video on YouTube or in Reach's data files. Just because Reach is hiding from us doesn't mean he's dead. He might have sold the info to PsyLED."

Reach had been the best researcher in the paranormal world. He maintained he had been tortured for his data and then had disappeared, not that we had undisputed evidence of his claim. We had acquired most of his files, and Alex, the electronic genius of Yellowrock Securities, had married the files into our own, making Alex the researcher at the top of the heap.

"His scent," I said, laying back my head on the sofa and closing my eyes against the headache. I was exhausted and even the hazy daylight through the windows still hurt. "He has a natural floral scent. Just like the vamps said." There had been a yellow-eyed Cherokee in the city over a hundred years ago, and she had smelled like flowers. "I don't think my Tsalagi birth name or my clan name is on record anywhere. Aggie One Feather hasn't shared it. I insulted her when I called to ask. And Beast called him littermate. He's my kinsman. If not my brother, then half brother. Cousin at the very least. But I was an only child. I didn't have a brother or sister; only hints and blurred images of my mother and not much more of my father. I don't know how . . . I don't know anything." I raised my voice though it sent a spike of pain through my head. "Edmund, you making nice-nice?"

The shelving unit blocking the vamp's stone-lined sleeping quarters opened just enough to allow his voice to emerge. "No, my mistress."

Ayatas shouted from the same place, "I'm not letting a fanghead suck on me!"

The door shut. I was Edmund Hartley's mistress—not his lover, but his master—and I could have ordered the vampire to drink Ayatas down and read him like a book. But I hated the idea of abusing a PsyLED officer, even one who had tried to kill me. I also detested the idea of forcing Ed to do something that he found to be inexcusable. "I loathe the very concept of drinking down someone who might be your brother. This is family and family are sacrosanct, even when they try to kill us," he'd said. Which was weird, but knowing Ed's history, the statement sorta made sense. He was right. I was ashamed.

I laid an arm over my eyes, and a moment later Alex murmured, "Lift your arm. I have a cold compress for your head."

I dropped my arm and something cool and gel-like settled in its place. No one said anything else about my little problem. My headaches were scary to the boys, since they might mean the genetic damage that had resulted from playing around in time had given me some kind of brain trauma. Or not. Maybe I was just getting migraines. Time-walking and headaches didn't have to be cause and effect.

Eli's cell rang. "It's Soul. Okay if I do the talking?"

"Knock yourself out," I said.

"Eli Younger here. Thank you for calling us back. We have a visitor, a man who claims to be PsyLED." He didn't mention that Alex had already been inside PsyLED's databases and confirmed Ayatas's identity and employment records and the claims about his personnel folder. "Claims he's Rick LaFleur's boss and your direct underling. Ayatas FireWind."

"That is correct." Soul's voice came over the speaker. We heard clicking as she tapped on a keyboard. "He was originally in charge of five western states, but last year he requested a move to the eastern seaboard. The transfer was granted only a few weeks ago. I see from an e-mail earlier today that he was going to request assistance in meeting Leo Pellissier from Jane." There was an odd tone in her voice, an eagerness I hadn't expected. "Is that why you're calling?"

"Not exactly. He tried to kill Jane."

There was silence after his words, and if silence had a sharp edge, this one would have cut the air. "An officer of PsyLED tried to kill the Enforcer of the Master of the City of New Orleans?" Soul was carefully using titles now. I had to wonder why. "He was unsuccessful? How?"

"Yes and yes. With his service weapon."

"Why?"

"Said her scent triggered something in him. Couldn't really say."

"I see. Jane's scent is . . . unusual and—" Her voice cut off abruptly. "FireWind is dead?"

"No. Jane dodged the bullet."

"Dodged a bullet. I see." There was another silence as Soul put things together. She knew I could timewalk. That was the name she had given to what some species could do, including her species, the arcenciels, or rainbow dragons. We had chatted a week ago, getting me up to speed on what was happening to me, though I hadn't told her about the headaches. Soul wasn't part of Yellowrock Securities, so that was still under wraps.

"He can't dodge bullets?" Eli said, asking if Ayatas could step outside of time.

She didn't answer the question, saying instead, "Ayatas had hoped that his possible relationship with Jane would speed a meeting with Leo. Time is short."

"You know Leo. Rick LaFleur knows Leo. Why does PsyLED need Jane?"

"PsyLED has tried three times in the last week to arrange a meeting with the Master of the City of New Orleans, through formal channels, and we've been shut down."

That was interesting, but not surprising. Every law enforcement and government agency from the feds down wanted to talk to Leo ASAP, if not sooner. Plus . . . Leo currently had possession of Adan, a witch-vampire everyone wanted access to. Adan had once kept a skinwalker as personal blood-servant, making him high on my personal chat list. He'd also imprisoned an arcenciel, one of Soul's species, and forced her to timewalk for him, making him high on Soul's personal chat list. So personal, business, and legal reasons all at once. Everything Leo did had multilayered reasoning. "Why does PsyLED need to chat with the MOC?" Eli asked.

"Not just PsyLED, but FireWind in particular. Ayatas is more than a special agent at this particular point in time. He is the liaison between PsyLED, CIA, FBI, and ICE for the European/American blood duel."

Soul had told me nothing useful, except that Ayatas had a lot of pull to have the backing of so many federal agencies. I figured she was giving me bits and pieces in hopes of info on the Sangre Duello. Leo was working hard to keep the government out of the duel. And—Ayatas was here to use me. I had known it. Yet, some small piece of innocence and hope died inside me. The coffin that was my chest ached.

Eli said nothing and Soul continued. "We understand that the Sangre Duello may be held offshore. Normally, of course, no one in a government position would be involved in anything offshore, in foreign countries or international waters."

I lifted a corner of my eye cover and Eli gave me a wolfish grin. He'd been in combat in places where maybe he shouldn't have been sent. The government wasn't always true to international law. I pushed the gel pack away and sat up, ignoring the spears that lanced through my brain and throbbed like a heavy metal band of agony. Eli was watching me. I blinked and forced my eyes to focus together.

"Titus Flavius Vespasianus and Leo Pellissier officially requested permission to have the blood battles to the death in Louisiana," Soul said, "and, as the challenged party, it was Titus's right to do so according to Mithran law. Fortunately for the safety of our citizens, it was not his right according to United States law. When the request for the duel to be held on U.S. territory and land was refused by a myriad of government institutions, the Mithrans shut the door to all of us. Now Pellissier is no longer answering our calls. In fact, not one single vampire in the entire United States is returning our calls."

I knew all this. The number of U.S. legalities involved had been too long to deal with, from duels being illegal in most U.S. states to ICE and the federal government working to ensure that these particular European vampires were never allowed on U.S. soil, even for a visit. As Leo's Enforcer, a position of power in vamp hierarchy, and as the Dark Queen—a title I was still learning about—I knew most everything going on. And I could tell Soul none of it. I said, "Tell me that doesn't surprise you. The government flipped off paras and then expected the para leaders to keep in contact with them? You're a para. You know better."

Soul sighed over the connection. "We've asked the Robere twins and George Dumas to liaise with us on this matter and they refused. We've brought in the governor's office, several maritime organizations, including the Coast Guard, and half a dozen other agencies. Rick LaFleur is traveling internationally more than he's here, so he's little help. But Pellissier won't talk to anyone now."

One of the Roberes was a lawyer. George, aka Bruiser, my boyfriend, had been Leo's primo at one time and still had a lot of pull with the MOC. And all three were Onorios, which we needed at the fight with the Europeans. They were the judges and the keepers of the peace. Did the government know that last part? Sure. Why not? This thing had been FUBARed from the beginning. And Rick . . . I hadn't known that my ex was traveling. That was interesting too, if not pertinent to this convo.

Leo had pulled in his nets and gone back to port, as the fishing metaphor went. He had walked away from the government, a government that refused to recognize his species as equal to humans in protections under the law. So now the government and law enforcement were at my door, claiming a personal relationship to get my help. Ducky. The coffin door in my heart slammed shut.

Soul went on. "Titus and Leo have since requested permission to broadcast the battles, though no traditional broadcast networks have picked up on it. However, no one can stop the broadcast via Internet pay-per-view, despite the violence, and a number of providers are bidding on the rights with Leo. George and the Roberes are also involved in these high-level talks. And they are not calling us back."

And you can't make them, because the government in general refused to work with the suckheads and their humans. Yeah. Soul knew a lot more than I expected. I nodded to my partner and he said, "Okay. Still listening."

"I just discovered that the Europeans are planning to hold offshore gambling on the matches and have agreed that the tax income from the bets won and lost will go to Louisiana, if the state will partner with them."

My eyebrows went up. That was a surprise.

"This is likely to result in a great deal of money," Soul said over the cell connection, "and it seems that someone high up in the Louisiana state government is suddenly interested, which means we are scrambling. It's all tangled up in federal and state law with everyone wanting a piece of the action or to be seen as politically strong, fighting to keep more bloodsuckers out of the U.S."

"Right," I said, headache spiking again, feeling tired in every bone of my body. "Everyone's scrambling for power."

"My personal concern is that if Leo leaves Louisiana and goes into international waters, aboard a European ship, to fight, who will be in control of his lands while he is away?" Soul asked. "Who will inherit if he loses? What will happen to the humans and the political balance we have established so far? It's precarious, especially with new laws being proposed in Congress for paranormal citizenship. I want someone with Leo to handle all of that and Ayatas has the experience, the charm, and the diplomatic know-how. But not if he lost control and tried to kill one of you."

"He says he's related to Jane," Eli said.

"I see." Soul paused, perhaps in thought. "I have been unable to confirm or deny this in any official records. The records of Jane Yellowrock began the day she walked out of the mountains at a supposed age twelve." She hesitated and then went on again, as if feeling her way through what she wanted to say. "Aya's records appear when he supposedly entered an orphanage at age four and ended when he ran away at age fourteen. He reappeared at a supposed age twenty, having changed his name, and acquired an education by taking classes in three different universities, two online, graduating with a degree in criminal justice. There are photos of him at only one of those schools," she added, telling us that his history might have been faked. "And in the one photo we have of him at the orphanage, his ears appear to be shaped differently."

Children's faces altered drastically as they grew, but the shape and placement of ears never changed except by surgery. Ears were as individual as fingerprints. What Soul was describing stated that Ayatas had assumed the identity of a dead child, a runaway from the orphanage. It was typical of the way long-lived paranormals maintained a legal position in the world. Ayatas was likely older than his papers claimed. I had guessed that all skinwalkers were long-lived. That my father died only because the white man had shot and killed him before he could shift and heal. And that all skinwalkers were yellow eyed, like me. All assumptions, but with some small amount of evidence to support them. Ayatas could be far older than he looked.

"As to whether he is related," she said, "no one has done a genetic comparison to determine a relationship. Some creatures recognize one another's familial scent. That didn't happen?"

He smelled like skinwalker, not like me. "No." Though

Beast thought so. And genetic comparisons wouldn't work anyway. I'd seen my DNA. It was a mess.

"So he's here. He's both lying and legit. He has a job to do," Eli said. "His shooting at Jane appears to be a mistake. Pretty big mistake for an officer of the law. Damn stupid," Eli said, letting ire into his voice. "He should be put on administrative leave. An internal investigation should be begun."

"Yes." Soul laughed softly, almost sadly. Her laughter had always reminded me of bells and woodwinds and it made me want to smile with her, and hide my own braying laughter. Now it just made my head hurt worse. "And when he tells an IA investigator that he drew on Jane because she smells like a dangerous cannibalistic paranormal creature? And Jane is once again put back at the top of the PsyLED's 'person of interest' list?"

Eli's eyes narrowed and he looked at me to make sure I understood that we had just been blackmailed. Soul had us over a barrel.

"I will need to discuss this with Aya, though I would prefer to keep it out of his record," Soul added.

Aya, I thought. She called him by a nickname. Soul liked him.

"We won't be making any reports," Eli said, but I could hear his unwillingness to let the attack go.

"Leo will not speak to any law enforcement agency or special agent. I would consider it a personal favor," she said, "if you would introduce Ayatas to Leo and smooth the way for negotiations."

"Copy all that. And we'll consider it a personal favor if Ayatas keeps his weapons in his pants," Eli said. "We'll be calling if he kills someone, and PsyLED can clean up the mess." Eli tapped off the cell and drew his weapon, looked at me.

"I can send the request to Leo's secretary," Alex said, glancing at me beneath his long curls. When I tilted my head a fraction of an inch in agreement, he added, "If anyone can get Leo to see a cop, it's Scrappy. That's what's called the fine art of delegation." He tapped on his official cell.

"Edmund?" I asked without raising my voice, hiding the gel pack under a decorative pillow. "You can let him out."

The shelving opened fully, revealing the small stone-lined room beneath the stairs, the revolving weapons-safe in the corner, the foot of the small bed, and Ayatas. He stumbled out, obviously having been pushed. The shelving door closed on the daylight, protecting my master-vamp primo from the sun. Ayatas looked a little the worse for wear, his long black hair snarled, his clothes rumpled, but no smell of blood on the air, no vamp blood and no skinwalker blood, which meant that the man calling himself my brother had managed to avoid getting rolled, hadn't allowed himself to be sipped from, and Edmund hadn't forced him to drink vamp blood, a trait I liked in my primo. Things had gotten a little physical, but there had been no forcing a blood bond. Forcing a bond was horrible. I knew that from my own personal encounter. I still had problems dealing with, well, lots of things, because of that experience.

"You people are insane," Ayatas spat out. He sounded remarkably like a cat and Beast peered through my eyes. I could tell she was captivated by the man and I wondered if my eyes were glowing gold. It happened.

"Why?" I asked. "We didn't kill you. The vampire didn't drink you down even though you shot at his master and we woke him from his beauty sleep. And we're providing you a room to clean up in. We've been really nice hosts." Except for the whole squishing his balls and keeping him cuffed and tossing him into a lair with a sleepy vamp. Reporting him to his up-line boss and mentor. Yeah. There was all that.

Eli tossed him his cell phone and Ayatas caught it in midair without a bobble. "Call Soul," Eli said. "Then go clean up. The rest of your belongings are in the guest bedroom upstairs, front left corner. Clean sheets. Towels on the foot of the bed. Late lunch in twenty."

"It's Eli's white chicken breast Cajun salad made with capers and dill," Alex said, without looking up from his tablets, laptops, and personal desktop computer and Wi-Fi/cloud system with all the latest bells and whistles.

Desktops like this had to be hand-built and the compo-
nents had cost us over five grand, but it allowed us to act
as a hub for every computer system, security system, cell
phone, tablet, and GPS tracking system owned by Leo's
people. Alex was bent over it, tapping away.

"And if I don't like dill?" Ayatas asked, shaking his
hair back and wiping his face with his shirtsleeve.

"Starve," Alex said, again without looking up. I smiled
slightly, thinking, *That's my bro*.

Ayatas FireWind disappeared up the stairs, his fancy
shoes silent on the wood treads. Either he had special
soles or he moved like a cat. Or a hunting Cherokee warrior. I was going for doors number two and three. I closed
my eyes and dropped my head back again, pulling the gel
pack from beneath the pillow and laying it in place, eyes
closed.

"Still happy you didn't buy that bigger place?" Eli
asked, a little knowing spite in his tone. He had found a
traditional Creole townhome, only a few miles away, that
was roughly three times the size of this house. But this
was home, or as close as I'd ever gotten. Not that I'd told
him that. I'd just said the larger house was too expensive.
And it had been. Still was.

"Very. But we have to stop taking in strays," I said.

Eli and Alex both snorted.

Alex said, "We have almost everything integrated and
Bodat will be in town later today to help me finish up."

That was good news and bad news. With the new system, we knew where every one of Leo's people were at all
times, who they were chatting with, and what burner devices they were using to try to keep their activities secret
from the MOC. The Kid—Alex—had devised several al-
gorithms to keep the information from being too overwhelming, but even so it was not a one-man job. If
Yellowrock Securities was going to survive the Sangre
Duello and stay in NOLA, we needed serious geekish
help. We were going to have to outsource or hire someone
in-house. Either would change the dynamics of our lives.
Again. So Bodat was the best choice, even if it meant we
had to find him a place to stay temporarily. No way was

he staying here long term. Just thinking about the garlic-smelling, doughy-fleshed teen was enough to give me the shivers and make my headache feel worse.

Bodat was one of Alex's World of Warcraft buddies who had helped us with a case in Natchez. He was a couple of years younger than Alex and lived in Mississippi. The pasty-skinned kid was planning to attend Tulane in the fall, which was where Alex was going for his doctorate, now that he was finished with probation. Bodat was a hacker wannabe and had a knack for scanning and compiling data. He was working hard to learn the back doors of computer hacking and also had a serious case of hero worship for Alex, which he tried hard to keep hidden. It was cute. But . . . Bodat. I sighed softly.

Alex and Eli put a blanket over me and went into the kitchen to prepare a late lunch.

"Why do you think Janie is your sister?" Alex asked.

Ayatas halted, spoon halfway to his mouth. It was filled with vanilla ice cream and blueberry-mango cobbler fresh out of the oven. Lunch had been carefully polite, with no mention of relationships or how Soul might have reacted to Ayatas shooting at me. Mostly the meal had been guy chatter about the weather, the difference between an Arizona winter and a Louisiana one, and sports teams. Until now.

He placed the spoon back in the bowl and looked from one to the other of us as if trying to figure us out. "According to her history, Jane appeared from the woods. My sister disappeared in a snowstorm, many years past. We are long-lived. Her body was never recovered. Why would Jane not have a long-lost brother?"

"Because she's a lot older than she looks."

"Alex?" This was not a topic of conversation I had expected to be having. This was my most personal information and Alex was on the verge of giving it all away. I put down my spoon, again sick at my stomach. Though the food, and maybe the OTCs, had helped my headache some, the pain wasn't gone, and nausea was one of the symptoms I suffered with the migraine-like agony.

Alex didn't look at me. "I mean, dude, she looks maybe twenty-five, but she's old. She could be thirty."

I wanted to laugh. He sounded like a typical teen, though he was twenty now himself and growing up. Mostly. And he was, not so subtly, pumping Ayatas.

"If we are siblings," Ayatas said, picking up his spoon again without looking my way, "then Jane is much older than twenty-five."

The words hung on the air for a dozen heartbeats. The odd emotions welled up in me again, a vortex of feelings that swirled together. Things like, *I'm not alone. The People still exist. They came for me. Finally. Finally. Finally.* Mixed with the hope and the fear and the unanticipated possibilities was a wash of anger and suspicion. Why now? Why did you wait so long? Only to use me? Is the skinwalker—the one who taught me to kill my first man and who pushed me into the snow to live or die—still alive? Is my mother still alive? I had posited that the skinwalker gene was X-linked, like with witches, passing on the mother's X chromosome. I had assumed that I'd gotten the gene from my father, passed down from his mother, but for Ayatas to be a skinwalker, and my full-blooded brother, my mother had to be a skinwalker too, since any brother would have gotten his only X chromosome from her.

I shoved down on all the emotions, useless passions that were obscuring the rational, reasonable parts of me, the parts that might let me find my way through the maelstrom. It was unlikely that any of my family were alive. A demon called *Kalona Ayeliski* claimed to have sucked the blood of a woman I remembered only as *Uni Lisi*, a term of respect meaning Grandmother of Many Children, and possibly actually my own grandmother or great-grandmother. The demon had been one of the *Sunnayi Edahi*, the invisible nightgoers in Cherokee tradition. The demon claimed to have killed the grandmother who had taught me to kill. I had believed that the woman I remembered as Grandmother was dead. But demons weren't known for telling the truth.

"Like, how much older?" Alex asked. "Jane's a woman. Women don't like to talk about their ages."

I might have laughed or rolled my eyes, but this was deadly serious, vitally important, and my headache was still pretty bad. Eye rolling was out.

"I'm telling you my history, my deepest, most personal story." He looked at me now, his golden eyes intense beneath hawk-wing brows. He pushed away the fruit cobbler and bent his elbows on the table, his fingers interlaced. Long fingers, very slender. Familiar. I clenched my fists together beneath the table. I didn't know the PsyLED cop who claimed kinship, but he seemed quiet, wary, contained, as if holding down emotional reactions until he could deal with them later, privately. Almost shooting me, a future confrontation with his boss about that attempted shooting, had to be weighing heavily on him, yet there was nothing of that in his demeanor.

"I'm telling you this because I hope you are my sister and there is no way to prove or disprove that hope unless I share everything with you. Things I have not discussed with anyone in decades."

I nodded, that peculiar, *Tsalagi* chin jut of affirmation.

"I was born on the *Nunna Daul Tsuny*. The Trail of Tears."

No one was eating. No one was even breathing.

"My mother told me that my five-year-old sister had been killed by soldiers after she attacked one of them with a knife. It was the lie they told the soldiers to keep them from searching for her. I learned later that my sister had attacked a man who raped a Cherokee woman, and grievously wounded him. The leader of our clan had forced my skinwalker sister into the form of a bobcat and drove her into the snow to save her from the soldiers." He knew too much. He knew things I didn't. Or claimed things.

But . . . it fit. It all fit.

"Who was the leader of your clan?" I asked, my words as soft as a speaker of The People.

"She goes by the name Hayalasti Sixmankiller."

It was an interesting choice of names he fed me. Hayalasti was one of the Cherokee names for "knife." If Hayalasti was the woman I knew so long ago, then I had been present for the deaths of two of the six men she killed.

"I just call her *Uni Lisi*," he added and smiled. "She scared me to death when I was a child." He pulled a cell phone from his pocket and placed it on the table between us. "Call her. She is still alive. She and a small group of her family and clan moved back to the Appalachian Mountains about seventy years ago."

Still alive . . . Small group of her family and clan . . .

I smiled, a twitch of my lips. I took a breath that moved air over my tongue, through my nose, filled my parched lungs. He scented of the truth. Yet, though everything this man said could be truth, and would fulfill the deepest unrecognized longings of my heart, nothing—absolutely nothing—could be proven. What he thought was truth could be lies he believed. "My . . . our mother? Human or skinwalker?"

His face fell into a vision of dour grief, old but potent. "Our mother was skinwalker-born, though she lacked the ability to shift and therefore aged as a human. She died while I was in the West. She was seventy-five years old, in good health, but one morning she simply did not wake." He seemed about to say more, but fell silent.

I looked at Eli and Alex, who were watching me. Kindness on their faces. Kindness that made tears prick my lids. I pushed away from the table without touching the cell. "Eat your cobbler. Leo will be up at dusk. Alex has sent an official request to bring a visitor. For now, I'm getting some sleep." Looking at Eli, I communicated a lot of things in one glance before going to my room, where I stripped and fell onto my bed. I didn't expect to sleep, but I did, dreams like a vortex of head pain and possibilities and half-recalled bloody memories.

My hand holding the crosshatched hilt of a knife. Bloody. Blood everywhere. Just like my entire life.

I laid out the slim black pants, black jacket, and white silk men's-style dress shirt on the bed. Added a silk scarf and black dancing shoes. The straps over the instep gave me excellent balance in case of unexpected attack, and the heels gave me an extra three inches over my six feet in height. With my weapons, I'd look lean, mean, and scary.

It was what Madame Melisende, Modiste du les Mithrans, my business and formal clothes designer, called dangerous business dressy, meaning it had slits, fake pockets, and loops, for weapons. I took a fast shower, pulled my hair up, and braided it into a fighting queue, so tight it made my head ache, but in a different way from the headache before my nap. I stuck silver and ash wood stakes into the braided topknot bun like a deadly crown. Satisfied that the hair was less of a weapon than it otherwise could be, I started dressing.

I strapped on a sleek harness around my waist, slightly to the right, inserting a tiny Walther PK .380 handgun into the soft leather holster. Kydex was nice, but not if I had to sit with the weapon cutting into me. The small gun would be easily available to me through the right pocket slit in my pants, and with a shirt that belled out around me slightly, and the scarf hanging to my hips, no one would ever know the gun was there. Scarves were dangerous in a fight and I didn't wear them, but this one had caught my eye, gold and silver and copper silk. Onto the same waist harness, I strapped two blade sheaths and secured them to my upper thighs for right- and/or left-hand extraction. Into the sheaths, I secured short-bladed, silver-plated vamp-killers with six-inch blades. I pulled on and adjusted a brand-new tactical sports bra with built-in dual underarm holsters for the matching HK45s. I adjusted the cant of each weapon and made sure there were no rounds in the chambers, even at the expense of the time I'd use to ready the weapons in the event of a firefight. I might not start a small war, but I could finish one—unless I shot myself in the boob. That hadda hurt. So, safety first.

I pulled on the outer clothes and slid bare feet into my dancing shoes, securing the clasps. I looked like a businesswoman. No weapons visible. The men's shirt appeared to have buttons but was closed with hidden snaps that I could rip through in a heartbeat to get to the H&Ks. Sometimes speed of draw is less of a factor than appearing to be unarmed.

However, my face still looked crappy. I put on makeup,

that thick, pasty stuff that makes sleepless and pained under-eye bruises less noticeable. Then powder, blush, and mascara. A dab of gold shadow at the corners of my eyes. I still wasn't good at putting on makeup, but I had learned a little.

On the outside of my clothes, I strapped on the Mughal blade my sweetcheeks had given me. It was ancient curved Damascene steel, fancy and decorative and sharp as death. And its scarlet-velvet-covered wooden sheath would draw attention from any bulges or other evidence of the real weapons. I wrapped the pretty scarf around my neck and adjusted the ends for more concealment. Rethought the scarf, which could be used as a handle to yank me around. Re-rethought it. Left it.

And . . . I was still wasting time.

I looked at the stack of protocol books on the table. There was one for each species, one for each social situation, one for dancing, and four that detailed different kinds of introductions. While the Sangre Duello used little that was contained in them, I knew I should use the exact wording and proper protocol to introduce Ayatas to Leo. But—nah. Crass was almost always better. I dialed the Mithran Council Chambers and got Scrappy. "Lee Williams Watts, Mr. Pellissier's personal assistant. How may I help you? Oh. Sorry, Jane. I didn't look at the screen. What's up?"

"Hey, Scrappy. How's the boss?"

"Pretty good. Though I have to say that taking dictation in his bathroom is new."

I breathed out a laugh. "His bathroom?"

"He and Katie and Alesha Fonteneau were all in the tub together, making up and making out. Lots of bloody bubbles, thank God."

"Oh." I couldn't think of anything else to say. Picking up my jacket with a finger in the collar loop, I opened my bedroom door and entered the house proper. I dropped a shoulder against the wide cased opening into the living room, talking, listening, smelling, and watching. There were four men and a pudgy kid in the room, and three of the group looked distinctly uncomfortable, as if I'd walked into the middle of something that was about to be unpleasant. Eli was scowling, a partially unsheathed blade in one hand. Bruiser was standing angled to the other two as if he might be about to launch into some martial art move. Ayatas's face wore an expression I'd call cop face—ready for anything. Clearly someone had done something to someone else and things had escalated.

I frowned at them, my expression saying, Really? Now?

Beast leaped to the forefront of my mind, peering out at the tableau. *Littermates have steel claws. Littermates play-battle. Beast wants to play.*

But Lee was still talking. "Right? There was lots of giggling and the presence of the bloody bubbles tells me they were having a good time. Way too good a time for a lowly human like me to want to be there for long."

Alesha and Katie Fonteneau were sisters, and Katie had been—until very recently—Leo's heir, while Alesha had been his Madam Spy and a traitor. Last I heard, they were both in the scion prison together, locked up for betraying Leo. Things in the vamp world changed at a glacial rate, one they called the long view. Until they changed fast. Then help the poor human or skinwalker who couldn't keep up. As a joke, Alex had e-mailed me a flowchart. I'd kept it and used it.

"I don't blame you," I said.

"Anyway, what can I do for you?" Scrappy asked.

"Alex send you a message?"

Scrappy said, "A personal message. Yes."

That said a world of important things in vamp hierarchy. "A nonhuman PsyLED agent named Ayatas FireWind wishes to parley with Leo. The Enforcer would like you to arrange a casual little tea with him, Grégoire, Katie, Bruiser, and my people. Tonight, early."

After a silence that lasted a beat too long, Lee said, "Enforcer," using my title. Making it formal. "We have an opening between seven thirty and eight."

"Got it," I said.

"Interesting mix of guests. Especially since Mr. Pellissier turned down a meeting with PsyLED multiple times this week."

She was fishing for info. I let a small smile cross my face. "I think so too."

Scrappy said, "Okay then. Do you need a car sent for you or your guest?"

"No. He'll be riding over with us. However, he'll need a place to stay. Would you make an arrangement with the Hotel Monteleone? One of the executive suites would do. Put it on Leo's tab."

"Consider it done. If that's all, I'll see the Enforcer and her guests in a bit."

"Thank you, Lee."

She hesitated at the use of her proper name and then said, "Thank you, Enforcer." Enforcer. Not Jane. Making sure we were still not personal when doing vamp business. Got it.

She ended the call and I tucked the cell into my jacket pocket, slung it over my shoulder, and slouched some more, one hand in a faux pocket that was really a weapon slit. The men were still in precombat positions, ready to fight. Stupid men.

Beast wants to play with stupid men.

"I don't see any blood yet," I said. "Didn't hear any shots fired. You want to tell me why my boyfriend, one of my partners, and my uninvited houseguest are looking like you're about to rumble?"

"A misunderstanding," Ayatas said.

"No misunderstanding." In his best, most ticked-off British accent, Bruiser said, "One week ago, Special Agent Ayatas FireWind called me for an introduction to Leo. I refused. Now he's in your home, claiming to be your long-lost baby brother, and he bloody well has not only an introduction but a casual little tea? That is, if I heard correctly the conversation that just ended."

"Hmmm," I said. "Yeah. He says he's my brother."

Bruiser shot me a look. "FireWind didn't mention that he might be related to you." He looked back at Ayatas. "However, yellow eyes and golden-copper skin are not a common combination. There is a familial resemblance." Bruiser eased back a step, relaxing from attack mode into something more like high alert. My honeybunch was wearing black tonight: black suit, black silk shirt, no tie, his hair slicked back with something that held it in place and also made it look darker. He looked scrumptious, especially with all his feathers ruffled in a "protect the little woman" attitude, instincts left over from his upbringing in England back a century or so ago. It was a cute instinct but unnecessary.

Eli was in black too, but black jeans and a T-shirt with a jacket. He fully sheathed his blade but left his battle face on.

That left my supposed brother, who had pulled a weapon once today, and currently one hand was positioned to go for his service weapon. All very odd for a cop, with their proscribed grounds for anything involving a weapon. His expression was tight and cold, body bladed to the others, knees slightly bent in defensive position against multiple possible attackers. This man had seen combat, no doubt about it. Maybe not this century, but recently enough for the reflexes to still be honed. I said, "If you draw a weapon in my house again, you better be using it to save my people. Otherwise I'll be shoving it up your ass and emptying the chamber."

"She said *ass*," the pasty-skinned kid said to Alex. "I thought Jane didn't cuss."

"*Ass* isn't cussing, Bodat. Sit down," Alex said, yanking his friend from behind the couch where he had been half-hiding.

A few seconds too many passed before Ayatas dropped his hand and relaxed.

"Any reason why you didn't tell George Dumas that you're my brother?" I asked Ayatas.

"I had planned that private, intimate moment with you," he said, sounding grumpy. It was a tone I had heard from my mouth often enough that it rang with familiarity. "None of my plans or actions have gone well since I got to New Orleans."

"You got into my home without getting killed first. Told me a lovely story about your past and mine with just enough details to not get you shot. Yet. And you got a meeting with Leo out of the deal. What's gone wrong?"

There must have been something sensible in my tone because both Eli and Bruiser slid gazes to me and to each other. Ayatas's expression shifted into wary-neutral. Progress.

"You're wily as *elaqua*," I said, "but without the rattles to tell me you're about to strike. I find nothing to like about you." I saw the skin beside Eli's eye relax, not something anyone else would have noticed. He was relieved that I hadn't been blinded, by hope and desire for a past, to the man's serious flaws. Ayatas, on the other hand, gave away nothing I could interpret. His black brows drew down slightly. That was it. Coulda meant anything.

I continued, "Except for your height, hair, and nose, we have nothing in common." And his fingers. His jaw. His attitude. All familiar. Not saying that. "Too much planning here, things that look like coincidence but aren't." I decided to jab and see how he took it. "I'm not sure if you have any honor at all." Ayatas's back stiffened just the tiniest bit and some small sadistic part of me found pleasure in the insult I had delivered and his reaction.

"A woman who sleeps with the Master of the City has honor?"

I laughed. He could hit below the belt too. Maybe it was a family trait. "I thought you had done your research. As a favor to Soul, I'll introduce you to Leo. You're on your own after that."

I glanced at the long doors on the side wall. It was dusk. But my primo's shelving unit was still shut. On purpose. Punishment for making him try to roll Ayatas. I deserved it. I was scum.

In for a penny, in for a pounding.

To Bruiser and Eli, I said, "Cuff him and throw him in the back of the SUV."

CHAPTER 3

My Life Was a Soap Opera with Fangs and Fur

Ayatas didn't resist, and when he was deposited on the parking area of the drive at vamp central, with his cell, his badge, and his weapon, he managed to still look like a fashion plate. He was wearing a suit, black, but with shimmering midnight blue tints when the light hit the fabric just right. His shirt matched the blue tints and his tie was a glistening black that perfectly matched his long black hair. Leo would get one whiff of him and want the man in his bed.

As Eli removed the agent's cuffs, Bruiser leaned to me and murmured, "You are wearing the blade I gave you, love. You look beautiful and deadly."

This man knew just what to say. I leaned my temple against his, watching my partner but stealing a quiet moment. With the shoes, I was right at Bruiser's height, and his skin was heated, a peaceful warmth. His Onorio scent filled my nostrils and I blew out the breath, more calm than I had been since my brother tried to kill me. No. Not my brother. Not proven yet. FireWind. Since FireWind tried to kill me. But the thought let me know just how much I wanted it to be true. Him. His stories. A past I might learn of, and might remember someday. Questions he might answer about who and what I was.

"You look amazing too," I said. "Can we just skip all this and go to your place?"

Bruiser chuckled and encircled my waist, pulling me closer. He had to feel the other weapons against his body, but he said nothing about them. We had come a long way since the time he kissed me on a limo floor and found a weapon strapped to my thigh. "Be safe, my love," he said. "Be wise."

"Ditto to you." I stood straight as he kissed me on the temple and I stepped out of his embrace to climb the steps after Eli and our prisoner guest. As Enforcer, I had a defined place among my people, but no way was I letting Ayatas FireWind behind me. We went through the front door, between the metal detectors, and directly into the bullet-resistant glass cage. The others started to remove weapons as part of the security measures, but I leaned into the mic on the wall and said, "Operation Wise Guy, by orders of the Enforcer."

Wrassler appeared at the front of the inner doors as they whooshed open, blowing in the scent of vamps and sex and something tasty like roast venison. Derek Lee stepped out from the area near the elevator. Both men wore charcoal suits and dove gray shirts with slightly darker dove-ish ties. The grays were Clan Pellissier colors, the livery of the clan for hundreds of years. It was disconcerting to see them in the clothing, though the special-order, thin, cut-resistant Kevlar-Dyneema-based body armor vests they wore beneath their clothes made me happy. I glanced around to see all the security types in similar suits and shirts, armored vests peeking out beneath. Derek stopped several feet back and waited, hands at his sides, less than inches from his weapons.

"Enforcer," Wrassler said.

I glanced at Ayatas and caught him sniffing the air, nostrils widening and contracting. Yeah. HQ was a full olfactory onslaught. I led the way out into the foyer. "Senior Special Agent Ayatas FireWind, of PsyLED, to see the Master of the City of New Orleans and the Greater Southeast United States. We have been scheduled in for tea, though we're early. We can wait in the green room." The green room was a decorative little sitting room with couches and a kitchenette with snacks, colas, coffee, and a variety of teas. It was also a room that could be secured from outside.

"His weapon?" Derek asked.

"Empty of ammo," Eli said. Ayatas gave a micro flinch and I smiled. The skilled PsyLED agent hadn't noticed the weight difference. He might look all smooth and calm and sophisticated, but his emotions had overwhelmed his instincts and training. It might be silly, but that made me like him a little.

"Mr. Pellissier is running a bit late," Wrassler said. "May I suggest a visit to the gym. He's integrating the Mithrans visiting from Canada. Our guest might find it instructional."

At my side, Bruiser shifted slightly, not happy with current events, especially the word *instructional*. Wrassler was a seriously big guy, his nickname derived from the World Wrestling Federation, for which he could have auditioned and become a star if he hadn't sworn loyalty to Leo. *But, instructional?* I thought. *Instructional for whom?* Inside me Beast chuffed. I was not going to ruin these clothes just to put on a show for Leo's guests. A sparring match would ruin my outfit. I liked these clothes. They were girly enough to be . . . well, not guy clothes. And they hid the weapons. I glared at Wrassler. He looked back at me with complete equanimity, even as he passed out the mini-earbuds and mics that would tie us to the comms system. Ayatas didn't get one.

When I didn't answer, Bruiser answered for all of us, saying, "The Enforcer, her second, the Onorio, and Special Agent FireWind would be happy to observe the activities in the gym."

"I'll sit it out," Eli said. He tilted his head to the new security room off the entrance.

Derek met my eyes, his questioning, asking if my guest was a danger to Leo. I shrugged slightly. Derek was Leo's part-time Enforcer and my immediate subordinate. We both knew my position was short term. Finish with the Sangre Duello and I was done with the vamps, but Derek wanted long-term employment and the blood Leo was feeding his mom to keep her alive. Even part-time Enforcer was way above acting as guide and bodyguard. Yet, he said, "If you'll follow me?" He touched his earbud and led the way to the elevator. I put on my mini-headset and followed at the back of the pack, ignoring the inscrutable look Ayatas sent my way. Tribal people did inscrutable well. I wanted to stick my tongue out at him, but I sent him a matching look instead.

We opened the door to the roar of voices and the *clack-clack-clack* of multiple wood staves. I took it in with a glance. All of the fighting rings were in use. There were five now, since the new mats had been delivered and installed. In the back of the room, Leo was sparring with Ro Moore, Katie's Enforcer. Katie was sparring with her sister. And in the ring closest to me, Gee DiMercy, my Enforcer—which still felt weird on my tongue and in my mind—was sparring with a tribal woman, a Canadian vamp.

The woman Gee fought was as tall as I was but with much stronger bone structure and enviable shoulders, with long hair the color of the night sky. Amusement and interest sparkled in her black eyes. Her name was Namida, which meant Star Dancer in Ojibwe, and my Enforcer had been enamored of her since the first time he laid eyes on the vamp in Canada. Judging from the smell of blood and pain on the air, the Canadians were learning how New Orleans's vamps fought. In a word, dirty.

Gee was gifted at personal glamour, and because Namida was so tall, he had made his human-shaped body taller and leaner, and his face more traditionally Anishinaabe than his usual Spanish. Two other Canadian vamps were fighting with local vamps. They were good, their technique different from the La Destreza taught in NOLA.

All the fighting pairs were using sticks instead of longswords, one in each hand, bruising hardwood. Bone-breaking hardwood. Some sparred with two long sticks, some with one long and one shorter. The longer staves had the length and balance and heft of flat swords. The shorter staves were styled to match the *caja corta*, loosely translated as "short box" or "short trap." Both kinds were made for killing Mithrans. And Namida was landing taps on Gee. My Enforcer was one of the best fighters in NOLA, and Namida was laying a hurting on him. She was fast, even for a vamp. But then, Gee might be executing some deceptive courting, letting her beat him up as foreplay.

I stepped inside and out of the doorway, beneath the camera over my head. The others lined up next to me and the door closed. The gym was old-fashioned, with ancient wood floors, patched in a few places since I joined Leo's team. (Beast's claws were hard on floors.) There were cameras everywhere, covering the entire room with its full basketball court, newly painted shuffleboard court, and the padded circular fighting mats.

Gee danced out of the way and I caught a glimpse of Ro in the back, completing a move I hadn't seen her use before. She swept across at Leo's collarbone with her right stick—a decapitation move—and then shoved Leo with the end of the left stick. Had she been wielding swords, she would have taken off his head and pierced his heart, two fatal moves against a vamp at once. As it was, Leo was shoved out of the ring and onto the wood.

He laughed. It was a pleased sound, silken, joyful, captivating. I glanced at Ayatas to see him narrow his eyes at the sensation of the laughter dancing along his skin. I couldn't be mesmerized, but I didn't know if it was a skinwalker thing or a Beast thing. Ayatas didn't roll over and pant for attention, but he did seem a little rattled. Leo's laughter made his people happy, ready to follow him to the ends of the earth. Ro Moore joined in the laughter and Leo said, "You are faster than I expected. The sharing of blood was well worth your healing. I am pleased." Ro clacked her staves together, crossing them without looking away from Leo. He wasn't above cheating. This time, he clacked his sticks together and held out a hand for Ro's staves, before turning to the doorway. "My Enforcer," he called. "You bring us a guest."

I gave him a small nod. Leo was wearing fighting clothes fashioned with a twist all his own. He was shirtless, to show the pure white of his scars, scars from wounds that no human could have survived, and not many vamps. Nudity in the fighting rings was uncommon among the Europeans and there had been a lot of chatter about Leo going naked for the entire Sangre Duello proceedings, just to shake them up. Sadly, that had sorta been my idea, when I suggested they play Petruchio and Kate in *Taming of the Shrew* to shake up the EuroVamps. I hadn't meant naked. I really hadn't meant naked.

There was also chatter about Leo leaving blood on his body after feedings and fights, and acting the crude, naïve thug, to throw off Titus's fine-tuned sensibilities. It would make a good show, but Leo was fastidious. No way was he going to be messy, bloody, or dirty or display unsophisticated or bad manners for any length of time. I was pretty sure Derek had a pool going for how long Leo would last unshowered.

The Sangre Duello was a more violent, less systematic version of Les Duels Sang, the codified legal duels that decided a vamp's place in clan and city. While it started out polite, Sangre Duello had no matches where the winner moved up in a predetermined order. The Duello meant death at the end as challengers dueled and killed opponents until the only vamps left were the most protected, the very best fighters, and the MOCs. First blood in the battles was meant to maim, and duels to the death were expected. There was no way to think of the contests as games. They required mental stamina, clear thinking, excellent understanding of tactics and strategy, physical endurance, and skill. And in the end, the willingness to kill.

When the European emperor's servants came ashore, onto Leo's territory, and attacked by means both magical and weapons based, Leo's U.S. vampire scions and human servants started dying in greater numbers, and Leo could see his power base slipping away. To keep his people alive and safe, the MOC felt he had no choice but to demand Sangre Duello. But if Leo lost, his loyal people lost and would likely be killed outright, as would all his blood-servants, blood-slaves, cattle, and every other para as Titus and his victorious fangheads rolled over New Orleans and took over the United States. Hence Leo's consideration of most anything to throw off the EV emperor's plans and reasoning.

Eli had suggested getting together with some former Navy SEALs and swimming out to the emperor's boat with enough explosives to sink them to the bottom of the gulf, but there were likely prisoners on the boat. Leo had nixed that idea, but it was still floating around the security types as a last-ditch strategy. And likely it was something the U.S. military was keeping on a back burner as a black ops possibility should Titus win.

Leo popped in front of us, moving with vamp speed and the distinctive sound of displaced air. His black hair had come loose from its fighting queue at the back of his neck and the old scars on his torso were bone white against his vamp-pale skin. His fangs were out. His still-human eyes were on Ayatas. "My guest for tea this evening," he said around his fangs. "My sworn ally Rosanne Romanello, from Sedona, has hinted that you are quite the warrior." He extended Ro Moore's staves. "Shall we?" It was more a demand than an invitation.

I turned to Ayatas. He had visited the Master of the City of Sedona? I knew Rosanne. I had probably helped to save her life. She knew what I was, and would have had no reason to keep any secrets from Ayatas. I gave the special agent a toothy expression that couldn't really be called amusement. More like *gotcha*. Holding his eyes, I said, "Have fun, Ayatas. And, Leo, watch out. He's sneaky as a snake."

"The better to spar with." Leo waggled the staves.

His face showing nothing, Ayatas slid out of his jacket, then his shoulder holster, and unclipped his badge, handing them to Derek. He pulled an elastic out of a pocket and pulled his hair back, tucking it into his shirt where the long strands couldn't blind him. The tail could still be used as a weapon, but it would take close contact to get a hand on it. Then he kicked off his dress shoes and peeled off his socks. Even his sweaty feet smelled floral as he accepted the staves and walked across the gym to the empty fighting mat.

The fighting mats cleared out and the number of spectators along the walls and sitting on the bleachers increased. Someone whispered, *"Prepararse para la muerte,"* which was Spanish for "Prepare for death." I said, softly, but loud enough for Leo to hear, "This man is a special agent of PsyLED and under the protection of the Enforcer." And he may be my brother. Or not. If Ayatas somehow hurt Leo, I might be able to keep him alive long enough to get him outside.

The men went through the meet-and-greet ceremony, a truncated version that skipped the names and titles and went straight to tapping staves together in a salute. Ayatas moved in and tapped Leo's staves, then back out, fast. Faster than human. Skinwalker-fast. I knew that speed. Without Beast, it was my own speed. Pulling on Beast's abilities was like skinwalker on turbo.

Leo backed away and his staves started circling in La Destreza, the cage of death, the magic circle. So did Ayatas's. Interesting and interestinger. Ayatas knew La Destreza.

They engaged slowly as Leo tapped Ayatas's staves, a two-tap with his long stick. Ayatas tapped back with lunges, feeling out his opponent. His feet were long and slender at the heels, wide at the toes, the shape of the feet of a man who wore moccasins in his youth, not boots or shoes, yet the skin of his feet was smooth—the feet of a man who got regular pedis. Or who shifted shape to an animal and then back into the form of his human DNA, with no calluses or scars. His knees were bent for balance, his quads pushing against the suit pants. He was poised, posture neat, his body stable, rock steady. The taps sped up, becoming clacks, loud enough to echo on the bare walls. No one was taking bets on the winner. Not yet. Ayatas landed three taps on Leo. The Master of the City laughed and tossed his shoulder-length hair. I realized he had left it down to give Ayatas an advantage. Leo's version of fighting honor.

The clacks sped. And sped again. I found myself moving closer, watching every move. Beast crouched at the front of my mind, panting, chuffing when one of the men landed what would have been a bloody deadly wound had they fought with steel. Leo's long stave caught in Ayatas's hair, ripping out the elastic, sending the hair in a swan-wing arc, free.

And then, with his hair flying, Ayatas raised the short stave back over his shoulder and threw it. Like a small ax. Like a tomahawk.

Time seemed to slow down for me. Not the Gray Between of time bending, but the battle time slowing that allowed me to see everything happening. The muscles in Ayatas's arm flexing and releasing. The spin of the practice sword. The stave hitting Leo in the collarbone, slightly to the left of middle.

And memory flashed over me.

The trees had been brilliant with fall colors. The smell of meat in the smokehouse and the wisps of hickory smoke had filled my lungs. The house was part cabin, part white-man house, with long, smooth boards over the outside, painted white, and chinked logs on the inside for warmth. It was Elisi's *house, on land she farmed. But* Edoda *was the hunter, and he had brought back black bear and two bucks, all three animals scored with claw marks.*

I wanted to hunt with Edoda, *not farm like* Elisi. Edoda *was humoring me. The clan women were butchering the meat, watching while* Edoda *taught me to fight.*

"Did you see?" he said. "The moment of release?"

I nodded.

Edoda *placed the smaller ax in my hand. It was a white-man ax, the head made of steel. It was very expensive and* Edoda *had bought it with the skins of his hunting and the* dalonige' i *he had found in the riverbed. White man's first love—gold—had purchased the ax and the new dress I wore, the spinning wheel, the hoe, and other farming tools for* Elisi. Edoda *pointed out the parts of the ax: "Head, handle. On the head is the poll, the eye, the cheek, the toe." He touched different spots on the sharp edge. "The bit or blade." He slid his long fingers down to where the head joined the handle. "Beard, shoulder, heel." His*

*hand reached the curved handle. "Belly. This curve is
what gives the ax its balance and its strength." He slid his
hands down the handle. "Throat, grip, knob." He placed
my hand on the grip. Adjusted it. Showed me how it felt
by swinging his weapon, grip only tight enough to guide,
not strangle, the wood. I swung mine.*

*Edoda nodded. I had done it right. He spun, his arm
flashing back, muscles tightening and releasing. His
larger ax flew. Bit deeply into the dead tree. I copied his
movements. My small blade sank in beside his. Not so
deeply. Only the toe of the blade. But it held.*

"Well done, Gvhe.*" He patted my head.*

His hand had been warm, smooth. I had been safe.

I blinked back into the gym, my body bathed in a cold
sweat, the memory a fleeting moment, now gone.

Leo laughed and I focused on the combatants. The battle was over. Leo had a bloody ear and Ayatas had blood
on his face and a busted lip. They had played rough. Ayatas shook an injured hand and Leo offered to heal him.
Ayatas refused with words that showed he knew vamp
politics. "I am honored, Leo Pellissier, Master of the City
of New Orleans. But my kind heal well on our own."

The men were bruised and one of the battle-hard
staves was broken. That was a first.

"You're both stupid," I muttered. But I must have spoken too loudly as they both shifted to me, bodies bladed,
two warriors facing a common foe, though relaxed, the
foe not attacking and of no real danger.

I turned and left the room, walking alone down the
empty hallways, leaving behind the echoing voices and
the smell of testosterone and blood. Remembering the
sound of my father's voice.

"Well done, *Gvhe*." *Gvhe*. Wildcat. My name had been
Wildcat.

I still had a few minutes before tea and wandered to what
once had been the conference room but for now was the
main security area. The walls of HQ had been newly
spelled, top to lowest basement, against flood and rising

water table by the local witch coven. There was a hidden weapons storage unit on the back wall behind a new shelving unit, one of four in the complex. There was enough coffee and tea for a platoon to survive a week-long hurricane. HQ was now equipped with three different methods of making power, plus batteries big enough to run all the computer systems and one coffeemaker for that same week. We had guns, computers, and coffee, everything we'd need in case of problems. We might go hungry, but we'd be well caffeinated.

The big view screens over the table and around the room were all lit, all showing images of different parts of the compound, captured on camera, divided as to location. There were a series of the grounds. Tex (a vamp) and his dog were patrolling. There weren't a lot of vamps who liked dogs and vice versa. Three humans and two more vamps covered the grounds with him, inside the tall walls. A loyal sniper provided overwatch on our roof and grounds from his hide across the street. Things were as safe as I could make them.

There was a series of views of the gym, the area outside Leo's office, and his new, more secure bedroom. There were two from inside the blood-servant rec room. A series of camera views showed the entrances and the elevators (including the ones that had once been secret) and the various stairwells.

I looked at the tea room screen. I was late. Pulling on Beast-speed, I took the stairs. At a dead run, pulling on Beast's power and the application of Newton's Laws of Motion—inertia and all that stuff—I raced down the halls and spun into the tea room off the gym, using the door-jamb to fling myself inside. The others were there—Leo; his primo, Del; Scrappy; Bruiser; Grégoire; Katie; Eli; and Ayatas. An eclectic bunch and too many people and scents for the small room. The table, laden with food and carafes, had been placed in the center of the small couches, and extra chairs had been shoved in.

To the guard at the door, I said, "No interruptions," and I locked the door. Breathing hard, I tapped off my earbud and started the intros, keeping them short and truncated, leaving off all historical titles and lineage, which was usually so boring to humans.

"Master of the City and the territories of Louisiana, the southeastern states except Florida, and holder of goodwill treaties of loyalty from six other Masters of the City from across America, Leonard Pellissier," I said.

"Katherine Fonteneau, formerly the heir to the Master of the City. Current status in flux. Grégoire, Blood Master of Clan Arceneau, and secundo heir to Leonard Pellissier. Also Blood Master of European territory and clans." Blondie had killed his EV master, but until the threat here was satisfied, he wouldn't be spending any time overseas.

"Adelaide Mooney, Leo's primo and legal counsel, formally a blood-servant of Lincoln Shaddock of Asheville." I caught up on a few breaths and sat in an empty chair, before continuing. "George Dumas, Onorio, former primo to Leo Pellissier. Lee Williams Watts, personal assistant to Mr. Pellissier. Eli Younger, of Yellowrock Securities, second to the Enforcer of Leo Pellissier. And the Enforcer, Jane Yellowrock." I pointed to myself.

"Mr. Pellissier and others, please meet PsyLED Senior Special Agent Ayatas FireWind, direct subordinate to Assistant Director Soul, in charge of the eastern states, recently promoted and moved from a western law enforcement territory. He is an unclassified, noncontagious, non-moon-called shape-shifter."

Leo said, "It was my understanding that Rick LaFleur was the PsyLED agent over my territories. Has he been deposed? Deceased?"

"I'm technically Agent LaFleur's superior in PsyLED chain of command. I expected him to be here for this meeting. He must have been held up." Ayatas gave a charming smile and added, "I've already discovered that New Orleans's traffic is difficult to navigate."

I managed to control my shock. Rick was coming here? When had Ayatas called him? A tap sounded on the door and a faint scent wafted beneath. Rick. Standing, I unlocked and reopened the door. "Special Agent Rick LaFleur," I said as my ex entered.

Rick nodded but didn't meet my eyes. The black were-leopard took the only other seat, beside mine.

Beast growled inside. *Bad mate. Did not scent-mark Jane. Did not look at Jane.* I ignored her. She thought at me, *Rick is not mate now?*

No. Rick is not mate. Not now. Not ever again.

I retook my seat and looked over the room, taking in the mingled scents. Six men, four women. Multiple paras and humans, in a room built for half that number of creatures. Rick looked different. His hair had been stark black. Now there were long, thick strands of silver-white all through it. His face was furrowed and lined and he looked as if he hadn't slept in days. I frowned, not knowing what it might mean but having no way to ask.

Leo inclined his head and added, "My Enforcer neglected to mention many of our titles and lands, including her own. Jane Yellowrock, Enforcer to the Master of the City of New Orleans and . . . the Dark Queen."

Rick slanted me a look, a sad smile on his face. Bruiser watched Rick watching me. Ayatas frowned slightly, obviously searching for some correlation for Dark Queen in his studies. "Means a formality in place for the upcoming duels," I lied. "Scrappy?"

Lee leaned toward the table, her red hair swinging at her shoulders, and prepared cups of coffee or tea to our usual specifications, and then cups for the guests, as was appropriate for low-level humans and low-level, nonvamp paras.

Ayatas said, "I am honored to have sparred with the Master of the City of New Orleans and even more honored to take refreshment with him and with his people." He accepted the coffee, black, and sipped. "The coffee is very good."

Huh. Not bad. I leaned back, cup in my left hand, my right in a faux pocket, fingers on the small weapon strapped there. I sipped, keeping my eyes on Ayatas in case I had read him all wrong and he was here to kill Leo or maybe all of us.

The scents in the room were overlapping and heavy. Vamp, blood, skinwalker, werecat, Onorio human.

I sipped and breathed through my mouth, tasting the scents. There was nothing of anger or hostility present, despite the testosterone and general irascibility, so I concentrated on the tea instead of the diplomatic chitchat. Boring, dull, tedious, and mind-numbing conversation. And thankfully, not dialogue the Enforcer had to pay attention to beyond listening for cues that could lead to violence, anything that meant I needed to shoot someone. If anything else came up, Scrappy would send me a memo and then beat me over the head with it until I read it.

Ayatas was droning on and on about the duel and the technicalities of the law regarding hosting and broadcasting and gambling. And the tax status of said gambling monies. He used phrases like the Interstate Wire Act, the Department of Justice, the Professional and Amateur Sports Protection Act, and the Bradley Act, some of which might have been the same things. Or not.

Ayatas wanted to be present, no matter where the Sangre Duello took place. Right. Like Leo was going to allow a cop on-site—unless he had claws in the cop's life and total control over him. Again, I got to ignore it all, which was a good thing, because booooring. And then the meeting was over and Leo and his cadre, including Bruiser, Rick, and Ayatas, stood for small talk.

I didn't look at my ex, slipping out the door as he greeted the other special agent and Bruiser. I might have stayed or pressed my ear to the door, listening in, but I caught a scent that made my hackles rise. Beast snarled and growled softly deep inside. *Werecat. Were-big-cat. Have smelled big-cat before. Am alpha.*

She was right. We were alpha to the werecat I smelled in the hallway. It was the scent of the black wereleopard Kemnebi, part of the International Association of Weres and the Party of African Weres.

Black wereleopards were from Gabon in the African Congo. Kem's mate had turned Rick. The female had then been summarily executed for the deed, leaving a lot of bad feelings between the survivors. To keep Rick safe from Kem, I had sorta become alpha over him and claimed my ex. It was complicated. And Kem was in HQ.

My life was a soap opera with fangs and fur.

I tapped on my comms unit. "Update on weres," I said. A voice I didn't recognize verified all I had deduced by scent. *Dang.* I trotted up the hallway and took the elevator, tracking Kem's personal aroma.

According to the scent patterns, Rick and Kem had met in the foyer, among a group of weres, several of whom were unfamiliar and not catty, and Kem had embraced Rick. That must have been awkward.

I sniffed, pulling in the air over my tongue as Beast would do, parsing the scents. Two African werelions, whom I had met. And . . . oddly, I smelled werewolves. Leo and the wolves still didn't get along, and most hated me, since I'd killed off an entire pack. The dogs and cats didn't get along. The mismatched group had a grindylow with them, one I hadn't sniffed before and who, presumably, had traveled with the Africans. Grindys were supposed to keep the peace, but they were good only for were-on-human violence. Were-on-were or were-on-vamp wasn't covered in the grindy's job description. According to the scents, the various para groups had separated and some had moved off to different areas of HQ.

"Legs? Everything all right?"

I looked up in surprise to see Wrassler standing over me. I put my shoulders back and dropped my arms. "How long have I been standing here?"

"Immobile? Hunched over, sniffing the air like somebody's brought in Hot-N-Now Krispy Kremes? 'Bout three minutes."

I explained the problem to Wrassler. "And if a law enforcement officer, say Rick LaFleur, dies here, on land that isn't technically U.S. territory, but technically belongs to Leo, then Leo also has to act as judge and jury and I have to be executioner. And we'll be right back where we were before Leo made peace—sorta—with the were coalition. We could have a war."

"So you think the weres are here to sabotage the duel?"

"Maybe?" I pulled my cell and texted Alex: *Werecats and werewolves in HQ. Check status.* To Wrassler I asked, "Where are they now?"

Wrassler limped to the doorway on his prosthetic leg and called to the woman at the small room to the right of the entrance, a room that held a compact version of HQ's communication and security control system. "Location of the weres?" he asked.

"On the elevator," a woman's voice said. "Hell. It's going down. Should be going up to the library. No weapons on the scanner or pat-down. Dogs and cats in same elevator. Guided, guarded by Tequila Antifreeze." She cursed foully. "Elevator cam shows Antifreeze is out cold."

To access any of the floors, the elevator required a palm print, but the print could be made under duress. I met Wrassler's eyes. "SOD," we both said at the same time. Side by side, we whirled for the stairs.

"SOD's guards?" I asked.

"Two. Human. You can move faster than I can," Wrassler said. "Go! I'll get a team to meet you there."

I pulled on Beast-speed and raced down the steps, my feet barely touching every third or fourth tread, my hands shoving me off the landings and pulling me around tight corners. If they killed the Son of Darkness we could be in trouble. Besides, that was my job.

Slowing on sub-four, I let Beast into the front of my brain. She took over my footsteps and my body movements, making me silent. Stealthily, I moved to the bottom of the hidden stairs, in the shadows of sub-five. The lowest basement at vamp HQ had a claylike floor, poor lighting, and a distinct scent that combined stale walls, damp, mold, the herbal and funeral-flower-sweet stench of vamps, a hint of something tart, and the particular stink of the Son of Darkness. The elevator was to my right on the far end of the basement space and the SOD hung to my immediate left, shackled to the wall by silver. The bag of bones and goo was Leo's ace in the hole to any act of war by the Europeans. They had tried to get him back several times, but taking him by magic or dragging the heartless—literally—and broken thing up five flights of stairs while fighting a pitched battle had proven impossible.

The SOD had gone by many names in his life; the most recent was Joses Santana, preceded by Joses son of Judas, and before that, Yosace Bar-Ioudas. He was one of two sons of Judas Iscariot, the man who betrayed Jesus. Joses and his brother were the fathers of all fangheads. His blood was so strong that he had survived poisoning by a rainbow dragon, silver poisoning, and the removal of his heart. I was particularly proud of the heart removal as that had been my coup, but I should have broken my word and taken his head, because he was still a threat and a danger to us all.

I could hear people talking just ahead and below, and no more blood scent than usual. No battle. No danger. At the moment there was no threat of the SOD getting away and no humans or vamps to protect, so I eased up and pressed against the wall in the shadows to evaluate everything. Why were they here? What did they want? And why were they all together? I was downwind from the group. The stench of SOD and various were-creatures was overpowering, rushing up the stairs.

Two guards lay on the clay floor, bound and gagged, mad as heck, but not out cold. Over them was chained Joses Santana. The SOD had begun to heal, even without a heart, and looked human rather than like a sack of broken bones and slime. His legs and arms were in the right places, his joints aligned the correct way, and his eyes seemed to be focusing on the group in front of him, though his mouth hung open at an angle and his dry triangle of a tongue protruded to one side between oversized fangs. He was a little more hairy than once before, but that was likely just an oddity of his healing. Or of the werewolf who bit him from time to time. Life in vamp HQ was weird.

The mixed were-group stood in a small semicircle facing the vamp prisoner, but slightly to my left, in front of me. Asad, the African werelion, and his wife, Nantale, in human form, were in the forefront of the grouping. Were-creatures mostly corresponded with the body-weight-to-mass ratio, making Asad a huge man and his lion a midsized-to-smaller cat. He was black skinned, with coarse hair in shades of black streaked with lighter brown, and he wore white robes in the Arabian style. Asad looked human enough until you saw his eyes, a lion-

gold with a predatory gleam. The man was a war chief for
his human tribe, the Fulani, and his wife, Nantale, looked
like a Nubian goddess, even without the cloth of gold and
all the beaten gold jewelry she had worn when I saw her
last. She was tall and muscular with broad shoulders and
long legs.

The other werecat was my personal pain in the butt.
Tall and thin, his muscles were well defined, his ebony
skin stretched over a frame without an ounce of fat. Beautiful, he had the sculpted features of an ancient Egyptian
sarcophagus with full lips and tip-tilted eyes blacker than
a moonless night. Like Asad, he was dressed in the flowing white outer robe of an Arabian prince, and beneath it,
he wore black that vanished into the shadows, regal garb,
which . . . I stopped. Dang it all. Kemmie was wearing an
emblem sewn on his robes, a lizard eating his tail. I hadn't
seen that emblem in months, and hadn't paid much attention at the time, but the tail-biting lizard looked like
something that had been stitched into the clothing worn
by the blood-servants of Jack Shoffru, one of Leo's sworn
enemies, now dead. Some of Shoffru's people had survived, and the living and the dead had been wearing a
similar emblem embroidered on their inner shirts. Had
someone taken over Shoffru's clan, suborned Kem, and
come back for Leo? Was this happenstance or a declara-
tion of war?

There were three werewolves, four if I counted my
wolf. And I did. Brute stood in front of the SOD as if
guarding him, fangs bared at the grouping, growling low,
a sound that shivered up through the clay floor and the
walls like the vibration of a generator. He had seriously
huge teeth, and at over three hundred pounds, the white
werewolf was big enough to take on Asad and maybe live
to tell about it. He'd put on weight in the time I'd known
him, but even bulked up he couldn't defeat the whole
crew. I could envision the werewolves bearbaiting Brute
while the cats tore the SOD to pieces. Or stole him off the
wall.

Unless Brute timewalked.

The wolves were in human form, and I spared a glance

to take them in. Two white, one black, all of them young, hip, dangerous. There had once been half a dozen small packs in the Mountain States. Then a new guy had emerged, taken over, and united the packs from several states into the Bighorns, making a megapack. The social structures of were-creatures were nothing like human social structures, and werewolf packs were the most abnormal of the weird and strange, having no wolf females. Werewolves were temperamental, and without a strong pack leader, they fought. A lot.

On the floor behind the wolves was Tequila Antifreeze, putting a hand to his skull. Someone had knocked him down. He'd been injured the last time he followed orders. I didn't want him—or anyone—hurt like that again. For now, they hadn't killed Antifreeze.

Beast stared at the bad guys. *Beast is best ambush hunter.*

Eeny, meeny, miny, moe. I thought, trying to decide who to take out first.

Asad took a step closer to the SOD, licking his lips, his wife at his side. Had they gotten a taste of the SOD before Brute got there? I looked up at the cameras and made a mental note to get someone to check the feed.

The midsized grindylow hiding above the weres wasn't a surprise, as the creatures tended to appear whenever were-creatures went near humans. This one was bigger than Pea and Bean, but still the neon green of a juvie, and cuter than any steel-clawed killer had any right to be. She was perched on a beam up high, watching.

At that moment Brute must have caught my scent because he stopped growling and glanced at the stairwell. Into the sudden silence, the visitors started speaking.

"What is it?" one of the wolves asked in a British accent. It was the black guy. He leaned in, sniffing the SOD. To the wolf beside him, he said, "I can't believe that you brought me here to look at this. Pathetic artwork, if that's what it is. And the stench is dreadful. The vampire bitch must have no nose at all."

Vampire bitch? I thought.

"Not art. This thing is alive," Asad said. "The fanghead female told me it is very powerful. The blood drinkers value it greatly. If we take it and drink from it we will grow in strength and power and be able to defeat the bloodsuckers."

"Do tell. It bloody well reeks of several old vampires, rotting blood, and wet wolf."

"You smell the dog at his feet," Nantale said, dismissive.

"Call werewolves *dogs* again and I'll slit your throat and eat your entrails before you can blink," the British wolfman said with a patently false smile. "As long as we rescue the white wolf, I don't really care what you do with the artwork."

Rescue?

Stupid dog thinks Brute is prisoner, Beast thought at me.

The werecats took a collective step forward, crowding Brute. His growl came back, louder, deeper. His hackles rose, shoulders hunched.

"Phillip, I don't think he's a prisoner," one of the wolves said, warning in his tone.

The third wolf drew a weapon and racked back the slide.

The faintest footsteps sounded on the stairs behind me. Help was on the way. Beast-fast, I drew a vamp-killer and the Walther PK .380. Stepped from the stairs into the shadows, into a decent firing position.

"Bugger it all. Are you insane?" the Brit demanded of the wolf with the gun.

Overhead, the grindylow shivered and gathered herself for a launch.

The armed wolf pointed the business end of the gun at Phillip.

"What the bloody hell?"

Raising my voice I said, "Who let the kitties and puppies down here?"

The small group whirled to me. The wolf with the gun snarled. Stepped away to get a line of fire and pointed it at me, back to Phillip, then at Brute, indecisive, his body rotating slowly, leaving him open to attack. My own aim was steady on him, but I didn't want to fire into what sounded like internal werewolf politics. My killing a were in HQ could complicate a lot of things.

"Antifreeze, you okay?" I asked.

He mumbled, "I was taking them to the library. They said they had an appointment with Ernestine. It wasn't on the calendar, so I called her. She said to send them up, that she'd meet them there. After that, I don't know. I don't remember how I got here."

It hadn't been willingly. Ernestine was the vamp accountant, a withered, wrinkled ancient woman I called Raisin. People met with her all the time, but not usually in the library, and the mention of a female vamp indicated that the weres had had inside help in staging this FUBAR. *Dang it.*

The wolf with the gun growled; aimed it steadily at me. I whipped my blade into a modified La Destreza stance and took two steps, edging between them and the SOD and Brute. I gave them my best menacing grin. Beast glowed through my eyes, a bright golden shade. The wolves stared.

"Furballs and hairballs with guns, working together," I said wonderingly, giving the help behind me access and time to position themselves. "Who'da thunk it?"

Nantale stepped forward, ignoring my insults. "Jane Yellowrock. We are pleased to know that you still live. The Party of African Weres is happy to see you breathing."

"Really?" I angled the blade, spinning it so the light caught the edges, so the dogs and cats could see the silver plating. A lot of paras were easily poisoned by silver, including were-creatures and vamps. But I didn't have enough silver on me to take them all down. *Come on, Wrassler. Get here. Move it!* "The reason I disbelieve you, kitty cat, is because I recall you bringing Paka, a black wereleopard in heat, into NOLA and siccing the little kitty on my then-boyfriend."

"We were not informed that Rick LaFleur was involved in a romantic relationship. It was unfortunate you suffered because of the spell she wove."

Kem had known. I smelled, felt, sensed Wrassler and

at least four others moving into the stairwell behind me. Finally. But I needed to stall. "You knew that Raymond Micheika, the leader of the International Association of Weres, paid Paka to do exactly as she did. But you might not know that Paka had taken a prior deal, from Kemnebi, to spell Rick and bring him intense pain, turning him into his cat and then leaving him that way. Forever. Terrible thing for a were to do to an officer of the law, wouldn't you say?"

Asad slowly turned to Kem-cat, a question on his face. "Paka made parley with you prior to her agreement with us?"

"The woman lies," Kemnebi said, speaking of me.

"You are impudent," I said. "This woman is your alpha"—I tapped my chest with the hilt—"and though I never sent the video file to the Party of African Weres, I have you on film, groveling at my feet.

"Wrassler, now, if you please."

Blood-servant-fast, my backup boiled into the basement. Now we were more evenly matched and my heart was no longer in my throat. I slowed the pirouetting vamp-killer and holstered the H&K. Kept my vamp-killer pointed at Kem. "Tell them," I commanded.

"She smells of alpha. She smells of power and nothing of fear. Does she speak the truth? Is she your master?" Asad asked Kem, horror in his voice. Nantale looked at the SOD on the wall, indecision in her eyes.

"Not worth fighting all of us and a grindy to steal the bag of bones," I said. Letting Beast into my voice, I growled, "Kneel, Kem-cat. Kneel and give me your throat or you die tonight for the crime of disloyalty to your alpha."

Kem snarled and leaped at me.

The werewolf fired.

The Brit attacked him.

They tumbled onto the floor, biting, snapping. The gun went off again.

In the space of two heartbeats, everything went to hell in a handbasket.

CHAPTER 4

Not Everything in Were Culture Required Teeth

In midair, Kem's claws came out; his hands sprouted black fur. His fangs extended. Kemnebi screamed in fury and challenge.

I pulled on skinwalker magics. Pulled on the power that made me Kem's alpha.

Stepped aside at the last possible moment. Dropped low. Lifted the blade.

Slashed it across Kem's body. The scream changed, a high-pitched squeal of the dying.

I tore my blade out of him, altering his angle of leap. His speed carried him past me. Blood splattered against the wall and over the Son of Darkness. Kem slammed into the wall next to the SOD, hung there a moment, like a parody, and slid to the clay floor, a bloody half-shifted leopard.

The elevator doors closed, taking the scent and sound of fighting werewolves and one of the security guys with it. No one else moved. The only sound was the piteous mewling of Kem and the drip of blood. And the soft indrawn breath of the SOD. The stink of gunfire and the stench of werewolf blood.

Beast is best hunter. Beast killed leopard.

"Kem will live, if he shifts," I said, mostly to her.

Asad stepped closer and leaned down to observe Kemnebi, sniffing. "I don't believe that he can shift. Silvered blades?" he asked. He sounded amused and his expression was the same one an overfed housecat might wear while watching a mouse stuck in a trap.

I hadn't left any silver in him, but Kemnebi was prone to drinking lots of alcohol, maybe more than shifting could handle. If his liver was compromised and if I also cut his liver with a silvered blade . . . Well, *crap.* I said, "Make him shift."

"No," Nantale said. "By your own words you are his alpha. You are the only one here who might be able to affect a change to his cat."

I opened my mouth. Closed it. *Double crap.* I walked into that with both feet. Asad smiled at me, showing large white teeth in his very dark face. Yeah. He thought this was all funny. Not a lot of love between African lions and leopards in the wild. Not a lot in the wereworld either. And so far as I knew, no nonwere had ever forced a werecreature to shift shape. Meaning, I likely couldn't do it no matter how hard I tried, no matter that I was Kem's alpha and had magic of my own. Were-shifting was very different from skinwalker shifting. I used the genetic structure of another creature to shift into the chosen shape. Werecreatures *were* that shape, their forms altered and changed by the were-prion.

I nudged the gasping cat with a foot. Thought about how Leo sounded when he called his people. Mesmerizing, compulsive, compelling, demanding. I wasn't into convincing people to do what I wanted. I was more the stab-them-first-and-persuade-afterward kinda chick. That hadn't worked so well here. I glared at the dying werecat.

"Ja—Enforcer," Wrassler said, interrupting himself and going for professional instead of friendly. Not a good sign. "Kem did attack first; however, it would be . . . unfortunate if the leader of the PAW delegation were to die at your hand."

"Uh-huh." And then I had an idea. I was brilliant. "Get LaFleur down here. Tell him to run." All that boring reading about paranormals and the proper way to react within and between species would come in handy now.

I heard Wrassler repeat my command into the comms system and I prodded Kem again. This time I got blood on my shoe. "Stay alive." I almost added *please*, but that wasn't an alpha word, so I said, "That's an order." I didn't see an improvement, but maybe it helped. Who knew? While I waited, I cleaned my blade on Kem's clothes and put it away. Then cleaned my shoe. I sensed disapproval from the African cats.

Beast wasn't happy either, kneading my mind with her claws, a sensation that made me think my brain was bleeding. She had been in the mood for a good fight, and with Kem out so fast, she was being denied it. And now I was gonna try to save the cat she had almost killed. She was pouting. I ignored her.

Moments later I heard the elevator settle to the bottom. The doors opened and I smelled a female security guard and Rick. I didn't look up and he stayed inside the elevator, the bright lights illuminating the scene. Yeah. There was too much blood. I had messed up.

Bruiser stepped into sub-five, walking from the stairs where I had stood. I could smell his worry as he took in the scene. I didn't dare look at him. I was afraid I'd see a look in his eyes that would tell me how badly I'd screwed the pooch. Or screwed the cat.

"Rick, do you know this cat?" I asked, pointing.

"Yes."

"Specify the relationship."

The room went quiet again. Into the silence Bruiser asked, "Are you sure you want to do this?"

"Nope. Not at all. Rock, meet hard place." To Rick I repeated, "Specify."

He didn't ask me questions, which I appreciated. He crossed the distance of the basement to me, his feet cat-silent, his silver and black hair the only thing catching the light and gleaming. "Kemnebi had taken my maker, Safia, his assistant, as mate, though she didn't care for him. He never forgave me for seducing Safia's affections, if not her body. I have been in his fangs." The last line meant he had been at Kem's mercy for teaching and the words were laced with revulsion. Kem had been a cruel master to Rick.

"Kemnebi is my beta," I said. "I am his alpha. He attacked me without provocation and outside of proper hierarchy practices and traditions. It's my right to . . ." Not punish. The word came to me. "To rebuke him."

"You know the Merged Laws of the Cursed of Artemis," Nantale said, surprised.

The book of were law was on my bedside table. I had flipped through it, then read the most pertinent parts, like how to deal with were-creature chain of command, if the situation ever presented itself. Most of were law was bloody and full of domination tactics.

Beast had liked most of it. I hadn't. My Beast moved closer in my mind, listening with the same attention she gave a hunt.

I didn't respond to the catwoman, but continued speaking to Rick. "His actions against you, while cruel, were within his rights as spurned mate. But his actions against me were improper and constitute attempted murder of his alpha. He attacked without challenge. It's also my . . ." *Oh crap.* I went blank. "Ummm. It's my right to . . ." Not punish. And then it came to me. "My right to renegotiate his status as a way of saving his life."

I bent down to the dying cat. He was lying in a pretty big pool of blood and his breathing was getting more shallow. "I remove Kemnebi from his official status, placing him as my zed, the least of all my people. In retaliation for his attack, I seize all his worldly goods and all his subordinate cats. Rick LaFleur, you are now my second in command, my beta, and I give you Kemnebi. You are now his alpha."

Rick started laughing, a sound more like grief than amusement.

I glanced up at my honeybunch. Bruiser was watching me with unsmiling eyes. He had helped me research this part of were-creatures' social structure. He knew what I had to do to save Kem's life. I didn't like the cat, but still . . . "I wish my former beta to live"—*liar, liar*—"in shame," I added more truthfully. "I gift my new beta with all Kemnebi's worldly goods and status and cats." I looked at Rick. He was watching me. "In recognition of my gift of your augmented status, you will force Kemnebi to shift to his cat form and save his life, making him your blood beta and beholden to you." Blood beta was a tricky path to negotiate. It was a lot like winning a vamp's clan but more. I hoped Rick was up to it. "Do you agree?"

Rick was looking down at the cat who had connived to make his life a hell. "I do. But I don't like it at all."

"Can you force him to shift even with silver in his blood?"

Rick frowned. "Yes."

I leaned over and dipped the fingers of my right hand into Kem's blood and held out that hand to Rick. He clasped my hand in his and we shook on it. Not everything in were culture required teeth. "Do not disappoint me, beta."

Rick, still holding my bloody hand, said softly, "I will never again disappoint or pain my alpha."

"Ummm." That said a lot more than I wanted it to, but if Kem was to live, we'd have to renegotiate the wording later. I released my grip on Rick's hand and started to step away.

My new beta held on. His eyes were glowing cat-green and when he spoke there was a purring growl in his throat. "I've never done this, only read about it. It would be easier if I was in cat shape, and so I may need help." He dropped to his knees and shoved his free hand into Kem's wound. I felt were-power in Rick's palm grow, a buzzing, hot-cold mist-smoke of electricity. And then I felt Rick do . . . something. He drew on my own power, and I felt the Gray Between bend and stretch, the way it might if I had hooks in my flesh and he tugged on them. "This will do," he rumbled. He held the bloodied hand to his mouth and licked

Kem's blood. Our connection was so close I could taste the blood, sickly and silvered. *Gack, ick.*

Good werecat blood, Beast thought. *Beast is best hunter.*

I didn't respond.

Beast would kill Kem-cat.

Yeah, I thought back. *Not happening.*

Three limbed, Rick crawled over Kem's body, as if mounting the dying cat, and placed his mouth at the man's ear, saying, "My blood to your blood. My will over your will. Moon to moon." His voice dropped to a growl. "You are mine." Even deeper, the growl nearly as deep as Brute's: "Shift."

I felt the were-magics sparkle through me and over my skin like an electrified mist, scalding and frigid at once. Kemnebi's flesh began to lose cohesiveness. A pale fog sifted from his skin, blurring. Dark lights sparkled through the haze, looking like black crystals. Kemnebi was the first were-creature the human world had ever seen, the first I had seen shift, all on TV when the paras came out of the closet.

The black lights surrounding him darkened, deepened. His bones popped and crunched as they shortened or lengthened, the joints changing shape. Black hair sprouted over the visible part of his body and his spine curved in and then arched out. The feline canines in his gums elongated and his jaw and skull took on catlike contours. His flesh rippled, stretched. Rick released my hand and bent to the side, still crouched, still holding his own shape in the midst of the were-energies. Three minutes passed, and at last a breathing, black-coated jungle cat lay on the floor in the pool of blood and ruined clothing he had lost as a man. In the shadows, the muted spots of the leopard weren't visible at all.

Rick . . . held his human shape.

I stepped away. Checked the ceiling. The grindy was staring at Asad, as if he might taste good. He might have had vampire help, but I had a feeling that the alpha cat here, a bigwig in the International Association of Weres and the Party of African Weres, had engineered this visit to sub-five, though maybe the outcome had been a surprise. Had the werewolves been supposed to start a were-vamp war by killing the SOD or kidnapping Brute, further weakening Leo's power base and keeping him distracted from Titus's actions? *Crap.* Plans within treachery within peril.

Nantale joined Rick and the black leopard on the floor, Nantale pulling the large cat onto her lap and scratching his ears. Rick stood to his feet, looming over his former enemy, the man he had just saved, his hands fisted at his sides, his clothes bloody. My ex was a seriously pretty man, even caught up in whatever emotional whirlpool he was swimming in, even with the heavy silver streaks in his black hair and the deeper lines etched into his skin.

I took several slow steps back, closing the distance to Bruiser. I stopped when my shoulders nestled against the warmth of his chest. One arm closed around me again and he whispered, "I don't think anyone could have done better, considering that Kem attacked and the cats had been plotting something involving the Son of Darkness. You poled the waters well."

Poling the waters was an old Louisiana phrase that meant I had steered my way through the currents and the obstacles. I wasn't used to praise of any kind and I ducked my head in pleasure. This was as close to bliss as I ever got, being with Bruiser, knowing I was loved, accepted, approved of. But I had work to do. I touched his hand in apology and stepped away.

Rick knelt again. Kem batted Rick's hand with his large paw; head-butted Rick's chest, knocking him to his backside on the clay floor; crawled into his alpha's lap; and curled up, covering Rick's legs and most of his torso. He plopped his head on Rick's knee. Rick looked as surprised as I felt. "What am I supposed to do?" Rick asked, finding my eyes in the shadows.

"This is the tricky part," I said.

Asad explained, his voice no longer bored, as he bent and stroked Kem's side. "A blood beta is . . . domesticated. Tamed. He will do or be whatever you need him to be."

"But alive," I said. "Better than dead."

"His possessions, his position in were society, and his mates are yours," Asad said to Rick.

Rick jerked slightly, as if he'd stuck his fingers in a light socket. "Mates?"

Asad was clearly amused when he said, in a laconic tone, "Yes. Kemnebi has taken four mates."

"Four?"

Oops. I hadn't known about the mates. I had thought the woman who turned Rick was Kem's only mate.

"If you give them a choice, they will choose to stay with you, as they are accustomed to comfortable lives and will not wish to return to the wild and to hunting, even to find freedom."

Oh crap. My mind spun through all the possibilities. *Crap, crap, crap.* I'd screwed up big-time.

"Stay with me?" Rick repeated.

"In Gabon." Carelessly, Nantale said, "Two are pregnant, in human form, but are expected to have litters of two to four."

Rick looked as if he had been hit with a shovel and stared down at the oversized cat in his lap. He raised his hands from the furry body as if surrounded by police. "Four wives? Pregnant? I'm not moving to Gabon. No. No way."

"You will have to decide if you wish the kits to live," Asad continued, his expression suggesting that he was enjoying this tutelage, "or if you will kill the males at birth. If the males live to adulthood, they will challenge you for their father's place, so it is common for the new male to kill them just after birth."

Rick jerked at the violence and cruelty in the careless words. So did I, even though I'd read them in the Merged Laws. "Of course, any females born from Kemnebi's litters will be yours to take as mate if you choose," Asad said.

Rick looked addled. Stunned. Pretty much the way I was feeling. My ex turned horrified eyes to me, appalled, dismayed, disgusted. Betrayed. By me. I shook my head and said, "I didn't know about the wives."

The wolves had fled. Brute was sitting beneath the SOD, watching every move the heartless creature made. The SOD was hanging on the wall, shackled into place by silver. But things had changed. The SOD was gazing at the congealing pool of were blood near him and his desiccated tongue was lapping at the air as if tasting the scent. He was filthy, his exposed flesh covered in bite marks, some no more than scars, some seeping a watery bloody fluid, some bites Brute's, some vamp. Joses Santana was being inadequately fed and he had been repeatedly drained. Brute had been biting the bag of bones for weeks, and the grindy had never stopped the abuse. I had no idea what was supposed to happen to a vamp infected with were-taint, but Brute was probably acting under the orders of a heavenly angel—one with wings and everything—so I saw no reason to stop him.

"Jane?" Rick asked, his cat eyes glowing slightly green in his human face. "What am I supposed to do under were law? This is . . ." He stopped and swallowed, as if the words tasted bad. "A tamed cat is a slave."

Gently I said, "Kem has always wanted you dead. Me dead. I couldn't save him when he was dying just now. You could, but that act left him your slave. That's the way things are done in the werecat world according to the Merged Laws of the Cursed of Artemis. But there's nothing in were law that prohibits slaves from being set free. No were law says you have to keep him or his possessions. No one says you have to kill Kem's male kits or mate with female kits or be the same kind of evil they are."

Asad's head came up in what looked like affront.

Rick looked at Kem, the green in his eyes bleeding back to the Frenchy dark of his human self. He stroked the cat's ears uncertainly. "I can set him free?"

"Yeah. According to the Merged Laws, he'll always be your blood beta. That's part of a higher-ranking cat saving another cat's life. But I'm pretty sure you can determine the direction of the relationship. Pretty sure you could give him back his wives and determine how he treats his wives and his young."

Asad said, sounding bored, "But if you set him free and

send him home, he will be hunted and killed, and your new wives will be taken by the strongest male." Asad glanced at me. "It would have been kinder to kill him."

Bruiser murmured to Rick, "You could make him your *msimamizi*."

Rick let out a breath and the tension he had been holding. He raked his clean hand through his hair and said, "Yeah. I could. Kemnebi, I make you my *msimamizi*."

To me, Bruiser said, "LaFleur has been studying African werecat law, or he's been to Africa. *Msimamizi* is Swahili for administrator. Rick just gave Kem a job."

I studied my ex. He'd been traveling internationally. Had he been to Africa? Did that travel have something to do with his silvered hair?

Rick stood, pushing Kem aside. The black leopard looked at him adoringly. "Go home to Gabon and be kind to your"—his lips turned down—"my wives and your children."

Asad snarled. Clearly this was not what he had expected to happen. Beast snorted in derision and I grinned, showing blunt human teeth to the werelion. Asad had been planning something disruptive and dangerous as he tried to steal the SOD, maybe that war I had thought about. He had put tiles on a world-sized playing board, all perfectly arranged to topple for a predetermined ending, no matter where they started to fall. And then—whatever his plan had been—I messed it all up. That was clear on his face. Go, me.

The elevator opened to reveal more guards, which was my cue. Leaving the others and the mess of blood and interspecies politics, I slipped back up the hidden stairs, wondering where the werewolves had disappeared to. I freaking hated being out of my own Enforcer loop.

I needed a few minutes with Leo. As I rounded the stairs on the main floor's landing, I caught the fading stench of werewolf blood, then Ayatas's faint scent, Leo's scent overlapping both, but seemingly at different moments. Together, the fading scents went up the next set of stairs to Leo's office. Great. Leo had come out of his office lair and met the werewolves. Then had come back out and greeted the special agent. Ayatas got a private meeting with the MOC while I dealt with were-creature politics. I dropped my headset off at the foyer security nook and dropped into a chair with a tired sigh.

A low voice rumbled slyly, "Want me to rub your feet?"

I chuckled up at Wrassler. "You big ol' softie, you. Instead, let me see the security footage. Let's start with sub-five. I want to know who was responsible for the FUBAR down there."

Wrassler frowned. His expression told me that he had already watched the footage and wasn't happy about any part of it. The cameras mounted in the sub-five basement showed me most of what I needed to know, beginning with the elevator opening and a female vampire walking out. Pale hair and eyes, her face chiseled and cold, the stark beauty of a glacier in pink silk and ballerina shoes. Dominique. Grégoire's clan heir. She stepped onto the clay floor of sub-five, the werecats and wolves behind her, the wolves carrying Antifreeze, his head lolling.

Inside me, Beast growled low, odd tones in her voice, vibrating through my own chest.

Dominique, a two-hundred-year-old, powerful vamp, aimed a flat device like a television remote control at the camera. The screen went black. Then the other cameras went black.

"What happened?" I asked.

"We don't know how she did it," Wrassler said, "but she shut off the cameras on sub-five with that thing. The entire system covering the lower floor went black. Alex is trying to isolate the security loophole on his integrated system and we're going over the cam footage of people on stairs and elevators before the outage and after. But so far we have zip."

My fault, I thought. The SOD had ripped out Dominique's throat and I hadn't taken her head. The memory of her dead body at my feet was bright and clear as the vision of her on the screen before me. Leo and Grégoire had brought her back and restored her, hoping she would

lead them to her coconspirators. Instead, she had pledged
fresh loyalty and given them nothing until now. "Where
is she now?" I asked.

"Gone. I told Grégoire that his heir attacked HQ,
leading our enemies to the Son of Darkness. He's in a
rage. He had begun to trust her. Foolishly."

I let a soft breath go. "Crap." Vamps, especially old
vamps like Grégoire, needed their closest allies to be
faithful unto true-death. Betrayal cut deep. I checked my
cell. There was a text from Eli, telling me he and Ayatas
were with Leo. There was also one from Alex that said,
*Spotted an oddity on sub-five lasers before cameras went
out. Call.* It took a moment before I remembered. Alex
had done laser upgrades on the security at the entrances
and in the gym, the rec room, and sub-five, places where
we'd been attacked in the past.

I punched his number and Alex spoke fast. "Anomaly
from the lasers in sub-five. The presence of a witch under
an obfuscation spell."

"And? Tell me you caught the witch."

Wrassler whipped his head to me at the words.

"No. The witch left with Dominique. But the same
anomaly was in the gym earlier too, unmoving. I tracked
the anomaly back and discovered that it—she—came in
the front door with Dominique and some were-creatures
and left with her."

"Any way to alter the system to track this anomaly and
see it before it gets in?"

Alex hesitated. "I don't know how the magic works. I
could talk to Molly."

I thought about that possibility for half a second. "I'll
call her. I'm heading home in a bit." I hit end and told
Wrassler what Alex had discovered. He frowned and sat
in front of the system, punching buttons to see the anomaly for himself.

A familiar face appeared in the doorway, Shemmy, my
sometimes driver. "May I drive you home, Miz Yellowrock?"

My security measures had failed. I was suddenly tired
beyond bearing, my legs feeling leaden and my shoulders

drooping. I had lost my scarf in the fight and couldn't make myself go look for it. I did something I seldom ever did. I accepted when a security blood-servant offered to drive me home. "Yeah. Thanks."

As we walked through the doors together, a car swept in, and a vampire visitor emerged. She passed us on the front stairs, carrying a package addressed to Leo, the name clearly visible. The packaging looked vaguely familiar in terms of vampire business, but I couldn't remember where I saw the kind before or why. I stopped the vamp with an upheld hand and took the package. It was from Leo's biomedical lab in Texas. Not my business. I waved her on and slid into the backseat of the armored SUV and closed my eyes.

I didn't move again until I was back home, when Shemmy opened the door for me and wished the Enforcer a good rest and happy dreams. And then I looked up. And groaned.

I wouldn't be given a chance to sleep. The windows upstairs were open, the cold breeze blowing the curtains back and forth in the night. I thought about telling Shemmy to take me to a local bar. I couldn't get drunk, it wasn't in my physiology, but I could nurse a Coke and people-watch. Instead I said, "Thank you. Drive safely back to HQ." I blew out a breath and went inside, where I was met with the sound of electric saws running, nail guns thumping, hammers banging, Latin music playing, and men laughing. The cacophony echoed through the house. In my room, I took off the dancing shoes, pulled off the clothes, the sports bra, and the weapons, leaving them all on the bed, and dressed in a soft tee, a ratty sweatshirt, and leggings.

I sat on the bed, crossed my legs guru fashion, and made a call.

"Hey, Aunt Jane," Angie said, answering.

"How's my sweet girl?" I asked.

"I made a big butterfly. Mama punished me. I'm in trouble." But she sounded proud of herself for the entire episode, even the being-in-trouble part.

"How big did you make the butterfly?"

"Big as my feet."

My eyebrows went up. "That's a big butterfly."

"Yup. Mama was mad 'cause she couldn't see where I got the mass from."

My eyebrows went up higher. "You know what mass is?"

"Yup. Energy equals mass times the speed of light squared," she quoted. "Which means that magic and electricity and sunlight, which are energy, are the same stuff as things I can touch, which is mass or matter. And I can innerchange 'em 'cause they're just different forms of the same thing. But I didn't innerchange 'em."

My entire body had gone cold as she spoke. I was pretty sure my heart had stopped beating. "Okay," I managed. "So what did you do to make the butterfly grow big?"

"I didn't make one grow big. I jus' made a big one come to me. From one of the other places."

I breathed through my mouth in the beginnings of panic. "What other places?"

"There's bunches of other places. One has big butter-flies with pink wings and purple eyes and blue bodies and feet. I just pulled it over. Mama's mad at me," she said again, with pride.

"Give me that phone, young lady," Molly said in the background. "Go back to your room. And take that dog with you."

In the background I heard Angie calling her dog and trying to whistle. Into the phone, Molly said, "She told you?"

"About what sounded like she pulled a butterfly from an alternate universe into ours? Yeah."

"She's going to be the death of me." Molly sighed. "That butterfly was a foot wide and had a stinger the size of my little finger. I had to blast it with death magic to stop it."

"You okay?" My BFF Molly Meagan Everhart True-blood had a problem with the evolution of her magic and had lost herself to death magic once or twice. That was way scarier than pulling butterflies from alternate uni-verses.

"I'm good. I play a lot of Evan's music these days and I keep that dang cat close." The dang cat was Molly's familiar, though witches didn't have familiars. Ever. It was too cliché for real life. "What's up?"

"Two things. First, we had a witch under an obfuscation spell enter through the sensors. The lasers picked up the anomaly, but we only spotted it after the fact. It was too small a change to see it in real time. I'm wondering if there's a way to rig a ward or a magical something to alert us when someone comes in the door."

Molly was quiet and I could almost see her pursing her lips and squinting her eyes as she thought. "The entrances have the metal detectors and the X-ray scanners, like at airports, right?"

"Yes."

"And all the security setup is close by, with cameras?"

My heart thudded down. Right. Magic and electronics. Too much of either in the same place, and something was likely to go bang. Molly's next words confirmed that thought.

"Anything I might send would fritz out in short order. Someone could set up a *hedge* outside, but it needs to be hands-on with that many people coming and going. I could call Lachish Dutillet to set one up, but she'd have to stay there." Her voice sounded amused. Lachish was the head of the NOLA coven and she didn't like me much. Lachish didn't like vamps much either. So, no way would she provide security for us against another witch.

"Yeah. No thanks," I said. "Second, I'm pretty sure we're looking at the formation of Clan Yellowrock in the fanghead manner in the next few days. You still up for that? Being part of a vamp clan will give you and Big Evan power and protection from other vamps. It'll help to keep you all safe. Keep the kids safe." Keep Eli and Alex and all my people safe. But I didn't need to add that part.

"Janie, I'd suck vamp blood myself if it kept my children safe from the Europeans. Remember, I'm ready to come if and when you need me."

"This can be handled over an electronic connection. You stay where you are and take care of my next god-child. Understand?"

"I do. I love you, big-cat."

"I love you too, Moll."

We ended the call. I stared at the cell face for a while, remembering why I was doing everything in my life—to protect my godchildren. To keep them safe from blood-suckers who killed or turned every witch they could find and who would take Angie Baby and Little Evan and Molly's unborn daughter and . . . I stopped the visions that wanted to swarm through me. I didn't have time for them or for the fear that rode me every time I thought about the danger the children were in. Brick by mental brick, I blocked away the images and the panic.

Pulling out a notepad, I wrote a note to Alex to check on the injured guards and Tequila Antifreeze. I left it on his desk in the living room.

Barefooted, I traipsed up the stairs to the second floor and stopped at the landing. The hardwood-floored land-ing ran the length of the house from front to back, a wide hallway separating the four bedrooms into two on the left and two on the right, with old-fashioned bathrooms on each side. From the bathroom Eli used, I caught the faint-est hint of lemon, before it vanished on the air currents rushing through the house.

Paper had been taped over the hardwood and there was a load of lumber on top of it. A table saw sat in the middle of the room, three ladders of various styles were propped here and there, a skill saw lay on its side, and hammers, measuring tapes, pencils, cola cans, and fast-food wrappers were everywhere. A boom box played from somewhere out of sight.

Three men stood on the second floor with me and two on rafters above, where a hole had been cut in the ceiling to the attic, what would soon be the third floor, though in NOLA-speak it would be the atelier. But the hole was a lot bigger than I expected, covering the entire area from wall to wall. Way more demo than I had anticipated. I thought about weeping at the lack of sleep, but . . . I could survive being sleepy. I took in the smells: fresh pine wood with an underlay of garlic, beer, a little weed, hot peppers, and chili, from the men I didn't know. Even less obvious was the scent of vamp from the one man I did know.

Two beams sawn with right-angled cutouts for risers and treads were lying on the floor and the far wall was covered with penciled lines and scuff marks to create a narrow stairwell next to the stairs from the first floor.

I waved at the hole overhead. "Can I see up there?"

Edmund looked at me, and at the hole, and knelt near me, his fingers laced together and his hands cupped for my foot.

"I expected to climb a ladder," I said, my tone wry.

"It is an old house. The ceilings are twelve feet high and the ladders were not quite tall enough," Ed said. "We had to stand them on the stack of drywall and plywood to cut the hole overhead, and those stacks are now upstairs. Longer ladders are on the way. Until then, the men are pulling each other up. Please allow me to boost you."

I was tired. Vamps were strong. Beast was really good at catching us. I shrugged and stepped back, took a running start, and raced to Edmund.

My primo accepted and collected my weight without a bobble, tossing me high. I caught the rafters overhead and let momentum and Beast pull me into the attic. I heard the muttered comments of the crew as I landed, probably looking as if I'd flown up here.

"Bruja?" The men backed away, slowly, not turning their backs.

"Bebedor de sangre?" All the men crossed themselves. Several said, *"Madre de Dios,"* in tones of fear.

"Vampira." Pointing to me, not Ed, who was coming up behind me. Which was funny.

"Noooo," I said.

"Sí." More crossing.

"Noooo," I said back. "No *vampira*. No *bruja*. Just strong." I made a muscle.

"Black Widow? From Marvel?" a guy with a droopy paunch asked. It came out *Black Weedow?*

The other guy said, "Natasha Romanova," and shaped an hourglass figure in the air with his hands.

"Sorta kinda."

Being a superhero was way better than scaring the humans with the truth. They elbowed each other in approval, saying, *"Sí. La Araña Viuda. Sí. Sí. Sí."*

The space up here was amazing. There were dormers along one side of the roof system and the windows had been removed, leaving openings to the night. A new window rested below each opening, ready for insertion. Two-by-fours were up to indicate where the soundproofed walls would go, three smaller rooms on the back side of the house, with a minuscule bathroom and a large workout area on the front part.

After the walls were finished, the hardwood flooring was in, and the place was painted, the free weights and workout equipment would go up here, along with a rubberized fighting mat.

I nodded. Said all the appropriate things. And told them I had to get a nap. They laughed at me. I levered myself / dropped down to the floor below, dodging a man carrying an extendable ladder. I made another muscle, posing for him, trotted down to the first floor, and found my bed. Even with all the noise, I slept for hours.

I checked the weather when I woke, and the high today was supposed to be a chilly fifty-two degrees. I pulled on undies, leggings to protect my legs from the weapons harness, and a nice long-sleeved silk tee. Over that went the harnesses, the weapons, a skirt with slits for said weapons, a thin knit turtleneck tunic sweater that matched my eyes, and stakes in the top of my French braid. It was daylight, and I was overdressed for daytime in NOLA, but Bruiser was picking me up. It was lunch and business—the Gumbo Shop on St. Peter Street. I left a note for my partners, both of whom were still sleeping, before I tiptoed out. The sun was shining, the breeze was out of the south, and the weather was practically balmy. I texted Bruiser that I would walk in his direction to meet him, and he could pick me up. I initiated my GPS so he could follow my progress, and started down the street.

The sound of traffic was all around, a steady, never-ending roar. People talking. Music playing, some live from street musicians, some from cars as they passed, some from clubs. The smell of spicy food made with thick roux and onions and peppers, meat smoking on a grill, seafood fried in lard. Coffee. Exhaust. The mixed scents of water from the Mississippi, the bayous that ran through the city, and Lake Pontchartrain. Urine. Vomit. The city had hosted one of its ubiquitous celebrations the week before and we hadn't had a gully washer since a magic storm held the city captive. Few humans could smell it, but I could. I passed two homeless men sleeping in a doorway. Another slept on the ground in an alley.

A car with a mismatched paint job and spinning wheels rolled past and two kids wearing navy blue hooded jackets leaned out the windows, sitting on the window edges, cat-calling, telling me that they had some big . . . uh, things for me. I laughed and ignored them. If they tried anything I had some things for them too, and they were shiny and sharp with the word *no* written on them in blood.

They pulled away when they realized they weren't getting a rise out of me. I strolled past two- and three-story buildings, almost all with galleries and wrought-iron balconies, restaurants and storefronts and candy shops, selling kitsch or food or drinks or a combo of all three. A surprising number were closed, working shutters latched, doors padlocked and sometimes sealed with chains. Rents were high in the Quarter and times were hard in the city. There had been an influx of money in the years since the last major hurricane, but the city was still trying to recover.

I hadn't really liked New Orleans when I moved here. It was supposed to be a short-term job, then back to the mountains and my apartment in Asheville. And then I met Rick. And Leo offered me a more permanent job. And I found an excuse to stay for a while. I'd been stupid. Rick had "player" written all over him and I hadn't bothered to notice. I had needed to solve the mystery involving the missing witch children, then kill off the vamps who had been taking and sacrificing them for the power in their blood. The continuing danger to the witches had been another reason to stick around. I'd needed to find a way to keep the local vamps in power when big bad fang-bangers wanted to take over the city and its cattle, meaning humans and witches. Now there were the Youngers, my family by choice. And there was Bruiser. That man was a reason to stay here. I'd stayed. I'd cleaned up a lot of messes. If the Sangre Duello was the last mess I needed to clean up, I would have no reason to stick around. Except the Youngers and Bruiser. The Youngers were family. They had made it clear that they were in this for the long haul. Would my honeybunch want me to stay? We hadn't talked about it. Hadn't talked about what-ifs. Maybe things were too tenuous to plan ahead? To dream ahead? That left me feeling odd, empty. Maybe a little bit lost.

My Beast sent me images, one superimposed on the other, memories of snow piled two feet deep, pristine except for the prints of deer. Of tall waterfalls sliding between iced rocks. Of her lithe body leaping from an ice-crusted tree, thick tail rotating for balance and direction, landing on a buck racing down a steep ravine, sinking teeth in at his spine. Of dropping on one at a summertime watering hole, sinking teeth into its muscled throat, holding it until the prey passed out from lack of air. Of the spurt of hot blood and the taste of raw venison.

"There's something to be said for warm weather, lots of rain, and dining on gator," I reminded her. "But yeah. I miss the mountains too."

Hunt cow. Hunt cow in Edmund's car, she sent back. It wasn't going to happen. Edmund's car was worth over three million dollars. Beast didn't understand money or numbers greater than five and, like a cat, figured she could either wear me down or outsmart me into getting what she wanted.

I was halfway to the Gumbo Shop when I felt it. My predator responses zinging. The presence of someone watching. I was used to casual observers. The MOC's Enforcer got a lot of that from locals and tourists too. This was the interest of a hunter, my body in his sights. Or hers. A sniper had targeted me not so long ago and that experience had left some part of me hyperalert, always vigilant, in the back of my/our mind. Beast knew when we were being hunted.

Not speeding my steps, I jaywalked across the street and stopped in front of a window as if attracted by the silver jewelry on display. But mostly just watching my trail and the parked cars and the buildings across the way for anything or anyone suspicious. I saw nothing. Except the car with the teens in it, cruising back around the block. This time the windows were up, the hecklers inside, and the car was moving slowly, at a walking pace. My walking pace. Which begged the question, were they tailing me for purposes of their own or were they tailing me because someone paid them to watch for me and tail me?

Beast sent me an image of her leaping to the hood of the car and swatting at them. I sent her one of them shooting her through the windshield. She snarled, frustrated. I wasn't sure when Beast had developed this love of battle, but she was a lot more aggressive than before.

I tapped out a quick text to Bruiser. *Where are you?*

He sent one back. *Ten minutes out. Held up. Get a table. Be there soon.*

Too far away. Across the street, in a second-story window, I saw movement. The window was up about six inches. Something small and round emerged into the sunlight. Gun barrel?

I walked into the shop and quickly beyond the entrance. I pulled a twenty from the tiny pocket in my waistband. To the redheaded woman in the back of the shop, behind the counter, I said, "A car is following me. Can I get out the back?"

"Cop car?" she asked, reaching under the counter. "Or gangbangers?"

"I'm going with gangbangers. Clothes are alike."

She brought out a sawed-off shotgun and laid it on the counter. I froze until I saw it was pointing away from me. Sawed-offs had a hella kick, but the redhead was a big woman and looked as if she knew her way around the weapon. She had full-sleeve tats with skulls on both arms, a dragon on the left, and black roses on the right. The tats extended up her neck where blackbirds flew into her scarlet hairline. She asked, "Dark gray four-door sedan with a blue driver's door?"

I thought back, surprised. "Yeah."

She lifted a horizontal slab of counter and said, "Put your money away and get back here. That car has been up and down the streets around here for days. I've called NOPD every day, and they did a stop and frisk, but they got zilch. There's nothing they can do until the guys commit a crime. Get outta here. Back door leads to a long narrow courtyard and an apartment. My landlady lives there. Knock and tell her Andromeda sent you. She'll let you out to a covered passageway. Follow her directions out to St. Peter Street."

The Gumbo Shop was on St. Peter. There would be collateral damage if I was followed. I looked over my shoulder to see the mismatched car pull to a stop in the street. This wasn't accidental or coincidental. They were here for me. Beast moved to peer out of my eyes. *Fight? Can eat one?*

Seeing the car stop, Andromeda cursed and leaned down to press a red button on the side of the cabinet. Even her fingers were tattooed, with musical notes and barbed wire. "Silent alarm," she said. "The security company will contact the cops and we already have video running."

"I'm not leaving you here alone," I said to Andromeda. I sent a fast text to Bruiser, pulled the H&K nine-mil, and joined her behind the counter. The display cases were old-fashioned and though the fronts and tops were glass, the sides and back were constructed of heavy, old wood. I pulled my vamp-killers and placed them on the counter. "You ever fired that sawed-off?"

She looked at me, taking in the golden glow of Beast in my eyes. "You're Jane Yellowrock."

Three young men moved toward the shop, their gaits streetwise and threatening. Two of them hid their faces in their navy hoodies and reached into their jeans in a weapon draw. They were older than I'd first thought. Twenty-somethings, not kids. "I am."

Fight! Beast said.

"This is my daddy's gun. It's got a kick, but yeah. I can handle it." She withdrew a small nine-mil from below the counter too and racked the slide.

"Bloods? Crips?" I asked as the guys moved through the traffic. Behind them horns blared, but the mismatched car didn't move.

"No one's seen Crip or Blood for weeks. Word is that the fanghead MOC took them out." She shot me a glance. She meant my boss. "These are homegrown gangs, filling back in where the national boys used to be. Call themselves the Zips. They paint big navy blue *Z* graffiti everywhere. They're looking to make a name for themselves. My brother runs with the Razors, another local gang. This is Raz territory."

Out front, the young men gathered in a tight grouping, one talking, by his body language giving orders. He was wearing khakis, no hoodie. "This could get messy," I said.

"No shit, Pollyanna."

Am Beast. Not Pollyanna.

I chuffed in amusement, showing teeth.

The woman picked up the sawed-off and held it in a one-hand grip, the other hand holding the nine-mil, her feet spread. She knew how to make an impression. The modified barrel looked like a cannon.

The guy in front opened the door. Came in out of the glare, blinking, arm up, gun held in a street-style shooting angle, sideways. With that stance, if he hit us, it would be by accident. Andromeda said, "Stop or die." When they kept coming, she fired the nine-mil.

CHAPTER 5

I Can't Shoot a Suspect on the Ground

The round hit the wall at the floor, a deliberate shot. "Next one draws blood," she said over the ear-blasted dead air left behind.

"Give us the woman," Khaki Man shouted. His eyes were wide. He hadn't expected armed resistance. Or getting shot at.

"No," Andromeda said.

The men spread out in a small semicircle, blocking the front exit, two hoodies on the left, Khaki Man on the right. Andromeda shifted the nine-mil to the man on the far left. "I got the navy jackets. You take out the other one," she said.

I let Beast flood into me. My heart rate sped. My breathing deepened. I took a breath, smelling testosterone, aggression, and chemicals in their blood. And I caught an unexpected scent.

Of wolf.

The guy in the center fired. Time slowed, that battlefield awareness that showed me the angle of the shot. The blast stole the last of the silence. He missed us both.

Andromeda fired the shotgun. It deafened. Stole the air. Replaced it with a roiling cloud of gunfire residue. The guy in the middle stumbled and fell.

The other hoodie fired.

I firmed my aim. Fired twice. Andromeda dropped the shotgun and fired the nine-mil. All three men were on the floor, one with a large, circular shot pattern on his chest. Messy.

Fun, Beast said. *More!*

I raced around the counter and disarmed the three guys—even the dead ones—by gently shoving the weapons to the side with my foot. Carefully. People had died by kicking guns and getting shot. Out front, the gang car took off.

"What the hell?" Andromeda shouted, barely heard over the deafness of the gunfight, furious.

I tracked the unexpected scent I had caught just before the firing started, to the khaki-clad guy. Over the damage to my ears, I heard sirens and Andromeda cursing as she spotted the bullet hole damage to the walls and the jewelry cases. Scowling, she took in the damage to one cabinet: the wood that had once been beautifully carved, swans with long necks intertwined, and the antique glass, which was now all over the floor. She cursed long and hard at the damage. I took her weapon from her and set it with mine on the counter. Texted a fast *911* to Bruiser. Then, *Shots fired. Am OK. Cops on way. Call lawyer.* I added the address.

I got back, *There in 22.*

Twenty seconds later, Bruiser sprinted to the front of the shop and stopped. He was breathing hard, eyes wide and determined. He had been ten minutes away when this all started. He got here a lot faster, on foot, running. He opened the door, needing to see me, his scent washing into the room, over the smell of weapons fire, full of fear. I smiled at him and said, "I'm not hit."

He let a harsh breath go, gave me a nod, and let the door close. George Dumas, elegant and urbane, no longer out of breath or terrified, was standing there with his cell phone to his ear, talking, when the cops pulled up. There was something disarming about the appearance of the local celebrity, casually talking on the phone, and I could see the cops instantly decompress, though they came at him with weapons drawn. Bruiser held his arms in the air, and though my ears weren't healed, I could make out the soothing timbre of his voice. It was pacifying. Calming. In control of himself and everything around him.

The cops nodded, entered. Andromeda and I were standing with our hands up. The cops took in the three guys, looked at us, and looked back at the three guys. The one on the right was still breathing. "Jane Yellowrock?" the older cop asked.

"Yep." I pointed with one finger to the breathing guy. "Be careful. That one is werewolf. They can bite when they're in pain."

The cops shuffled back through the opening, though to give them credit, they did keep the door open.

"Werewolf?" Andromeda squeaked. And then she laughed, sounding half-hysterical, saying, "There wolf." When I didn't respond she added, "Movie quote."

I grunted. The guy on the floor was making strange puppy sounds and hair was starting to sprout on his hands and face. Reddish hair. And he was the only one of the attackers not wearing a navy gang jacket. Interestinger and interestinger.

"What are we supposed to do?" the cop holding the door asked.

"Get us out, seal the place up, and . . . Well, crap." I huffed in annoyance. "And call PsyLED. They have agents in town. I can give you the numbers of two of them."

The cops didn't ask for the numbers. They were still freaked at the idea of a were.

Bruiser reentered. His nostrils widened at the stench of werewolf blood; Onorios have better-than-human sense of smell, but he hadn't caught it the first time. His eyes searched me for signs of bite marks or torn flesh. I gave him a thumb up to let him know I hadn't been bitten. To the cops he said, "Medic is caught in traffic. If you can clear the street they can get in to help that one."

"We need a werewolf cage," I said again.

Bruiser frowned and punched in a number. "PsyLED has portable cages."

"If you have silver ammo," I said to the cop, "now's the time for it. If he gets shifted and is still in pain"—I glanced at Andromeda and half-joked—"things'll get messy."

Andromeda laughed, the sound only slightly panicked now that the shooting was over. "Call me Andy."

"Jane."

"I can't shoot a suspect on the ground," the cop said.

"You can if he's a menace to the public."

The cop looked at the wolf, at his partner, at me. "You shoot him."

"Not my job once the cops are here. I'd stake him if he was a vamp and a menace to the public, but not a furball. He's all yours."

The guy on the ground started growling. He must have had strong feelings about the direction of the conversation. More hair sprouted. The cop cursed under his breath and changed out mags while calling his supervisor.

After that it was disorganized organization, with the cops putting a round in the were's knee to keep him in a partial shift and out of action. The wolfman was seriously ticked off about being shot again. The local LEOs took our weapons. All of them. Even the stakes.

And my adrenaline dissipated enough for me to realize two humans had attacked me and now they were dead. Twenty-somethings, not children. Violent and ready to kidnap or kill me, or some violent combo of the two. But still. Humans. There was a time when killing humans would have broken my heart, sent me into depression. But there are just so many times one's heart can be broken before it hardens in some sad, fragmented, disarranged formation, where it doesn't work right anymore. I felt almost nothing and I was more sad about that than I was about killing the gangbangers.

Unconcerned, Beast thought, *Jane is war woman. I/we are Beast. Killed enemy.*

All the last of the battle energy drained out of me. I sat on a stool perched in the corner, sick to my stomach.

Rick walked in the door, his cat scent sending the

doggy on the floor into spasms of fury. He flashed his badge and ID, then glared and pointed a finger at me. "We need to talk about my new housecat." I nodded once. To the cops he continued, "This is a PsyLED investigation. I'll take over as OIC until my superior arrives."

OIC was "officer in charge." I started to relax when the cop who had reshot the furball said, "Sorry. Gang Task Force is here. They have jurisdiction."

Rick frowned. The cop grinned. He clearly found it amusing that the meddlesome bureaucrat-cop in street clothes was not going to get his way. And then Ayatas walked in with a portly man in a suit, and the cop's amusement faded away. "LaFleur," Ayatas said, "this is Gomez, GTF. He's been tracking the local gangs for two years." Rick and Gomez shook hands. Ayatas glanced at me and Andromeda but didn't acknowledge us. His hair was braided back and hung down the center of his spine. "GTF's had reports of strangers running with the Zips."

"Werewolf strangers?" Rick asked.

Gomez dropped to one knee and studied the downed were, comparing him to photos of men on his phone, one thumb flicking from pic to pic. He stopped on one and held the cell up to Andy and me. "He's a little too furry right now to be sure, but this him?"

"No," we said.

"This?" Gomez brought up another pic.

"No." I realized we were getting a quickie photo lineup, like in the basement of a cop shop.

"This?" Gomez asked.

"Yes," Andy and I said.

Gomez marked his screen, grunted, and stood. To Andy, Gomez said, "He's been seen with the Zips and with a guy who goes by the name Marco Agrios, white, just under six feet, brown and brown, sharp dresser. You or your brother know anything about Marco?"

Andy looked as if she would rather not answer, but she finally said, "I can ask around some. Gimme your card." Gomez held out a business card and Andy tucked it behind the register.

Gomez nodded, looked me over, and spoke to Ayatas.

"You got a safe place to store him until he heals? We don't want his kind in with the lockup pop, making furbabies outta the locals."

"Yes," Rick said, when Ayatas glanced at him. "We'll take care of it."

Gomez gave another grunt and left the jewelry shop. Ayatas studied me. I watched him back, wary. "Why would he target you?" he asked.

"No idea."

"If you need protection, I can arrange it."

I raised my eyebrows at him. "Really? For little ol' me? You want I should curtsy and clasp my hands to my chest? Maybe flutter my eyes and sigh some?"

"What about me?" Beside me, Andy dropped into a clumsy curtsy and fluttered her eyes at him. "I'll do a lot more than that to get you for my protection."

Ayatas laughed kindly, flashing pearly whites, clearly accustomed to people trying to pick him up. "A war woman can die too. Be careful out there."

"Yeah," I said.

"War woman?" She pointed at her right arm above her wrist. "I might have that tattooed right here." I just smiled.

Rick pointed a finger at me and said, "We are not done with cat business."

Moments later, Andy and I were hauled off to the Eighth Precinct and separated. My last words to her were, "I owe you a lawyer."

Her last words to me were, "Make him pretty."

We spent time in holding cells until lawyers could arrive and we could be interviewed. Leo had several lawyers on retainer, but Brandon Robere was my lawyer of choice, a graduate of Tulane Law, LLM, back in 1946. I hadn't seen him in a couple weeks. The Onorio looked good, though his suit hung on his leaner frame, he moved less fluidly, and his eyes were still a little hollow. It took time to get over being tied to a beam, tortured, and drained of blood. Sometimes life just sucked. "Jane," he said. "I've requested an interview room. Are you hurt?"

"No. I just hate cages."

"Yes. I know what you mean." He followed, silent, as

the cops moved me to an interrogation room, stood as they locked the door on us, and leaned with his back against the wall. He asked, "Is it true they targeted you specifically? Not the store owner?"

"Yes. There's security video. And one wasn't a gang-banger. He's werewolf."

"So I hear. Is it true you wish me to offer legal services to Andromeda Preaux?"

"Yeah. She tried to get me out the back door before the shooting started. Would you check on her?"

"In a moment. You do seem to attract heroes. How do you know they were targeting you?"

"Andy said the car had been patrolling the streets in the area for days. They hit on me and rolled past."

"Hit on you?"

"Offered me their services?" When he looked confused I said, "Offered to take me to bed, and not to snooze."

Brandon shook his head. "Horrors. Go on."

"Yeah. Then they came back. They followed me into the shop. They said, 'Get the woman,' or something like that. It wasn't hard to tell I was their target."

"They left and they came back," he clarified. "And they had been patrolling the area around St. Peter Street?"

Something was wrong here. More carefully, I said, "I hadn't seen them before. But that's what Andromeda said."

"When they came back, was their demeanor the same or different?"

"I'm not following you," I said.

He spoke slowly, as he might to a small child. Or someone he didn't want to upset. "I had Alex do a search of traffic cams. This car has been patrolling the area between St. Philip Street and your home. That area also encloses St. Peter Street and the streets between. However, no one knew you would be walking toward St. Peter Street."

"Okay." And then it hit me. Bruiser lived on St. Philip Street. Maybe they hadn't been searching for me. Maybe they had been after Bruiser. They had said something

like, "Give me the woman." Had I been nothing but a
lever to get to Bruiser? "They weren't after me, exactly?"

"It's possible that you were the means to an end, not
the end itself."

I sat down on the hard chair, going back over everything that had happened. They wanted Bruiser? Not me?
Bruiser. Rage flared up in me like a torch. Why Bruiser?
And then it occurred to me that Bruiser had been Leo's
flunky for decades. Together they had hunted and killed
werewolves; I'd once seen a photo of them standing over
a dead werewolf. There had been werewolves in sub-five
when the cats tried to steal the SOD. Those wolves had
wanted to steal Brute, who had been biting the SOD and
who had timewalking abilities. I hadn't been able to ex-
plore that aspect of this puzzle, thanks to Brute's inability
to shift to human and talk to me. Bruiser might have
been involved in "questioning" the werewolves who hurt
Rick. This could have been a snatch-and-grab attempt.
Or it might be a more complicated situation than a simple
kidnapping.

"Right," Brandon said, seeing my reaction. "I'll let you
think for a bit and see if Andromeda wants my services."
He left and came back moments later. "Are you absolutely certain that you want me to represent her?"

"Yeah. Why do you ask? Again."

"She told me I was pretty. And that she likes to sleep
with lawyers. She suggested a list of positions and toys
and games we could play." I tried to hold in a grin. It must
not have been successful because Brandon frowned. "I
like sex as much as the next guy, but some of the things
she said are downright scary." His eyes narrowed at me
when I laughed. "And her tattoos are Razor tats."

"Her brother runs with the Raz. Didn't know about
her. Don't care. This is vamp business. Leo pays her legal
fees."

Brandon gave me an abbreviated shrug and sat, placing a briefcase on the table between us. He pulled out a
pad and pencil. The Roberes were old-school. "Tell me
what happened again. Leave nothing out, no matter how

seemingly insignificant." Which was when I remembered
the open window and the barrel pointing down at me.
I talked through the sequence of events and when I
reached the part about the possibility of a shooter, Brandon left the room again and said something to the guard.
Moments later, a detective appeared and Brandon invited
him into the room. He was dour, tired, and supposed to
be off shift two hours before. I think he blamed me for
keeping him on the clock, but really, he should be blam-
ing the dead guys and the furry guy.

"Tell Detective Kerlegan what you told me. Be specific
about directions, locations, everything."

I did as I was told. Kerlegan took notes, had me draw
out the building across the street, and pinpoint the window where I had seen activity. I was specific and detailed,
if not artistic. I couldn't draw a stick figure, but I could
count windows. I circled the window where the gun barrel, if it was a gun barrel, had tracked me.

Kerlegan left and I told Brandon everything else.
"What happened to the wolf?" I asked.

"LaFleur called some people and hauled him off."

"And?"

"PsyLED and weres are not my concern," he said.

"They should be. There were three werewolves in sub-
five basement less than twenty-four hours ago, and they
seemed to be having an argument."

"What kind of argument? Bighorn Wolf Pack or the
new Montana Red Pack?"

"I got no idea," I said. "One wolf drew a gun on two
others, but I can't tell one pack from the other. They
came in with Dominique and a witch under an obfuscation spell, a good one. The lasers detected it, but not in
time to catch the witch."

"Leo parleyed an agreement with the Bighorns but
Montana recently split off from them. It's possible that
Montana came here with the intent of helping the Euro-
peans."

"I overheard the wolves say they were there to rescue
Brute, who wasn't pleased at the statement, by the way."

Brandon frowned, his brow crinkling, confused.

"They were on sub-five," I said, "with the werecat delegation from PAW and the IAW, who were there because of the SOD. You didn't know? About an attack by the werecats?"

He cursed succinctly. "No. I've been working on legal briefs for two days. Debrief me."

I did, and ended with, "Asad may have wanted to start a cat-wolf war, or a vamp-were war, or the kitties and pups might have joined forces temporarily to steal the SOD and Brute. Or something open-ended or more twisted. I don't know and I have no idea how we can find out." Brandon used his cell phone to call vamp HQ and knocked on the door as if alerting someone on the outside, like a prearranged signal. Detective Kerlegan reentered about the time that Brandon finished his conversation with HQ, and we three sat at the table. Upon advice from counsel I answered all the detective's questions, at length. Three times.

After the third time through the events, I said, "I'm done." I stood up and looked down at my lawyer. "Get me out of here."

"Charge my client with a crime or let her go."

Kerlegan sounded tired and jaded when he said, "She's both a person of interest and a possible suspect in the deaths of two humans and the injury of a werewolf."

"You have video of the shooting," Brandon said. "You have police corroboration of the threat of the gang members. She has been totally cooperative. Jane Yellowrock is not a flight risk and she hasn't eaten in hours. You have a mountain of evidence saying that the deaths were self-defense. And she told the senior officer on scene that there was a werewolf on-site, one who was shifting and could have posed a danger to the officers and to the public. She was helpful in keeping local law enforcement safe."

The detective placed his open hands on the table. "We can keep her for seventy-two hours."

I shot him a look that said, *No you can't!*

"All that will get you is her clamming up and refusing to help NOPD ever again." Brandon leaned in, over the table. "That would create a danger to the city and you know that. She's helped officers in the past. She saved the life of the chief of police. She helped those officers today. Don't screw up a system that works."

Kerlegan stood and knocked on the door, which opened immediately. "Make sure she doesn't leave town," he said as he left the room.

"I have to go see Andromeda," Brandon said. "God help me."

I just smiled and let him lead me out of the interrogation room. I accepted my weapons and put them into the tote bag that Kerlegan magically produced for me. Checked my cell to discover Alex had sent a dozen texts while I didn't have access to my phone. The only one that mattered was the one that said T. Antifreeze and the guards who had been injured when the weres went to sub-five were okay, healed by vamp blood and downtime. That put me in a better mood.

I left the Eighth, exited into the chill and the early dusk, and told Shemmy to take me back to Andromeda Preaux's jewelry shop. Traffic was horrid and after I texted Bruiser to meet me there, I took a speed nap in the backseat.

Bruiser and I went into the building across the street from Andromeda's and up to the unoccupied second floor to inspect the hide used by the possible shooter. The building had been cleared by the cops, and as we searched I told him my concerns about the gangbangers and the wolf with the gun, and the were-creatures in sub-five, also one with a gun. And how the wolves seemed to be at odds. We talked over other possibilities, some far-fetched, some downright scary. Together we concluded that there was nothing we could do and no way to discern the truth for now.

Bruiser ended the discussion by calling Leo. I wandered around alone for a while.

There was no electricity in the untenanted building. The room where the round thing had appeared in the open window was empty except for a metal folding chair. The chair and the window sash had been dusted for fingerprints, the powder easy to spot in the olive green room, dusty in Beast's sharp vision.

The place had been filled with too many cops and crime scene techs for me to get a specific scent, but I caught a whiff of lemon on the chair when I bent over it. The scent seemed familiar, but the memory wouldn't come. Other than that, there was nothing.

From the doorway, Bruiser said, "NOPD thinks the person who was in this room had been here for days. A squatter, most likely. Kerlegan said that CSI hauled off several dozen sealed pee bottles and one sealed five-gallon container of feces." He sounded aggrieved at having to say the words and I let my mouth curl up at the tone. "This entire building is empty and there are signs the person or persons have been in every room."

I wondered how many other buildings had squatters in them and how many of the squatters were actually shooters. How widespread was the search for Bruiser or me and why? We wandered the second floor and I caught the fading scent in several places. "I know it's stupid, but I smell lemons. Real lemons, not synthetic like in dish soap."

Bruiser stopped, thinking, head tilted, his skin and eyes silvered in Beast's vision. *Mate,* Beast thought happily.

He said, "There is a Mithran clan that scents of lemons, but there are no indications that Clan Des Citrons has left France to join with Titus in the Sangre Duello. If this shooter is one of their humans, then that opens up a number of possibilities, none of them good."

"Vamps are ready to jump into the fray at any point where they can benefit," I said. "Or at the end of the blood duel when they could declare war against the winner and take over." And then I remembered. "I smelled this scent before."

Bruiser's eyes moved to me, waiting.

"This person has either been in my house or was standing on thin air outside Eli's bathroom." The window had been open. The entire house had been breezy. "Or maybe they followed me home and were standing on the brick wall outside the house, listening. Watching. Also I caught a faint whiff of lemons in HQ. On sub-five."

Bruiser shook his head. "Someone is watching all of us?"

"And that someone had access to HQ. I'll put Alex on it," I said. "We'll find them."

"Derek can dedicate a few security personnel to your neighborhood." He shrugged, looking relaxed, but I had a feeling he was a lot more concerned than he pretended. Casually, he added, "Dinner, then. And we'll keep an eye out for trolling gangbangers and errant shooters."

The Creole platter at the Gumbo Shop consisted of a large platter of shrimp Creole, jambalaya, and crawfish étouffée. I had two platters, inhaling the first one so fast I only noted it as a blistered sensation on the back of my throat. Bruiser had the red beans and rice with a lovely smoked sausage and the chicken espagnole with extra sides and a half bottle of wine. That was a total of four entrées between us and a mountain of dirty dishes when we were done. The waitress stared accusingly at my skinny frame. I had spent the last few weeks shifting too many times and not eating enough calories to replace the energy usage. I often wondered what might happen if I had to shift many times with no food in between. Would I shrink to nothing? Find myself stuck in one form until I found food? Was that what had happened when I first stole Beast's body and shifted to human only now and then to heal? Beast called it the hunger times.

When we were done with the food, I accepted a half glass of wine and sniffed and tasted. It was okay. Bruiser was trying to educate me about the finer things in life and he described it as I sipped, saying, "This Cabernet blend has a healthy level of tannins, is full-bodied, with a medium level of acidity." He twirled the wine and it ran down the glass in skinny trails. "It has good legs. It's good with food. The oak has brought out the flavor of"—he paused and sipped noisily—"currants, a little black pepper, and tobacco."

I sipped, watching him over the rim of the glass, holding it in front of me as I spoke. "Still. Nothing can beat the Boone's Farm Fuzzy Navel, served in your best crystal. In your bed."

Bruiser's glass halted halfway to the table. The pulse in his throat sped; his breathing deepened; his face took on color. His brown eyes lost focus for a moment before they snapped to mine, his pupils expanding. His Onorio scent reached my nose, warmer than only a moment past.

I smiled, letting my lips widen slowly. Took another sip. "Not bad. But not as . . . good."

"Well. There is that." Bruiser returned my smile and took my hand in his, running his fingers along my knuckles. The pad of his thumb was heated, slightly rough on the inner side where some weapon had calloused his skin. He held my gaze as he stroked, telling me things he'd rather be doing, very wonderful things. So very, very slowly. The rough area scraped gently across my flesh. Heat spread up my arm and into my body like a slow-moving flood of need. Goose bumps quivered over me. My breasts tightened. My belly warmed and grew heavy. My lips parted and swelled as if Bruiser had kissed me. My breath deepened. My bones liquefied.

Magic . . . I couldn't see it. No sparkles. No Gray Between mist of energies. But the scent was all Onorio: spicy, a little citrus, more blood orange and lime than lemon. This time maybe a little smoke, the scent of sweetgrass charred into the glowing embers of a long-burning fire. He kissed me, his lips and tongue heated.

Mate, Beast thought. *My mate . . .*

The scent of smoke rose, aromatic with sweetgrass. Bruiser chuckled low, the way men do when they know the effect they're having on you. At the sound, my body thrummed, a boneless, trembling, shuddering need. I couldn't have stood without assistance, let alone fight. "Oh, woman. What you do to me."

"Ditto," I managed.

"We should perhaps save this," he said softly, "for the limo ride."

I blinked. Blinked again. "Limo?"

"Lee postponed our appointments. I thought you might

like a ride"—his lips tilted up again, his voice dropping on the last word—"around the city tonight. There is a blanket, a spare pillow or two, and a bottle of chilled Champagne in the limo out front. I'd like to be doing this to other parts of you."

"Oh," I tried to say. It came out as a sigh.

"And I'd like my mouth on you." His eyes dropped to my breasts and they tightened painfully. "I'd like to taste you. Everywhere."

Magic caressed me, velvet and the feathers of hawk wings, the prickle of nettles and dried leaves. Soft and stinging all at once. Icy and heated together. I was breathing too fast. *Holy crap.* If Eli had been here he would have told us to get a room. "Only if I can taste you back."

"I'm counting on that. It might be a very . . . very . . . long night."

"I'm counting on that," I repeated to him.

Not taking his eyes from mine, Bruiser held up his hand. The waitress approached from behind me. Bruiser gave her two crisp bills. "Keep the change." He stood and pulled me up with him, against him. It was a dance step, and my left thigh pressed between both of his. Torso to torso, hip to hip. Bruiser was more than a little happy to see me. I might have moaned. He chuckled again and everything in my body quavered.

He stepped back. Taking me with him, half holding me up. His arm around me. And then we were outside, sweeping past the driver and quickly inside the limo. *The* limo. The one he'd first kissed me in. I slid along the seat, my eyes on him. Only him. The door closed. The privacy shield was up. The driver, whoever it was, was closed away, unable to see, unable to hear. Bruiser slid his hands along my body, his palms hot and raking. Closing on my cell, taking it and tucking it into the small refrigerator. Adding his. Closing the small door.

"Brilliant," I murmured.

"I had the limo swept."

I took his shoulders and pulled him back on the long seat. Yanked off his jacket and then his shirt, over his head, sending collar and sleeve buttons popping.

"No listening devices," he said. "And the driver's intercom is disabled. No one can listen in." He shoved up my tunic and his mouth fell onto my breast, hot and wet, through my silk tee. My nails pressed into his shoulders in shock. He sucked hard.

Magic shot between us, scorching and frigid. Everything inside me clenched. I gasped.

Mate, Beast thought. *Want mate. Want more.*

"Yes," I said. "Oh God yes."

Bruiser bit harder. Just beyond the instant when pleasure turned to pain. Scalded and frozen, pleasure and pain whipped through me. "Come," he whispered.

I came. Throwing back my head. Growling his name, gasping. Shudders raced through me. Electric and fiery and throbbing.

Mate . . .

I screamed. It was the beginning of a long, very long, night.

Dawn was lighting the eastern sky when Bruiser half carried me into my house and into my room. I fell into my bed, where I rolled, facefirst on the pillow, unable to move. He tucked the covers over me. "I love you, Jane."

"I uv ou oo," I managed.

"I'll pick you up at ten for the visit with the broadcasters."

I grunted. And fell deeply asleep.

I was still boneless but full of energy and feeling pretty spiffy when Bruiser pulled up in front of the house at ten. The workers were banging and hammering and shouting in Spanish on the third floor. I was dressed in slim pants and a fresh silk T-shirt with a black cowl-neck tunic sweater over it, constructed for access to my tactical holster sports bra/T-shirt for easy access to the weapons harness and holsters near the outsides of my boobs. Jacket. Scarlet lipstick. I wore my hair straight, long, down to my butt. I never wore it like this, but at some point in the long night, Bruiser had told me I had the most beautiful hair he had ever seen. So . . . Down. Long. A straight fall of shimmering black hair.

It wouldn't be practical if I was fighting. But a business meeting was a different kettle of fish.

Hunt fishes? Beast asked.

Not today. Today we hunt businessmen across a conference table.

Eat businessmen?

Only if they attack us.

Without looking at Bruiser, I slid into the passenger seat. I could feel the heat on my face as I closed the door. He didn't pull away. I knew he was staring at me. Waiting for me to say something. I opened my mouth. Closed it. Opened it again, hoping something intelligent would fall out. Instead I said, almost casually, "Last night was fun."

I could hear the laughter in his voice when he said, "The best part was when you shoved me to the floor. And climbed on top."

"Ummm."

"Or maybe when you screamed yourself hoarse. That was good too."

"Ummm. Yeah?"

"Yeah." Finally he took mercy on me and pulled the SUV into the traffic. "Although the part where you took me in your mouth . . . I was quite keen on that part as well."

My breath hitched, remembering that part. "You are an evil, evil man."

"I am. You seemed to like it."

"Oh, I liked it." I let a small smile play across my mouth. "Can we do all that again soon?"

"God in heaven, I hope so."

I laughed.

CHAPTER 6

"The Shoes," I Whispered

Thanks to the little contretemps in sub-five, the meeting with the broadcasters and the camera crew was being held in an office in the Warehouse District on Tchoupitoulas Street instead of at HQ. Because, to cement paranormal relationships, Leo had hired the Bighorn Pack for the job. While Leo often kept his enemies closer than his friends, this time he wanted his Enforcers to check out the company firsthand.

Leo owned the entire block of three-story red brick buildings with tall windows, sun-faded green shutters, and tiny gallery porches. When we pulled up, Wrassler and Derek were standing out front, the big guy in a short windbreaker-type jacket and Derek in a long trench coat, both open to reveal suits and ties in the Pellissier colors of charcoal and dove gray. We parked and exchanged nods, Bruiser and me following them inside. It was too warm and we all tossed coats and jackets, which revealed that Leo's part-time Enforcer and his head of security were both heavily armed. Good. So was I. I looked around,

finding the unisex bathroom, stairs that led up, and a hallway leading to the back exit.

The ground floor was tile throughout in a neutral tone
and there was a large conference room to the left of the
entrance with a simple rectangular table and wood-
framed chairs with fake-leather upholstered seats. The
room was set up for PowerPoint and not much else. Bare-
bones, very un-Leo-like. Also un-Leo-like was our little
group, what might—in a business situation—be called
power players. Enforcer, part-time Enforcer, head of security, and former primo were all in one meeting with
Del, Eli, the Tequila boys, and the Vodka boys keeping
watch over HQ. It was Operation Shutdown, a plan I had
devised to cover any situation where the top security
brass were all silent or inactive (meaning dead) and the
second-level ops people were in charge. They were prac-
ticing, while we were dealing with contagious tail-waggers
who might have a traitor on board.

There was a coffee bar near the entry, and Derek
started coffee. There were certain requirements in Louisiana business and society, and coffee was always near
the top. As he worked, he filled us in. "The meeting is
expected to last three hours, to include four wolves, discussions of up-front money, advertising, ease of public
access, broadcast requirements, and parental controls.
The Roberes will be here," Derek said, "to sketch out the
contracts and handle negotiations."

Wrassler pulled out chairs in the conference room and
we all sat as the coffee started to trickle through the
grounds. He dropped down with a grunt and a sigh, as if
his prosthetic leg was causing him more discomfort than
usual. He said, "Leo approved of them, but Bighorn Pack
has references from jobs in Mexico City and Guadalajara.
They offered a bundled project with an offshore gambling organization."

I leaned in, finger tracing the pack's timeline across a
tablet screen, through the last few weeks and months.
"Mexico references might intersect with known enemies
and hazards. Bighorn Pack split after the gigs there. Is it
possible that one pack or the other has been working with

a new MOC of Mexico?" The previous MOC had been Jack Shoffru, of the tail-biting lizard emblem. There had been a huge power vacuum when Jack died true-dead and the resultant internal war had been bloody. So far as I knew, no victor had been confirmed. "If the wolves had been there and if they worked with the Mexican fangheads, is that a red flag of some sort?"

Wrassler rubbed his palm over his pinkish bald scalp. "I don't know. But gambling and Mithrans fighting to the death? Perfect for any MOC who might be looking to move into a vacancy created by the Sangre Duello. Or take out the winner. Maybe the wolves are part of a plan to infiltrate. That's why the meet and greet here instead of HQ. We make a nice target to draw in, ID, and terminate potential enemies."

"Oh," I said. We were bait. Nothing new there. I looked around the area. "No security cameras. We got anything here? Something I'm not seeing?"

"No," Wrassler said shortly. "Not a damn thing." The fact that he used language in front of me suggested that he was significantly upset about the lack of security measures.

I took another look around. The furnishings were bare-bones—the kind of slick surfaces that were easy to do a forensic cleanup in case of blood spatter. "Sooo . . . What are we doing here?"

Derek brought in coffee and I took a cup of dark roast since tea wasn't offered. He said, "As we've said, Leo wants us to take their measure before he signs anything." Right. The official stance. But his eyes were worried.

The Robere twins entered and took places at the table, greeting everyone by name, getting out paper and pens, and adjusting suit coats. Both Brian and Brandon—the B-twins, as I called them—were armed, their Onorio scents like caramel and their NOLA accents even thicker. Wrassler turned on the PowerPoint. "Let's take a look at our research into the Bighorn Pack." He hit a button and Del appeared on-screen, elegant and severe, her blond hair upswept in a smooth French twist.

"Good morning, everyone. I'm sorry I can't be there

in person. Let's get started, shall we? First order of business. As you know, the broadcast company that offered the highest bid for filming and distribution rights is owned by the Bighorn Pack. Here's what we know about them and their internal power structure." A graph appeared on the screen. I leaned in and listened, but also opened a file on my cell that was tied directly into Yellowrock Security's databases for a deeper read.

The highest bidder for the televised Sangre Duello was possibly the same bunch who had me in their target sights. The same group who had entered HQ with the werecats and Dominique, the traitor.

Del had dossiers on every one of the Bighorn Pack, but they were slim reading, not much more than age, DOB, ancient driver's licenses, faded passports, and job specs. And there were no current photos at all. Someone had wiped the web of all social media presence, someone very good at that job. Even Alex didn't have anything better.

So I actually listened to every word Del said. Not that I'd be running the business end of this meeting. I was here for effect. Leo's badass Enforcer. While she talked, I braided my hair into a long tail and made sure I was satisfied with my weapons' placement. Del ended the briefing with the words, "Leo saw the leader of the Bighorn Pack after the event in sub-five. Alone. I do not know what transpired."

The broadcaster / camera team arrived early, two convertible sporty cars, tops down, pulling up out front. They were young, looking no more than their early thirties, male, fit, and energetic. There was a blond, two gingers, the African Brit with ringlets, from sub-five, and two vaguely mixed-race guys with black hair, and the drivers, who stayed behind the wheel. They had a collective surfer-dude vibe, or a whitewater-paddler vibe, from home. The men had perfect skin, wind-tousled hair, and they were laughing as they leaped over the car doors to the street and sidewalk. I happened to be standing at the door as they landed, holding a bag of trash. I got a good view of them all. They each had a laptop. Thicker than usual. Old models. The top-down cars pulled quickly back into traffic. One of the men turned in a circle, watching the perimeter.

My honeybunch came up behind me. "What?" he asked.

"The black guy is a Brit. He was definitely one of the wolves from sub-five, in HQ to rescue Brute. What do you think?"

"Their suits are inexpensive," Bruiser said. "Brand-new Brooks Brothers, the Golden Fleece collection, perhaps three thousand each."

I gulped. Three K did not sound cheap to me.

"Nicely tailored. I think I recognize the hand of Mr. Lee's alterations in the drape of the suit pants."

Mr. Lee was a local guy and he handled the alterations of off-the-rack suits for many local businessmen. It was kinda weird that I knew this. I had been in New Orleans for too long.

"English-cut, slim-fit, two-button, dual-vent jackets. No cuffs on the pants. No bulges indicating weapons."

"But . . ." I stopped. I wasn't sure I'd ever seen a werewolf in a suit. "They bought suits here. Why? They're from up north." I sucked a breath as it hit me. "The shoes," I whispered. "Suits and Timberland hiking boots."

The smell of his shock hit the air. "The soles are for traction. For an attack." Bruiser leaped back into the conference room, shouting for Wrassler and Derek to take cover. As he hurdled the depth of the room in a single bound, I tossed the trash bag to the corner and drew a nine-mil, racked a round into the chamber. Drew the other and racked the slide.

"Jane! Get back here," Bruiser said.

"No." Back there wasn't my job. I focused on the hands of the blond man who reached for the door handle. Hairy. Hairy hands. Hairy backs of his fingers. Thick blunt nails.

Werewolf. Pack hunter. Beast flooded strength into me.

The wolf opened the door and I shoved one muzzle into his face, the other to his side to cover the body directly behind him. If he had reacted, he could have trapped one arm and batted aside the other. He could

have grabbed my hair braid and snatched me away—
stupid, stupid, to have left it down—but he hesitated. Too
late. He froze in indecision. The scent of werewolf filled
my nostrils. The wolf's pupils went wide and hard as he
breathed in my own scent. I recognized another wolf who
had been in sub-five, looking over the Son of Darkness.
"Howdy, puppies," I whispered. "Why don't you set down
the laptops, strip off the jackets, and step inside, slowly.
Then you can assume the position. Or I can shoot you
and let you shift to heal in front of all the security cameras on Tchoupitoulas Street. Up to you."

The one with the gun barrel pressed to his head
growled. "What the fuck you doing, bitch?"

"*Bitch* might be polite in your world, but it isn't in
mine. And foul language is definitely not allowed in my
sandbox, puppy. Put. Down. The laptops. Take off your
suit coats. Drop your cell phones. Now. Or bleed. You'll
be Internet sensations."

The guy close enough to kiss started to say one of the
verboten words and I tapped him with the muzzle. Maybe
a little too hard to be polite. "Uh-uh-uh," I said.

From the back, the voice with the British accent asked,
"May I ask why the Enforcer to the Master of the City of
New Orleans has drawn weapons on our pack?"

"Two reasons. Three wolves visited the HQ of the
Master of the City of New Orleans, intending to steal
Brute, a white werewolf in my employ. Then two of you
visited with Leo, or so I hear. But somewhere in my recent timeline, a ginger wolf and some local gangbangers
attacked me. The gangbangers are dead. The wolf is not,
and is in the hands of PsyLED."

"Jax. It must be," the same voice said on a sigh. It was
the tone of a parent over a defiant and foolish child. "May
Artemis strike him dead." He looked at his group. "All of
you. Do as the Enforcer says."

Glaring, bending his knees, the wolf in my sights set
his laptop on the sidewalk at his feet and peeled out of his
jacket. He wasn't wearing a T-shirt under his dress shirt,
and ripped muscles and a six-pack were clearly visible. I
might have a sweetpea of my own, but I could still appre-

ciate a well-made man. And the fact that he was unarmed. The others followed his lead and I stepped back,
into the office building, motioning them after me and
into a clump where we could see them all at once. I
stopped the last one, the security guy. He was beefier
than the others. Hairier too. "You get to stay outside with
the coats and stuff." I let the door close and pretended
not to hear his rumbling growl.

Derek and I shared a hard glance as he and Wrassler,
both with weapons drawn, moved in, and Wrassler patted
down the wolves. "They're clean, Enforcers," Wrassler
said. "I'll check their clothes and electronics." I waited
while he stepped outside and went through all the suit
coats, examined the laptops, and patted down the last
wolf, before ushering him inside and tossing in the clothing and electronics.

The door closed. It would have been polite to put down
my weapon. I didn't. Neither did the men at my back. I
said, "You want to tell me about this attacker you call Jax?
And why we have six tail-waggers at a presentation that
stipulated four? Why you're wearing brand-new suits but
unlaced, worn boots? Why you smell"—I drew in a short
burst, over my tongue and through my nose—"like battle
pheromones and werewolf blood? Like wild boar? Dead
meat? And swamp?"

The British man/wolf blinked, thinking.

I added, "Why you were at HQ with the werecats and
a werewolf who drew on me? And last and maybe most
importantly, why we have a pack in a city, on the streets,
with humans, and no grindylow in sight? Eh?"

"I am honored to meet Jane Yellowrock, though the
situation seems to be growing more and more unfortunate," the dark-skinned Brit said. I slid my eyes to the
man. He met my gaze, freeing his magic, sharp and musky
on the air. They were all pretty, but this one was more.
This one smelled of alpha, of power, of dominance. He
was mixed ethnicity, African and East Indian maybe,
slender, about five-ten, with the muscles of a dancer and
the face of a model. "I'm Phillip Hastings, leader of the
Bighorn Pack."

This was the wolf who had taken over several smaller Mountain State packs and consolidated them into a four-state powerhouse called the Bighorn Pack. Who, according to a source in Knoxville, Tennessee, had taken in some *gwyllgi*—devil dogs—and had the power to meld them all into a single, dual-species megapack. This guy had done that. He was überpowerful. But then the pack had split. Sooo . . . I wasn't sure how that fit in.

"You were asked questions," I said. "I'm listening."

"We brought six wolves because precisely twenty minutes ago, we were attacked in our hotel by a rival pack, led by Jax's alpha, Prism, and we found it prudent to move. Prior to that, my beta and I went with the cats and the wolf Toots to a prearranged meeting with the Master of the City. The invitation was issued by Asad, who said the MOC was untrustworthy and that he kept a white werewolf chained in his basement. I quickly discovered that both Asad and the wolf had lied. I killed the wolf. I then laid the body of the betrayer at the feet of Leo Pellissier and presented my belly to the Master of the City."

I blinked. It fit, barely, in the timeline.

"We carry our laptops because they are safest with us and because Adelaide Mooney asked us to provide additional information at this presentation. Because of the attack and the move, we didn't have time to collate it onto one system, hence we each brought our own laptops. We smell as we do because we hunted last night to run off the frustration of being in a city, of losing our luggage, which is currently in Hawaii, of having to sleep in a hotel instead of our den, and of being in a foreign place, surrounded by predators who Could. Eat. Werewolves. For snacks," he said, the last words harsh. Softer, he added, "We are accustomed to being the apex predators with land to roam in wolf form."

It wasn't succinct, but it was thorough, and I didn't know what to say to any of that. My scent must have changed in surprise. The skin around his deep brown eyes crinkled with laughter. "Puppies? Tail-waggers? I'm deeply insulted." But his tone said he wasn't. He was laughing at me, at a predator with two guns drawn.

"Grindylow?" I asked, not yet willing to let them be okay. "Shoes?"

"For reasons I can't explain, our furry green executioner chose to stay in the car. Grindys are inexplicable at the best of times and ours is too young to have language, so we can't ask. Our luggage will fly here tonight, but not soon enough for this meeting, even with the extra day to prepare. We paid a Mr. Lee a fortune to alter off-the-rack suits for us, for this meeting." Wryly, he added, "We didn't think about shoes until far too late to go shopping."

One of the black-haired men said, "I've never had a gun pulled on me for a bad fashion choice before."

"I have," the other dark-haired man said, with a distinct Southern accent. Maybe Georgia. "Of course, that was back in the nineties, when RuPaul and Elton John were working on 'Don't Go Breaking My Heart.'" He batted his eyes at me. "I must admit the ensemble was over the top, even for me."

I realized he was wearing eye makeup with sparkles. And glittery earrings. And something lacy under his dress shirt. An openly gay werewolf? The fact that all female werewolves were insane and were usually killed on sight, even by males of their own species, and that males could be eviscerated for having sex with humans meant that, if the wolves had sex lives at all, it would be with each other, so the idea of a gay wolf wasn't surprising. I could practically hear my housemothers at the Christian children's home where I was raised reacting in judgment. Except Belinda Smith. She had been pretty cool, putting "Thou shalt not judge" as rule number one in the group home.

I took a breath and tasted their magic on my tongue, familiar and yet alien magic. It was similar to Brute's magic, but long and fibrous, the brown of polished agate. If I had to describe the magic of the Bighorn Pack, it was braided stone, slick and hard and glossy.

"They shot you because of the way you were dressed?" I asked.

"They missed."

"I won't."

"Noted, darlin' girl. You're hot. You know that, don't you?" He air kissed me and I fought my grin, which was surely his intent.

The Brit said, "Would you be so kind as to put your weapons away? I'm beginning to feel unwelcome." No growl, no attitude.

I realized that the wolf with the makeup had calmed everyone down. He had magic, big magic, and it had curled around us all, calming and palliative. The wolves were big and bad, especially the beefy, hairiest one, but Makeup Wolf could be the most powerful, regardless of his place in the pack. "Not yet," I said. "Tell me about Jax. I don't like being shot at."

"Prism was my beta," the black man repeated, "and Jax my third. I kicked them and a dozen of their followers out of the pack some time ago for tracking a human girl. She wasn't hurt, but the grindy flashed steel. Their actions were grave enough for me to act, and harshly. The wolves who participated in the tracking of the human challenged me. There was a battle and the remaining wolves were taken to the edge of our territory. They disappeared.

"I did not know they were here until I was approached about a werewolf in captivity to a vampire, something no wolf would ignore. However, one might suppose that their fledgling pack decided to ruin our entrée to Leo Pellissier and to New Orleans. The banished wolves knew about the trip and our purpose." He shrugged.

"Before we make nice-nice, there's one question you didn't fully answer, Phil. How did you get into the basement at Mithran Council Chambers?"

His mouth tightened and his wolf eyes glowed with irritation. "A vampire woman led us and the werecats to the basement. The werewolf was roaming free, there by choice. Cats are liars, disloyal by nature, and so was the female vampire. I now assume Prism arranged for us to be there in the hope that it might appear we had allied against Pellissier. We have not," he said distinctly. "Fortunately, the MOC accepted our bellies as proof we were not involved with the cats. We have signed loyalty agree-

ments and discussed a potential business contract to be
negotiated by Leo Pellissier's primo and Onorio attor-
ney." He tilted his head, his long ringlets shifting like
hound ears. "And other agreements granting us the right
to broadcast the Sangre Duello. Clearly Pellissier did
not fully believe us when we yielded to him, hence this
armed standoff, like something from an American cow-
boy movie." He shrugged again. "I would not have believed us either."

Phillip huffed out a breath, sounding like a large playful dog, and said, "And this meeting, while difficult under
the circumstances, is still necessary. We met with the
Louisiana Gaming Control Board this morning and we
have broadcast and distribution agreements signed, nota-
rized, and filed." Phillip managed to look smug as he said
that last part. "Pellissier will do well by a financial agreement with us, and we gain a safety net from a rogue pack
by this arrangement."

"The female vampire who led you to the basement.
Did you know her? Did you know her position among the
vampires?"

"No. She reeked of fruit. Blond, glacial personality.
Beautiful."

Vamp games. Hated 'em.

And then it hit me. "Leo thought the other werewolf
pack would wait to attack and follow you here. Attack all
of us here at once. Where his armed people would be
prepared to protect you."

Phillip shrugged slightly. "Or he thought we had lied
and that all of the werewolves in New Orleans would attack you here, and that you would kill us all at once, freeing him to negotiate another deal should we prove
disloyal." Phillip stared at me, a wolf's predator gaze. "I
gave him my belly. I am loyal."

I stepped back, slowly went through the proper procedures to safe my weapons, and tucked the extra rounds
into my sports bra. Makeup Wolf was watching and said,
"Oh, honey, do you have one of those new tactical wom-
en's sleeveless holster shirts?" At my blank look he said,
"I have one in black mesh lace. It is to die for. Of course

it's with Queen Bitch, lost in the belly of a plane somewhere in Hawaii. My QB got to go to Hawaii without me.
I am so jealous."

"Queen Bitch? Hawaii?"

He fluttered his hands and explained, "Queen Bitch is
my wardrobe and my stage name." He stuck out his hand
for a shake. The hand wasn't hairy, which meant he had
been body-waxed since his last shift. Just . . . ouch. His
nails were painted in a sparkly black that matched his
hair.

I took his hand, which crushed mine in a manly competition, and I had to pull on Beast's strength to avoid
bruising.

"Love the hair," he said, beaming. "It's so eighties
Cher."

I thought it was a compliment. Maybe. And that also,
he might be telling me he was a . . . drag queen?

New Orleans had had drag queens openly onstage for
decades before the rest of the nation even knew what the
flamboyant stage performers and cross-dressers were. I
had never been around a real honest-to-goodness drag
queen; not even Deon, Katie's chef, claimed to be a drag
queen, just a queen, and there was clearly a difference.
Gender pronouns for drag queens could be fluid, and I
suddenly didn't want to insult. "Okay. How do I address
you, pronoun-wise?"

"When I'm properly dressed, you will call me QB,
which I totally am. And the proper pronouns would be
she and *her*." He gave me a girly hand flap with the crushing paw. "When I'm in a suit, I'm *he* and *him*. Since we're
all besties now, you can call me Ziggy, my puppy name."

They had given Leo their bellies. Therefore they were
puppies to Leo and to us as well. *Crap. Puppies.*

Derek cursed softly under his breath. Ziggy batted his
eyes at Leo's other Enforcer. "And you must be Derek.
Honey, you are gorgeous. I've always had a thing for the
lean, mean military man." Derek glared but shut his mouth.

Phillip asked, "Do you know where Jax's wolves are?"

I said shortly, "Jax is under PsyLED control. I have no
idea about the others. Why was I attacked by Jax?"

"There's not one simple reason, but rather a plethora of them. Jax's sire died in New Orleans some months ago, in a bar called, I believe, Booger's." His tone went faintly disgusted at the name. "It's said he died of a blade at the hands of a woman called Jane Yellowrock. As a young wolf, he watched Leo and George Dumas"—his dark eyes flashed Bruiser's way—"hunt down and kill a wolf who had bitten a human. He hates bloodsuckers, but that hatred exploded when he heard that Leo Pellissier might have a werewolf chained in his basement. He came for vengeance, and because he cannot control his wolf even in human form. And he is a very, very powerful wolf."

I had a feeling Phillip had left something out, but I went with what I had so far. "I killed a lot of wolves back then. They were led by a bitch in heat and the entire pack was violently psychotic. Leo hunted down and killed a lot of wolves back before the U.S. had grindylows to keep the peace." No one shifted stance or changed scent, so my blunt statements weren't a surprise.

"PsyLED has Jax," I repeated. "He's out of the picture. How many more are going to attack me?"

"Jax will not be in custody for long, unless they keep him drugged or full of silver. He doesn't have the emotional control to be an alpha, but he has . . . skills. He'll be back on the streets in less than twenty-four hours."

"You seem pretty sure of that," I said as Bruiser pulled his cell and started texting, probably texting Rick or Soul about the danger of the ginger werewolf in custody.

"I am," Phillip said distinctly, his magic sharp as broken stone on the air. "My drivers left the cars and went hunting. Bighorn will find this misbegotten pack and teach them obedience."

I almost said, *Newspaper to the snout,* but I managed to hold it in. "This is Pellissier's city. If you need assistance, just ask."

Phillip tilted his head, a doggy gesture. "I would be honored if the white wolf would join us in this quest."

"I'll have someone ask him. I don't tell him what to do. No one does. Would the other pack join with the Euro-Vamps?"

Phillip hesitated. "Possibly. I haven't had time to address that possibility. Scout, Bear, go help track. Make sure the grindy is with you all."

"Yes, sir," both wolves said. They grabbed their gear and left the room.

I gestured to the conference table. "For now, we have contracts to discuss and security measures to consider."

Wrassler brought in more chairs. We sat around the table, Ziggy taking the chair beside me so we could "girl talk," though I think he wanted to be there so he could magic me down if the need arose. His presumption should have ticked me off, but it didn't, which was probably a big indication of his considerable magic.

We all introduced ourselves, with proper names, but Ziggy filled me in on the puppy names. There was Boomer, Scooter, Champ, and the two who had left to hunt, Scout and the hairy one, Bear. The drivers were Bandit and Rocky. Phillip—Champ for obvious reasons—ignored Ziggy's not-so-sotto-voce intros. Ziggy was the only openly gay wolf or drag queen in the group, but I guessed there would be others.

Champ made it clear to us that the pack swearing to Leo meant that Leo's share of the profits in the broadcasts had gone way up, that his problems dealing with the gaming board had just disappeared, and most importantly, that the pack would stand by us should war with the emperor, Titus Flavius Vespasianus, result from the outcome of the duel—no matter who won or lost.

Leo was expanding his power base in the vamp way, getting others to do his dirty work—like tracking down dangerous wolves in his city—while also using the same people to accomplish negotiations with the powers that be in pay-per-view and the gaming board. The MOC had been playing five-card stud with life and undeath again.

And . . . because there were no European vamps onshore to cause trouble, until we had a venue for me to secure, people for me to vet, or werewolves to kill, I was twiddling my thumbs. I needed something to hunt. I wondered if Scout and Bear wanted company tracking the errant werewolves. I texted Alex a recap of what had happened and sat there, thinking about where I'd go if I was a werewolf pack on the loose in NOLA, waiting to parley with the EVs and join the war against Leo. It was unlikely that the Zips would take in a pack who had already cost them two gang members. But the rogue wolves had made the acquaintance of Dominique and therefore with the vamps who were turning against Leo. They might be given a lair to sleep in. Except that Alex had all the known lairs wired for video and audio. He'd have caught something by now, even if it was just a misspoken phrase.

However . . .

There was a huge homeless population in NOLA, hundreds, maybe thousands, living under the overpasses, sleeping in alleys, in private gardens. If I was looking to hide out, I'd join the men and women there. Yeah. If I was an evil werewolf, I'd go hunting and bite a few humans. While an overworked grindy was busy with the Bighorn Pack, I'd make a bigger pack. This sucked.

CHAPTER 7

I Failed You

The meeting was cordial and useful, especially when we brought Alex on electronically, face-to-face, to discuss the possible necessity of setting up satellite transmission of the fights and to settle on the best ways to financially secure the online gambling transactions.

The wolves were extra affable and congenial, probably because of Ziggy's antics, pack dynamics, and the stronger wolf—Champ—showing Leo his belly. Whatever the reason, the groups merged well; Leo had planned it all out, giving us a path to meld us into a single pack under my leadership. And—despite Ziggy's claims—because I was the only woman in a group of men, that made me the queen bitch. Werewolves followed the queen everywhere.

The appointment ended when Bruiser got a call and headed back to vamp HQ.

I saw the rest of us out, which meant time I had to chat—not my forte, especially in the face of Ziggy's friendliness. I turned down an offer of a drink at Café Lafitte In Exile with the Bighorn werewolves, dancing at Oz, and hunting rogue werewolves. The café was low-key and unpretentious, a place where local gays socialized, according to Ziggy. Oz was another matter entirely, with bar-top go-go boys, high-energy music, and a laser show that was reputed to leave the dancers in a frenzy. "You love to dance. I can tell," he said, dragging a fingertip across his lower lip. "And then we can hunt Prism down and eat his liver."

"Ummm. Yeah. No. But thank you." I was certain that I couldn't keep up with wolves in a gay dance bar, and I had work to do that limited my time to hunt. He insisted. I desisted. When I finally convinced Ziggy that I really wasn't going off with the pack, he kissed me on the cheek and hopped into one of the topless cars, fingers fluttering in a wave as they drove off.

As the rest of the guys closed up, I ordered a car and texted my plans to my partners. *Have a few free hours. Need some alone time. Back after dusk.* When the driver arrived, I told Shemmy to take me to HQ.

It was daylight and I went through the usual security measures, accepted a comms unit, and headed to sub-five to have a chat with a white werewolf. The elevator doors swooshed open and I stepped out onto the clay floor. The lights were focused on the SOD on the far wall, leaving the rest of the huge room dim, but my eyes adjusted quickly. I moved across to the SOD and the white wolf at his feet.

The subbasement reeked of old blood, the odor of damp werewolf, and the peculiar stink of the Son of Darkness. The sour, bloodless, heartless creature hanging on the wall would have garnered my pity if I hadn't seen video of him drinking down and killing a barroom full of dancers and partygoers. The thing I hadn't been allowed to kill was watching me, his dark eyes dull yet full of malice. That was new. I'd hoped me cutting out his heart and giving it to a cop would have kept him totally down and out. He was healing. That sucked.

At his feet, Brute was watching me, head on paws, looking sleepy, crystalline eyes content. There were two stainless steel bowls on the floor a few feet away. One held water. The other smelled of raw roast beef and blood.

I dropped to one knee beside him. "Hey."

He yawned, showing me his killing teeth.

Beast perked up. *Fight Brute?*

No. He's on our side. I think.

Beast padded away, her tail twitching, catty and irritated.

"Werewolves came here because they thought you were being held against your will."

Brute chuffed and his big mouth grinned, tongue lolling.

"I know, right? You can timewalk, so there's no keeping you anywhere you don't want to be." I could change time back to before something awful happened if I wanted. If I was willing to risk the time-paradox possibilities. I'd done that a few times by accident already and it was scary. Brute could do that too. I studied the wolf, who was watching me back. We hadn't fought on the same side very often, and one of those times he was being eaten by a demon, so I doubted he remembered my part in that. "The angel who saved you, Hayyel? He left you in wolf form so he could give you the ability to timewalk, didn't he?"

Brute blinked and yawned again. Bored.

"Hayyel wanted you here, to guard the Son of Darkness, didn't he?"

Brute slanted his eyes to me, suddenly interested in what I had to say.

"He wants this psycho thing alive for some reason that's more important to the timeline than human lives are."

A low vibration trembled up through the clay floor into my knee, and I realized Brute was growling so low it wasn't audible, even to me. Brute shook his head no, a foreign human gesture on the huge wolf head.

"Ooookay. So you're here to bite the SOD? That's it?"

Brute's eyes narrowed, but the growling stopped, so I went on.

"The werecats might try to come back and steal the SOD."

The werewolf's eyes narrowed further in an expression that said the cats could die trying.

"Right. Okay. FYI: There are two different wolf packs in town and one of them may be the crazy kind."

Brute raised his head, chuffed, and licked his lips.

"The other pack seems to think you're something like royalty and would be honored to have you hunt the crazy pack with them."

Brute dropped his head, as if bored by the suggestion. "Yeah. Well. Thanks for the chat." I looked up at the thing on the wall over me, speaking to it. "Someday Leo won't be around and I'll take your head. Just so you know."

Joses Santana, the SOD, stuck out his tongue and curled it up at me, as if licking the air. And then he laughed. It was silent but mocking, his desiccated lips curling up and the flesh around his eyes crinkling. Brute chuffed up at me as if the idea of my killing the SOD was long overdue and I might save us all a lot of trouble if I just killed him now. Or maybe that was my fond imagining and the wolf just had indigestion. What did I know?

I took the elevator up, checked out, and took an SUV from the motor pool.

I drove by my house and spotted a PsyLED car out front, a tiny sticker on the back window the only clue. I slowed and rolled down the window, taking a sniff of the car, expecting to scent Rick. I got Ayatas instead. *Dang.*

I drove on past, thinking about the unfriendly werewolves loose in New Orleans and making pacts with gangs. About Ziggy and the friendly werewolves. About the Sangre Duello and the emperor, who I had ignored for hours as I dealt with were problems. Titus Flavius Vespasianus had been a powerful Roman general who became the Roman emperor. As a human, he and his human second in command, Tiberius Julius Alexander, besieged and conquered the city of Jerusalem. Inside the besieged walls were the Jewish, Christian, and Mithran defenders. The siege ended with the sacking of the city, the destruction of the temple, and the enslavement of what pitiful humans remained alive inside the walls. Titus returned home and gained the throne, ruling Rome for two years before he was turned by his vampire concubine, a woman captured from the fall of Jerusalem. He became the undisputed ruler of the Roman Empire and the European Mithrans. He had ruled for two thousand years. Technically, Leo owed him fealty. The legal chal-

lenge of Sangre Duello meant Leo was aiming to behead
the king in personal combat. But Titus had been fighting
with a sword for hundreds of years longer than Leo. To
win, Leo would have to cheat. Fortunately he was pretty
good at that.

Miles away from the city, my weapons and shoes left behind in the SUV, my feet in flops against the mud, I
stepped along the path to the bayou, conscious of the
tracks of raccoon, dog, deer, turkey, and boar, and evidence of hog destruction, all around me. Wild hogs used
their tusks to dig up edibles and left the signs behind. A
single wild hog could destroy large swaths of otherwise
useful habitat. Beast had killed a boar once and had been
badly injured from the experience, but that only increased her desire to hunt and kill another one. This one
was in heat, and her musky odor seemed to have settled
across the ground all along the path, into the foliage all
around, even into the mud itself, obscuring the scents of
the other prey and predators.

Hunt boar. Or alli-gator, she thought. *Hunt and kill
and eat. I hunger.*

You're always hungry.

Yes.

I found the low-hanging branch of a scrub tree and
stripped, wrapping an extra pair of flops, my shorts, shirt,
and throwaway burner cell tightly in a zippy in my gobag,
which I secured around my neck. Adjusted the gold nugget
and *Puma concolor* tooth on the doubled gold chain necklace. I sat on the low branch and rocked my feet back and
forth, securing my flops in the mud to give me a balanced
tripod perch on two feet and my backside. I relaxed. Closed
my eyes. Sought the Gray Between of my magics.

Skinwalkers weren't traditionally moon-called, like
were-creatures, but the time of day and phase of the
moon did make a difference. It was easier to shift on the
three days of the full moon. Easier to shift at night, and
harder to shift in the daytime—unless I was dying and a
shift meant survival. And the shifting wasn't a balanced
thing. It was a peculiar effect of my skinwalker magics

that while I could shift from human shape to Beast in daylight, I was unable to shift back to human until night. I wondered if Ayatas had that problem. The thought pushed the Gray Between away from me.

I admitted that I was feeling weird. Different. Emotionally different from my normal. Because of the man who claimed to be my brother. Who had been at my house just now. And I had run away from him.

Coward, Beast thought at me. *Must make peace with littermate.*

It was the same word she used to describe Eli and Alex. I asked her, *Littermate. Like from the same parents or littermate in the same way the Youngers are?*

Beast didn't answer. *Dang cat.* But that might be why I wasn't ready to face him, to make peace with him, yet. I wasn't sure he was the man he said he was.

Coward, Beast thought again.

I blew out a hard breath and turned my thoughts inward. This time I gripped the *Puma concolor* fang on the gold chain and sank into the genetic structure stored there. This time the gray magics rose. This time I slid sideways into the magical forces, studying the new Vitruvian shape of my energies. They looked stable, like an illustration on a wall in a nuclear reactor.

Beast, ever impatient, reached out and extended her claws. Pricked the magics. The shift took me. *Pain, pain, pain.* I grunted breaths as my back arched and whipped forward, throwing me to the mud. And then I was lost to the shift.

Beast sat on Jane's shoes, front paws in mud, sniffing, pulling in air over scent sacs in roof of mouth. It was good to be puma form. It was good to be in hunting territory. But it was also bad. Jane had seen prints in mud on track. Jane had smelled hog in heat. Jane had not looked beside track, in green plants. Where hunter had paced. Where hunter had followed deer, days past. Hunter on Beast's territory. Jane had not smelled scent of trespasser.

Jane still slept. Beast did not know yet what to tell Jane.

Beast leaped into low tree and climbed high. Perched and scented. Hunter was werecat. Three werecats. One was female lion; one her lion mate. One was black were-leopard. Werecats had been on Beast's hunting grounds. Werecats had pissed and shat, leaving spoor. Werecats had scratched on trees to sharpen claws. Werecats had left Beast and Jane messages on Beast's own territory.

Asad and Nantale and Kem-cat had chased Beast's deer but had not killed them. There was no scent of blood or death on air and no buzzards circled over old kill. Asad and Nantale had sharpened claws on trees and pissed on ground where Beast had pissed. Asad and Nantale had left message to say they knew where and when Beast hunted. To say their claws were long and could have killed Beast or Beast's prey. It was threat, but it was weak like watered blood.

Weak because hunt on Jane's land had occurred before Jane/Beast had hurt Kem-cat. Before Jane had torn claws through Asad's plans and left them dead and ruined.

Kem-cat had wanted to be more than beta to Jane. Had wanted to kill Jane. Kem was now house kitten, mouser cat. Tamed to Rick's hand. Threat that was no threat. Rick had pride to mate with and to protect like African lion. Kem was threat no more. Rick was Beast's beta.

Asad and Nantale were humans in cat skin. If they challenged Beast, Beast would kill them. Beast thought about ways to kill lions. Must fight one at a time to win. Or grindy might fight and kill them.

Beast had much to think on but was hungry. Leaped to ground, landing silently. *Pawpawpaw* to pile of scat on ground. Beast bent and drew in scent, what Jane called flehmen, pulling air over scent sacs in mouth. Kem had smelled healthy and full of male hormones. Also of anger and hunger and frustration and longing.

Kem was tamed. But Kem had access to witches. If Kemnebi did not stay tamed, if Kem-cat came back, Beast would kill him too. Kill him and leave his body to rot and to feed buzzards. Jane might not like this, but Jane was asleep and Beast would not share territory.

Beast turned away from spoor and leaped into trees, moving from branch to branch toward water.

Beast hunted alli-gator from trees, along water that coiled like snake. Leaping limb to limb. Silent. Beast found sleeping alli-gator, stretched out on bank of water, half-buried in mud. Alli-gator was longer than Jane body. Alli-gator was longer than Beast body and tail. Female alli-gator was big. Beast hungered after shift. Needed food. Beast territory had been invaded. Beast needed to kill. Beast needed to fight. Wanted to fight and kill and eat.

Gathered paws close beneath body. Slowed breathing. Stared at place on back of alli-gator neck, just below head/skull. Place where spine joined head.

Beast dropped.

Landed. Four paws to mud. To either side of head. Fall gave fangs and jaws power. Slammed down, mouth open. Bit down on alli-gator.

Alli-gator whipped whole body. Rolled. Rolled over Beast, through mud. Beast bit deeper, through hard skin. Through flesh. Into bones. Gator rolled. Rolled. Trying to throw off Beast. Rolled toward water. Other alli-gators were there, watching. Beast fought roll. But Beast paw was too close to alli-gator teeth. Gator teeth bit down on paw. *Painpainpain*, like shifting but more. More pain. Alli-gator shook head, tearing Beast flesh. Holding Beast paw, alli-gator rolled. Beast shoved down with three paws to stop roll. Alli-gator would roll into water. Would drown Beast and feed Beast to all alli-gators if she could. Beast did not let go of alli-gator. Alli-gator did not let go of Beast paw.

Alli-gator thrashed. Whipped tail. Hurt Beast. Would win if Beast did not kill now. But alli-gator skin was harder than last alli-gator Beast had hunted. Alli-gator was bigger than last alli-gator.

Beast bit down and down and down. Clamping jaw tight. Bones crunched. Teeth passed bones and into spongy meat. Was brain. Alli-gator mouth opened. Dropped Beast paw. Gator closed eyes. Opened eyes. Thrashing slowed. Stopped. Except for tip of tail. Was dying. *Beast is best hunter.*

Limping, Beast carried/dragged long alli-gator into brush. Dropped alli-gator on bluff of ground and lay on top of prey. Licked paw. Was bad bite. If Beast could not shift into Jane and heal, Beast would have only three legs. Beast would die. Injury had happened before, many times, when Beast was alpha and Jane was beta. Shifting to Jane had kept Beast alive. Beast had learned to be glad that Jane had stolen body. But Beast had not told Jane this. Would not tell now. Beast licked own blood and chuffed at thinking human thoughts. Beast was more than puma.

I woke to the sound/scent/taste of fresh-caught gator being devoured. Fangs ripped through hard, knobby, armored skin into meaty flesh. Mud was everywhere, all over the gator and all over Beast, a thick, gummy, drying, crumbling, dark mess. Blood was mixed with the mud, a deeper, darker gray in Beast's sight. Flies were buzzing me/us, lazily dropping to feast and lay eggs. I caught a glimpse of two buzzards in a tree, patiently waiting for Beast to finish her meal. The sky was less bright, the sun only a few inches over the horizon. It would set soon. It was time to get back to HQ, to work, to politics which I hated, to security measures which I loved. But it was peaceful here, in the mud. Calm, despite the death that made the meal valuable.

I felt pain, however, and when Beast blinked, I saw the damage to her paw. Two toes were ripped nearly off, claws hanging. The central pad of the paw was torn. Not all the blood was the gator's. *The gator got you. That your only injury?*

Beast tore through entrails and gorged on organ meat. It was an odd taste combination of intestinal/fishy/livery/lung-ish meat.

You not talking to me?

Beast is best hunter.

I know. I caught sight of the tail. Wait a minute. How big was this gator?

Was big. If Beast had kits, would take tail to den to teach kits how to eat meat.

Holy crap. This thing was, like, twelve feet long.

Was big.

It bit you, but you sound pleased with yourself.

Alli-gator bit Beast. Alli-gator is dead. Beast is best hunter.

Okay. I agree. Crap, that's a big mama gator.

Beast is best hunter. Beast must kill Kemnebi.

I went still and quiet. *Kem is tamed.*

Kemnebi has hunted in Beast territory. Kem left spoor. Challenged Beast. Beast must kill.

I thought how to explain the danger her plans presented. *To kill Kemnebi outside of self-defense means Ricky-Bo would have to fight Beast. And Rick is PsyLED.*

Beast stopped ripping flesh. Swallowed a large gobbet of meat from tail. *Rick would fight Beast? Rick could become alpha over Jane? Put Beast in cage?*

Technically yes.

Beast will kill Kem-cat where Ricky-Bo cannot find kill. Or in what Jane calls self-defense. Beast tore more food, thinking. *What is self-defense?*

If Kem attacked Beast in cat form, for no reason, and Beast killed Kem, that would be self-defense.

Beast licked her jaws. Flipped the tip of her own tail at the buzzards to show them alligator food was still Beast's. *Will think on self-defense. But will kill Kemnebi if Kem-cat comes onto Beast territory to hunt again.*

I figured it was the best I was going to get. *Okay.*

Want to go home. Home to mountains.

I had nothing to say to that.

At dusk, I woke up in human form in a decent place, no mud, not lying in the middle of a dead gator, which I had halfway expected, and close to my SUV. That part was fortunate because Beast had spent so much time rolling in mud that the gobag was muddied through and through, including my clothes, which had somehow come out of the plastic zip bag. I had more clothes in the SUV.

Standing in the falling light, I dressed in the chill of early evening, feeling the familiar gnawing pangs of hunger. I could have gone back to the extra pair of flops in the mud, but I could also get them next time. Hunger helped me decide on not going back into the swamp after the flops, though the thought that I was littering on my hunting grounds bothered me.

Dressed, warmer, I got in the cab, feeling pensive. There was a protein bar in the glove box. Three, actually. I ate them all without tasting them, which was likely a good thing. I could have bought Popeyes and now be eating cold fried chicken, but I hadn't. Not poor planning, just . . . I hadn't wanted to stop.

The drive back to the city was silent, the radio off, no music through the system. Thoughtful. Worried, just a little. About Beast. About Ayatas. About tonight and my schedule. It was full and it was all going to be difficult.

When I got home, I found a parking spot a half block down the street and walked to my door in the early dark, barefooted, carrying my muddy gear. Sniffing for the scent of lemons, the smell of werewolves. But the scents were the same as ever: food, urine, dust, mold, water on the muggy breeze. Because I was so close to Beast, I smelled him even before I got to my door. The floral scent of Ayatas.

He was still in my house.

Moving silently, I keyed open the door and slipped inside. The lights hadn't been turned on in the foyer and there were enough shadows to hide in. I smelled Ayatas, Eli, Alex, Edmund, and Gee, pretty much the main members of my vampire clan and my maybe-brother. And the garlicky smell of Bodat. Their voices came from the kitchen and the living room. I moved into my room and showered off the remaining mud. Dressed in a long black skirt and jacket and a starched white shirt. I made up my face, going for dramatic, with black eyeliner and lots of mascara though it made my eyelids feel heavy. Scarlet lipstick. Working clothes.

I pulled on a thigh rig weapon harness and weaponed up, adding the Mughal Empire dagger Bruiser had given to me, on a small harness on my hip. The hilt was gem-set jade; the scabbard was velvet-covered wood. The knife had been made in the 1700s, in India, with a slightly curved blade, a central ridge, and double grooves. It had a gold-overlaid palmette and cartouche at the forte. I had made it my ceremonial blade, wearing it when I wanted to make a statement. The blade was watered steel and it was said that it had magic, being charged with a spell of life force, to give the wielder the ability to block any opponent's death cut. Bruiser had said about the spell, "Pure balderdash, but it makes a nice tale." Still. Sometimes a history and reputation were magic of themselves.

Barefooted, I walked silently into the living room. Alex and Bodat didn't even look up. They were bent over several tablets and laptop screens, with the big-screen TV in front of them divided into various views. It was all security video of HQ. I didn't bother to study anything. Pulling on Beast's stealth and ability to move unseen, I stepped into the opening of the kitchen and stood there. Watching. Listening.

Gee was at the table, sitting in my place. Edmund was standing near the sink, opening a bottle of wine. Eli was taking a huge chicken pot pie out of the oven. I knew the menu by the mouthwatering aroma. Ayatas was standing with his back to the side door, at an angle where he could see all the others but couldn't see me, wouldn't see me unless he turned his head or smelled me and searched me out. I was counting on the chicken pot pie—which smelled heavenly—to cover my scent. Ayatas would have a skinwalker's scent glands, mostly human, whereas Beast had taken in the genetics of a dog's scent glands and the part of the brain that analyzed and remembered the scents, from when we shifted to bloodhound. She was way better than *any* old skinwalker.

Littermate, she thought. There was a sound of longing and wonder in the single word.

Ayatas said, "You were telling me about the video footage."

"No. I wasn't," Eli said.

"I could bring you in for questioning."

"You could. You won't." He set the Dutch oven on the table, on a wood rack I hadn't seen before. My stomach cramped. I hadn't eaten much after the shift and I was starving.

"And why wouldn't I?" Ayatas asked.

"Because Leo has his talons in every law enforcement agency and politico in the state and a good many in D.C. Because you want Janie on your side. Taking me in, Alex in, Jane in, is not the way to build good relations. It's a way to burn bridges you haven't decided to burn yet. Bridges with Leo. Bridges with Jane. Bridges with Soul." Eli took a long-handled spoon and cut into the pot pie's crust, releasing steam and chickeny goodness. I pressed a hand to my middle. "You're a smart guy," Eli said. "But you're also stupid."

On the surface, Ayatas didn't react with offense, but his scent changed. A faint spike of anger. Insulted.

"Here's what I think happened. You came here in your capacity as PsyLED to oversee the Sangre Duello. Smart. Necessary even." Eli looked at Ayatas to make sure he was listening and back to his pot-pie work. "You had heard about Jane Yellowrock. Seen some YouTube video. I figure you had researched through PsyLED databases and questioned your family about the long-lost sister. And then Soul came into the picture and gave you more info, more than you found in the databases. The Europeans came. Things heated up here. You decided to apply for a job transfer, with the opportunity to meet Leo, and, on the side, to see if Jane is that sister. Combining two purposes into one trip isn't stupid by and of itself. But that made Jane an afterthought." He looked at Ayatas again. "Just a note of caution, counsel, whatever—Jane Yellowrock is never an afterthought."

I smiled, seeing Eli's tension as he said that, his jaw tight. No one else might notice his anger, but I did.

"If you put Janie first you might get somewhere. If you can figure out how to do that, and still complete your investigation, you might like your life a lot better and live a lot longer." Eli began to scoop up servings into the bowls around the table. We were having the pie, salads, and a loaf of herbed bakery bread. Enough for all of us, but I was so hungry that I wanted to kick everyone out and eat it all myself.

"Live a lot longer. Is that a threat?" Ayatas looked

amused. He was leaning against the wall beside the butler's pantry, where we kept our tea and coffee equipment. He looked relaxed, but his scent said otherwise.

Gee said, "No. A fact. The Mithrans in NOLA are always dangerous. Apex predators."

"And Jane," Eli said, "is their Dark Queen, which means she's the biggest, baddest cat in the city."

My eyebrows went up. Me? That was crazy. Wasn't it?

"So what is the Dark Queen?"

"Not totally sure," Eli said. "A mystical, powerful creature that can use all sorts of magical items, witch, vamp, were. She can take positions of command and authority for herself, rearrange power structures. Sorta like a wild card in a full deck."

"You're calling her a Joker?"

"More like a Queen of Spades with the powers and unpredictability of the Joker."

I smiled in the shadows. I liked that description. It fit most of what we knew about the position of Dark Queen.

Ayatas said, "She shifted into a half cat / half human. I have to find out how she did that. How she shifted into parts of something."

"For the agency? Or for yourself?" Eli nodded to Ed. My primo began to pour white wine into the glasses. Eli went on. "Because I'm guessing you can't do what Janie did and you want to find out how. You want to learn how to shift into fighting form yourself." Eli smiled, a tiny quirk of his lips, and carried the Dutch oven to the sink, then stood straight, his hands at his sides. It was the smile that warned me. And warmed me. He said, "You may be Janie's brother or you may not. But you're a selfish bastard. And we won't let you hurt Jane. That? That is a threat." He raised his voice so Alex and Bodat could hear. "Dinner is served."

I waited a good five seconds before rounding the corner. "I hope there's enough for me. I'm hungry as a Beast." It was a way to tell Eli that I'd been a cat and needed to replace calories used up in shifting.

My partner gave me a look. It might have meant most anything. I smiled at him blandly and nudged Gee out of my chair, saying, "Up, my Enforcer, unless you want me to take a bite out of you." To Eli I said, "This smells yummy. I hope you made two." I'd need more than a single serving to make up for lost calories.

As the others took their places, shoving chairs around and bumping knees at the too-small table, Eli nodded his head and said, "There's plenty."

I looked at Ayatas, the only one who hadn't moved. "Even for him?"

Eli made a pretense of looking around the table. "I guess I could set another place. He could squeeze in next to Bodat. If you want him here."

I looked at my br—at Ayatas. "It's the way of The People to feed guests. To see after their needs." Eli had another place setting ready and set it near the garlicky gamer kid as everyone scooted chairs closer.

Ayatas was staring at Edmund, not moving. "I thought Mithrans preferred blood over normal food. Human food."

Placidly Edmund said, "We consume a variety of foodstuffs. Blood is the favored food, but I do not sip from my mistress or her family. And Eli is a splendid cook." Edmund turned to me. "Do you wish to offer thanks, my mistress?"

We had started praying over meals after the angel Hayyel had reappeared in my life. It might be nothing more than covering my bases, or it might be something significant, but it made me feel better. I nodded and closed my eyes. The others quieted. "We are thankful for the blessings of this day. Thankful for family. For clan. For food."

Eli, Alex, Edmund, and Gee said together, "Amen." Bodat looked confused. Ayatas looked surprised. I passed the bread around and dipped a spoon into the pot pie. And *Oh. My. Gosh.* Ignoring the men gathered around the table, I ate. And ate a second serving. And then ate a third serving. Fortunately Eli had more than one loaf of bread, and the second pot pie in the oven. It was, nearly, enough.

By the time I was finally fullish, the others had long finished eating and Bodat and Alex were washing dishes. Eli had slipped to the third-floor construction site with

Gee and Edmund, their muted voices coming down the stairs. Ayatas was sitting to my right, his gaze on me. I pushed my chair back from the table, meeting Ayatas's eyes. "Alex?" I said. "Would you mind leaving the dishes?"

"We're mostly done." He looked back at me and said, "Oh. Come on, Bodat. Let's give them some privacy. We can finish this later."

My entire face softened. Only a few months before, Alex wouldn't have understood what he was being asked. Now he was adulting. They left the room. I picked up my wineglass and sniffed the contents. It had a nice crisp aroma. Even good wines tasted a little vinegary to me, and unless I was cuddled with Bruiser, I didn't typically enjoy them. However, as an Enforcer I needed to know about them even if only a rudimentary and passing familiarity. I hadn't touched the glass while I ate and it was a little too warm to be perfect now, but I sipped anyway. It had a nice balance of acid and earth and oak. I swallowed. Eh. It was still wine. I put the glass down. I had dithered enough. "I heard you talking to Eli."

"They are very protective of you."

"They're family."

"You have a family."

I said nothing.

Slowly he leaned forward and rested his arms on the table, lacing his fingers together. His sleeves were folded neatly to midarm, exposing skin that was the same golden shade as mine. He said, "Where were you all those years you were missing? Why . . . why didn't you come looking for us, once you grew up?"

"The early reports were correct. Amnesia. No memory, no language, no social skills."

There was no smile in his voice when he said, "Raised by wolves."

I shrugged. "I'm sure you know my childhood history. There's enough public record to make that part easy. When I turned eighteen I left the Christian children's home where I'd been raised and moved to Asheville, where I got my training in security and lived for several years. While I was there I rode through every small town where The People still lived in North and South Carolina, into Tennessee, looking, listening. Wondering if I had family, if someone among The People would recognize me as a missing daughter, sister. Would take me in. When I did come upon someone who looked and smelled and sounded like what I remembered, they had no interest in a skinny Cherokee chick. And no one knew of a kid who had been lost in the mountains and never found. I rode through the territory of the Western band once. It was even more foreign." I took a breath and asked the question that I'd wondered for so very long. "Your questions work both ways. If you're not lying to me, creating an intricately layered fiction, if my family are all skin-walkers, if they are all as long-lived as you seem to be implying, then why didn't . . ." I let my words trail away, thinking, *Why didn't my family come looking for me?*

There. That was my real reason for running away last night. Ayatas FireWind claimed to be what I was, claimed to be family, and he hadn't come right away. Latent shock boiled up inside. Pain, loneliness, betrayal gushed after it. A geyser of misery that went back to a single day in the snow that I could barely remember. The day an old woman forced me to shift into a bobcat and pushed me into a blizzard to live or die alone. I had been five years old.

I swallowed hard, forcing down the pain. Forcing it back into the darks of me. Yet, tears gathered in my eyes, hot and stinging. I blinked them away too. Calmed my breathing and let go a breath that smelled of old despair and suffering. I knew Ayatas had smelled the pain. I knew that gave him some kind of power over me if I let him take it. Instead I pulled all my suffering deep inside and crushed it into stillness. Emotionless, sounding almost detached, I stared into Ayatas's eyes and said, "Eli is right. If my family still lives, why didn't you come for me?"

"We didn't know you existed until the videos surfaced. Until we saw you on the television as a warrior woman working for the vampire master of New Orleans. Until we saw you kill a demon, the Raven Mocker, on television. *Uni Lisi*, who is one of the Keepers of the Secrets, said we must watch and wait to be sure you were not *u'tlun'ta*.

They had to research and share the old stories. This took time. Time to be certain that it was possible. The Elders do nothing in haste."

At the mention of the Elders, I thought about Aggie One Feather, the local Elder who was helping me to try to remember my past. There was no way that she had been left out of the loop. They had called her. I was sure of it. And I was equally certain that she had told them nothing. Personal privacy was sacrosanct to an Elder. But did it work both ways? Why hadn't she talked to me about it, unless she couldn't?

"Why should I believe you?" The question was harsh and disbelieving, but inside, deep in the soul of the lost little girl growing up in a children's home, I wanted to believe. I wanted this more than I wanted breath or vision or sanity. Valued it more than I valued the sanctity of my own soul. And that was a weakness that another could exploit. That was—

"*Gvhe*," Ayatas said, the syllables more breath than air.

Tears flooded my eyes, hot and painful. I focused through them on his laced fingers, thinking, reasoning past the unbridled emotion the single word created in me. How had he known? I had only just remembered my child name. I had told no one. I didn't blink. Didn't move. I held in the tears by force of will, breathing deeply. Not looking up. Only someone who had lived then would know that name, my baby name.

"Wildcat," Ayatas said. "Or *We-sa*, Bobcat. According to the old tales, our father called you both."

My gaze turned inward, backward, to a past I no longer consciously remembered.

I was standing on a precipice of rock and loam. Inches from my bare toes, a sheer cliff fell off into a chasm. At the bottom, a fog swayed, so dense it seemed impenetrable. A cloud upside down. Below us a hawk soared. At the bottom the cloud parted to reveal racing water, a river running wild, white water roaring.

A hand held mine. Heated. Long fingered. Golden skinned.

A hand like Ayatas's. I said nothing, but I knew this

place. It was a real place in my childhood memory. I knew this place.

My father's voice came to me out of memory. "Gvhe. Your mother carries my child, a brother or sister for you, one of her clan. I charge you to remember this place, this moment. I charge you to promise to care for your mother and your brother or sister. They are yours. Your heart is strong. You are strong. You are enough to protect them should something happen to me."

I stared into the chasm. The river rumbled. The ground was chilled beneath my feet. My father loved this place more than any other. He had wanted to fight for this place, for this land. For this water called Nvdayeli. The yunega, the white man, was stealing it and all the land which no one could ever own. America was stealing it. And there was nothing the Tsalagi could do about it. We would have to leave. Forever.

Because the white man had discovered yellow rock here. Gold, like my true, full birth name. And the white man lusted after it.

My father said, "Your mother will name our child after this place. Nvdayeli. And you will care for the child of your mother's womb."

This memory, this place was the origin of my brother's name; the name meant Land of the Noonday Sun, a gorge so deep, so sheer, that the sun reached to the valley floor only at midday. Nantahala. *Nvdayeli*, in the language of The People.

And . . . Yellowrock. Yellowrock, the gold for which my people had suffered. Gold—the curse for which I had been named.

I blinked and the tears spilled over my cheeks, scalding and salty. My breath came faster. Shorter. I whispered, *"Nvdayeli Tlivdatsi*, of Ani Gilogi. Nantahala Panther of the Panther Clan. *Ayatas Nvgitsvle*, One Who Dreams of Fire Wind. Your sister welcomes you. I welcome you to my home."

Ayatas reached out and touched my hand with one fingertip, a sliding caress. "Sister."

I said, "I failed you."

"How so?"

"Before you were born, our father told me your name. He told me to take care of you. Instead, if your tales are right, I attacked and injured a white soldier, and I was forced into the snow to live or die. I let my anger endanger you, after our father took my word that I would protect you."

"You were a child of five or six."

Ayatas's finger was still touching the back of my hand, the sole point of contact between us. The touch was warm and unexpected. "I failed."

"I . . . You . . ." He stopped and began again. "You need forgiveness, but I don't need to forgive. There is nothing to forgive."

I shook my head. I didn't know what I needed. What I wanted. But my tears and my inability to meet the eyes of my brother said I needed something.

He said, "In the way of the *yunega*, I offer you pardon and absolution. You should not carry this burden any longer, my sister."

I shook my head. I hadn't carried the burden of taking care of Ayatas. I hadn't remembered it until the single word triggered the memory. *Gvhe.*

I believed. And I didn't. I halfway believed because Ayatas had the proof of words and partially remembered tales, and I had fragments of memory. I halfway believed because I wanted it to be true. I disbelieved because the timing of it was too convenient. Because magic might fool me, or he might have heard old stories that he had made his own. But mostly I disbelieved because Eli had been right. Ayatas hadn't come for me. The man claiming to be my brother could have come months, even years earlier. He could have told the Elders to stuff it and come anyway. It's what I would have done. He could have made the pilgrimage to meet me when it wasn't killing two birds with one stone. When Bruiser hadn't turned him down for arranging a meeting with Leo. When I was not an afterthought. Would a brother make finding his sister an afterthought?

These deliberations allowed my breath to come easier.

My tears to dry. I slid my hands to my lap and raised my eyes to his. I inclined my head in the way of The People, an acknowledgment without agreement. "I have work to do. I hope you will understand and excuse me." Polite, as The People are unfailingly polite except when they kill their enemies. I stood in preparation to go to my room, the kitchen chair scraping across the floor.

"Jane."

I stopped. Tilted my head so I could see him from the corner of my eye, my hair falling across my vision, hiding my face.

Ayatas was sitting so that his long black hair tumbled forward in a shimmering veil. It coiled on his thigh and dropped below the chair seat. Hair just like mine. "Even if you will not believe that I am your brother, I know you accept that I am skinwalker."

I nodded. "I accept that."

"I know the timing is bad, but—" He broke off as if wanting to stop. But he couldn't. "I'm asking you to teach me the half-form that you fight in." The words came out rash and almost angry.

Maybe I should have gotten mad at his presumption, like the lost child I had been, and told him to get out. Maybe I should have been nice, like the sister I might be, and said yes. Instead, I felt nothing, and so answered as the woman I was, with all the formality of the job I had. "Your request has been made known to the Enforcer of the Master of the City of New Orleans. It will be considered at a time of my choosing and you will be informed of my decision."

Ayatas rose from his chair. "Ayatas FireWind awaits the decision of his sister. Not the Enforcer of the Mithrans." Quietly he left the house.

CHAPTER 8

You Can Try, Little Kitten

The SUV's tires ground on the wet pavement, one of New Orleans's too-common rains pattering down. The windshield wipers squished back and forth slowly. The air in the vehicle was close and muggy and the presence of Eli beside me was comforting.

The day had taken a lot out of me. Emotionally I was wrung out, tired, feeling a little faded, like a rag I might use when I worked on Bitsa, my Harley.

Ride Bitsa, Beast thought.

Not tonight.

Soon, she said. *Need wind in my/our face. Need scents in air. Need growl of power beneath us.*

I smiled, my face turned away from Eli as he drove so he couldn't see my expression. *Yes.*

Tonight we will make kits.

What? No. No kits. We aren't making kits at all. This is vamp clan stuff. We're attending ceremonies at vamp HQ.

Making Jane clan. Jane clan will depend on us for teaching. For food. For care and training. For fighting and life and death. Kits.

Ah. Edmund was a better fighter than I'd ever be. Eli took care of me like the brother I had claimed. Alex had mad skills I'd never have. But still. Beast had a point. I supposed so, then.

We will have kits again, she thought.

I let my smile widen and said aloud, "Beast thinks tonight will make you my kits."

Eli chuckled. "Tell Beast I love her."

Beast sat up and forced me to look at Eli. I could feel her padding to the forefront of my brain and staring out through my eyes. Eli smiled, a real smile, not that soldier flick of humor that was left over from too long on a battlefield. Beast studied him and then shoved down on me, hard, forcing me out of control of my body. *Beast! Stop!* I had no idea what she would say, but it wouldn't be me saying it. I struggled against her.

My voice in a lower register, she said, "Beast does not understand love. Beast understands killing enemies. Tracking prey through deep snow. Taking down fat deer. Eating. A full belly. Clean water that shouts as it falls through rocks. Mating. Kits. Not love. Love is for Jane, not Beast."

Eli put on his blinker and took a right. Beast waited. Eli said, "That feeling, that need, and hope and dependence that kits feel toward their mother, that is love. That feeling that a mother puma feels toward her kits, the desire to protect, to feed, to share, to teach, that is love. You think we will become your kits tonight when we join Janie's vampire clan. Therefore I love Beast. And Beast loves me."

Beast scented the air. Tasted his sincerity. Tasted the truth in his words. "Beast did not understand love. But Beast loves Eli." She turned my head to the backseat and the three who sat there. I could see her golden eyes reflecting in theirs. "Beast loves Edmund. Beast loves Alex. Beast loves Gee, though Gee is wily like a fox and might have to die someday at Beast's claws and teeth."

Gee's eyes went wide and he laughed. "You can try, little kitten."

Beast turned back to stare out the front windshield. "Beast accepts kits into Jane's clan." She released my mind, padding back into the deeps of my soul home. I felt her leap onto the ledge where she used to live, back when we first came to New Orleans. She curled into the small hollow of rocks. She blew out a breath and said to me, *Beast is happy to have kits again.*

In the backseat Alex said several of the words that were prohibited in our home. I didn't make a fuss about it.

Eli turned into the front drive at vamp HQ and rolled down his window. Spoke into the mic and the security camera, and the heavy iron gate rolled ponderously open. He parked. I said nothing. Didn't move. Not even when the others got out and went up the steps. Eli came around and opened my door, took my hand, and led me out of the SUV and up the stairs. Softly, just for my ears, he murmured, "Tonight? Is going to rock."

Eli and I entered the Mithran Council Chambers—the actual room where the council met, as opposed to one of the proper names of the entire building. The room had seats in a semicircle, stacked like a small theater facing the dais. At the front of the room on the dais were carved black chairs behind a narrow, curved, half-round ebony table; a black rug was on the floor there. The wall behind the table of judgment had recently been painted black and was centered with a tall grandfather clock in ebony wood. The room had new black marble tile flooring, with a drain in the center of the slightly sloped floor. There was something foreboding about a drain in the room of judgment.

Little brass plaques lined the table's front edge, engraved with clan names, only four of them now where once there had been eight. Leo of Clan Pellissier, Grégoire of Clan Arceneau, Innara of Clan Bouvier, and Bettina of Clan Laurent, with the name tag of Sabina Delgado y Aguilera, the outclan priestess, in the middle, presiding. Time had been rough on the vamps. Or I had. Almost half of the chairs would be empty for tonight's ceremonies.

I went to the table and tapped on the mics hidden behind the plaques. They were all live. This meeting of the council would go live throughout the building.

Sitting in the audience chairs were a number of early

arrivals, and some were a surprise, primarily Ming Zoya, formerly Blood Master of the now-defunct Clan Mearkanis. At her side was her sister, Ming Zhane of Clan Glass, out of Knoxville, with Zhane's primo, an Asian man named Cai. Koun sat at the back, his arms out to the sides as if claiming the chairs on either side of him. Koun had declared he was a Celt and maybe he was old enough for that, I didn't know. We didn't really get along, but in a fight, I'd pick him at my back. He was fast and powerful. Alejandro, another vamp I didn't know well, entered and sat with Koun, their heads coming together as they chatted.

I nodded cordially to the vamps just as Amy Lynn Brown entered and took a seat against the wall in back. Amy was a young vamp, seemingly too young to be important, but vamps had gone to war over her because her blood could bring a Mithran scion over from the devoveo—the madness vamps entered when first turned—in less than the average ten years. Feeding from her blood had even brought a few of the long-chained back to sanity. Amy was valuable for her fortuitous but inadvertent and involuntary blood kiss, however, not for anything that she was. She was untalented, too young to protect herself, and had a big red target painted on her forehead. Every master vamp in the world wanted her for themselves. Not one of them wanted her for who she was except her master, Lincoln Shaddock, back in Asheville. Isolation was turning her inward and making her solitary. That was the kind of lonely vamp who would one day, far too soon, walk into the sun.

Just after Amy, Shiloh entered. Shiloh Everhart Stone was my BFF's witch-turned-vampire niece, her long straight hair pulled back in a thick tail. Big surprise to see her. At her side was Rachael Kilduff, her red-headed, tattooed, primo blood-servant. Rachael had been working out. She looked buff and toned and dangerous. Shiloh came over to us and Eli stiffened, an almost imperceptible reaction, one I couldn't interpret. "Jane," she said. "Why am I here?"

I frowned. "You don't know?"

"No. I got this and I figured you sent it." Shiloh held out an envelope that bore Leo's clan watermark. The envelope was made of extra-heavy rag paper, paper made with linen or cotton, and the flap had been sealed with red wax, which was still attached to the envelope tip. Leo's seal had stamped it closed. I looked around. Several people were holding identical envelopes.

I pulled out the note, and it made that soft rich sound of very expensive paper scrubbing against more fancy paper. In exquisite calligraphy, the note said, *Your presence is requested in Mithran Council Chambers upon rising.* It was signed, *Leo, Master of the City.*

Shiloh said, "I mean, it can't be from Leo, so it has to be from you."

I stuffed the note into the envelope and handed it back to her. "Leo handwrote that." When Shiloh went still as a dead cat, I chuckled.

She whispered, "What could the master want with me?"

"Go. Sit. You'll know soon enough. And I expect you to do whatever makes you happiest."

Shiloh took a seat one down from Amy Lynn. The two vamps didn't acknowledge one another, which was sad. There were always so many lonely people in here. I walked over to them. "Amy. This is my BFF's niece, Shiloh. She's a witch turned vamp and master vamps want her because, since she survived being turned and survived the devoveo, she'll be powerful someday. If she lives long enough."

Shiloh flinched slightly at my blunt words.

"Jane," Eli breathed, faintly horrified.

Not very diplomatic of me. I guess I could have been more tactful, but . . . sometimes plain words were best? "Shiloh, this is Amy. She's the vamp whose blood brought you back to sanity. Every master vamp in the world wants her for that. You two would make—" I stopped as an idea hit me and a devious expression melted over my face. Both girls went wary and worried. "You two would make a very powerful coalition." They looked from me to each other and back again. That was why they were here, I was almost sure of it. Leo was working the short view this time, protecting his assets. The girls considered each other. I let Eli pull me to a seat in the middle of my clan members.

Other vamps and blood-servants wandered in, and in the midst of them were Katie—once Leo's heir—and Grégoire, arm in arm. Behind Katie trailed Alesha Fonteneau, her sister, once known only to me as Madam Spy. The two women had spent a lot of time in the scion cages after Katie rebelled against Leo to protect her sister, but their freedom and the glittery jewelry they wore suggested that they had been forgiven if not restored. Real diamonds and sapphires and emeralds sparkled on their necks and fingers and ears. I hadn't been aware that Grégoire was in town, but the Sangre Duello had meant a recall of outlying forces. Leo wanted his best around him. Dacy Mooney, the heir of Clan Shaddock, took a seat and moments later Leo's primo blood-servant and Dacy's daughter, Adelaide Mooney—Del—took a seat. Del was taller than me, a blond beauty with long lean legs, her fingernails painted green to match her dress. The whole gang was here.

The place filled up fast as the grandfather clock gonged seven p.m., the herbal stench of vamps and sex and blood mingling on the air. The doors behind the long table opened, and the VIP vamps filed in and took their seats. The three Onorios filed in after and took places against the walls, where they stood at military parade rest, hands clasped in front of them. Bruiser found me in the audience and his eyes stared hard in warning, though his somber expression didn't change. Something was up. I gave him a scant nod that I understood there was a problem and opened my senses, smelling, tasting, watching, listening. I thought I caught a trace of lemon. My eyes shot around the room, trying to place the scent, but it faded and was gone. Someone had eaten lemons. Or washed their hands in lemons to get seafood stink off them. Or there was a danger here I didn't yet see. Nothing else seemed out of place. Everyone here belonged here. The vamps at the dais sat except for Sabina and Leo.

The men up front were dressed in tuxedoes, the women in black floor-length gowns, except for the outclan priestess, who wore stark white, even to the gloves that hid her fire-blackened hand. The last time I saw Sabina, she had been blood-drained and weak; now she fairly glowed with power, her skin glistening palely in the soft lights. Sabina was old, with a beaked nose that suggested Mediterranean ethnicity. She looked powerful, imposing, and serene.

My eyes traced back over the crowd. Everyone seemed as expected. No one was visibly armed beyond teeth, fangs, and talons, weapons they carried with them all the time. I took a seat again with the Youngers and my people, on the second row.

"The executive council is called to order," Sabina said as she took her seat. "The chair recognizes Leo Pellissier, acting in his capacity as Master of the City."

I figured that meant he would not be acting as master of Clan Pellissier. Interesting but not enough to cause the look Bruiser had sent me.

Leo shot his cuffs and walked around the table to stand a step down, in front of his usual chair. He was a lithe and elegant man at all times, but in a tux, with his hair loose and hanging on his shoulders, he was gorgeous. He paused, his French black eyes taking in the room, waiting until every eye was on him. Something glinted through his hair and I realized he was wearing diamond studs in his ears. He also wore two gold rings, one on either hand. Two diamond studs were in his collar points and his cuff links were large onyx with tiny diamonds. I'd never seen Leo in this much jewelry, and it only accented how pretty he was. And then I realized how human he looked, instead of pale as bone and cold as death. All the council members had fed and fed well. Bruiser had warned me about something with that glance. Was this the reason? Prickles of unease feathered down my body. I tried to catch Bruiser's eye, but he was watching Leo, his face impassive.

"My people," Leo said. "Tonight we *gather*." His power shot into the room, serrated and hot. It was like being dragged through a flaming cactus patch, naked and blind-folded.

I sucked in a breath. This was the reason for Bruiser's

warning glance. Eli nearly went for his weapon and I placed a hand on his arm, murmuring, "It's okay. It's not an attack. It's vamp magic."

Alex cursed softly. The spectators sat back, tense and wide-eyed. A *gather* was one of the most sacrosanct of vamp rituals, sharing and exchanging energy, working for a purpose. Except for the people behind the dais, who looked fine with the proceedings, Leo hadn't warned anyone. The spectators were uniformly rattled.

The vamps all stood, lifting their hands to the dais. Their humans shrank back, breathing too deeply, eyes shocked. The reek of dead flowers intensified, the smell of papyrus and lavender and ink and black pepper growing strong enough that I had to breathe through my mouth to keep from sneezing. I kept a hand on Eli and put one on Alex's arm too. Gee could look after himself. Edmund, however, was standing with the other vamps, his arms at his sides, and Leo was watching him.

"Edmund Hartley," Leo said. "Though you are not of my bloodline and soon will no longer be of my clan, you have been named my heir. State your loyalties."

Ed raised his hands to Leo. "I am primo blood-servant to Jane Yellowrock. I accept the honor and responsibility as primo heir to Clan Pellissier, and primo heir to Master of the City of New Orleans and associated territories, to care for its Mithrans and protect its cattle. My shoulders are strong and my sword is true. I swear fealty to my mistress the Dark Queen, to the city, and to its master."

Leo didn't react, but something suggested it wasn't exactly the response he had been expecting, or maybe it was the order of importance he didn't like. Me, then the city, and Leo last. After a pause that stretched too long, Leo said, "That is acceptable. Take your place beside me. Drink of me, and I will drink of you."

Oh crap. This was gonna get icky.

Edmund bobbed a kneel in front of me, one of those half-bow things people do in a Roman Catholic church. "My mistress," he murmured. "Your leave?"

I almost said sure, but caught myself at the last moment. "The Enforcer of the Master of the City gives you leave." I carefully didn't give him leave by the power of the Dark Queen. No way.

Ed gave me a cheeky grin before wrapping a solemn demeanor around himself. He turned and knelt before Leo, this time down on both knees, which seemed to please the MOC.

"Our city's Mithrans have been weakened by internal strife and civil war, by kidnap and imprisonment, by perfidy and betrayal. Attacked from without, by other clans and other masters. Attacked from within by those we should have been able to trust. Yet we have survived. Now we have cemented new alliances with the witches, and with the werewolves of the Bighorn Pack, we've affiliated with the Mithrans of many cities, and our territory has grown to include Atlanta. With Sangre Duello imminent, we must choose wisely those with whom we ally ourselves and our clans.

"Edmund Hartley. You have proven yourself wise in leadership, wise in the webs of Mithran politics, and far more capable in La Destreza than anyone knew." There may have been a hint of irony in Leo's tone. Yeah. Ed was quite the fighter. "Should I fall in battle, will you accept the weight of responsibility for my clan, my city, my territories, my Mithrans, and my cattle?"

"I will."

"Should I fall in battle, will you take up my sword and my war?"

"I will."

"Should I fall in battle, will you seek to find peace with the conquerors?"

"If there is no way to win and all would die otherwise, I will."

"Should I fall in battle, will you seek to protect the alliances and the Mithrans I have sworn to protect?"

"I will. Moreover, I will avenge your life and your true-death should you fall."

Leo smiled at that one, and clearly he hadn't been expecting it.

"I will govern wisely, I will listen to counsel, I will elevate the wise and teach the foolish. I will carry the long view as my master has foreseen it, has dreamed it, to fruition."

"I have chosen wisely," Leo said, surprised.

"I have served with honor, my master, and that will never falter nor fail."

Leo slid a hand into his tux jacket and removed something small and green, a jade knob, about the size and shape of a golf ball. He cradled it in the palm of his hand, and between his fingers a small, wicked blade protruded. Ed held out his hand and Leo stabbed downward, puncturing Ed's thumb. Bright blood welled. I wondered who Ed had been drinking from to have such good skin color and such bright blood. He had a female blood-servant, Maryanne. I seldom saw her, but Edmund had to drink from someone.

Leo lifted the thumb to his mouth and captured Ed's eyes with his own. The level of magic in the room rose, spiky and blazing, my skin itching. Leo took the thumb into his mouth and closed his lips around it. And sucked. Ed bowed his back without breaking Leo's gaze, as if the sensation of Leo's mouth sucking on his thumb was unanticipated. There was nothing erotic in the action. The smell of vamps rose on the air, suffocating. The magic intensified with it until I wanted to scratch off my skin to get to the itch in my bones. Eli frowned hard. Alex shook his kinky curls and shivered.

Leo pulled his mouth from Edmund's thumb and punctured his own thumb. He placed it at Edmund's lips and Ed sucked in a ragged breath before taking Leo's thumb into his mouth. He sucked, eyes closed. He shivered. The magic crept up another notch. The temperature in the room went up a few degrees and it was getting hard to breathe. I was pretty sure my skin was turning red. The air felt charged with electricity. My body ached. Beside me, Eli opened his mouth as though he was having the same trouble breathing as I was. His skin was glistening with sweat. Alex, on my other side, was breathing hard, as if he'd run several smiles at a dead sprint. I tensed, ready to grab up my partners and carry them from the room.

And then it hit me. Leo might expect something similar from me tonight.

Will drink Leo's blood, Beast thought at me.

No.

Will drink Leo's blood.

No.

Will—

No!

Beast fell silent and I knew she was playing with me like a cat with a new toy, batting me around, biting me a little, and batting me some more, watching me ricochet into the corners.

Beast chuffed with amusement as Leo pulled his thumb from between Ed's lips.

Leo said, "Tonight I officially appoint Edmund Hartley as my clan heir and as heir to my position as Master of the City of New Orleans and her territories."

The magic blasted out. Pain like forge-heated razors. I gasped, stood, and grabbed the boys, one beneath each arm.

The pain fell away. The room chilled so fast the sweat on my skin felt like ice water. Alex sucked in a breath and started coughing. Eli shoved me away, his chin dropping with irritation as he peeled my arm and hand off him. Former Army Ranger didn't need saving, not now, not ever. Right. I dropped Alex too. We all sat. We were okay.

But . . . *dang.*

Leo pulled Ed close and guided him around the big desk, to the back, toward a chair on the end. Leo flipped a small brass nameplate up. It said HEIR OF NEW ORLEANS and, below that, Ed's name. Edmund looked drunk. Great. A blood-drunk primo. Just what I needed. Not. Ed walked behind the dais and fell into his chair, sticking his thumb into the air. It was still bleeding, just a bit, a single drop that spiraled down his thumb, despite the fact that vamp saliva clotted blood quickly.

Leo, back around front, said, "Katherine and Alesha Fonteneau. The Master of the City requires your presence." This was said without a rise in magic. And without a hint of a smile.

The sisters, looking more alike now that they were well fed and healed of their injuries, came to the dais. The two blond women dropped deep curtsies, long silk dresses shushing in the still-as-undeath air.

Leo pulled a sword that sounded as if the blade were taking a breath in the silence. "Katherine and Alesha Fonteneau. You have dishonored your vows," he said. "You have worked with our enemies, those who came from Europe to harm us, to conquer our territory, first by stealth and witch magic, by the raising of revenants, and now by the Sangre Duello. Katie, you did not trust us to save you or your sister, Madam Spy. You aided our enemies instead. You have endangered us all. How do you plead?"

I looked at the drain in the floor. I tried to catch Bruiser's eyes, but he was staring at the place where the edge of the blade rested on Katie's shoulder, at her neck. Katie. Leo's lover. Leo's friend.

"I plead guilty, my master and my friend," Katie said. "I did not trust that you would find a way to fulfill your vows to the city, defeat your enemies, and still save Alesha. I was a fool."

"Yes," Leo said, his face human in his hurt. "Are you disloyal, my Katherine?"

"Never, Leo, my love, my best friend, my master."

"Do you trust me now, Katie?"

"I trust you with my undeath. With my heart." She leaned into the blade and a sliver of blood appeared at her neck where her shoulder sloped. She was cutting herself on Leo's sword. My entire body tensed and I prepared to leap to protect the bare necks of . . . of two who were technically Leo's enemies. His friends and lovers. But enemies. Who had shared a bath with him only recently. Right. But. Indecision raked me with claws. Before I could decide to act, Katie continued, "With my blood. With my true-death should you demand it. I ask only that you protect my sister when you take my head, Leo, my love."

And danged if Leo, the Master of the City of New Orleans and most of the Southeastern United States, the baddest of the big, bad fanged uglies, didn't have a pale

pink tear gliding down his face. "Will you come to me
with your fears and with your heart?" Leo asked her.

"Always. I will never fail you again. I will trust you. I
will fight with you. I follow your orders without fear."

Leo lifted the sword and placed it on the ebony table,
where it settled with a rattle of steel on wood. He held out
his hand. "I will drink of you and you of me. We will
know one another blood-to-blood, heart-to-heart, before
these, our friends." Katie placed her hand in his and
stood; with the little knife, Leo stabbed down. Then he
stabbed his own thumb and, as he took her thumb into his
mouth, she took his. Katie groaned as if they were alone
in bed. Her head went back and her knees went weak.
Leo caught her and held her close. Katie's back arched . . .

Just *ewww*. It was a little too much sex and blood for
me. I looked away and kicked Alex to look away too. He
ignored me. Katie moaned again. *Ick*.

When the public mutual licking and moaning was finally over with, Leo said, "Katherine Fonteneau, you are
heart of my heart."

"And soul of my soul," Katie whispered to him.

"But I cannot allow you to remain with me."

"No," she whispered. "Leo, my love, no!"

Leo took a breath that sounded thick and painful.
"You are banished from my clan home, you and your sister Alesha." Katie, who had been mostly standing during
the blood reading, fell to her knees, one arm outstretched
as if pleading, her hand still in Leo's. Her face blanched;
her mouth hung open. She sobbed silently.

I could smell her horror and her fear. I had read about
banishment. Being banished meant being taken to a wil-
derness and set free, far from the nearest human. Not
that there was such a place in this day and age.

"You are now"—Leo smiled gently at her—"Blood
Master of Clan Fonteneau and banished to Atlanta,
where you will take up the mantle as Master of the City."

"No!" Katie shouted, her fists bunching as if to sock
him. She jerked back on the one in Leo's hand, whipping
against him. He held firm and she struggled, almost
growling, "I refuse to be master of clan or city."

Okay. That was a surprise. A vamp refusing power?
Alesha, at her side, was still as stone, her eyes slowly
vamping out.

Katie's voice rose and she yanked against his hold. "I
refuse the city. I am made for pleasure, not boardrooms.
I am made for beds, not negotiations. *Tu sais ça!*"

I recognized the phrase. *You know this.* I had been
among the French-speaking vamps too dang long. I was
understanding French.

Leo actually laughed and, with the back of his free
hand, wiped his face clean of the tear track. "Dearest
Katherine. Katherine, *mon amour*, you have ruled this
city and her humans for a hundred years, through the web
of hedonism and decadence. Did you think I was so foolish that I did not know? Did you think me unaware that
Katie's Ladies was the center of your web? That you had
spun silken snares about your clients and victims? That
they smiled in pleasure and desire as you strangled them
in a snarl of coercion and bled them dry of favors with
extortion? You have been my hand to power for far too
many years to count. You have served me, even as you led."

Katie went still, standing, her body bladed to Leo, as
if she might yet fight. Or as if she might pull away and
run. Or as if she might pull a weapon and kill her master.
"Je ne régnerai pas." I will not . . . something.

"You will," Leo insisted. "You will rule as Master of
the City of Atlanta, as the Blood Master of Clan Fonteneau, with your heir Alesha at your side and your Enforcer Ro Moore as your sword and Tom as your primo."

Katie's eyes were wide and frenzied, shooting to every
person and every corner of the room as if looking for allies or a way out. And then Katie heard what Leo had
said. He had given her an Enforcer only a few days past.
He had now given her an heir. He had . . . he had been
planning this for a while. Leo was making a new clan, one
loyal to him.

Then it hit me. The MOC was making more than one
new clan tonight. He was rebuilding his power base.

Leo smiled into Katie's dawning realization. "You
have all you need to govern and control Atlanta. You will

care for her Mithrans and convert her murderous Naturaleza to the way of the Mithran. You will ensnare and protect her helpless cattle, her politicians, and her moneyed and powerful." He paused. "And you will swear to me as master and ruler of the Southeastern United States of America."

Katie's eyes flashed black fire. "You bastard," she hissed.

"Au contraire." Leo lifted her hand and kissed her fisted fingers. "I am the son of my father, planted in my mother's belly, born in wedlock. My name is listed in the family Bible and recorded in official parish papers." Leo was laughing at her.

Katie's fangs dropped down slowly with a faint click of the hinges. Her eyes vamped out—the sclera bled scarlet and the pupils went wide, eclipsing the irises, black holes in a bloody sea. "For how many years have you planned this?"

"It was never planned, my love, but this move has been on the board forever."

"I refuse! You need me here. You need me to fight at your side. You need me to ensnare our ancient enemy once again. I will not leave you."

Leo pulled her into an embrace and said gently, sweetly, "Then I will have my Onorios take you and your sister to the mountains of Georgia, far from the nearest habitation of cattle, far from the nearest protection from daylight, far from food and safety. They will drain you both, in the Onorio way, and drop you from a helicopter."

"La faute est à moi," Alesha said. Katie whipped her head to her sister, still standing at her side. I had practically forgotten her, in the soap opera of Leo and Katie, playing out on a public stage. Madam Spy was biting her knuckles with her own fangs. Clear, human-looking tears ran down her face. She shook her head. *"Je suis la coupable. Tout est de ma faute. Tout est de ma faute."*

"Katherine!" Leo demanded, his voice low.

Katie whipped her head around to Leo.

He said, *"Nous vous offrons le salut. Acceptez notre miséricorde."*

I had learned a lot of French just being around HQ,

but I must have looked confused because Edmund said from the dais, to me, "Alesha says it is all her fault. Leo offered her mercy."

Leo said, *"Ne me forcez pas à vous tuer toutes les deux."*

Edmund said, "Do not make me kill you both."

"Nous acceptons votre offre et jurons fidélité," Alesha said.

Edmund translated, "We accept your offer, and swear loyalty."

"C'est pour cela que je suis née."

Edmund murmured, "I will govern. It is what I was born for."

In English Alesha said, "Your conniving lover made certain that I was trained in duplicity and governance. Ask him."

"You!" Katie leaned away from Leo, who tightened his arm on her waist. She whipped her eyes wildly around the room as if she felt a noose closing over her neck. Her hair slid out of its coil in an ash-blond swoosh. Her shoulders hunched, fangs flashed in the pale lights. Then she blinked. Slowly, as if understanding was dawning. Katie turned her head in one of those inhuman motions the fangheads had. In a totally different tone, she said to Leo, "You!"

Leo shrugged lightheartedly and kissed the back of Katie's fingers again. "I must needs come to visit my most loyal servants." He uncoiled her fist and lifted her index finger; kissed the tip. "There must be comfortable beds and well-trained servants." He lifted the middle finger. Kissed. "And deep baths."

Katie laughed, half-hysterical. Her shoulders, which had hunched up for battle, dropped. "No, Leo. Please do not send me from you."

"I must. You have betrayed me. Do you accept your chastisement, your sentence, and your elevation in status?"

"Tu es une créature maléfique."

Edmund said, "You are an evil creature."

Leo said, "I am."

"However," Katie said, *"j'accepte ton jugement."* I got that one all by myself. I accept your judgment.

"Call for your blood-servants to pack your clothing,

Katherine, and go to Fonteneau Clan Home and the Council Chambers of Atlanta. You and your traitor sister have much to heal there in the wake of the previous Master of the City, and his Naturaleza ways."

Katie threw herself into Leo's arms and sobbed. "You send me to a dreadful place. They do not even speak French there."

Leo chuckled and unwrapped himself from her. "They are not so without culture. At least it isn't Charlotte with its nouveau riche or Charleston *avec ses touristes and Yankees*, or Richmond with its . . . nothing these days." Leo had just insulted three of the South's largest and most powerful cities. I suffocated a grin. He looked at Brandon and Brian Robere, standing beside Bruiser. "Take them. See that they are in Atlanta by morning. My jet is fueled and awaits you. And if *mes deux espions* attempt to convince you to hide them here in the city or to stay with them in Atlanta, you will stake them in the bellies until such time as they are ensconced in their new clan home." Katie shot Leo a murderous look and gathered up her skirts in a righteous fury. "Tomorrow night," Leo continued to the twins, amused by her actions, "you will see that the Georgian Mithrans swear fealty to her, and that any remaining Naturaleza, who refuse to sign the Vampira Carta of the Americas and swear loyalty to their new mistress, are beheaded. I believe that Grégoire has provided you a list?"

Vampira Carta of the Americas? That implied Leo had created his own document.

They nodded again, though this time a bit reluctantly. They were swearing to kill vamps, creatures they loved and served. Onorios could kill easier than I could, and without a single weapon. Bruiser's gaze had moved from Leo to me, watching my reactions. I tilted my head to show I understood. That I could deal with it. And really, how could I do anything else? I'd killed so many fangheads since I came to NOLA that some vamps referred to me as the Enforcer Executioner. I had so much blood on my hands that I had befouled a baptismal pool when I jumped in. I was something and someone to be feared and hated. I tightened my lips, fighting a self-disgusted quiver, and looked back at Leo, who was still talking to the Roberes.

"With the second dawn, when Clan Fonteneau is entirely in power, you will return here. Alesha will remain in Atlanta to rule. Katherine will return with you for a fortnight. Do you understand?"

The Robere twins nodded once, the actions mirror images.

Katie's mouth popped open and fangs retracted as she laughed. She threw her arms around Leo. "You are allowing me to return for the Sangre Duello?" Leo speared Katie with a look that held centuries of passion and trust and emotions I had no name for. He nodded and she said, *"Je t'aime."*

"And I you. For my Katherine I have one last task. To stand by my side as I fight and live, or fight and die." Leo released Katie.

The two women curtsied, deeply and gracefully, and remained in that position of obeisance for ten Mississippis before the B-twins stepped forward and each took a hand of the Fonteneau women, lifting them to their feet. As a group, they stepped back and swept from the room.

"The long view," I muttered. Leo had just punished Katie and Alesha by giving Katie the one thing she didn't want—responsibility—provided a stable rule for Atlanta by making sure Alesha was there to do the political stuff, permitted Katie to return to NOLA so she could participate in combat, and reset a clock that he could twist in many ways. "Wily and devious and scheming."

"That was freaking cool," Alex whispered. He was right, it was. Leo was a snake in the grass. I feared it boded badly for me.

CHAPTER 9

Huggy Huggy Kiss Kiss

"Ming Zoya, former Blood Master of Clan Mearkanis, and Ming Zhane of Clan Glass, rise and kneel before me," Leo said, clasping his hands together behind his back.

This was unexpected. I looked again at the drain in the floor, but Leo had no reason to want the Mings dead. So far as I knew.

The Asian sisters stood and walked down the aisle to the front, where they knelt at Leo's feet. Ming Zoya was wearing unrelieved black—pants, shoes, and a jacket that was woven to show a large dragon shimmering across the back when the light caught it just right. Her face was made up with rice powder, scarlet lipstick, and strong black eyeliner, her hair piled high on her head in an intricately braided bun. She was a very different woman from the starved, skeletal, raving insane vamp pulled from a watery pit.

Ming Zhane of Glass was wearing scarlet. Their colors clashed and blended, like lava and stone. The Mings were graceful, delicate, and they carried themselves with deadly balance and purpose, even kneeling.

"Ming Zhane of Clan Glass," Leo said, "I give you

leave to petition the Master of the City of New Orleans for position of Master of the City of Knoxville."

Ming Zhane fell still, the marble statue stillness of the undead. She took a breath needed for speech and bowed her head to the floor. "My master is gracious, wise, and kind to this most unworthy Mithran. I will file all necessary petitions posthaste." The sisters started to rise, but Leo spoke again.

"Ming Zoya, former Blood Master of Clan Mearkanis," Leo said, "will you swear to me to protect and guard my city, to guard me, to fight by my side, to avenge my death, should I fall and die true-dead?"

Ming sucked in a shocked breath, as did all the gathered. "Master?"

"I asked you questions, Ming Zoya."

"I do. I will. Always and forever."

"You lost your home. Your people. Your scions and your cattle. Your clan. Yet you showed no fear, you refused to relent, you refused to give in to your captors. I would have you back at my side, as Blood Master of Clan Mearkanis. What say you?"

Ming started to shake. Bruiser looked nonplussed, and then a wide, delighted, surprised smile swept over his face. Ming said, "My master. How? My clan has been disbanded, my scions and properties dispersed."

"In the last months, you did not rule well, Ming Zoya. Your people were afraid and your clan home was controlled by fear, yet, there are fourteen Mithrans of former Clan Mearkanis who have spoken for you and are willing to return to you. Are there others among my people you would claim for your clan, if they and their Blood Masters are willing?"

"I—" The word broke sharply and Ming stopped, her shoulders going back with almost military posture. When she spoke again it was with the formality of fangheads in ceremony. "I pondered much while buried in water with the dead. I request the time to choose scions and blood-servants who are willing to join Clan Mearkanis. I will do so over the next twenty-four hours and present them to the Master of the City tomorrow night at this same hour."

"I proclaim it so," Leo said. "Your former clan home is empty, and the witches, to whom it was offered, have been approached and are willing to accept another property. Mearkanis Clan Home awaits you." He looked back and forth between the sisters. "You must rule with kindness. With the awareness and understanding of failure and error. With mercy."

"Forgive me, my master"—Ming Zoya dropped her head in a bow—"but Clan Pellissier has never ruled with mercy."

"I too have learned much in these last three years."

Eli slanted his eyes at me and his lips did a little quirky smile. I sat back in my chair. Three years was about how long I'd been in NOLA.

"I now demand all of my sworn Blood Masters follow the new guidelines, amended to the old Vampira Carta. Will you so swear?"

"Without seeing these new ways of thinking and acting?"

"Yes."

Zoya answered, her reluctance almost imperceptible. "I will trust my master to require only the possible. My sword is yours, my loyalty is yours, my heart is yours, and if I have a soul, it too is yours."

Leo pricked his thumbs with his blade. Pricked both Mings' thumbs. They each took the other's thumb into their mouths and sucked. There was nothing sexual in this blood exchange, though I knew Leo and the Mings had been more than friendly in times past. They all closed their eyes and leaned closer, as if each using the other for balance.

I checked the time. This was all huggy huggy kiss kiss, but boring. I had things to do, werewolves to hunt, and creatures to fight.

Leo and the Mings stopped the blood exchange and swallowed. Leo said, "Ming Zoya, your loyalty is rewarded. Clan Mearkanis is reestablished, with all attendant properties and rights and incomes. Go. Attend to your restored clan. Build it. Protect your people. Ming Zhane, provide petitions for Master of the City status."

The Mings backed away and bowed so low it looked as if their heads might touch the floor. Vamps are really limber. "I am yours," both Mings said, mostly in unison. "May my clan and my progeny die forever true-dead should I ever be disloyal."

The Mings swept out of the Council Chambers.

Just wow. Leo called two other vamps to the front for some small approval, which I ignored. Until he called Callan to the front. Pretty Callan, young vamp with a boxer's shoulders, cyclist's thighs, and angel's face. The vamp who had kidnapped me in the middle of a magical storm and hidden beneath a boat on the Gulf of Mexico, waiting for the sun to set so he could drink me down.

Leo asked, "You are accused of betrayal, conspiracy, and traitorous actions. How do you plead?"

Callan tossed back his beautiful locks and stood straight and tall. "Not guilty, for I serve the master of all Mithrans, Titus Flavius Vespasianus."

Leo stared at Callan, unmoving in that creepy, vampy, still-as-a-graveyard-statue way. Then he took a fluttering breath and said, "Judgment shall be decreed by the outclan priestess."

I had pretty much forgotten Sabina and the others on the dais behind the black table, because they didn't breathe or fidget or blink. Typical undead. Sabina stood, her robes making a starchy shushing sound, and said softly, "For your crimes against the Enforcer and against the rule of Mithran decrees and the law of the Vampira Carta, you will be beheaded."

In his Carolina accent, Callan sneered, "Unsurprisin' judgment by a pickaninny and the coward who owns her"— he threw back his shoulders and finished—"against an unarmed man."

"Oh, he didn't," Alex whispered.

"Or you may test your skills against the Master of the City, here and now," a woman's voice said. Vamp-fast, someone behind me tossed Callan a sword. And I caught a whiff of lemon. Everything happened *fastfastfast*.

The condemned vamp snatched the sword out of the

air. Vamped out. Fangs schnicked down. Eyes bled scarlet, centered by widening pupils, blacker than death.

Edmund leaped into the crowd. After the sword-throwing woman.

I was sitting forward, drawing a weapon. I stood.

Before I could blink, Callan whirled the sword and stabbed at Leo. He leaped back. Sabina took the sword thrust. She jerked to the side. Just a fraction. Just enough to miss the center of her throat. The blade struck through the left side of her throat near her collarbone. It exited her nape, bloody. Callan twisted the sword, cutting to the side. Taking out the left carotid, jugular, tendons. Still twisting, he yanked back on the sword. The blade came free.

Sabina toppled.

Leo leaped over the table to catch her.

I screamed. What came out was, "Mine!" I hurdled between and over the chairs in front of me. Raced to the front. *This. This I can do. Vengeance for Sabina.*

"Attack most foul. This is the responsibility of the Enforcer Executioner," Leo said from behind the table where he cradled Sabina.

Callan stepped back, watching the rear of the room, his face frozen, eyes wide. Whatever was happening back there, it wasn't what he expected. And I smelled lemons on the air. Someone sworn to Clan Des Citrons was here. I never took my eyes from Callan.

Eli stepped close and took my gun, scooping Leo's longsword from the tabletop and placing it in my right hand. Beast-fast, I drew a vamp-killer for two-handed fighting.

"Prepararse para la muerte," I said. And I attacked. My swords swirled and circled, steel edges glittering in the lights.

Beast murmured deep inside. *Killing claws.* I stepped inside Callan's guard. Beast swept out with a killing claw and cut across Callan's chest. We stepped back. "First blood," I said.

"Little bitch. Always in the way. Damn wolf shoulda killed you."

Wolf . . . The red wolf from Andromeda's jewelry

shop? Or Ziggy's and Champ's pack? I cleared my mind, letting the meditation of the skinwalker shape-shift fill me with the emptiness of battle. My blades whirled faster. Meeting and sliding and grazing apart. My feet settled into perfect balance, long and short transverse steps sliding me inside his reach and out. Callan lunged. Again. Again. Our blades clanged and shushed along the length, gently, as I knocked his aside. Trapping his blade with my vamp-killer. Cut at his neck. Shoulder. The wrist of his sword arm. The Zen of battle.

The room around me faded. Disappeared. There was only the single blade before me and the movements of the creature who wielded it.

Cut. Cut. Cut. Blades a percussive steel melody. Edges sliding, shushing, tapping. My body dancing, dancing. Moving through the forms of La Destreza, feet spread, weight balanced. Focused on one thing. This dance.

"Jane Yellowrock. Desist."

Cut. Cut. Cut.

"Jane Yellowrock," the words roared. "Desist!" Leo. Commanding.

I laughed, showing teeth.

He said other words, softly, then, "*Dalonige' i Digadoli.* Stop now."

I cut and cut.

"*Dalonige' i Digadoli. Halewisda. Howatsu.* Stop. Please."

I blinked. Stepped away. From Callan. I was blood splattered. Callan was sliced into ribbons. I felt a blinding pain on my right side. Callan fell to his knees on the marble before me. His blood trickled into the drain. Instantly, I understood what I had done. In meditation, I had reverted back to the punishment I'd dealt to the first man I killed. Sickness rose in my throat, but I forced it down.

I lifted the longsword back, across my body. With all Beast's strength, I cut.

Callan's head toppled. Fell. So did Callan's blood-slick body. His sword hit the black floor. I stood over him, watching as his blood puddled between the marble tiles in geometric patterns, flowing toward the drain.

Alex clicked off his phone, but before he did, I saw Aggie One Feather's name on the screen. He had called her to get Tsalagi words to make me stop. He had given the words to Leo.

"Bring Edmund to me for healing. Find Dominique, who tossed a sword to the prisoner, and bring her to me," Leo said. "If she is still in Council Chambers, her true-death is now mine to give."

Dominique. The traitor brought back from near-true-dead. Dominique and Adrianna—an archenemy I had tried to kill for years—had been lovers. I had recently killed Adrianna and that gave Dominique a big reason to want me dead. And she was here at the same time as the scent of lemons . . . Ahhhh. That was why Leo and Grégoire had brought Dominique back and set her free—to track who she had been working with. Dominique had sworn to Clan Des Citrons. A tiny puzzle piece fell into place. Finally.

"Jane?" Leo was wearing that blank vamp expression. There was a reddish haze around him and I blinked, trying to clear it away. Raised my hand and wiped my eyes. My wrist came away bloody. I realized there was blood in my eyelashes. In my hair. "Eli. Take Jane to heal."

I felt the world shift and I realized I was in Eli's arms. He carried me from the room, moving fast through a dizzying maze of hallways, into the locker room across from the gym. He placed me on a bench and a woman knelt at my feet, removing my shoes and cutting off my clothes, wrapping me in white sheets that quickly turned scarlet. I watched for a while until the pain and the stench of my own blood brought me around. I looked at my stomach. There was a deep cut there. Callan had been a mediocre swordsman. I was actually better. But just there at the end, when I stepped away and before I positioned for the final cut, he had lunged. I hadn't blocked or parried. Callan's sword had run me through.

Jane used killing claws. Jane is good hunter. Trespasser in hunting territory is dead. But Jane is stupid kit. Should have used ambush and taken head first.

"Can I be both?" I asked aloud. "Good hunter and stupid kit?"

"Don't know. But you are for sure bleeding to death," the woman said.

I knew her. She had helped me dress the first time I put on the proper fighting clothes for blood duels. I couldn't remember her name.

"I'll take it from here," Eli said. The woman didn't move and his voice took on a tone I wasn't accustomed to hearing from him. Command voice. "Get out."

The woman rose and left the room.

"Jane. Shift. I'll bring Beast a plate of steaks."

"Oatmeal for after. With sugar and milk."

I could hear the amusement in his voice when he said, "I remember how you like it."

"Today has sucked," I said.

I fell forward and let the Gray Between take me.

Beast kicked out of bloody cloth. Stretched through hips, front legs out, chest and belly. Shook pelt. Stretched again. Looked over parts of body. Looked in mirror. Liked mirror. Was better than water in lake. But lake had beaver dam. Remembered beaver dam. And beavers. Hard to catch but fun to chase in water.

Looked for Eli. Looked for cow meat. No cow. Chuffed. Eli did not appear. Went to door and chuffed again. Was hungry. Made kit-sound, peep and mewling.

Door opened. Eli looked down at Beast, laughing. "Poor hungry kitty cat."

Beast snarled, showing killing teeth.

"Be nice. I have a roast fresh from butchering."

Beast backed away from door, sniffing, nostrils opening and closing. Sat and waited. Eli entered and placed big metal bowl on floor, full of blood and meat. Not watery blood. Real cow blood. Beast licked and slurped and tore into meat. Was good.

"Don't laze over your food too long," Eli said. "Leo has plans."

Beast looked up from blood and licked jaw, raspy tongue cleaning lips and muzzle. *Like Leo. Have seen Leo fight in drops of water. Leo is like kit. Must be protected. Will give drop of time water to Jane and see what Leo does.*

Finished dead cow. Was good dead cow. Belly full, Beast lay down on cool floor and woke Jane. Gave body over to Jane.

I came to lying on the floor. "Dang cat," I grumbled. I stood and went to my locker. I hadn't checked it in a while and I had no idea if it still had clean clothes in it or not. I found a dark gold sweater and black slacks. A pair of dancing shoes. Undies, thankfully. I wasn't in the mood for commando. I dressed and braided my hair in a sloppy single braid, hearing a knock at the door. "I'm decent."

When I turned around, Eli stood in the doorway holding a bowl of oatmeal. He came in, placed the bowl on a small shelving unit, and pulled a long bench up to it. I sat and scarfed down the oatmeal. Heaven in a bowl. I used a lot of calories shifting into any form, so no matter how well I ate in one form, I needed to eat again when I shifted back.

"Update," I said around a mouthful of oats and sugar and milk.

"Dominique tossed Callan a sword. You sliced Callan to pieces and beheaded him. He got in one good stab and nearly killed you. Edmund attacked Dominique bare-handed and took a dozen stakes to the belly and heart. Dominique got away, up through a ceiling tile and a tunnel we didn't know was there. Leo healed Sabina. Dacy Mooney healed Ed. You shifted."

I grunted. Ate some more.

"Alex saw an anomaly on the screens during the fight. There was a witch in the Council Chambers."

My head came up.

"Alex says he's talked with Molly and she can't think of a way—other than the lasers—to get tech to recognize magic."

I grunted and shoveled in another bite. "Where's the witch now?" It came out like *Ere ee wit now?* but Eli understood.

"The anomaly fled Council Chambers. We caught sight of it near Leo's office. We have the MOC and Sabina under Derek's personal protection."

I grunted again. Ate some more of the sugary delight.

"We heard from Phillip Hastings." His voice was tone-less and sere.

I looked up at him. Battle face. This would be bad news.

"Bighorn Pack tracked down three of the rogue pack. The rogues had targeted NOLA's homeless population and the grindylow had already killed them. The grindys and the wolves gathered the bitten humans into an empty boxcar to await the full moon."

The full moon. When the humans would change and then—if they had no control over their werewolves—would die at the claws of the grindys. Or stay human and live. I looked back at the oatmeal. Wondering if I could do something to stop that, knowing that I could not. Knowing that the humans' fate was already decided by the were-taint in their blood. I shoveled in more oatmeal, though now it was tasteless.

"Bighorn Pack has set up a feeding regimen and show-ers and portable toilets for the bitten men. They'll be well cared for until the full moon, but they will be prisoners."

I grunted. Hating this. Hating not being able to save people who would die because of no fault of their own. This sucked.

"You meditated when you fought," Eli said.

"Zen," I said. Though it came out *Chhhsssin*.

"And in a meditative state you are a fighting beauty to behold."

"Ducky," I said. Or tried to. It came out sounding ob-scene and Eli chuckled. I swallowed and said, "I sliced and diced him to pieces."

"And took his head. And your rep as a fighter just went through the roof. Five challengers from the Sangre Duello just dropped out." He watched my face and an-swered before I could ask, "Yeah, word got out fast." More softly he added, "Andromeda Preaux is dead."

I looked up in confusion.

"Andromeda. The woman in the jewelry shop. She's dead. Her store was shot up this afternoon in what looks like a gang shoot-out. Six victims: three gangbangers,

Andromeda, a blood-servant who smelled like lemons, according to the surgeon who worked on her, and a homeless man who had been sleeping in the doorway."

I closed my eyes, remembering the woman who had offered me a way out the back when she believed I was in danger. The woman who had been willing to defend a stranger. I pushed down the need to hit something, to save a woman who couldn't now be saved.

Hate pack hunters, Beast thought.

Yeah, I thought back. *I hate helplessness more.* Hiding the need for vengeance, I asked, "And the lemon-smelling woman?"

"She was still under from anesthesia when she disappeared from the recovery department. They think she was carted out in a laundry basket right in front of the sheriff's deputy on watch."

"Des Citrons got her back."

"Looks like it. Let's go. We have more ceremony tonight."

I wiped my face and gathered up my weapons harnesses. "I'd rather be chasing down and cutting up Clan Des Citrons. Ceremony is boring," I said.

"Not when you're around."

I grunted a final time and led the way to the elevator.

Back in the Council Chambers, I studied the hole in the ceiling and the small brick-walled tunnel beyond it. The space was maybe thirty by thirty inches and black as pitch. Eli craned his body around and sent a tight beam of light into the hole. Mr. Prepared always had a flashlight on him. The tunnel went straight up for about fifteen feet and then angled hard to the left. Right at the angle there was a smear of black. I sniffed and thought I caught the faintest scent of old fire and fresh lemons. "Soot?" I asked.

Eli said, "Boost me up to your shoulders." I bent my knees, hands on the floor. He stepped on my shoulders, the hard rubber of his boots cutting into my muscles. I didn't complain, and stood to give him height, watching as he fingered the brick at the lower edge. It was broken and shattered evenly all around. "Hammers. I'd guess

there used to be a fireplace in this corner and it was removed during some renovation."

"There was," Leo said calmly from behind us. "In 1917."

"Where does it go at the angle?" Eli asked, stretching
to the left, his light shooting a thin beam of illumination
up the shaft.

His voice carefully unemotional, Leo said, "Down to
the small library on this level and up to the fireplace in
my office."

I bent my knees again and Eli leaped to the floor. I
brushed off my jacket and stretched. "Let's check out
your office," I said grimly.

Derek said, "I'll check out the library."

Leo's office had been trashed. Upholstered furniture had
been ripped open, the hanging draperies that hid the lack
of a window in the inner room had been yanked down and
lay in piles in the corners, and objets d'art had been shattered against a wall. Said wall was full of fist-sized holes.

"Nothing of value was taken," Leo said softly.

"And you know that how?" I asked, standing at the
end of the small hallway, where the space opened out into
the office proper.

"Because the wall she punched through is new. The hidden storage place is empty." Leo pursed his lips and walked
closer to the destruction. He scraped a finger along one
hole and then held it up to the light. There was a smear of
soot and blood on his hand along with the dust from busted
wallboard. Leo sniffed. "Lemons." He looked back at me.
"The storage area was removed after the police conducted
the investigation into the death of Safia, the black wereleopard who bit Rick LaFleur. Within it were papers related to the families and histories of many of the Mithrans
in my domain, including Dominique's."

"And?" I asked.

Leo shrugged slightly and sighed. "And there were once
two *objets de magie* hidden here. The amulets were removed and now reside with Sabina in her lair."

I texted Alex to check on the vamp cemetery, where
the outclan priestess slept by day, and got back a nearly

instantaneous response of, *Nada. Cameras show silent as
the grave. LOL.* Then he texted, *Our house is fine.*

Next I texted Derek about the library. He texted back,
*Pair shoes in front of fireplace. She came in here. No sign
returning this way.*

"Leo, would you be so kind as to open the secret tunnel from your office?" I asked.

"Secret?" he asked. "Hardly." Leo walked to the wall
beside the desk and tapped the lever that opened the access to the formerly secret tunnel. Everyone knew it was
there now, including the several law enforcement agencies from that investigation into the death of the woman
who had bitten Rick. The small doorway opened and the
scent of lemons whooshed out.

My cell dinged with a text from Alex. On the screen
were the words, *Got it. Dominique didn't disable cameras
in Leo's office. Took nothing so far as I could see. Took
escape tunnel and out through outer wall. Into dark SUV.
Got plate. Running/tracking through traffic and security
cameras. NOTE—anomaly was with her. Got a partial
visual. Cleaning it up.*

What was she looking for? "Alex is on it. I'll take off
and—"

"You will return to the Council Chambers," Leo said
in his command voice, a kingly, brook-no-refusal tone.
"We have unfinished business."

I wanted to disagree, but . . . "Yeah. Okay." What the
heck. Alex could run this search through his tablet from
the chambers. It would be a long night.

Back in the chambers, I ignored things for a while and
let Leo's politics and the fallout run through my mind,
combining tonight's actions with the coming Sangre Duello. He had cemented things with NOLA's previous four
clans and restored a NOLA fifth clan, and he'd given
himself loyal Masters of the Cities of Atlanta and Knoxville, to add to the loyalists in Sedona, Seattle, and other
vamp-cities. And he wasn't done yet.

"Jane Yellowrock."

Pulled from my reverie, I narrowed my eyes at Leo,
but otherwise I didn't move. The business had progressed

to smaller, less consequential things and I thought Leo
had forgotten about us. Looked like I was wrong. Snake.
In. The. Grass.

"No 'Yes, my lord and master?'" he asked.

"No."

Leo laughed. He raised his hands and his magic coiled
into the room, less painful than before, but still hot and
biting. "Jane Yellowrock, Enforcer to the Master of the
City of New Orleans, approach and kneel."

Beast peered out of my eyes, and I could see their yellow glow reflected in Leo's. *Leo would be mate.*

Leo would be and do a lot of things if I let him. I stood
and walked the few steps to the dais. I wasn't real excited
about kneeling to anyone, but I was taller than Leo, even
with him on the step, so it wasn't as bad as it might have
been.

Beast took over and dropped me, but I caught myself
as she started to roll me over. *Beast shows belly to alpha.*
No. No freaking way. I held myself upright on my knees.

Turning to the clan masters of the executive council,
Leo said, "Jane Yellowrock cannot be bound. Jane Yellowrock is loyal by choice. Jane Yellowrock will know that
the Master of the City is loyal as well." With his little
jade-handled blade, he cut his thumb again and turned
back to me.

I stared at the welling blood. *Crap on a cracker with
toe jam.* He expected me to suck his thumb. Which for
some bizarre reason made me think of Leo sucking on a
pink pacifier, which brought a grin to my face. Suddenly
I was laughing.

And Beast ripped through the Gray Between. The
half-shift was instantaneous. Violent. I would have
screamed with the pain, but I had no breath. My back
arched, then bowed, snapping both ways. My body threw
itself to the floor, ramming my head on the stone. I saw
stars. But no way was I lying on the floor at Leo's feet. I
put both hands out and shoved myself to my knees. My
hands were half-Beast/half-human, knobby knuckled,
furred on the back, with retractile claws, already extended. Swallowing down stomach acids and a taste so

sour it made my cat nose quiver, I stood. I was taller, shoulders broader and bony. Waist thinner, hips rangier. My clothes still fit, though the shoulders were stretched out and the slacks were hanging on my hip bones.

Leo, eyes piercing, extended his hand and offered me his thumb. It was his right thumb, healed since one of the Mings had tasted him.

Alpha offers blood, Beast thought. *Is not mating gift. Is not meat. Alpha offers blood. Blood is food but not meat food. Vampires are strange predators.*

Staring at the blood dripping down his thumb and pooling in his palm, I dredged through what little I knew about blood sharing and blood offering. I'd fed on Leo's blood when I was dying. On Ed's too. I'd fed when Leo tried to force a binding, but that had included him forcibly taking my blood. This wasn't a binding. There would be no pain, and without my blood as part of the bargain, no way to force anything.

Leo binding failed, Beast thought.

Yeah. He failed. And I/we are a lot stronger now. He could try to bind me again, but I had a feeling that my own magic would stop anything. Especially in half-form. I relaxed with a single exhalation and sank into my soul home. The cavern was palely lit, as if the sun was just beyond the stone walls, shining through, glowing, the way light glowed through the nacre of a pearl. In the cavern, I heard water dripping, steady and certain, the same speed as my heartbeat. I laughed again, and my laughter echoed off the stone walls, steady and confident. I looked up, to the angel wings that originated in the center overhead and feathered down the walls. Hayyel, standing guard. Yeah. I was safe.

I blinked and was still standing in the Council Chambers, still chuckling. I knelt and opened my mouth. Captured Leo's eyes with my glowing golden ones. He might have flinched just a bit, hesitated just a microsecond, but he recovered. He placed his thumb between my lips and fangs.

Leo's blood was salty and sweet. Tart. He reached out and cupped the back of my head in his other hand. He leaned down, breaking our gaze, and placed his lips on my forehead. I swallowed the blood of the Master of the City.

His magic shot into me. But this time I was ready.

Ice and fire, the heat of a volcano and the frigid air flowing from a glacier, twining together in a tornado of power. His magic whipped me, seared me. The pain of forge-heated needles stabbed and cut me. I reached out with a clawed hand-paw and put my magic over his. Pressed down, my claws cutting into his power. Held it still. Studied it the way Beast studied the movements of prey.

Leo magic is in his blood, Beast thought.

Yes. And he can control what he does with it. He can heal. He can seduce. He can bind. Probably other things. But this time, there was no attempt at binding, no attack.

Instead, with my claws hooked into his energies, images lanced through me.

Leo and his brother at play by day, racing on horseback through fields and woods.

The night they were turned, a night of fear and excitement, as they were sold by their father, who had two too many younger sons. The rage of the devoveo, *the madness and thirst.*

Later, fanged, the brothers rode finer horses, galloping by the light of the moon.

Leo and his uncle, reading by a campfire.

Leo and Katie, the night they first met. The instant attraction. The immediate desire.

Grégoire, the first time Leo saw him, old, though still in the form of a teen, on his knees, forced to service his master, in public, a shame and humiliation that was ruining him, destroying him. Leo's instantaneous and urgent vow to free Grégoire from Le Bâtard. His uncle's hand on his arm, the crushing grip stopping him from drawing his sword and challenging Le Bâtard to Duel Sang—personal combat—on the spot. Amaury telling him that Grégoire had gotten away once, had been free for over two hundred years. And when Le Bâtard found him, the old pedophile tortured the Mithran rescuer and laid waste to his entire town to teach the world a lesson.

The night Leo stole Grégoire away from Le Bâtard, the two of them riding through the darkness of a new moon night, racing their horses twenty miles before the sun rose. Falling into bed together in the safe house before dawn broke. Waking together, Grégoire crying with relief and fear and murmuring over and over, "Je suis libre. Je suis libre." I am free. And Leo holding his new friend in his arms as Grégoire wept.

Battlefield after battlefield spread out before them— wide and clanging with the clash of war, or the boom of cannon, or empty, the army on the far side. Fires everywhere in the night. The sound of music and singing. Laughter. The smells of smoke and bread and gunpowder and human blood, of fear so strong on the air it was sour. Over and over, war after war.

Leo and Katie and Grégoire on the docks of New Orleans in the deeps of night, having been rowed ashore by blood-servants. Amaury Pellissier stalked just ahead, disappearing into the dark. The smell of the city and her sewers in the heat of the summer night. The clouds of mosquitoes. The sounds of revelry. "We are safe here," Katie said. "We three, safe at last."

Leo's first sight of George's mother. Then of George, in a small room near where his mother was dying.

The sight of Amaury dying, after drinking the silver-poisoned blood of George's mother.

Holding George the night the boy saved his own sister and killed her attacker.

Dancing with Katie at Katie's Ladies. Group sex and feeding in a room upstairs.

His first sight of a color television. Of seeing the sunrise on the screen. The shock and wonder and deep desperation to see it himself, with his own eyes, even if it meant true-death.

The sight of his brother dying, Leo's sword in his side. Then his brother's head flying from his shoulders as Leo beheaded him.

The darkness of depression and despair as the years spread out before him. Empty of the sun. Filled with only blood and those bound to him.

Leo's first sight of the woman Jane Yellowrock. Her scent that screamed of danger, of predator, of the ruination of all his plans. The shock when the damned woman branded him with a silver cross. A lesser Mithran would have been scarred forever.

The sight of his son, dead on the carpet in the doorway. A monster. A beast of darkness, half sabertooth cat, half Mithran. Dead at the hand of the woman he'd brought into his lands and charged with killing that same darkness.

His decision not to kill her. But to force her to love him.

Months later, the attack by his enemies, when the Naturaleza had been draining him dry. The woman led the charge to save him. When later, still drunk from his healing, he attempted to bind her by force. George's rage and ferocity. The woman's resistance. His realization that he had erred, the sensation of a small part of the soul he feared he no longer had, slipping away. He had never told her that she had bound him instead.

A vision of Jane, on the dance floor, a warrior woman of her tribe, dressed in vibrant silks. Dancing. Whirling. As sinuous as a snake.

The feel of her body against his as he led her in a dance of passion. Her refusal to become his in truth. Her ability to thwart him at every turn.

Her honor.

His honor.

Leo slid his thumb from his mouth.

I blinked. No. Not Leo's mouth. Not . . . Leo's.

My mouth.

The sensation became my own, his thumb sliding across my lips, the taste of Leo on my tongue. I blinked. Found I was gasping. Crying.

Alex grabbed my arm and dragged me away from him, whispering harshly, "Bruiser staked the MOC to protect you."

The room was in an uproar. People shouting. The smell of blood and anger and battle. The ebony table was empty of clan leaders except for Sabina, wearing fresh whites, healed, her fangs *schnicking* down, all five inches of them. Her jaw was still unhinged. I was leaning limply across the table, entirely too close to the outclan priestess. Eli and Bruiser were squared off together against Leo, who was sliding to the floor in a boneless heap. It was the blood of the MOC that I smelled.

I wrenched my arm free and croaked, "I'm okay."

Alex's face said I wasn't. I scrabbled, fighting for balance, my bare paws on the cold floor. I'd lost my shoes when I half-shifted. I fought for control. Bruiser raised the bloody stake high. I pulled the Mughal blade. Shouted, "Stop!" But my throat was dry, voiceless. So I pulled a gun and shot into the only thing dense enough to safely stop a fired round, damaging the antique carved table that was probably worth more than my house. But it worked. The table stopped the round, splinters flew, and the Council Chambers went still and silent. "I'm okay," I said. "Bruiser. He didn't attack me."

Alex asked, "Janie?"

"Leo, did you give me that or did I take it?"

"I gave myself to you," he said, as his blood pooled on the floor beneath him.

I smelled his truthfulness. Saw it on his face. I said, "He didn't try to bind me. Stand down." No one relaxed from combat mode, but I ignored them. I was still holding a blade and a nine-mil. I checked in to my soul home. Everything there was peaceful. My soul was still my own. I was slightly deaf from the gunshot, but otherwise I was good.

"Leo," I said. "How badly are you wounded?"

The Master of the City slid his hand into his black jacket and it came away scarlet. "Nothing immediately mortal," he said, with the faintest of smiles. His fangs clicked back into the roof of his mouth; his eyes bled back to human.

Eli said, "Janie? You're sure?" He still had a gun aimed at Leo. Bruiser still held the stake.

He had fought the MOC for me. That was so sweet it made tears gather in my eyes. "I'm good. He"—I looked at Leo again—"gave me a gift, I think. I'm fine." A little teary eyed, a little weepy, a little off-kilter, but mostly okay.

Leo huffed out a breath he might actually need, and, with two fingers, removed a neatly folded white hankie from his pocket. After wiping his bloody hands, he folded the hankie and pressed it against his side. He said, "Jane Yellowrock, I cannot bind you. I cannot even know your mind. But you now know mine. Will the Dark Queen swear to me, to protect and guard my city, to guard me, to fight by my side, to avenge my death, should I fall and die true-dead?"

Except for the Dark Queen title, the last part was essentially what Leo had asked Ming. This was part of the swearing-in ceremony of a blood clan. My breath went fast and my heart rate sped, things I knew Leo could detect. This was the creation of a new clan. Of Clan Yellowrock, in the way of the Mithrans. *Holy crap.* This was really happening. And then it hit me. As Dark Queen, I could avenge his death . . . Plans within plans.

I looked at the floor, at the feet of the Master of the City of New Orleans. At the feet of the creature who had abused me. Who had crowned me. Who would always want to use me, whether I agreed to that use or not. Who would do evil in the name of good, horrible evil to protect his people. A creature who was rebuilding his own power base even as I was building my own to protect my people. In his shoes would I do any less? Softly, not sure who I was talking to, I quoted, "Because I'm a Scorpion. It's in my nature."

"From the traditional tale of the Scorpion and the Frog," Leo said. "But scorpions are creatures of instinct. I am a man. While it is my nature to use you, I will not do so unless the need is urgent. I have learned and changed and evolved, thanks in large part to you, my Jane."

It wasn't likely, but it was remotely possible that Leo had grown emotionally and might change. Me? I was the city's champion. Which was utterly ridiculous. I am an idiot . . . But I'm NOLA's idiot. One who might, one day, do evil to protect it. "Yes. And yes, I accept and I so swear."

As if I hadn't kept him waiting while all that raced through my mind, Leo said, "George, please bring Edmund Hartley, Jane's primo, back into the room. Mean-

while, Gee DiMercy, do you accept the position of
Yellowrock Clan Enforcer?"

Gee dropped from the ceiling to the floor, landing beside me on the balls of his feet and one hand, like a mon-
key leaping from a tree. It shocked me so much that I
nearly shot him. He flowed to his feet like a snake. "I do,"
he said, holding out his hand. Leo cut downward with the
blade. That was getting to be a pretty unhygienic, unsan-
itary thing and I was glad my part in the cutting was over.
Except it wasn't. Gee offered me his thumb to suck on.

"Oh, come on," I said. "Really?"

Gee waggled his thumb at me, blood trailing down it.
And then he grinned as if this was the funniest thing ever.
"Just think of it as sushi, my mistress," he said.

"Bird blood? I hope you washed that thing." I opened
my mouth and Gee hesitated, meeting my eyes. The grin
slid from his pretty face. The blood on his hand shifted
from scarlet to sapphire blue, its true color. There was
something vital, weighty, even imperative about the misericord of the city offering me his blood unglamoured.
Black eyes intent, he placed his thumb into my mouth. His
blood was thick and bright, sweet like agave syrup. Beast's
synesthesia flared, giving Gee's blood the chill of deep
blue water; the smell of midnight in a winter forest, thousands of stars overhead, shimmering through naked
branches; the sound/vision of indigo or woad splashing in
a vat, staining a pair of hands. The sensations shimmered
into taste and texture of ground lapis lazuli and sugar on
my tongue, the sound of sapphire wings in flight.

"I am yours, my mistress, my little goddess," he whispered.

I encircled his wrist with my long knobby fingers and
pulled his thumb away. Irritated, I said, "I'm not a
goddess."

"As you say, my mistress. I swear loyalty to you above
all others, in every circumstance outside of my misericord duties. In your absence, I swear to your clan and to
its scions and cattle."

"Backatcha, little bird." But it didn't come out flip-
pant, as I intended, but somber, unsmiling, and resolute.

Gee stepped back and when he was about five feet away, he bowed, bending one knee and sweeping with one hand, as if to push a cape back. Or his glamoured wings. He took a seat.

Crap. This was getting heavy.

Leo said, "Edmund Hartley, you have claimed to be bound to your mistress. Is this so?"

I whipped my head to the side and saw Edmund, a nondescript, brown-haired, brown-eyed man, small statured, at least compared to modern-day norms and my own height. He had been healed of the stakes in his belly and was now sober, wearing a tux, when Eddie had been drunk and wearing a navy suit last time I saw him. Edmund looked pretty good in a tux, his dark hair swept back with goop, his expression strangely gentle.

Ed stared at me, his lips up in the smile that had surely been the reason he was turned. "It is. We are bound. She called me back from true-death and I answered."

It hadn't been my intent. I didn't want a slave. But it had kept him alive and at the time that had been a bargain worth making.

Leo said, "You have sworn privately to Jane Yellowrock. Do you renew those vows now?"

"I do." Ed's smile widened and he pretty much quoted what he had said more privately, not so long ago. "Jane Yellowrock. I, Edmund Killian Sebastian Hartley, do hereby swear fealty to you and to yours, to your entire extended and many-peopled and many-creatured family, and to Clan Yellowrock. I swear to provide for, protect, care for, fight for, and die true-dead as you may need. I place all my needs second to yours and to theirs. I place my hunger second to yours and to theirs. I place all that I am and all that I can be and all that I can do at your disposal, into your hands, for the duration of the next nineteen years. I am yours in life and undeath and in true-death."

Those danged tears gathered in my eyes again. But Eddie wasn't done.

"I swear fealty to the Everharts and Truebloods, for as long as Jane Yellowrock is theirs and the Everharts and Truebloods are yours, one clan, placing my own well-being beneath your own. I promise that I shall protect your godchildren and their parents and their children's children unto the laying down of my own undeath."

Edmund smiled slightly. "Since I first spoke these words, I have become heir to Clan Pellissier. Jane Yellowrock has become the Dark Queen and I am primo to Jane Yellowrock. You no longer must protect me, my mistress. It is my job to protect you. Our lives are now intertwined. My blood is yours to spill."

Leo stabbed Ed's thumb. Red blood welled and ran down, fast, faster than most vamp blood would run, since their hearts didn't beat much. I had been fed Edmund's blood. I knew its taste, its power. I took his wrist and guided his thumb to my mouth, wondering for a single instant what outsiders would think of this ceremony, so nonhuman, so foreign to any culture of any group of humans, so . . . sacrificial.

Such blood drinking had guided the actions of Torquemada and the Inquisition for so many years, fueling fear and hatred and torture. And then Ed's flesh was in my mouth, between my fangs, his blood on my tongue, his power open and moving, fast as a mountain stream. I swallowed and took in his magic. It was a river of might, raging but held in check, the way water thundered down a gorge, kept in its bed between massive boulders. Whitewater, powerful enough to destroy, but full of life. Held into its course and purpose by tall and mighty rock walls.

In his blood, I saw myself as Edmund first saw me.

On a night battlefield, bodies piled high behind the female warrior, flames leaping. Gunshots sounded in the distance. The reek of bowels that had opened as humans died, the particular odor of Mithran death, smoke, blood, and the stink of gunfire hung on the air. Koun was stepping from an ambulance, the broad-shouldered man wearing only a loincloth, a sword at his hip, and Celtic tattoos, dark blue and black. He was pale. He had lost blood. Or given it.

"I left my master's fight to heal a human," Koun snarled at the armed warrior. "You owe me a boon, woman." The warrior was a woman. Black haired and golden skinned.

Jane Yellowrock, the woman Pellissier had hired for some obscure reason. Koun pulled his sword.

The woman stepped back, going for a handgun at her side. But Koun was on her in an instant, moving Mithran-fast. His longblade sliced for her throat. Her eyes blazed golden. Edmund moved closer, to watch.

The blade cut into her throat just as she leaped. She dropped away, tucking into a shoulder roll. Officers shouted, "Put down the weapon! Police!" They fired and Koun stumbled before coming upright. He stood over the golden-eyed woman, his sword in both hands, the blade pointed at her belly. "A boon!" he demanded.

Edmund expected her to scream or cry or wail. She shouted, "What boon?"

"I am weakened, and the primo requires yet more blood. You will fight in my place."

"Done," the woman said.

Koun stepped back and the woman, Jane Yellowrock, rolled to her feet, the motion more fluid than a Mithran's, as impossible as that seemed. "How many are there?" she demanded. "Who are they?" And then she fought. Ed-mund had followed, protecting her rear. Watching.

I swallowed again. Yanked Edmund's hand away from me. From where he . . . kneeled at my feet. Which I freak-ing hated. I reached out and placed a fingertip beneath his chin and lifted his face to my half-lion face. "I swear loyalty to you," I said.

"Yes, my master. And I to you."

Mistress. Master. I had bound Ed long ago. I had sealed that binding now. I was a monster. I almost ran out of the room.

CHAPTER 10

My Fangs Were Bigger Than His

Leo said, "Eli Younger and Alex Younger."

"I'm not sucking on their thumbs," I said, just as the Kid said, "I'm not sucking on Jane's thumb. It's got hair on it."

I snorted. Leo laughed aloud.

"Eli Younger. You have warred," Leo stated. "You have fought and won and fought and lost. It is the way of the warrior. You have survived with honor, though the scars you carry are heavy, and you walked away from the battlefield. If needed, will you war beside Jane Yellowrock?" It was a formal question, with an equally formal response.

"If Jane asks me to war," Eli said softly, his dark eyes moving from Leo to me, "I will war. If Jane is attacked, I will war. If Jane's friends and those she has sworn loyalty to are attacked, I will war."

"She calls you brother. Will you guard her and keep her clan safe? Will you make certain that she takes time to think and to plan, to strategize, to know all the weaknesses and strengths of her enemy?" Leo asked.

"I will."

I frowned. Leo had just said I was foolish and stupid and needed a protector and teacher. I didn't. I had done pretty good flying by the seat of my pants all this time. Then again, I was snarky to beings who were more powerful than I was, who had more magic, bigger teeth, and sharper claws. Maybe Leo was right.

I glared at Eli, who smiled back at me with the exact same expression I'd seen him use on a lost puppy in the street. He shook his head at whatever emotions had crossed my face. "Babe," he said, in a long-suffering tone. In an entirely different tone, he said to Leo and me, "I will care for Jane Yellowrock. I will be her second when she is challenged or when she challenges another. I will keep her safe. I will be her friend and her brother. Being part of Jane's family has made life worth living again, when battle had stolen all my joy and my belief in goodness." Eli's somber expression disappeared and he grinned widely. "Even when she has fangs and a cat nose and a pelt. Even when she insults the powerful and the mighty and steps all over their egos. And I will love her as sister of my heart."

Sister of my heart was a formal vamp saying that meant adoption. My own heart melted into a puddle of goo and mush.

Alex said, "I'll do the same. Except for the being-her-second part. I'd suck at that."

I turned the sappy face on the Kid.

He shook his head. "Janie. Please. Don't get all girly. It'll ruin my image as a bon vivant, a lady-loving man-about-town."

Eli snorted. I snorted. Alex looked as if he was fighting tears.

Leo said, "For ten years, until the clan can support itself, Clan Yellowrock will be paid an annual stipend to be negotiated with Alex Younger. Clan Yellowrock will be given a property for a clan home commensurate with Jane's status as Enforcer to the Master of the City of New Orleans. Clan Yellowrock will be given property that is currently unused, or was never rebuilt after Katrina, to build upon and invest in. Clan Yellowrock is established."

"I have a house," I stated.

"You have a personal home," Leo clarified, "which you may keep. But you need a clan home large enough for scions and the humans who will feed them."

I thought about the house, the new rooms upstairs, the construction, and the crowded feeling, with people everywhere. How much worse if Leo stuck me with lots of fangheads and their dinners. It would be good to have fewer people in the house. "Ducky."

"Ducky," Leo repeated, as if sticking the word and its usage as an affirmative into some spot in his brain not currently occupied with important stuff. Maybe one labeled "Bizarre Modern Words." "Choose a home from among the Mithran properties. One not currently occupied." Leo gave me a wolfish grin. "And one not currently claimed or used by a clan."

Leo had me figured out. I had been gonna take his clan home on the west side. I gave him back a grin, and currently my fangs were bigger than his. Take that, master suckhead. I said, "I'll take the Rousseau house in the Garden District not far from Grégoire's place." If I was gonna get a house, then I wanted one with a pool.

"Oh yeah," Alex breathed.

"Unlike Ming, who must rebuild her clan from the ashes of what once was, Yellowrock has options. You will choose your clan members from among my own and from among the clanless, those dispossessed by the war that saw the decimation of four clans. Are there those you would choose?"

"Koun," I said, "if he'll accept." Koun didn't like me, but he was a good fighter. And Leo had known I'd want certain people. He'd sent personal invitations to them. The sneak.

"Brute, the white werewolf. Kemnebi, the African black wereleopard."

Leo's left eyebrow lifted just a hair. "Will they accept?"

"Brute just got a new dog bed. He won't care. Kemmie

has no choice. He's zeta to my beta. I claimed him so I'm stuck with him. Same with Rick LaFleur. Pain in the ass, but there you have it. I didn't kill them when I should have and now I'm responsible for them. Twenty-twenty hindsight and all that." Yeah. I'd had to claim my ex and his slave. That sucked.

Leo looked at me with the most peculiar expression, which I couldn't interpret and so I ignored it and went on. "Evan Trueblood, Angelina Everhart Trueblood, Evan Trueblood Junior, Molly Everhart Trueblood, and the baby she carries."

I thought Leo was gonna choke on his own fangs in surprise. Yeah. Suck on that one, MOC. I got a witch family willing to join my vampire clan. "Shiloh Everhart Stone and her friends and blood-servants if they are willing. I haven't asked them. Tex."

"Who?" Leo asked. I could tell he was off-kilter at the list of names. But it wasn't as if I hadn't been thinking about all this.

"Tex. The fanghead from Texas who has the guard dog. I don't know his name." I figured Tex could handle Brute if the wolf lost all humanity and became pure wolf.

"Ah," Leo said. "You will need that bigger clan home." He was teasing me.

"Yeah, whatever. I'll take any of Katie's girls who want to stay in New Orleans as long as they understand that they have to go to school, sign on with a vamp as personal blood-servant, or get a job. A real job, not a pay-for-sex job. And I'll accept résumés from people wanting in."

"Will you, now?" Leo asked. "Résumés."

"Yeah. Pieces of paper with job histories—"

"I know what a résumé is." Dry, wry, amused.

"Right. Sloan Rosen and his family." At Leo's confusion, I said, "He's NOPD. He has a price on his head by gangbangers."

"I see." But it was clear that Leo didn't see.

"Deon, Katie's chef, if he wants to stay in New Orleans rather than travel to Atlanta. Up to Katie and Deon, but I'm interested. And Wrassler. He's honest, capable, and my friend." And he'd been injured because I hadn't done enough to keep HQ safe. But I didn't say that. "And lastly, I want Bruiser. George Dumas. I know he can't swear to me any more than the Roberes can swear to Clan Arceneau and Grégoire. But he's mine. Not yours."

Leo's eyes flashed; his scent flashed too, taking on the acrid stink of scorched parchment. I thought for a moment he was going to vamp out and that I'd have to stake him too. But Leo managed a breath and said softly, "George Dumas. How do you swear?"

Bruiser moved around the table and up to us, his footsteps silent, his scent heated and calming. "I have signed a legal contract with the Master of the City of New Orleans. If the Master of the City will release me from said contract, I will swear to the Dark Queen and to Clan Yellowrock. To the Master of the City of New Orleans through the Dark Queen. And to New Orleans through her."

Leo was good at hiding his emotions, but even I could see the pain in his expression. "Your loyalties have changed, one who was once my primo."

Very precisely, speaking slowly, as if he too had seen Leo's reactions, Bruiser said, "I am Onorio, Dominantem Civitati—Leonard Pellissier, Master of the City and Hunting Territories of New Orleans and the Greater Southeast. I am Onorio. I am loyal." But he didn't say to whom he was most loyal and that seemed to tick Leo off.

"If there is war?" Leo asked, his voice silky and far too soft.

"So long as my position as Onorio does not prohibit me, I will fight beside Jane Yellowrock and Leo Pellissier, for the city of New Orleans and her Mithrans and her cattle."

"And if my territory alters?"

"Then we will decide what to do, my dearest, best friend."

Leo tilted his head. "Friend?"

"I will always, for as long as the sun rises and sets, so long as I live, be your friend." Bruiser held out his hands to Leo, his arms open. Expressions flooded across Leo's face, emotions that ranged from surprise to fury to grief to hope to some things I couldn't name. Leo looked at

Bruiser's open hands and arms and looked up into Bruiser's face. Carefully, slowly, Leo stepped toward his former primo. Bruiser's arms closed around Leo, Bruiser a good nine inches taller, broader, more muscular than the slight frame of his former master. They stood that way, the positions awkward, stiff, as if they had never hugged before as equals.

And then Leo exhaled and dropped his head against Bruiser's chest and relaxed. "I have always been your . . . friend, my George." The odd pause before Leo said the word indicated its human peculiarity. Vamps had associates and sex buddies and servants and slaves and scions and drinking pals, but did they ever have friends?

"I know," Bruiser said. "Relationships change, Leo. Ours did. But that relationship is still bloody strong and faithful."

"I am uncertain how to have a . . . friend. My last friend was my brother, El Mago. He turned against me and I killed him. Twice. I do not grieve for my brother, George, but I would grieve for you."

"Then I must make certain that you never need to kill me, my friend." There was laughter in Bruiser's voice, the kind of laughter that was also full of tears. "Will you release me from my contract?"

"I will have papers drawn up and sent out today, releasing you from service one day after the end of the Sangre Duello."

"Thank you," Bruiser said softly. "You honor me with your trust and your love."

Their arms dropped. Leo stepped back and away from Bruiser's embrace. His black hair had come loose and fell around his face in dark wisps. He looked at me, his eyes more human than I had ever seen them, tears pooling in the Frenchy-black depths. "You will keep my George alive. You will protect my friend."

"I so swear," I said, knowing that if I got Bruiser killed, my own life was forfeit. Of course, if I got Bruiser killed I'd want to be dead anyway.

Leo said, "Bring me a cell phone and dial the Everhart-Truebloods. I will accept a verbal swearing for now should they decide to join Clan Yellowrock." He held out a hand and a blood-servant placed a cell phone in it. It was on speaker and it was ringing.

"Hey, Unca Leo!" Angie said, delight and happiness in her greeting.

Leo's brows, both of them this time, shot to the ceiling. Then his eyes went wide as shock morphed into something else. Something like wonder.

"This is Angelina. Mama!" she screamed. "It's Unca Leo!"

I smothered a grin. *Uncle Leo.* Holy crap, that child was brilliant.

"Unca Weo!" Little Evan shouted in the background. "Unca Weo! Unca Weo!"

"Dear, Blessed Mother of God," Leo whispered. He sounded horrified.

"This is Molly Everhart Trueblood," Molly said, sounding wry. "I take it this is Leo Pellissier of New Orleans."

After a pause that went on too long, Leo said, "It is."

"Jane said we were being adopted into a vampire clan. Her clan. This call is about that?"

"Daddy! It's Unca Leo! We're being adopted by Aunt Jane!" Angie Baby shouted in the background.

I managed not to laugh at the expression on Leo's face, but it was a near thing.

"Evan, this is Leo," Molly said. "We need to swear to Jane."

"I always swear when the head bloodsucker calls," Big Evan said.

"Shush. Be nice." We could hear feet stomping in the background, as of children jumping up and down. Together the older Truebloods said in unison, "We agree to adoption into Clan Yellowrock. We swear fealty with the use of magic, and loyalty and love from our hearts, our minds, and our spirits, to Jane Yellowrock. We will work to keep her and all her people safe."

I jerked. That wasn't what they were supposed to say. By this adoption, I was supposed to keep them safe. But the words were spoken. I said, "I pledge, undertake, and guarantee that I will keep you safe unto the giving of my life."

Leo said softly, "Your vows are hereby recorded."

"'Bye, Unca Leo!" Angie Baby shouted. "Hey, my Edmund! I love you!"

Leo flinched again, as if something in her words told him things he hadn't known. Leo ended the call and turned to Edmund, who stood just behind me, still as an undead statue. Something passed between them but was gone before I could understand it.

Gee said quietly, into the silence, "The Dark Queen has changed us. Has changed us all."

"Thank you," Leo said. "You are dismissed. I'll be along in a bit. The werelions and black wereleopard are in the gym, sparring with my Mithrans. I needs must check in with them." He slid his eyes to me. "I shall inform Kemnebi that you have claimed him for your clan."

I made a sound of disgust. I'd asked that Kemmie be included so that I could keep an eye on him. Keep my enemies close, to use Leo's wisdom.

Leo nodded to us and ducked out the back door of the Council Chambers. Sabina, her throat healed but marked with a thin red line, opened the first of a stack of papers. "Your signature, Master of Clan Yellowrock."

"How many siggies?" I asked.

"Forty-seven," Sabina said.

I huffed an irritated breath and took up the pen. Started signing. It took a while.

When I was done, I checked with Alex. His head was bent over his tablet. "Update on Dominique and the shielded witch?"

He shook his head, curls bouncing, and stood. "Male driver. Facial rec program in progress. Dominique in the passenger seat. Others in the car, faces unrecognizable. Wove through the streets and got on I-10, headed east. I'll update when I find them again."

"Good."

"Plate issued to Mithran Council Chambers," he said. "I'm running a search for anyone who might be missing.

Someone let them into the chambers and into the library." What he didn't add was that it had to be someone from inside, likely a member of the security team. *Crap.*

Gee held out his arm the way a game show model would and I walked toward him, aware of the others behind me, following in a single line as we left the Mithran Council Chambers and headed down the hall toward the elevator, silent. I was deeply, profoundly aware of the people at my back. Of the names I had spoken when I created my clan. Of the weirdness of it all. I had walked out of the mountain woods when I was twelve years old, naked, scarred, scared, with no language, no social skills, a wildling, with nothing at all except a gold nugget clasped in my hand.

Now I had a clan of people who had sworn to me, people I needed to protect. And there would be more. Maybe lots more. A cold chill skittered down my spine at the thought of keeping them all safe and cared for. Gee stopped and asked Eli for his headset. I leaned my back against the wall so I could see up and down it, the cold chills growing worse. Eli leaned against the other side, pulling his brother to his left, into the safest place, though the Kid was tapping into his cell, head down, oblivious. Eli's hands went to his weapons, his face taking on that still, expressionless mask of the warrior, watching me for clues that might explain my foreboding. I searched up and down, sniffing. I couldn't see a reason for Eli's disquiet, for my feeling that something wasn't right. Trying to keep the *scree* of sound silent, I sucked the air in through my mouth and over my tongue but detected nothing out of the ordinary.

The elevator door opened and though it was going down before we could go up, we filed in. Gee said, "I have sent word to the people who were invited into Clan Yellowrock. We expect replies and vows soon."

Or not. I heard the unspoken words. I knew most of my potential clan members wouldn't be able to swear face-to-face due to distance and time constraints, but I figured most would become my people. *Holy crap.* My people. The biggest part of me wanted to go back to bed

and pull the covers over my eyes. The smallest part told
me to pull up my big-girl panties and act like a war
woman. Not that war women traditionally wore panties.

The elevator door closed and dropped. Came to a
stop. And began to open.

Screams clawed down the hallway, high-pitched squeals
and low-voiced growling.

My hands shot out and rammed the doors open. I
dashed into the hallway. Catching a glimpse of Eli and
Gee pulling weapons, racing after me. The scent of the
gym hallway was mold and old sweat and traces of old
blood, some of it mine, shampoo and deodorant and
locker rooms. I blew through the gym doors.

The stench of wrongness hit me just as Leo himself
caught me around the waist. Time stuttered. Leo grabbed
me again. Time stuttered. Leo grabbed me again. Leo,
holding me. Together we fluttered in and out of time.

Time went flat and still. Returned to normal. My momentum nearly threw us both to the floor, but his vamp
strength twisted us until we swung around one last time.
He caught our balance and stopped us, like an ungainly
dance move as my feet touched down. "My Jane?" Leo
breathed. "What was that?"

"I don't know. Magic?" I lied. But I did know. Time
had done something funky. My head spiked with pain, so
bad I wanted to close my eyes.

Larry, Leo's personal manservant, looked at us oddly.

I stopped. Took my own weight and pushed away from
Leo. Shifted to the side. Eli and the others stopped too,
studying the room, securing weapons. I swept my eyes
around the gym.

Three werecats were fighting vamps. A sparring match.
Bodies were flying, falling, rolling, and leaping back to the
bare-handed/bare-pawed/bare-clawed fight. I caught my
breath, watching as they sparred.

The door behind us opened. The smell of lemons
swept in, but no one was there. The anomaly. The witch
was here.

Before I could shout a warning, a werelion in half-form looked Leo's way, Asad in half-form. He roared. It was a chuffing, reverberating thunder that stole all other sound from the air. The hairs on my arms and back of my neck stood up in some primal horror that said I was about to die horribly. To Eli I said, "Lemons."

"I smell them. Searching."

"Ditto," Alex said, fingers dancing over his tablet.

The stench of lemons increased and the burn of magic boiled into the wide room. The werelion chuffed, twisted his head on his thick neck, and shook himself. Magic, familiar, somehow. Asad turned. Picked up a vamp. And threw her across the room. She screamed in surprise, hit, bounced, rolled, and lay still. Blood pooled beneath her head. Leo tensed.

The werelion roared again, clawed paw-hands in the air. Asad whipped his whole body to the doorway, his nasal folds opening and closing with each breath. He hadn't seen me when he looked this way, his eyes on Leo then. This time he saw me. Our gazes met and stuck together like glue.

He threw back his head and roared, this time in unquestioned challenge, fangs white and massive. Beast ripped into the front of my brain. *Predator!* By instinct, my muscles bunched and my hand found a vamp-killer strapped to my thigh. I pulled it free of its hidden sheath. I was still in half-form. Fighting form. Beast snarled, showing killing teeth.

Kem was closer to our group than the other weres. Pulled a blade that was strapped to his human thigh, screaming a leopard cry. Kem was supposed to be tamed. What had happened to him? Magic . . . Growing heavy, hard to breathe. A staged sparring match had suddenly become real. Kemnebi screamed a challenge.

Leo's swords swept up. He shouted, "You dare!"

I smelled the bloodlust on Kem-cat. "Predator!" Beast screamed again, this time from my/our throat. Beast gathered control of my body, taking over. She stepped to the side of Leo, protecting her alpha from Kem's attack. I scrabbled for control as she screamed a cat challenge.

Kemnebi screamed, mouth open wide, snout back in snarl, fangs white. Shifting fast, into a partial half-form. Raced to Jane/Beast. Raised steel claw.

Beast shoved down on Jane.

Ducked under Kemnebi blade. Fell to floor. Stabbed up, into Kem belly. Tore up and side to side. Kem's belly opened. Blood sprayed. Beast rolled beyond wounded cat. Up to back paws. Standing like Jane. But Kem, wounded, turned on Leo, reaching with leopard claws. Fully cat. Larry jumped in front of Master of the City. Protecting him.

Jane/Beast stabbed Kem in back. Kem dropped to floor. Trying to shift back from leopard form to human, to heal. But blade that struck him had been silvered and had sliced into spine. Kem was trapped in cat form. Was dying.

Larry was on floor. Bleeding. Most of throat gone. Leo was bending over Larry, cutting own fingers to heal human. Thought at Jane, *Do not understand.*

Thoughts raced through Jane's mind. *Betrayal. Magic,* Jane thought. *No grindylow anywhere. And Larry tried to save Leo. He might have were-taint.*

Beast screamed challenge. *Hate pack hunters! Kill pack hunters!*

Jane pushed Beast back from control. Fought for alpha position. Beast screamed, *Will not be beta to Jane alpha!*

Stop! Jane thought. *Stop fighting me. I don't know what's happening, but this isn't over. I'm a better fighter with a sword.*

Beast let Jane take over. Pushed power into half-Beast/half-Jane form. Screamed challenge. Asad and Nantale, in half-lion fighting form, attacked, each of them spinning two swords. Eli stepped in front of me, raised a gun, and shot Nantale. She dropped and writhed on the floor. I smelled silver and were blood.

Asad roared, grief and fury in his tone. And the smell of lemons flared brighter. Asad, golden eyes gleaming, attacked. Eli fired. Edmund and I moved around him and engaged the werelion. Asad, king of the Fulani, an alpha male and experienced fighter, took us both on. Edmund ripped him to shreds in seconds. I sliced Asad's throat. Asad slowed. Blinked. Looked down at his swords as if puzzled. The leader of the Party of African Weres tripped, stumbled, slid to the floor. And died.

Leo stood as Gee and Larry—Lawrence Hefner, not Larry; he hated Larry—were carried off the floor. Gee's arms and legs were wrapped around the man, Gee's Anzu magic a sapphire and indigo haze, already healing. Leo slanted his eyes to me. They were vamped out, scarlet sclera and wide, black pupils. Silkily, his accent more French than usual, he asked, "Why did the werecats attack us? We welcomed them into our chambers. We had signed accords." He was using the royal *we*, which was always scary. It meant he was royally ticked off.

"I smell lemons. Smelled lemons. The scent is fading. As to why they attacked, ask Nantale about Clan Des Citrons," I said. Now that the battle was over, my adrenaline began to break down and the pain in my head spiked again. Nausea rose like a hurricane tide and I swallowed it down desperately. I would not hurl in front of these people.

Alex cursed softly to himself. "I can't figure out how to find the witch. Nothing's working." Leo strode to the half-shifted African lion and knelt over her. He lifted her head in his hand and stared into her eyes. "Why have you attacked my people?"

Nantale swallowed and swiveled her eyes to find her husband dead on the floor. Tears leaked from her eyes. "Asad and Kemnebi and Raymond Micheika, our supreme cat, signed a pact with the emperor Titus Flavius Vespasianus for the were-creatures of Africa and Asia. We were given into the claws of a vampire as her tools. I had no choice and no say, but my husband was foolish. And now I am dying." She swallowed again, and this time there was blood on her lips, bubbling with her breath. Her lungs were compromised. "Micheika will take my kits and kill or enslave them. Swear to me that you will protect my kits and I will tell you where the papers of parley are. And you will know your enemies."

Leo said, "I will arrange to take your kits to safety, with others of their kind."

"The papers are in Asad's bag in a hidden compartment. At the Royal Sonesta."

That was a NOLA five-star hotel. Nantale reached up and grabbed Leo's hand. He returned the grip; Nantale's skin went pasty, and then quickly ashen. She spasmed, coughed. Just that fast, Nantale died. Leo stroked her face once and gently placed her head on the floor. It was over, whatever it had really been.

I looked around the room. Vamps were standing in small groups, and I memorized who was with whom, who had weapons drawn, who looked happy and who looked disappointed at the outcome. I opened my mouth and scent-searched for lemons, but the smell was gone. Good thing. My head hurt too bad to fight a witch right now.

Leo stood, spitting mad, and rounded on one group of vamps. He addressed Tex. "You will go to the Royal Sonesta and find the papers of parley. You will bring the offspring of our enemies here, to safety. You will treat the kits with kindness and respect, as valued guests."

Tex slanted his eyes at me and I gave him a small nod. To Leo, he said, "I will, my master." Which gave Leo control over some of the most important African werelions on the planet. Kits he could shape and raise as he wished. Nice move, I thought, if he brought up his foster kits to believe in personal freedom and responsibility. *If.* I guessed that being fostered by a vamp was better than being killed in the claws of an adult big-cat.

"Once Nantale's kits are safe," Leo went on, "I will contact the Party of African Weres. PAW may want the bodies for burial." He lifted his chin slightly to Kemnebi, a very French gesture, full of disgust, but he spoke to me. "You will deal with your traitor."

Beast peeked back out and sent me a vision of sinking our fangs into Kemmie's back just below his skull, shaking him until his neck broke, before picking him up and carrying him away. Instead I remembered the stench of lemons and the heat of the spell that had set off the fighting. A familiar taste of magic.

Leo gave me an enigmatic look and gestured to his

blood-servants. "Take the leopard to the playroom. Our Jane may use the scion lair."

Playroom. Right. Only a vamp would think of a room full of cages and with a drain in the middle of the floor as a playroom. Leo said, softer, holding my eyes with his dark ones, "I thought I had healed the rift with the were-cats. I thought you had tamed the leopard beneath Rick."

"Magic," I said just as softly. "Familiar magic. Some-one found a way to override the bond, and fast."

"Ahhh." Leo knew about the anomaly's presence in HQ and our inability to see the witch in real time.

I looked back at my people, Eli's face closed and cold, Alex a little more blanched than I expected of the player of violent video games. But then, he had recently been attacked and left nearly dead. His hand was around his throat, fingering the new scars. I seldom even noticed them these days, but being human, he'd healed far more slowly than I did, even with all the vamp blood in him.

"I'll handle moving the werecat," Ed said softly, from beside me. "Rick LaFleur should interrogate him."

My adrenaline washed away. "Right. Okay. Do it."

And then I remembered the image of Asad and Nan-tale licking their lips the first time I saw them in front of the SOD. Had they wanted to drink the ancient vamp blood? Had they been in HQ tonight long enough to ac-tually do so? Had they been in sub-five while the ceremo-nies were taking place? Had they drunk SOD blood tainted by werewolf bites? I had to wonder what that blood would do to them, if it would make them fall under spells of aggression. "Leo. Take a whiff of the lions."

Leo looked at me oddly, but he bent over the lions and sniffed.

"They scent of Joses Santana, the Son of Darkness, and of magic."

I nodded, a scant motion against the migraine. "Yeah. That's what I figured. I think they've been trying to get to the SOD since the first time they came here. And I think they finally got what they wanted. I think—maybe—that they aligned with Dominique and Des Citrons, and

at some point before she tossed Callan a sword, Dominique led them to sub-five, beneath a strong obfuscation
spell. She had magical help, the spell big enough to hide
them on the stairs. And they drank SOD blood, tainted
by werewolf saliva. What would it do to them? Would it
alone make them crazy enough to attack? Or was that
from the witch's and/or Des Citrons' magic in the room?
Or both, working together?"

Leo shook his head. "This I do not know."

"Eli, with me. Alex, get to security. Check the footage
and find out what happened with the anomaly. Find out
when the cats got to sub-five and why we weren't noti-
fied." I pointed at a security guy. "You. Go with him. No
one travels alone in HQ." Alex sped away, his scent suggesting he was happy to be out of the blood-splattered
room, the security guy on his heels. I turned on my paw
and padded down the hallway and the stairs to sub-five.

I'd kicked off my shoes when I half-shifted and the
floor was cool to the touch on the stairs to the lower basement. I looked around fast, taking in everything: old
blood, werewolf-stink, SOD, and mold. The cameras
were off. The last time Dominique was here, she had
turned them off with a remote device.

There were no uninvited weres present, but the SOD
wasn't alone. A dozen HQ security, armed and twitchy,
stood with weapons raised at three women, who were
standing in a semicircle studying the human-shaped
thing on the wall. They looked almost human, but were
all likely arcenciels: not Soul, who I knew best, but Opal
and Cerulean and one I hadn't met. Brute was there too,
Brute biting Joses Santana's foot, drawing watery blood.

The SOD had changed even more, and I guessed that
he had been fed, possibly the blood of the vampire and
the witch who were hiding in HQ. He was fully human
shaped, his face no longer slack jawed. His eyes were
open and he was laughing silently at his wolf tormentor. I
ignored him and said to the security types, "Stand down.
Return to your posts, by order of the Enforcer."

They didn't look happy about it, but after a moment

they left the basement by way of the elevator. Gee stepped out of the stairwell and bowed to the arcenciels, his face lit with joy. "My goddesses. Greetings." In unison, they nodded to him and Gee assumed his place beside me, taking in the tableau.

"Brute?" I asked. "We were just attacked in the gym by werelions and Kemnebi, the black wereleopard who was injured here"—I shrugged, not sure of the day—"not long ago. Is it possible that they got a taste of the SOD recently?"

Brute snorted then nodded, his head moving up and down, the gesture un-wolf-like and odd on his huge form.

"Today?"

He nodded.

"Were they with Dominique?"

Brute shook no.

"Were they here with someone who smelled like lemons?"

Brute tensed and nodded.

"Well, crap. They divided up?"

Brute stared hard at me and nodded.

"Would the taste of SOD do anything to werecats? Make them crazy?"

He snorted and vocalized something that sounded like, "Aroouuu." Maybe it was an answer, but I didn't speak werewolf.

"You got any idea why no grindylow showed up in the gym?"

He snorted and vocalized again. "Ooommmeee. Ooommmeee." The tone was different, the length of the snort was shorter, but again, I didn't speak werewolf and I couldn't figure out how to ask all my questions in simple yes/no form.

The SOD was looking at me, still cackling, silently. Hard to do with no heart. Hard to be undead with no heart. I figured it had grown back somehow. He lifted his head away from the wall, his long black hair sticking and coming away with a soft *squick*. His jaw unhinged and his fangs unfolded. His fingers flicked open and I caught a flash of gem and gold. He took a breath that sounded like a coffin opening. Hoarsely he said, "Yellowrock. *Ut omnis, mortem.*"

I tensed to throw myself behind the doorway. But . . . nothing happened. The SOD had just spoken a *wyrd* of power and . . . nothing. No magical power swept the room; no magic tore and seared the air. I frowned, trying to figure out what had happened. The SOD rattled his entire body on the wall, the silver chains clattering. *"Ut omnis, mortem!"* he screeched.

And again, nothing. The arcenciels put their heads together, and I had the distinct impression that they were chattering among themselves, silently. Mind power crap. *Ut omnis, mortem?* The last word I knew. It meant dead or death. But the first two words were less clear.

"To everyone, death," Gee translated thoughtfully. "It was a *wyrd*, and it should have killed us. Well, some of us. The curse failed." He looked at Brute. Then at me, studying me in my half-form. Without turning his head away from me, Gee asked, "Brute. Did you bite the Son of Darkness to take away his power?"

Brute wagged his tail and sank his teeth into the SOD's bare foot again. It wasn't an answer, but the SOD screamed in frustration and banged himself off the wall and back, the chains clinking more loudly.

Gee asked again, his words a little different. "Brute. When you bite the Son of Darkness, do you take away his power?"

Brute chuffed. And then he nodded his head up and down in the human affirmative, bouncing once on his front paws. Brute spun to me. His silver-blue eyes less wolflike than I had ever seen them. Human intelligence gleamed in them. And I knew. Over the sound of the SOD's raspy screams, I whispered, "Hayyel gave you the ability to time-walk and to incapacitate the magic of the Sons of Darkness. With your bite."

Brute gave me a doggy grin, his tail wagging even more fiercely, and turned his attention back to the SOD. He bit down again and again, his wolf fangs piercing the bare feet of one of the fathers of all vamps. Biting. Biting.

Giving one of the two most powerful vamps in the world the were-taint. And no grindylow was stopping him. I walked to the SOD and grabbed his nasty, slimy hand. On his index finger was a ring, a faceted brown diamond in a simple setting. A magical amulet. "Did Dominique give this to you today?" I asked.

Joses gurgled with laughter and clenched his fist. Brute nodded and vocalized again, "Ooommmeee." He was trying to say Dominique, the vamp I hadn't killed well enough. *Crap.*

I gripped the SOD's hand and pulled on the ring. He made a fist to stop me, and so I broke his finger and pulled off the ring. Tucked it in a pocket as he screamed hoarsely. I turned from the drama in sub-five and pattered back up the stairs, texting Rick that his zeta cat had just attacked Rick's alpha at HQ. He texted back that he would be at HQ in four hours. Then I found some Tylenol and a handful of ibuprofen for my headache. I managed to keep it down.

In the scion lair, the playroom/prison where Leo, or some other suckhead, once kept his scions in the devoveo, I walked past Eli and Edmund, who were standing a good six feet away from a silvered cage. Inside was my new buddy, Kemnebi. My silvered blade was still buried in the middle of his back. Kemmie couldn't heal until the silver toxins of my sword cuts had flushed from his system. The stuck silvered blade made that impossible and shifting to either of his forms unattainable. He was trapped in cat form, paralyzed by a silver blade, his guts still spilled out on the floor. Alive, but in pain. I could smell it on the air, hear it in his panting breaths. Guilt, my old nemesis, raised its head. Kem would kill me in a heartbeat, but I was sick at the sight of him there. Being tortured.

I opened the cage door, pulled a vamp-killer, and squatted on the floor in front of his cage, balanced on my toes, my elbows on my knees. I leaned in and growled. It was a deliberately masculine position and a challenging growl. My lips pulled back, exposing my fangs. Letting my voice drop into Beast's growl, I started with the easy questions, saying, "Did Dominique and a lemon-scented witch cast a spell on you to free you from your tamed state?"

Kem hissed at me, cat style.

"Did you harm the grindylow who was supposed to watch you?" I placed my blade at his throat.

Kem snarled, showing me his cat fangs.

More slowly, I said, "Did you, somehow, kill your grindy? You and the lions attacked when humans were present. The grindy should have killed you all."

The half-man/half-cat spat at me, the only gesture he could make with silver in his spine.

"Why did you attack? How were you and the cats planning to disrupt the Sangre Duello? Nod that you'll answer these questions and I'll pull out the blade so you can heal." He lifted his lips, showing me his teeth; deliberately he shook his head no. I stood, closed and secured the cage door, and said, "No food, no water, no medical help, and no one removes the silvered blade until he's willing to tell us about the grindy and about what's going on with the weres." I turned my back to the cat, a cat insult, and left the room, Eli on my tail. So to speak.

In the hallway, the playroom door closed and I could smell Eli's anger.

"You're leaving him in agony."

I steeled myself to answer. "This isn't war. He isn't human and isn't covered by or protected under human laws. He's a werecat. He won't die. He'll suffer a bit, that's all."

"Jane—"

"No. Too many seemingly unconnected things are happening right now. Too many possibilities all leading back to the EVs and ahead to disaster. In the last few minutes, we've been attacked by werecats who acted crazed or spelled or both, one of which should not have been able to attack at all, too tamed for anything except getting his belly rubbed. We've smelled lemons. Dominique, who allied with Des Citrons—but might, possibly, be acting outside their wishes—has gotten in and out with ease and she tossed Callan a sword. Callan attempted to kill the outclan priestess. A witch is floating around HQ and no one can seem to find her.

"I'll make sure Alex is researching them, but though they're an old clan, Des Citrons has managed to keep out of the historical eye for centuries. The clan may or may not be aligned with the EVs. They may be hoping to sit back and watch and then pick up the pieces later. Rick will be here in four hours. Rick, as alpha, can make Kem talk. Four hours to think about his sins." And then it hit me. I ducked my head to see directly into Eli's eyes. His were haunted. "You saw injured enemy combatants tortured, didn't you?"

"Aggressive interrogation." His lips twisted down. Confusion filled his face. "It's—" His words stopped abruptly.

"Inhuman and inhumane?" I leaned in to Eli, my shoulder touching his. "His grindy is missing. He may have killed it. Her. That's assuming grindys can be killed. But his grindy is a baby grindy. *A baby.*" They looked like kittens, neon green kittens with steel claws, but kittens. They were cute little killers. "He wanted to kill humans. Tried to kill Larry and may have turned him into a furball. And Kem is my pack. It's my right to demand answers."

Eli shook his head, but answered in the affirmative. "Yeah. Okay. For a werecat who didn't think twice about harming Larry." He made a fist and placed it on the door between Kem and us. "Okay. Four hours."

Eli walked away, leaving me thinking about how much I had changed, about how easy it had been to slip away from humanity, away from thinking about mercy and kindness. Mercy and kindness were hard. Hurting others was easy. The door opened and I met Ed's eyes as it closed. It was a thick door. Heavy. It sealed with a little whoosh of sound I hadn't noticed when I entered and left. It was a door created to keep the screams of those inside from disturbing others in the hallway. It was a room built for imprisonment and torture. "I'm a horrible person," I said, speaking to myself rather than to Edmund.

"Yes, my master. You are."

"But if I set him free, again, he'll hurt the ones I love. Again."

"Yes, my master. He will."

"I have to take care of the people I love. That means . . ." This was the hard part. The part I had realized several times over the last months. "That means I have to become a monster."

Gently, Edmund said, "Have you not always been a monster, my master?"

I took in a breath that hurt as if I had been stabbed. I turned from the room where I was actively torturing an enemy and started to walk away. Faint screams came from the room behind the heavy door. My heart leaped into my throat. Ed slammed the door open. We both raced inside. Kemnebi lay inside his cage, his throat sliced away, his blood emptying out, toward the drain in the middle of the floor. His cage was still secured. The grindy was standing atop the cage, her neon fuzz bloodied, her ankles and neck showing ligature marks where rope of some sort had dug into her flesh and abraded off the hair. She had been tied up. She had gotten away. And killed a wereleopard inside his cage. Right. Not exactly a kitten.

Eli appeared at my side. "Well, hell," he said.

Vamps and weres and their blasted layers of conspiracies within plots within intrigues within treacheries. "I need to see the parley papers. We need to talk to Leo."

CHAPTER 11

QaStaHvIS yIn 'Ej Chep

We were walking into the foyer when a man's voice stopped us, saying, "Legs?" The nickname meant it was one of the longtime security guys. Team Tequila or Team Vodka. "Hey, Antifreeze," I said, slowing. "It's good to see you up and moving. How are you?"

"Not bad, Legs. Suckheads pay better for injuries than Uncle Sam and don't dump you for wounds." He held out his good hand and there was a folded note between two fingers. Folded but unsealed meant it had been seen by everyone, that it wasn't private. "From the MOC."

I unfolded the paper, seeing my long-fingered hands move. I hadn't even noticed I was still in half-form. In Leo's distinctive calligraphy were the words, *The Master of the City requests that the Master of Clan Yellowrock join us in my office before you depart.*

Master of Clan Yellowrock, not Jane, or my Jane, or Enforcer. Names and titles meant something to vamps. This was city or clan business, and fortuitous since we needed to chat with him. I passed the note to Eli, who gave his service smile, a twitch of lips. I chuckled and the sound was half-Beast. Antifreeze flinched just the tiniest bit. Right. I was a monster and living with monsters never got easier.

"Let's go visit Leo in his office," Eli said, his voice hard and emotionless. It was the voice he used when he planned to beat up someone. It made me feel all warm and fuzzy. "Thank you," I said politely to Antifreeze. On my bare paw pads, I climbed the foyer stairs to Leo's office, Eli on my heels. Knocked. Entered when he called out *"Entrez."* I walked through the entry with its fireplace and expensive rugs and wall hangings to find Leo at his desk, me still in half-form, Eli wearing his battle face.

Leo was sitting, leaning back in his leather chair, his legs outstretched, shoes off, and ankles crossed. Papers rested on his chest. A gold-plated pitcher dribbled condensation onto a gold platter. A cut-crystal bottle, the label reading MACALLAN 1824 SERIES NO. 6 SINGLE MALT, was at his elbow, a glass beside it, the scotch legs still draining down the side of the empty glass.

His hair was loose on his shoulders, his clothing blood splattered. There were even a few drops on his face. The stench of old blood had to be horrible to an apex predator, but he hadn't cleaned up. And he was drinking scotch. His hands were uncovered except for the bandage on his fingers. He'd lost some in a fight recently and they were still reattaching. It was a vamp thing.

He didn't look up as we entered. I stood there for a moment, watching, evaluating. Then I leaned over and took the papers off his chest. It was the werecat parley agreement that someone had retrieved from the Royal Sonesta. The pages rustled softly as I flipped through them, scanning, Eli reading at my side. The opening paragraph was like a thesis statement, saying that three parties were aligning in a triumvirate of power: the European emperor, the were-creatures (African werecats and a small pack of rogue werewolves), and two vamps. Dominique Quessaire and—Bancym M'lareil.

"Ahhhh," I breathed, putting things together. Cym had caused the anomaly. That was why the magic in the gym had felt so familiar. That was why the weres had attacked. I knew Bancym M'lareil. She had mind magic. She had an obfuscation spell unlike any other I had ever seen.

Cym was both witch and vamp. She had been the heir of Jack Shoffru, the Mexican MOC, a pirate vamp, one of many fangheads in the last two years who'd tried to take over New Orleans. Bancym had kidnapped Molly. Had hurt Molly. Had nearly killed Eli. During my fight with Shoffru, when Eli nearly died, I had staked Cym. But I hadn't taken her head and she had disappeared. Clearly, she had been dragged off the battlefield and healed.

The rogue werewolves had always been Leo's enemies, as had Titus, the EVs, and Cym. Dominique was the glue that held them all together, and she had sworn to Clan Des Citrons, which was not mentioned here. A clan would have their own parley agreements, not one tied in with the hoi polloi. Dominique and Bancym had their talons in a lot of pies, the least known and understood, Clan Des Citrons. I needed to find out about the clan, who they were, what they wanted, where they were, everything.

The summary was the part that mattered. They had all signed and agreed to pacts of aggression against their enemies. When Titus defeated Leo, he would destroy the Bighorn Pack and give the huge territory to Prism, Jax, and their pack. Titus would also grant all of Leo's territory to the two female vamps, making them, together, the two most powerful vamps in the United States. I dropped the papers on the desk.

Leo didn't look up. Softly he said, "The weight of years, the weight of my enemies, the weight of betrayal rests heavily on my shoulders." It was the tone of depression, melancholy, and failure.

Eli glanced at me and gave me a quirky half grin. He leaned over and took Leo's glass and the decanter, holding them to the lamp. "This goes for around sixty-five hundred dollars a bottle." He sloshed a bit in the glass and swirled it. Sniffed. Added a few drops of water from the gold pitcher. Swirled and sniffed again. Leo slowly turned his head, one of those nonhuman, snaky gestures they did, watching my partner. "I did not offer you my scotch, human."

Eli sipped, swirling the liquor in his mouth, swallowing in tiny bursts, breathing down the fumes. "Not bad. Not better than a thirty-five-year-old Balvenie, but not bad." He sipped again, watching Leo.

Leo said, "I have a forty-six-year-old Balvenie, 1968, cask seventy-two, ninety-three, in my cellar."

Eli nodded. Sipped again. "Nice. Since you're all whiny and giving up, can I have the Balvenie? I'd hate for Titus to get his paws on it." Eli glanced at me. "Begging the pardon of the pawed and pelted."

"Pardon granted," I said, letting my amusement tell in my tone.

"Whiny?" Leo asked, his eyes slowly vamping out. "You are asking to raid my estate? I am not dead." His fangs schnicked down.

"Not yet. And you've got the home advantage. And you now know all your enemies. But you sound defeated. You sound as if you've given up. What you believe about the outcome is three-quarters of the battle, so you've already lost. You're dead, old man." Eli sipped, sizing Leo up like a young recruit on the day of battle. "And I'm drinking your scotch without your permission." Leo shot out of the chair, straight at Eli.

His jaw landed on my fist. The pop of displaced air and the thump of chin to fist overlapped. Leo dropped back, sitting on the desktop, shaking his head. He started laughing and his fangs snapped up. That was three-quarters of the battle won back. I could've kissed my partner.

Leo looked us over, his gaze taking in my human clothes and my cat face, hands, and feet. I could see him thinking about asking me how much of my other parts were cat shaped. "Don't," I said. The skin around his eyes crinkled with amusement. He slid back into his desk chair and Eli and I took chairs. Maybe it was rude to sit without being asked, but I was tired, as if the little bit of fighting I had done had taken a lot out of me. When he didn't object, I put my paws up on the small table as if it was an ottoman. Leo let me get comfortable. "We need to chat about—"

Leo held up a hand, stopping me.

Quesnel, the sommelier, entered the office, carrying a tray with a dozen bottles of beer on it. All of the bottles and cans were cold and sweating with condensation, the way Americans liked beer, which meant this was not part of the taste testing that went along with being the MOC. Quesnel set the tray on the table near my arm and indicated it, as if telling me to take a pick. "Our Master of the City is pleased to toast your ascension to clan Blood Master. What would you like?"

I pointed to a can of local NOLA Brewing Company beer. The Mecha brew had a red dragon on front that was eating part of the uptown. And then I pointed to the Irish Channel Stout by the same company. Quesnel opened both cans and poured each into a frosted beer glass, the pair of which he placed on the table at my other side. He produced a new glass for Leo and poured the scotch and water. Leo sat back in his chair, examining me in my half-form. There was no distaste or judgment in his eyes; rather, there was that hint of delight.

Leo's enjoyment of my form fell away, leaving him pensive again. "I have no way to properly toast you, my Jane. The appropriate toast for a new Blood Master of a clan is from the jugular of a virgin boy or girl, with the words 'Long undeath, prosperity, scions, blood, and cattle.'"

I looked at my beer. "Yeah. Beer is better. And how about 'Live long and prosper.'"

Leo gave no indication that he found me funny as he lifted his scotch in a toast. Eli followed the example, with his glass. I picked up the Mecha, holding it out and slightly up. Leo repeated my words, "Live long and prosper." Hearing the Vulcan blessing from Leo's lips was giggleworthy, but I managed to smother the laugh.

Leo drank and ate a few nuts. Eli and I followed his example. In companionable silence I finished my beer. Then Leo refilled the scotch glasses and pushed my second beer to me. Leo said, "However, I prefer *QaStaH-vIS yIn 'ej chep.*"

I stopped with the beer held in the air, ice water dripping from my fingers. Eli said, "Klingon? You did not just say 'Live long and prosper' in Klingon."

"Oh, but I did. And I do hope that my Jane may live many decades more and prosper greatly." He held up his free hand in the Vulcan V salute, gave an abbreviated nod, and sipped.

Holy crap. Leo knew about *Star Trek*. A lot about *Star Trek*. Alex would have a cow.

Eyes gleaming, Leo sipped again and I remembered to lower my arm and drink too. Leo said, "I was informed that the white werewolf was biting Joses Santana."

Finally we were getting to important stuff. "Yeah. And werewolf spit seems to make the SOD less magical. Does he taste different?"

"I have not tasted Joses in recent days," Leo said, wryly. "I understand that the werecats who attacked us had fed from the Son of Darkness prior to them attacking us in the gym. Were you aware of this?"

I said, "I figured it out. Dominique let them in and destroyed the cameras along the way. We don't have video footage."

"Why did Dominique Quessaire betray her sworn oath to Grégoire and to me, after we forgave her trespasses and restored her to us? This has troubled me for . . ." He rotated a hand as if to say, *For a long time.*

"Magic, again? Lemon-smelling magic." Tiredly, I asked, "Does it matter?"

Leo pondered this and then shook his head. "No."

"You have the parley papers between the EuroVamps and Dominique and Cym and what I hope will soon be a dead rogue werewolf pack. The Bighorn Pack is hunting for any werewolf remnants still in the city. Alex will concentrate on Bancym, Clan Des Citrons, and Dominique. When he finds their lair, I'll take it out. That leaves only the EuroVamps. Easy peasy."

Leo smiled slightly and set down the remainder of his scotch as if it had lost flavor. "We will fight. Within two nights. It will be, as you Americans say, winner take all."

"Which will make you the emperor of Europe." I studied him. "For all that you're a selfish narcissist with tendencies to see everyone on earth as tools to be used or discarded, you'll rule well."

Leo laughed, but it was a vamp laugh, all pathos and no human humor. "You honor me. Honor I do not deserve in the human understanding of the term, for I harmed you, my Jane, my Enforcer. My Dark Queen."

For once I decided not to object to the titles or the possessives. He knew how I felt about them all. I sipped. After a moment Leo sipped again too. Eli watched us like a hawk, eyes piercing and steady. "You guys decided where the fights are gonna be?" I asked. "You've left me out of that decision-making process."

"Such decisions are . . . above your pay grade."

Well, wasn't that just ducky. "I need to get the venue's security in place."

"I have not kept you in the dark without cause. I have used you for the purposes I need."

He swirled his drink again, watching the scotch legs drain down the glass. "As of two hours past, the decision has been made to situate the Sangre Duello on one or another Chitimacha tribal island not far from Port Eads," Leo said. "There are three tribal islands with houses that have been shared with Clan Pellissier since the early 1800s, and the tribe has allowed us to maintain the homes and the grounds for a reasonable fee."

I thought about that, sipped the last of my beer, and said, "As tribal lands, the islands fall under non-U.S. lands use? So you can dock there and so can Titus."

"Correct. It can be argued that, technically, the U.S. government has no jurisdiction there."

"They might dispute that," I said. "In court."

"They might," he agreed. "However, as we will not be announcing the exact locale, the Duello will be long over by the time the government decides how to apply the law to us, the Chitimacha, and Titus, put the proper paperwork together, and go to a judge for legal writs to charge us or to stop us."

"Or they could just blow you out of the water as soon as you all arrive. Drop a bomb on the island or napalm it and be done with the biggest, baddest vamps on the planet." Leo didn't reply to that one, still turning his crystal glass. "You're planning that by the time they figure out where the fights are taking place, Titus's head will have rolled. But the military has satellite capability and radar and missiles." Leo still said nothing. "You got a map of the places with GPS?"

Leo pulled up a topo map of the toe of Louisiana on his computer and turned it to me. Three places were fuzzed out, the way U.S. military installations are fuzzed out on satellite maps. I frowned at him and Leo said, "Some time ago, I arranged to have them . . . pixelated?" His tone questioned the term. "Money has its privileges."

"Île des Eaux," I said, reading the name of one. "Island of the Waters." Leo looked impressed that I could translate the French, but *île* and *eaux* were pretty easy. "Spitfire Island and Contempt Isle. So when do we go?"

"A few housekeeping and landscaping blood-servants were dispatched a week past—just in case an island proved acceptable to Titus—to each of the three islands, along with a well-paid construction crew, to determine the houses' suitability and state of disrepair. Security went down with the construction crew to evaluate those concerns. As soon as the final venue is decided upon, you will, of course, go down and oversee preparations for security.

"The crews involved with the immediate evaluation and cleanup don't know they are there to begin initial preparation for a possible Mithran occupation. They have had no contact with the outside world since they arrived at the islands. Each house is primitive by modern-day standards: no cellular, no Internet. We may not have hot and cold running water or indoor toilets. Minimal electricity, all solar. We will have a small staff, most of them camping. Those of us who have been challenged will either stay on-site in light-safe rooms or be flown in by helicopter. On-site bunkroom space will be provided for Clan Yellowrock and a security team and blood-servants. Other bunkrooms may be available as needed, though the occupants may need to switch off, as you say."

"I'm not concerned about the sleeping arrangements. I'm concerned about the security. Why was I not involved with this?"

"Your Alex has been an active participant, looking over all three sites. He has a preference, and I am doing all I can in negotiations to accommodate him and the security needs."

And Alex hadn't told me.

Leo let a tiny human smile cross his features. "When a leader has trained his capable and loyal people well, my Jane, it is then time to let them go and perform the tasks one has assigned to them. I needed your skills and protection here at Council Chambers, not on an island many miles away."

I scowled at Leo, but he had a point. Alex was growing up and doing his job without being asked.

Leo went on. "Titus and his people will anchor offshore and arrive after dusk each evening via motorized dory to the repaired docks. They will depart before dawn in the same small boats."

I put my paws on the floor and stood. "You got any other news you want to share?" Leo stretched back and removed a sheet of paper from his printer, folded it once, and leaned to me, holding it out. I narrowed my eyes at him and took the sheet. I opened the fold and glanced down. It was a list of opponents and fights. My name figured prominently. "This is gonna suck."

"I hope so, my Jane," Leo said, the twinkle back in his eyes. "I do hope so."

"Not what I meant."

The partial smile slid away. "No. Not what you meant. These next few days will be difficult. But you asked me if there was other information you needed to know. Yes. There is."

"And?"

"As you requested when you brought him here, I met privately with the man Ayatas FireWind. He requested to be present at the Sangre Duello. I refused. He grows persistent."

"We don't need PsyLED on the island in any capacity. They would be legally bound to try and stop duels to the death."

Leo inclined his head as if to say he had taken that into consideration. "And yet, in the event of my true-death, the presence of officers of the law might prevent both a bloodbath onshore and any action by the United States Navy or Coast Guard."

"You think the military will take us all out if you lose."

"Accidents happen. Even a deliberate bombardment of an inhabited island in the gulf is not unheard of. Ask Eli Younger. He knows of such things. Ayatas FireWind has been kept apprised of all happenings in my city. I will think on this carefully and will discuss plans with you."

Softer, Leo said, "I have taken the scent of FireWind. And I was gifted with a single drop of his blood as pledge of his honor, if not his loyalty." Gently he added, "He is your brother in truth."

I blinked. Felt as if the world tilted and that I might fall. I took a breath to steady myself and the air was too dry, too cold. "What?"

"I have taken the scent of the man claiming to be your brother. You were born of the same mother, sired by the same father. He is your full-blood brother."

Both of the Youngers were relaxed in the living room, Alex at his desk and Eli lying on the couch, where he had thrown himself when we entered, now looking deceptively tranquil and sleepy.

I was standing in the entry, still in half-form, cranky and annoyed. To Alex, I said, "You knew about the Sangre Duello being at one of three islands, and didn't see fit to tell me?"

"That's his job, Jane," Eli said, watching me from lazy eyes, his hands behind his head and feet crossed. "If you had known, the first thing you would have wanted to do was fly out and look around. You're busy. You have to delegate, but you suck at that. So I did the look-see. Alex oversaw the security. Now, tonight, you need to know. Not before."

Very softly, I asked, "Is there anything else I need to know that I wasn't told?"

Eli sat up from his sprawl. "You're really pissed. Why?"

Ayatas is my brother. Not said. I wanted to hit something. Hard. I felt Beast leap to the forefront of my brain and glow golden through my eyes. The look I sent him had Eli standing, his body angled to fight me, ready for me to hit him. He took a step back, clearing the space between us, giving himself room to block and plan, his eyes lit with delight. Eli always enjoyed giving me a chance to blow off steam, and he gave me a little "come on" wave as if urging me to hit him for real, the way he did when we sparred. "That's our job, Jane," he said, moving around me for a better attack angle. "To evaluate a site and put a plan together. Your job, especially at this particular time, isn't the nuts and bolts. It's following the leads back to Leo's enemies. So you aren't mad about the islands. What are you really mad about, Janie?"

I frowned, not taking the hint to let out some aggression sparring. I was feeling . . . helpless. Yeah. Helpless. And I hated that feeling. "Crap." I dropped my stance and let my shoulders droop. "Sorry. Did you find the SUV that took Dominique away from HQ?" I asked Alex.

Alex ducked his head over his tablet.

"Alex? Kid, what's up?"

Quietly he said, "Rona Hogg and her sister Mazie."

I vaguely remembered Rona. She was one of the Atlanta recruits, training for a possible security position in the new Atlanta clan. In Katie's new clan. Weird. "Okay."

"Her sister's a gamer. I sorta . . . know Mazie."

Eli and I went still as hunting cats. "Know in the casual sense or the biblical sense?" Eli said.

"Not sure what that means, bro. But we got to second base on gamer night a few weeks back. She had questions. I gave her answers. Lots of answers. She's trying to get on as part of the security team too, so . . . I thought it was okay."

"She made you feel important," Eli said.

"She made goo-goo eyes at you, let you feel her boobs, and you caved," I said.

"Sorta," Alex mumbled, his dark-skinned face going red. "Rona and Mazie Hogg helped Dominique get in and out the first time. I got a good still shot from a street cam. They were in the car with her, Rona driving."

"Where did they go?"

"They ditched the SUV off I-10. I lost them."

I said something my housemother might have slapped my face for. Alex's eyes went wide.

"You need to see Aggie One Feather," Eli said, not unkindly.

"I'm busy," I said, my voice reverberating.

"And you need to take Ayatas with you."

The last statement was like being slapped across the face for real. "What?" I said. My shoulders dropped, my face wrinkled up, and I took another step back, further widening the space between us.

Eli hadn't relaxed his stance. "A man claiming to be your brother appeared out of nowhere, alleging things that were confusing and frightening. He appeared when it was convenient to him, instead of making a ceremonial visit that would have shown you he cared. Leo just confirmed Ayatas is really your brother. You're not acting like yourself. You're acting like a pissed-off cat, all claws and attitude. Too much aggression and not enough thinking. Too much cat."

Beast reared up in me, my eyes glowing. I growled softly.

"Yeah. See?" Alex said. "Growly and catty."

"I'm not going to see Aggie. I don't have time for a sweat."

"Fine," Eli said, sitting down on the edge of the couch. His action seemed purposeful, as if to deescalate the tension in the room. "But I called Ayatas and told him Leo confirmed your relationship. You can talk to Ayatas with or without the tribal Elder. Either way, Ayatas is here. You want answers. He wants answers. Aggie is an Elder and she can give them to you."

"And she's waiting," Alex said. "Eli called her too."

Four knocks sounded on the front door. *Tap, tap, tap, tap.* Ayatas's knock.

The urge to hit something swept me up, taking me over

for maybe a half dozen too-rapid heartbeats. I clenched my fists to keep the claws retracted and swallowed down my own emotions. Breathed. Forced the rage down. Down, away, and back. Eli was right. I was angry for all the wrong reasons. I needed to get the information about my supposed brother. I needed to settle this personal thing so I could deal with the Sangre Duello. When the fury had passed I asked, "What does Leo get if Ayatas is my brother? Why drop this on me now, before the Sangre Duello?"

Eli frowned. So did Alex.

"Right. Leo shared info without a quid pro quo. He gets something out of this deal. Leo always gets something out of any deal. If Ayatas and I become chummy, then Leo has another talon hooked into PsyLED. And Leo said something about how having PsyLED at the blood duel might keep the Navy and Coast Guard from dropping bombs on us if Leo loses."

Eli gave his battle-face frown. "Bombardment isn't likely, but I'm keeping my ear to the ground."

"And if Ayatas is your brother and Leo was just being nice?" Alex asked.

"Really?" I moved to the front door, my back to them, but speaking over my shoulder. "Leo? Nice?"

"Good point," Alex said, sounding vaguely surprised. "Huh. Follow the money and the political power." He was already banging away on his tablets and his laptop.

I opened the front door, half-cat and spitting mad, to see the topic of the conversation on my front porch. I blocked his entrance with my body, watched the shock on his face as he took me in and almost went for his weapon. I gave him a cat smile, all fangs and fur. "Hiya, baby brother, if that's who you really are. Get back in your car. We're going to sweat." And I slammed the door in his surprised face. Whirling to Eli, I grabbed a gobag and said, "You're driving."

It took the entire ride to Aggie's, while strapped into the backseat, to shift into full-human form. It was slow, a bone-breaking, tendon-snapping process, and I whined and moaned the whole way. It hurt.

After telling me to "man up," Eli put on music so he didn't have to listen. Man up? Really? Evil man.

When I looked like me again—like Jane again—I let myself out of the seat belt and changed into warm, baggy sweatpants and an oversized sweatshirt, crawled up front, and slumped in the passenger seat. Eli was listening to a Joe Bonamassa album, playing "You Left Me Nothin' but the Bill and the Blues." Music I liked.

I tied my hair in a knot and let it hang down my back and leaned my head against the seat, giving my muscles time to stop quivering and aching. When Joe was finished playing "Drive," I clicked the music off. Silence filled the car and I could smell my own pain and disquiet. "Are you mad at me?" I snapped my mouth shut. I sounded like a twelve-year-old girl whining to her besties.

Eli said, "Babe," in that tone that told me everything was okay between us, and shook his head. "No. I'm not mad at you, Janie. I'm worried. You have a lot going on right now, personally and professionally. You have Ayatas. You have all the magical trinkets in the closet. You're still getting over being struck by lightning. There's the construction. The new clan master position. In a couple days we'll be on an island in the middle of the Gulf of Mexico, an island with questionable GPS coordinates and no secure landing field. On an island with no backup and no way off except an unarmed and unarmored helicopter or two, and Uncle Sam's Navy in the nearest port."

"Officially," I conceded.

"Officially what?"

"Well. Bruiser has a boat."

Eli glanced away from the road. "Does he, now?"

"I was on it. It has a cabin and a teapot and everything."

"And it'll be moored nearby?"

I looked away from Eli, out the window at the night. It was cloudy, the kind of clouds that portended a harder rain than the heavy mist. "It's Bruiser. What do you think?"

Eli might have relaxed a hair. "Good to know. Maybe I'll text him and ask for a sitrep."

Leo had said to let my people do their jobs. "I'm micromanaging everything, aren't I?"

"Yep. Trying to."

Eli was on the job. Alex was ahead of the job. Bruiser was always on the job and tended to plan in advance like a vamp. I wasn't alone anymore, but I was still acting as if I was. I'd been flying by the seat of my pants so long I was surprised my undies didn't have wings. We made the rest of the trip to Aggie's, the quiet settling between us like a lazy cat, and tiny, misty raindrops settling onto the windshield. It would have been pleasant except that I was always aware of the headlights behind us, the car driven by Ayatas FireWind. Who might truly be my brother.

I knocked on Aggie's door as the sun grayed the sky and the stars began to vanish. The front porch light was on and the windows were lit with a pale glow. I smelled cedarwood smoke and coffee. Aggie and her mother were up and moving around, which might have been part of the younger Younger brother's call or part of Aggie's early-to-rise lifestyle. Eli pulled out of the drive and headed back up the road. Ayatas parked on what was technically a cul-de-sac and dimmed his headlights. The car door opened and closed.

Aggie opened the door.

"*Egini Agayvlge i*," I said, speaking her name in *Tsalagi*, "Elder of The People. I seek your counsel."

"*Dalonige' i Digadoli*," Aggie said. Then she looked at the man walking up the steps behind me. "You must be *Ayatas Nvgitsvle*, the one who claims kinship with Jane, according to the Elders of the Eastern *Tsalagi* and the brothers who have adopted her as sister, brothers who stand at her side in battle."

I sorta thought that put Ayatas in his place and I felt a little of the stiffness in my shoulders ease. Ayatas didn't answer.

Aggie went on, "Do you seek counsel as well, One Who Dreams of Fire Wind?"

"I do, *Uni Lisi*."

"*Lisi* will do. Are you both fasting?"

I nodded. I assumed Ayatas did too.

"Go. Wash. Dress. Wait for me in the sweat house."

I started to ask for separate waiting areas, but Aggie closed the door in my face, pretty much the way I had done to Ayatas but with less ire in it. *Great.* I didn't want to be alone with Ayatas, which was probably why Aggie made it happen. Elders were sneaky.

I looked back at Ayatas and jutted my chin to the sweat house. "Hope you like cold showers."

Ayatas sighed. "I'd rather have the coffee I smell."

"I'm a tea kinda gal, but yeah. Coffee would work."

Coffee. Common grounds? Ha-ha?

Side by side, our weapons left behind, we trudged to the sweat house, a wood hut with a metal roof, located at the back of the property, in the winter-bare limbs of trees. In the rear of the building, I pointed to the spigots and Ayatas dipped his head in a half bow. He said, "You first, my sister. I'll wait until you're inside." He stepped back to the front of the building. His words were careful, as was his body language. There was something there in his manner and words if I could only figure out what. I stripped, hung my clothes on the empty hook, and turned the water on. And managed not to curse as the icy water drenched me.

Not bothering to dry off, I pulled on the undyed cotton shift hanging on the nail, braiding my hair out of the way. The shifts were better than the undyed lengths of cloth tied above my boobs I had used on other sweats, especially with a man in the room. I stopped. I had never been to sweat with anyone other than Aggie and her mother. I wasn't sure how this was supposed to work. I didn't like not knowing what to expect. I tied off the tip of my braid with a bit of string pulled from the inside seam of the shift, my fingers suddenly and unexpectedly clumsy.

I opened the low door and stepped inside. The sweat house was already warm and I shivered at the change in temperature, though the winter air outside was warmer than anything I had been accustomed to in the Appalachian Mountains.

So maybe it wasn't the cold that made me quiver.

I heard the water come on and Ayatas's inhale, shocked at the cold.

I sat in my usual place on the clay floor, crossed my knees, adjusted the shift to cover everything important, and leaned back against the split log seat behind me. The seat was hand-carved for the Elders or the injured to use when floor seating wasn't practical.

The coals in the pit before me threw back heat, glowing red and cracking apart, and the rocks lining it in a circle were hot to the touch. I had been here often enough that I slipped easily into a meditative state. A memory came back to me, warm and soothing, of Aggie's soft voice speaking about circles. At some point in a previous ceremony, when I was relaxed on one of her concoctions and in a deeply meditative state, Aggie had told me the purpose of the rock and fire. In my memory, I heard her say, *"Rocks in a circle are ceremonial, part of the Four Directions, the Cords of Life, and the Universal Circle. The fire center leads Tsalagi into accord with the Great One, into harmony with Nature, and into harmony of relationships with each other. It also leads to healing of self, mentally, physically, and spiritually."*

I didn't understand what any of that meant, but this fire had burned a long time. I figured Aggie had taken someone to sweat during the night. I didn't like it when she took two sessions back-to-back, especially since some sessions—unlike my own—lasted days. Aggie looked and acted young, but deadly dehydration was a real possibility in a woman her age. If I said that, she'd likely thunk me over the head with something.

Ayatas opened the low sweat house door and, like me, he had to duck his head to enter. He moved like a cat in the dark of the windowless space. Ayatas wasn't wearing a shift. He was wearing a loincloth, one that was clearly his own.

Memories hit me fast.

Edoda, Tsaligi for *my father*, wearing a loincloth, his legs, hips, and outer buttocks bare in the traditional Cherokee style, his loincloth damp, his body muscled,

long, and lean. Striding catlike through the cold water of
a splashing stream, his feet in moccasins, his calves
wrapped in tall cloth and deer hide sleeves to his knees as
protection from sharp rocks. He had been bending and
lifting stone, building a rock weir to trap fish.

I remembered.

Edoda in his loincloth, as he pulled in a net full of fish,
looking back at me and laughing, white teeth shining.
Edoda cleaning fish with the steel knife he had traded for
with the *yunega*. *Edoda* dipping a bucket into the stream
to gather water. *Edoda*. My father. A vigorous man.

And then my last memory of *Edoda*, dead on the floor
of the cabin. His blood cooling, congealing in the weave
of the cloth of his shirt, as I dipped my hand into it. The
slick swipe of blood as I wiped it across my face, giving
his killer a blood vow of vengeance, staring into the man's
blue eyes. That single moment of promise had set my entire life into motion, every decision since, every thought,
every drop of blood spilled, every death. I had been five
years old. A child full of hate and anger and willing to die
so long as I took my enemies with me.

The visions were intense, vivid, shocking as the cold
water of the spigot.

The loincloth *Edoda* wore when working in the creek
water had been a brightly colored, woven belt tied high
on his waist and passed through his legs, covering the
center part of his buttocks, with a small square skirt
hanging from the belt in front.

So much like the one Ayatas wore. The same colors in
the belt. The red and yellow and blue woven into a long
narrow length, wrapped and tied just so, that left the
body bare and unencumbered for work or sweat.

But Aya's skirt was fringed and tasseled, and a similar
small skirt hung in back. Not as traditional as *Edoda's*.
Why the difference?

Ayatas sat a third of the circle away, his eyes on the fire
pit. Like me, he had braided his long hair and it hung over
his shoulder, wet and dripping on the clay of the floor. His
chest was still dripping from the shower, water beaded
and reflecting the fire. A leather medicine bag hung

around his neck on a leather thong, black on one side, green on the other, stuffed full of his spirit guide items. The bag was so similar to the one I wore in my visions of my soul home that I looked away. I had no medicine bag, nothing marked the herbs and stones and bones of my passage through life. I had no medicine bag because I had no family. No history with The People. Jealousy spiked through me, so strong that my chest ached and my breath came fast.

Jane and Beast are family. She sent me a vision of kits almost two years old, hunting together in a small pack. *Not pack hunters. Family,* she insisted.

Tears filled my eyes. *Yeah. I guess we are.*

Ayatas and I didn't speak.

A pile of split cedar logs were to the far side near where Aggie usually sat. A basket filled with bundles of fresh and dried herbs was nearby. A pitcher of water sat among the heated rocks, the clay formed, worked, dried, and fire-cooked, in the ancient Cherokee tradition. A water bucket with a ladle sat in the shadows near a roll of cloth strips and a shallow clay bowl. A narrow lap drum with a small, hide-covered drumstick were next to Aggie's old boom box.

Outside, the water came on and went off again. Aggie entered and walked to the east wall, where she lifted a five-foot-long pole and used the tip to open a small wooden slot door, up high in the small gable. I realized that there were a series of tiny slot doors there and I had never seen them. She sat across from us, crossing her knees as I had. Moving slowly, she added a single split log to the coals and the fire flared up for a moment as the flames teased across the dry wood. Light and shadows danced on the wood walls. Cedar scent filled the sweat house, and thin smoke hung near the ceiling. The heat built as we sat in silence and sweated. Time passed, but it had little meaning here in this place. Sweat slid and pooled and dripped. The fire burned lower, hotter. Aggie added split oak. Much later, another. My mind moved deeper into the slow, meditative state of ceremony, my eyes heavy.

Aggie shifted her body slightly upright, the rustle of
fabric and her indrawn breath telling me she was ready to
begin. She raised one hand, palm up, over her head and
slipped into the cadence of the Tsalagi Elder and healer
speaking English. She said . . . not what I expected. "We
are grateful to the Great One." Her open palm moved in
front of her. "To the East." Her hand moved. "To the
South." Her hand moved. "To the West." Her hand
moved again, making a circle. "To the North." Her hand
returned overhead, finishing the circle. Still holding the
hand high, but where we could see it, she cupped her
other palm beside the first, as if pouring something into
it. She leaned over the fire and dropped a few sprinkles of
wild tobacco into the flame. It brightened in bits before
vanishing. Reaching behind her, Aggie pulled a cloth-
covered bundle out of the shadows and positioned it beside her without untying and revealing it.

"Wah doh," she said softly. "You are here for counsel.
For mediation." She looked back and forth between us and
recognition filled her eyes, a peculiar expectation. "We
will begin. I am *Egini Agayvlge i,* Aggie One Feather. My
mother is *Ani Waya*—Wolf Clan—Eastern Cherokee, and
my father was *Ani Godigewi*—Wild Potato Clan—Western
Cherokee. My great-grandfather was Panther Clan."

"I am *Ayatas Nvgitsvle,* Ayatas FireWind. My mother
was *Ani Sahoni,* Blue Holly Clan. My father was adopted
into Panther Clan, part of Blue Holly Clan, when he married my mother and moved into her home."

I said, "I'm Jane Yellowrock, rogue-vampire killer. I
am also *Dalonige' i Digadoli,* Yellowrock Golden Eyes.
Panther Clan, I think. But I've been gone too long." I
stopped sharply. When I spoke again, the words that
came from my mouth were, "I am an orphan of time and
place. I have no Tsalagi clan, not really. Not anymore."

Ayatas shot me a look that might have meant most
anything, a look that an Elder might have given me. And
I realized that he was nearly as old as me. But he had a-
hundred-seventy-some years of memories and I had less
than thirty years of memories. I looked away from him.

Aggie watched my face and seemed satisfied with

whatever she saw taking place there. She said, "I will tell you of the world, through the bear and the deer. The bear, who is the body of the universe, lives its life eating and defecating and sleeping as comes naturally, with no cares for any other being, except for the messages recorded in the cells of his body."

My head came up. That sounded a lot like the snake in the center of all creatures—Skinwalker wisdom and knowledge—mixed with instinct.

"These messages tell him what to do and when. All the messages and memories of time are recorded there, in the body of the bear. And the bear listens."

Time? Time is recorded in the cells? Beast crept close to the center of my mind, listening. My palms tightened on my knees and I had to force my body to relax, had to force myself to breathe slowly, and to listen with all of me, and not just my ears. And I realized that to listen with all of me was to listen in the *Tsalagi* way.

"The deer is the mind of the universe. The deer is sacred," Aggie said, "a cunning animal. It sees and hears all things and we can talk to the deer. The deer listens to the messages of the mind of the universe as well as to the body of the universe." She looked to Ayatas. "Have you conditioned your body to listen to the messages of the universe, of the Great One, to receive knowledge and wisdom, as the Sacred Deer does for Mental Healing?"

"I have traveled far, and listened to the deer and to the bear and to the jaguar. To the wolf and the mountain lion. I have listened. And sometimes the universe, the Great One, has spoken to me."

"And have you followed the wisdom of the visions?"

Ayatas hesitated. "Not always, *Lisi*. I have been stubborn. I have thought my way was the better way. I have feared to follow the path before me. I have looked to the past. I have held on to the past and to those I have lost. I have been a child in the face of Grandfather Rock, many times. But now I wish again to learn. To see the right and healing way again."

Aggie looked at me. "Your past was lost to you. Will you be deer or bear?"

Deer is prey, Beast thought. *Bear is too big to be prey. Bear can kill big-cat.* Beast padded closer to the forefront of my mind. *Beast would be big-cat. Faster big-cat. Big-cat with sharper killing teeth and stronger claws. But Beast will not be deer or bear. Jane will not be deer or bear.*

I shook my head and pulled on the most formal speech I could manage. Words and phrases and mannerisms I had learned in the children's home. But more importantly, words and phrases and mannerisms I had learned in Leo's household. "Grandmother. There is wisdom in both ways. The way of the mind of the universe and also the way of the body of the universe." Because the body has time stored in its cells, I thought. "Body and mind should be—no, they are—together, one thing, one power, one energy, as even the foolish white man now knows. *E* equals *mc* squared."

Aggie nodded slowly, hearing my words and the feelings that lay beneath.

I said, "I would choose the wisdom and the messages of the cells and the wisdom and the messages of the universe, the mind and the body combined, the wisdom and messages in both, together. I would serve my family and my clan and my tribe by leading them into war if peace was not possible. By bringing them meat to eat, including the deer and the bear. By sharing what wisdom there exists in my cells and what wisdom God would reveal to me, and that I understood. But I think I would not give my body to be eaten as a way of service. I would not choose to become prey. I am not prey."

Beast is not prey.

Right, I thought. *I/we are not prey.*

Aggie seemed satisfied and disturbed at my answer in equal measure and uncertain which one to address, but finally she nodded again, as if accepting what cannot be changed. She reached into the basket, took out a fresh pine bough, and placed it on the fire. The stink of blazing pine filled the air. "We come for healing, for the right way. For reconciliation." Aggie looked back and forth between us and said, "How may I help?"

Ayatas said nothing, so I did. Maintaining a formal tone, I said, "This man came to my house. He tried to kill me. Then he says he's my brother, and a skinwalker, and wants me to use my connections for an introduction to Leo Pellissier."

Ayatas recoiled, the skin of his back cringing when I spoke his secret. But Aggie knew all my secrets, and no way was I keeping Ayatas's.

Aggie frowned. "This is a twisted path we walk, with many byways to tread. First, Ayatas, are you Jane's brother, part of her family and clan?"

"Yes, I believe so."

"Jane, do you believe him to be your brother?"

I didn't want to reply, and I may have sounded sulky when I answered. "I have a partial memory of my father talking about a baby I was supposed to take care of. And the Master of the City says that beneath the skinwalker scent, he smells like my full brother."

"For now, we agree that you are blood kin?"

Reluctantly, I nodded.

"Ayatas FireWind. You tried to kill your sister?"

"She did not wear the scent of Tsalagi, but of predator. Of magic not associated with . . . my people. I reacted on instinct. I ask forgiveness."

"Forgiveness is a difficult thing." Aggie looked at me. "Would your Redeemer God forgive his brother?"

I scowled at her. "I didn't kill him when I had the chance. I helped him in his request to see Leo Pellissier. I can forgive an instinct and a reaction to magic."

Aggie nodded slowly, considering. "Yet your anger and distrust persists."

"Yeah. He's known about me for some time and decided not to come visit until he could combine business and meeting me; coming now is awfully convenient. Maybe that's some of that wisdom he says he ignored. I don't know. But his explanation lacked full disclosure, and his apology, if there was one, was inadequate. And it may be petty, but his loincloth has a skirt in back. It's not traditional and that bothers me."

She ignored my last complaint. "By not making the

trip to see you, and you alone, Ayatas offered insult to your relationship, which is more painful to you than your brother trying to kill you."

Which made me sound the next best thing to psycho and Ayatas scornfully rude.

Ayatas frowned at Aggie and then at me. Eli and I had said much the same thing and Ayatas had thought nothing about it. Let a tribal Elder say something and he listens.

"Do his words and stories have the ring of truth?" Aggie asked me.

I frowned back at Ayatas. "He tells just enough to make any lie sound like the truth. He's a cop. They're professional liars."

"You were in love with a cop," Ayatas said.

"And he was a liar."

Aggie raised her hand to stop me before I could continue what already sounded like a childish squabble. "Ayatas. How do you respond?"

"My wife was a white woman with red hair. We lived among the tribes of the West for some years. Things in my life changed because of that. I acquired new concepts, stories, and wisdom from the Paiute and the Navajo and the Apache. The extra skirt and covering made my wife happy. She was a woman of her time and she didn't like the nakedness of the savage.

"I meant no disrespect to my sister. This woman does not smell like skinwalker or clan. She smells like predator. Yet, this woman *is* my sister."

Aggie nodded. She knew why I smelled like I did. "Do you agree that she speaks the truth about your insult to her? That you should have, and yet did not, come to greet her sooner?"

Ayatas's face went cold and unyielding, the look of a hunter facing danger. If I'd been Aggie, I'd have been squirming. Aggie simply sat there and waited. And waited. Sweat became slick trails moving slow, down my spine, between my bent knees, down my chest, across my scalp, and down my face. I blinked to keep it out of my eyes, but it stung, salty-sharp.

Ayatas took a breath and blew it out, and when he spoke, it was with the same measured formality that Aggie was using. "She speaks the truth. I put off coming. I didn't know what to say or how to say it. I heard the messages of the universe, of Grandfather Rock, and the candor of the deer, and I did not listen with my whole self. I turned away. I have been a child in my thoughts, to run away from truth and wisdom, ignoring or following the Elders' wisdom and the Great One's messages as I chose. Seeking my own way." This was a Tsalagi way of speaking and The People do not lie, even to the white man, never to an Elder. This was *truth*.

"I combined the trip with business in the white man way. I didn't treat the relationship with honor. My apology was not heartfelt because I justified my actions."

His words made me feel better, though in his place, I'd have just barged ahead, driven to NOLA, and banged on his door, letting the chips fall where they might. Maybe his way was better. Or maybe his way was cowardly. Or maybe a combo of the two.

Aggie said gently, "You have both violated relationship. You have strayed from a good medicine path and dishonored one another."

I frowned at the floor, letting her words try to make sense inside me. Among tribal peoples, medicine wasn't drugs. It was a method of right relationships: spiritual, mental, physical, and with the natural world, in terms of nature, the Earth, tribe, clan, and family. I wasn't sure how I had violated anything, but I sure could see how my bro had violated it all.

"Jane. Your *uni lisi* violated the path to harmony when she led you to kill your father's murderers."

Ayatas whipped his eyes to me. Yeah. I had told her. So what? I ignored him.

Aggie went on. "You were too young to understand the way of the war woman. Her teaching led you to believe that violence and death was the answer to all things."

I opened my mouth to argue and just as quickly snapped it shut, feeling the sweat in the creases around my mouth, tasting salt and smoke. Aggie was right. I

frowned harder, not wanting to agree. But. I had entered
the sweat house in honor, which meant I had no choice
but to be led to reconciliation.

I should have just shot Ayatas and been done with it.
Dang it.

"Yes, *Lisi*. If Ayatas is to be believed, I continued in
the way I was taught. I violated the path of harmony when
I tried to kill a white man rapist on the Trail of Tears." I
frowned harder, as an image came to me of a pale face,
dark with white-man beard, lined and saggy, too thin.
The knife in my hand as I stabbed him with it. The vision
of his fist coming at me. Then nothing. "He was *yunega*.
He hurt a woman. I thought . . . I thought that meant he
deserved to die at my hand."

"You were a child, led down a path that was for a
grown woman. You are now that woman, standing on a
bridge over a roaring river, where you can see upstream
to your past, down to your present, and downstream to
your future."

I nodded, but instead of seeing a river, I saw a path
through a dark wood, one running with blood, and with
the bloody, muddy footprints of the passage of my life.
My past. I looked the other way and saw a short, rock-
strewn path mostly hidden in a rainstorm, lightning jag-
ged through the sky. Thunder boomed. Rain beat the
earth like a timpani of drums. The path leading into the
future quickly vanished into the mist of pounding rain
and lashing trees. Rain. And lightning. And time . . .

I blinked my eyes open, surprised that they had shut.
"My past is a path that runs with blood," I said, still
speaking in a formal tone.

"Yes," Aggie said gently, "and in your present you
work for Europeans, for white men, white bloodsuckers.
You take their money and kill when they say to kill. Your
present is a river running with blood. Your future is unknown and you may take it in any direction, the same
bloody path you now tread, or something else. Something
different. Something that is not dependent on the grandmother who taught you to kill."

I wiped the stinging sweat from my eyes. I'd thought

pretty much the same thing myself. After a little too long, I blew out a breath and said, "Yes, *Lisi*. I have taken a blood path. I am mired in it. My feet stand still, unmoving, not walking, submerged in the blood of my enemies and the enemies of the vampires." I looked into Aggie's dark eyes, eyes that saw too much, ignoring my brother's yellow ones.

When I spoke the next words aloud, where my brother could hear them, I gave away much of what made me tick. But this sweat was sacred, almost holy, and it seemed the time to share my own heart. "I took this path to protect my godchildren, whom I have sworn to keep safe. To protect all the witch children in the Americas. Perhaps there was a better path, one that would have accomplished the same ends without so much death." I dropped the formal tones and speech patterns. "But I don't see it, Aggie. I don't see any other way I could have gone, except through the heads and hearts and blood of my enemies."

Aggie nodded thoughtfully and passed us pottery cups filled with cool water, smelling of mint. "Drink," she said. "You have taken a path through blood and death. Have you done so with honor? Have you been kind and compassionate for the lives of your enemies? Have you given back to the Earth for the blood you shed? Have you treated all of Nature with honor in all of your ways? Have you taken a path with respect for the Earth?"

"Mostly. Life of the living, human life, yes, mostly. Life of the undead? Not so much."

"Why should your brother, who knows only what he reads in his reports, trust one who deals in death? He does not know for a surety that you killed to protect the innocent. He does not know that you have not killed simply because the vampire requested a killing."

Crap. To kill or not to kill? That is the question. And that was the crux of the whole of my life. I closed my eyes and salt stung them. A time passed, marked only by the sweat that ran off my body. I looked again at the vision of my future, as it disappeared in rabbit trails through the rain and forest—in the fall of rain/time and the life of the Earth. I said, agreeing, "The path I walk is not the only

one through the forest. I may have been set on this path
by the grandmother who should have taught me differently, but now I am grown. I can see clearly how the path
of my future might alter."

And there was that bear and deer story. *Holy crap.* I
could see the future through the messages of the body
and also through time . . . "I have the right to choose how
I should go forward. The path is mine to make." I looked
at Ayatas. He was sitting with his eyes closed, sweat
streaking his body. His nose was shaped exactly like
mine. His eyebrows exactly like mine. His irises were yellow. Exactly like mine. That was the recognition sparking
in Aggie when she first entered the sweat house. She had
seen the resemblance. I said, softly, "I would make peace
with my brother."

If Ayatas heard me he didn't give anything away. He
might have been asleep for all the reaction he gave.

"Ayatas," Aggie said. "You knew of Jane Yellowrock.
You knew she was likely your sister. Yet you chose not to
come." Gently, her words slow and kind, Aggie said,
"Your path was one of jealousy and insult."

Ayatas's mouth tightened.

"Your path was based upon the tales and stories you
had heard as a child, the big sister who killed her enemies, who went to war when just a child. You could not
live up to her. You did not believe that you could walk her
path. And so you avoided her until you had need of her.
Until you might use her as a weapon. Just as did the
grandmother who taught her to kill. This was your insult."

The silence stretched out, tight as a drumhead.

Aggie placed a pine bough on the fire. It caught,
smoked, and blackened in the flames until its core glowed
red and it fell apart.

My stomach growled. We drank more water. I had to
answer the call of nature. We all slipped into the cold and
came back. We drank again.

More time passed. Ayatas sighed, long and low, lifted
his head, and looked at Aggie. "Yes, *Lisi.* In my heart I
still harbored the childish jealousy of my youth." He
turned his eyes to me, and this time, I saw Ayatas FireWind,

the man he was in this moment, and hints of the man he might someday become, deep in his eyes. "I am sorry, my sister. Sorry that I treated you with disrespect. Sorry that I did not show you the great value you hold in our clan. I am ashamed that I didn't honor the Great One and the gifts of this life by coming to you the moment you were revealed to me. Your stories are still told around the fires of the old ones. But I never told your stories. I never shared them. I was weak and foolish and I did not put away foolish things when I became a man." He took a slow breath. "I ran away from all the childhood things that challenged me in my youth. All the skills and stories and dance and ceremony that I was not successful at. All the things that were hard. And though I have been successful in all the things I have done as a man, I have never stopped running. I have never looked back and made the things of my childhood right."

Aggie dropped her chin, indicating that she was satisfied and that we could move ahead with the mediation ceremony. From the basket, she took a small mortar and pestle, stripped some wilted herb leaves off a stem, added some dried leaves, and ground it all together. She took two wooden cups and put half of the herb mix in each and poured heated water into them. She set the decoctions aside to steep and settled herself as the Elders always did, a relaxing of the facial muscles and shoulders, knees, and hips, though her back was still tall and straight.

Aggie's eyes were sunken. Her skin was wrinkled and desiccated from sweating. Salt crystals were white in her hairline, brightening the few silver strands interwoven in the long bob that had grown out to hang at her shoulders. Her eyes were black, skin olive and copper. Tsalagi . . . The sight of her and Ayatas together spoke of home. Of the home I had lost when I was five.

Something washed through me, a flash flood of ice and fire, of fury, a torrent that left behind only emptiness. The deluge of emotion was accompanied by an echo of wailing and grief, a sound I remembered, not a sound of imagination. It was a howling, weeping cry from my childhood. The sound of my mother and the other women wailing over the body of my father the night he was killed and my mother was raped. This memory was an inundation—longing and loneliness and the resonance of the grave. I sucked in a smoke-filled breath, blinked, and the memory was gone. But I could find it again. Would find it again. This memory of my past.

My path from the past to the present and into the future had begun with the wailing of grief.

I reached back and ran my hands along my braid. It was both wet and stiff with salt. We had been here longer than I realized.

Aggie set three lengths of sage on the coals. The leaves curled and the smell rose on the air, crisp and earthy. Ayatas, his face impassive, watched every move Aggie made. I had no idea what he was feeling, and that bothered me. Not being sure why I was bothered, bothered me even more.

CHAPTER 12

He Asked Me to
Have a Three-Way with Leo

The smell of flaming sage rose on the smoke. Aggie handed us each a cup. "Drink. Then we will find a path through the things that you seek."

Ayatas drained his cup and said, "I come for counsel about my sister, who is remembered in our clan, who was mourned. For all of my life I heard about *Dalonige' i Digadoli*, Yellowrock Golden Eyes, the sister who killed the white men who murdered our father. Who wore the blood of our father, the blood of her vow, until the two men were dead. She was five years old when she made her blood vow and carried it out. *Dalonige' i Digadoli*, who attacked a white man on the Trail of Tears and was banished into the snow in the form of *gvhe*. Bobcat." He looked at me. "*Dalonige' i Digadoli*. Golden Eyes. Our eyes are the gift of our heritage."

"Skinwalker eyes," I said. "*Uni Lisi* of Panther Clan had eyes this color, though she may not have been a grandmother by blood and birth."

Ayatas nodded, agreeing. "This was the woman who was grandmother to me, as well."

"There was another woman like us, here in the city a hundred years back or so," I said. "She had gold eyes too. And she smelled like you. Floral. Sweet. There was also one *u'tlun'ta*. This was before I took the blood path that I walk today. *U'tlun'ta* was stalking Aggie and her mother and the bones of their ancestors buried out back. He was killing humans and vampires."

"You killed it," Ayatas said. "This is good."

Time passed again. Aggie added a small split log to the fire and then ladled water from the bucket over the hot stones. Steam billowed and rose.

Sweat gathered and ran across me, taking the toxins out of my flesh and opening my mind. Sweat ran across Aggie's face and darkened the fabric of her shift. Sweat ran across Ayatas's bare upper body and down his legs. He sat cross-legged, eyes closed, waiting.

Aggie paused and motioned for me to finish my drink. It was yucky, like heated pond water, but I knocked it back and swallowed, then spat a leaf out of my mouth, into my palm, and wiped it on my shift.

Aggie smiled slightly at my *ick* expression and said, "The first time I brought Jane here, I told her that blood chased after her. That blood rode her. That she pounced on her enemy, like a big-cat onto prey. I told her this long before I knew her nature or her spirit. But even then I knew that she was not *Callanu Ayiliski*, the Raven Mocker who likes to steal hearts. Nor was she liver-eater or spear finger, *u'tlun'ta*."

She stopped. Aggie had also told me that I walked a fine line between light and darkness and that I could fall into the evil of the skinwalkers, but she didn't say that to Ayatas, not yet. It wasn't kindness. Aggie wouldn't keep an important warning or potential problem hidden. Being kind wasn't the job of an Elder. So when she continued I wasn't surprised.

"I have heard it said: 'The skinwalkers shared the blood of The People. The liver-eaters stole it.' You both are skinwalkers, from the stories told by the oldest among us, from the time before the white man. You are protectors. Warrior and war woman. You are from among the skinwalkers who led Tsalagi into battle. But all skinwalkers walk the line between light and darkness. It would be better for you to walk that line together."

Ayatas looked at me from the corner of his eyes and I could tell he didn't like that idea. So I stuck out my tongue at him. An eruption of laughter exploded from low in Ayatas's belly, a clear and free tone of merriment, the laughter of a happy childhood. Aggie's eyebrows went up at my deliberate childishness and Ayatas's response.

My mouth curled up and I sounded deliberately snarly when I said, "I never got the chance to do that when we were kids."

Ayatas's laughter fell away and he tilted his head to study me. "I should have come to you right away."

"Yeah. You should. Why didn't you?" I asked. "I mean, really? The real reason."

As if thinking, Ayatas shook his head, his long braid slinging against him. "Aggie One Feather is right. I grew up with this tale of the five-year-old war woman. The old women would sit around the fire in winter, talking about her, telling family stories of my sister who should have led her clan, who would have sat on the war councils with the chiefs and the Elders and led her people to war."

Aggie said gently, "You wanted to wait until your jealousy passed."

Answering Aggie, but still speaking to me, Ayatas said, "I saw the YouTube video of you walking out of a mine entrance with a massive scar across your throat and a dead police officer slung over your shoulder, one you had tried to save. Your eyes were glowing gold. I knew you were that sister. That war woman sister." He glanced to Aggie and back to me. "Yours were big shoes to follow, when I was young, until I found my way and my place in the world. And so I waited. I let things get in the way; I put that visit on the back burner. I ignored my heart's urging to come see you. I'm sorry. Really, very sorry."

I blinked against the sweat that dripped down my face, again stinging my eyes. The room had lightened with the nearness of dawn, pale gray light creeping through the small cracks of the building and along the roof system overhead. We had been here twenty-four hours. "How can you be my brother?" I asked, hearing the desperation in my voice, remembering standing with my father above a roaring river. Remembering my promise to care for the expected child. "After all this time. After all these years."

He had said the words before, but ceremony required complete candor and understanding. "Our mother was pregnant with me when our father died. I was born on the Trail of Tears. The Great One has timing that doesn't always make sense to us."

Aggie asked, "Jane. Are you satisfied with Ayatas's words?"

"Yes."

"Ayatas, are you satisfied with Jane's words?"

Ayatas considered me. "Where were you all those years, sister?"

"I'm sure it's a long story, but I don't remember much of it." I pointed to my head. "Amnesia. The stories the newspapers told about me were real. I spent a lot of time in mountain lion form." I didn't mention Beast's soul inside with me. That was black magic and I needed to know him better before I shared that. Since Aggie didn't volunteer that information I figured she was okay with a delay. "Stick around. I'll tell you my stories."

"I can't stay long enough to hear the tales of that many years," he said, his expression oddly kind, an expression I might have seen in the eyes of the Keepers of the Secrets, the most elder of the Tsalagi. Which he was. "But when I leave I'll be going to Asheville. Hayalasti Sixmankiller has requested my presence. Maybe you should come with me."

Shock zinged through me like a pinball, an electric bruising. Hayalasti Sixmankiller was our grandmother. "Maybe I will." If I live that long.

Aggie said, "It is dawn. We will close with a blessing." She reached for the bundle at her side. I had forgotten it was there and was surprised when she lifted a rock out of its folds. Or not a rock, but a huge, clear quartz crystal. There was a central spire with a multifaceted pointed top.

Two smaller spikes were on one side. The three rose together from a base of smaller crystals and a curved bottom of stone. I tensed, eyes darting, searching for trapped arcenciels. There was nothing. Just the clear crystal.

With both hands Aggie pushed aside the fire-warmed river rock that was closest to her knees and placed the crystal in the depression. She held her cupped hands over the crystal and said, "Like the quartz, we are clear of strife, clear in mind, body, spirit, and natural space. Like this small piece of Grandfather Rock, we are part of Earth, safe in Earth, protecting Earth and her plants and creatures. Great One, we offer thanks for what gifts we have, thanks to the Four Directions and the power of the universe."

Her voice took on a chant cadence as the sweat house brightened still more. "I give thanks in a traditional prayer, altered for Jane's spiritual path:

"To the Spirit of the Fire who is the East,

"To the Spirit of the Earth who is the South,

"To the Spirit of the Water who is the West,

"To the Spirit of the Wind who is the North.

"To the Redeemer who forgives, whose path Jane follows, who Jane worships.

"We pray and we give thanks to you, Great One.

"We pray. We give thanks for Mother Earth.

"We pray. We give thanks for Father Sky, Grandfather Sun, and Grandmother Moon. For Jane's Redeemer. For all life, all gifts, all joy, all wisdom. And we pray that we may exist together in peace, with harmony, with balance in all our relations. *Wah doh.*"

As she spoke the last two words, the dawn sun passed through the small door in the eaves, the door Aggie had opened when she entered. The dawn light illuminated a path through the air, lighting the dust and residual smoke with its muted ray. Alighting on the crystal on the earth near Aggie's knees. Brightening it, sending the dawn light out in a prism of color and a rainbow of hues. This was Aggie's version of the traditional Blessing Way. Not exactly something I remembered from the scant years of my childhood, but it was close enough.

*   *   *

Ayatas waited at the fire while Aggie and I showered in
the frigid water, dressed, and walked to stand beside his
car. Aggie stared at her house, looking as wilted as the
herbs from the mediation ceremony. "Will you ride with
him or do you need to call your brothers to pick you up?"

"I'll drive her home," Ayatas called from behind the
sweat house. Skinwalker ears.

Aggie smiled, nodded to me, and walked up the steps
to her front door. She moved like an old, worn-out woman,
exhausted by life. I had done that to her. I should go back
and pour water on her fire pit and wood. Use enough water
and she would have to let the pit dry out before she could
work again.

Ayatas strode from behind the building, his eyes taking in the way I lounged against his car. "Get in. I'll take
you home," he said. I opened the door and eased into his
cop car, a gray four-door SUV. It smelled like Christmas
trees and commercial cleansers and old cigarette smoke.
The back was filled with cop gear, including one of the
new psy-meters, the kind that measured all sorts of magical energy.

"It meet with your approval?" he asked as he executed
a three-point turn in the street. I couldn't tell if he was
being sarcastic or curious so I just shrugged. He said, "I
poured the bucket of water on the fire. It'll be at least a
day before it dries up enough to take anyone to sweat."

"She was tired," I agreed, finding it odd that we had
been thinking along the same lines, but that Ayatas had
actually done something about it while I had only thought
about it. "That stuff about our clan talking about me. You
know it wasn't like that at all, right?" He didn't respond.
"I mean, yes, I made a blood vow. But I didn't know what
I was doing. I was five."

"Our stories tell of you running through the cornfields
and through the woods to the clan longhouse and waking
everyone. Then climbing on the back of a horse, riding
with *Uni Lisi* as she tracked the men, then waiting as she

shifted to *tlvdatsi* and trapped them and caught them. Brought them to a cave on clan lands."

I blinked, remembering the power and speed of the racing horse beneath me, the smell of *Uni Lisi's* body, the smoke trapped in her clothes, the acrid smell of herbs, the sickly sweetness of old blood. The memory vanished, as if I had popped a balloon with a pin. Later memories flashed in front of my mind, like flipping the pages of a gruesome picture book.

"I watched our mother and grandmother torture and kill one of the men. And I killed the other one. *Uni Lisi* put the blade in my hand and pushed me at him. I wanted to do it. I wanted the white man to die. But it wasn't glory or honor. It was kidnapping and torture and murder."

Aya nodded and made a turn, his blinker bright yellow. "Things were different back then. Society was different. More blindly, casually cruel. Despite what people call the conservative, fascist, racist, sexist world of today, people were worse in the past."

I shrugged. "Perspective is everything, Aya."

He grunted. It sounded like one of mine. And I realized I had used the shorter term. *Aya.* I stared into the dawning light. A few miles later Ayatas asked, "Are you going to tell me where the Sangre Duello is being held?"

"Asking as cop or brother?"

"Does it matter?"

"Yes."

"Then I guess you won't be telling me anything."

"Guess not."

"What's the history between you and Rick LaFleur?"

Ohhh. That was a zinger from out in left field. I could ignore the question. Or I could answer it and see how he reacted. I turned in my seat, pulling one knee up, to watch his face in the glow of the dash lights as I spoke. "We were a thing. He was undercover and was seducing a wereleopard for info. He got bit. She got executed by a grindylow. He got kidnapped by werewolves and tortured. I rescued him and killed the wolves. He turned. Became a black wereleopard, despite the amount of wolf saliva in his bites. We were still a thing. Sorta. Then he was magically seduced by a wereleopard in heat in front of dozens of people. He left with her. I should have killed her, or stopped him some other way. I didn't protect him. I let him go because my feelings were hurt and I was embarrassed. We were no longer a thing. It's uncomfortable and complicated."

Aya nodded. I realized his hair was still braided and it had left a wet trail down one side of his clothes. "When you killed the wolves," he said, "it opened a chasm that has since been filled by the Bighorn Montana Pack, with whom Leo has sworn an alliance."

I shrugged and said nothing.

"Tell me about Rick and Kemnebi. Kemnebi attacked you?"

"Cop or brother?"

"Cop asking." The slightest of smiles settled on his face. "This is awkward. If I had come before now, we would know one another and I wouldn't have to be both brother and cop."

"You screwed up."

"Yes. And because I did, I now appear to be a top-tier jerk."

I didn't argue. I wasn't going to talk to him about Kem's demise or Rick's elevation in status, his wives, or Clan Yellowrock. I was vamp-careful when I answered. "I'm the head of the local wereleopard clan."

"You're not a werecat."

"Nope. But problems arise and have to be solved."

"Leap of leopards," Aya said. "Not clan."

"Leap. I like. Anyway, Rick is now highly ranked in the leap, so he can handle things any way he wants."

"If Rick loses control of his leopard, that could make for an awkward international incident."

"Cop talking for sure. And I don't care."

Aya sighed. "I don't know how to blend both the brother and the cop. I feel awkward and foolish and all my words are clumsy."

"I noticed." A small smile accompanied my words.

"Yes. Well." He drove in silence for a while before he

sighed. "I don't have time to build a relationship with you before the Sangre Duello."

"You may never be able to build a relationship with me."

"This is true. But I will try. Until then, I have a job to do too."

"Go for it."

"As a part of that job, I have to find a way to be at the Sangre Duello."

"I'm not in charge of royal vamp protocol."

"That's Leo's Enforcer talking, not the sister."

"Potato, potahto. I have a job too. Talk to Leo's se-cundo heir, Grégoire, when he gets in from Atlanta."

Blandly, Aya said, "He's back from Atlanta. And I tried. He asked me to have a three-way with Leo."

I snorted. I didn't mean to. It just blasted out. My laugh felt vastly different in tone from Aya's. My laugh was stilted, sarcastic, stiff, as if I had never learned to laugh as a child. Or had forgotten how a hundred seventy years ago. Still, the grin I gave him was bright and teasing and at least it felt natural.

Aya glanced at me and back to the street, his own lips turned up. "According to Adelaide Mooney, Grégoire is totally 'gaga' over me, and I should consider myself caught in the crosshairs of an intense and concentrated seduction once the Sangre Duello is over."

"You should be scared. Very, very scared."

"I am not a homophobe," he said. His lips curling higher. I knew that smile. It was mine, seen in the mirror. "The Cherokee Nation accepted same-sex marriage back in 2016. Among the speakers of Diné, the Navajo, the two-spirited are referred to as *nàdleehé*, or the trans-formed. The Lakota call the two-spirited the *winkte*. To be two-spirited is a commonly accepted truth among a lot of tribes; the Mojave, Zuni, Omaha, Aleut, Kodiak, Zapotec, and Cheyenne all accept multiple forms of sex-uality. But I'm straight. And even if I wasn't, there is no way in hell I'm doing a three-way with two vamps."

"Chicken."

He laughed, that amazing, carefree laugh. The laugh I might have had except for two white men who killed my father and raped my pregnant mother and then had the misfortune to fall into the clutches of a war woman skinwalker and her blood-vow-bound grandchild. "Yes," he said. "I accept that judgment. Back to my job. They call you the Dark Queen. Want to tell me why?"

"That?" I said. "That was a cop move. And though I might have told my brother all about it, I'm not telling a cop. Figure it out on your own. And by the way, you must suck as an interviewer." I shook my head, disgusted.

Rain spattered on the windshield, growing stronger. Lightning flickered in the distance. Silence settled on us, uneasy, though not exactly troubled. We shared genes, no history, no common ground.

"It seems I have no finesse when it comes to you," he admitted. "But, I have something for you. It's in the glove box, in a white bag."

I frowned at him. He got me a present?

As if he read my mind, Aya said, "*Uni Lisi*—Sixmankiller—overnighted it to me."

My frown grew deeper, darker, and I stared at the glove box as if it might hold a water moccasin. When the box door didn't open all by itself and something venomous didn't slither out, I pulled the handle and spotted car rental papers and a brown-paper-wrapped package. I studied the return address and the name: Hayalasti Sixmankiller, with a PO box number in Robbinsville, North Carolina. The box was light but not empty. I tore the paper, careful to keep the address whole, and set the paper aside. The tape on the box broke easily with my fingernail and I lifted the top off, shoved aside the cotton padding, and saw a medicine bag. It was old—ancient. It was the bag I wore in my soul home. I knew instantly that it was my father's.

Green-dyed leather on one side, rougher rawhide on the other, much like Aya's, but so old it was dry-rotting. It should have been buried with him. Or given to his eldest child. Me.

"Oh," I breathed. And caught his scent. Tobacco, sweetgrass, cedar. The faint but still present scent of the Nantahala River. Tears raced down my face. I touched the bag, and though the edges were crumbling, the center was still pliable enough to take the slight weight. There were hard things inside. A bone? A quartz crystal?

"*Uni Lisi* put something in it for you. For when you're ready."

I nodded. Not ready. Not ready just now. Maybe not ever. "Thank you," I whispered.

At the house, I leaped out and raced through a sudden deluge to the door. Soaked to the skin, I worked the lock as my brother drove off into the storm. Lightning cracked down, one of the ubiquitous lightning storms of the Deep South.

I finally got the lock open and dashed inside, into chaos and screaming and commotion. Edmund—up after dawn, probably only because of the storm and the darkness it gave the day—and Eli were fighting a woman, both men covered in blood, as were the walls and the floor. With the two of them fighting together they should have killed an attacker in the first two seconds and they hadn't. Yet, this wasn't a sparring match. It was too bloody for that. Their opponent was a blond vamp, all claws and talons and rage. It was a testament to my exhaustion that I didn't even blink at the brawl, though did think that it would be a pain in the butt to get the blood off the walls. Again. But I did smell lemons.

I opened my mouth and let the flavor of her blood flow over my tongue and the roof of my mouth as I slouched in the entry, watching, trying to remember the vamp. And then it hit me. Bruiser's scion. Nicolle. I frowned, not able to remember her last name, if I'd ever heard it. Bruiser had drained her energies and taken her memories and then gifted her to Ed. I had no idea where Ed had been keeping her, but somewhere not close enough. Someone had gotten to her and claimed her for Clan Des Citrons.

I parsed the scents, smelling lemons and the sharp, sour, stagnant pond scent of madness. Her wrists and ankles bore ligature scars the way vamps' skin looked when it had been burned by silver.

"Where is she?" Nicolle screamed. "I'll rip her heart out!"

I figured she meant me. Just a wild guess.

Ed vaulted across the kitchen table, his talons ripping at her. More blood on the walls. *Crap.* If the lemon clan set her free and tracked her, then they knew where we lived. If she had gotten away—which her scarring suggested—then if I shifted to blood hound, I could follow her back to them. If I was willing to risk losing myself to the hunt and never finding myself again. Becoming blood hound was dangerous.

Beast thought at me, *Ugly dog. Good nose. Do not want to be ugly dog tomorrow and tomorrow and tomorrow.*

I slid my hands into the slits in my clothing and pulled weapons. A wood stake and a semiautomatic nine-mil. It was loaded with regular ammo, but it should slow her down. Nicolle was a young-ish vamp and they tended to be less resistant to weapons of all kinds.

I hesitated, remembering the path of blood Aggie had shown that I was treading. But. I wasn't killing. I was swatting down a crazy-assed vamp.

"Nicolle!" I shouted.

Everything stopped. And then Nicolle leaped at me, totally vamped out. I raised the gun and fired. Mid-center body mass. She didn't die but she did scream, that awful ululation of a vamp dying, or thinking they are. She dropped to the ground, landing in a three point balance, a tripod, both feet and one hand. When she thrust herself up, I stabbed low, into her belly, hitting her descending aorta, or whatever passed as such for vamps. She fell. Lay there, paralyzed, leaking onto the wood floors. If our house was ever a crime scene, the cops would think the place had been the home base of a couple dozen mass murderers.

Ed and Eli fell back, exhausted. Ed pushed off his perch almost instantly and went to Eli. "Let me heal you."

My second set his weapons on the kitchen table for cleaning and pulled off his T-shirt. His dark chest was scored with talon marks and too much blood. Ed sliced his fingers with his blade and went to work healing the bleeding mess. Neither man looked at me.

"Somebody want to tell me what's happening?" I asked.

Edmund huffed softly through his nose. I was pretty sure he was breathing to make up for the battle and his own blood loss. "She came in through the back. Over the brick wall. From Katie's." Fear slammed through me. I turned that way and Ed said, "Dion called. Everyone is fine. He locked the girls in the kitchen and threw holy water on Nicolle."

I toed her over and spotted a scald on her shoulder and neck. Nicolle glared at me. It was all she could do with the ash wood in her belly. That and leak.

"And she wanted . . ."

"To kill you," Eli said. "Natch."

Natch was my word and I shook my head at him.

"She was dropped off at Katie's by a dark SUV," Alex said. "Plates reported stolen an hour ago."

I shifted my body forward to see him and Bodat coming out of the laundry room where they had taken shelter. The Kid was armed with a handgun. Bodat was carrying a broom and was more pasty than usual. He also stank of fear.

"No way to track her back to the enemy," Alex said.

"Is there always this much blood?" Bodat asked, his voice shaky.

"This is nothing," Alex said, his voice light but his eyes hard, maybe remembering his own near-death.

"Alex, please call for the Council House's cleanup crew." Ed bent and lifted Nicolle into his arms, which must have shifted the position of the stake in her belly because she swiveled her head to me in one of those not-human moves that's a lot more like a lizard or a bird than a mammal.

"George is mine," she whispered, the smell of the lie on her breath, leaking from her with her blood and the scent of lemons. "We love each other. We have been lovers for weeks." When I didn't react she shouted, "He's mine!"

"She's been turned by Des Citrons," I said. "We need to know where they are. How many they are. What their plans are."

Edmund hesitated as if weighing my unspoken command to drink her down. "I will discover all that she knows, my mistress, assuming that she knows anything at

all." That sounded as if he agreed with my unspoken request, so that was good. "Rosanne Romanello has decided not to participate in the Sangre Duello. Therefore,
I will have Nicolle shipped to Sedona at sunset."

Nicolle screamed, "Nooooo!"

Ed carried her deeper into the living room, where he
opened the hidden door into his sun-protected hidey-hole
and slipped inside. The shelving unit closed behind him,
cutting off her scream.

"Eli?" I asked.

"I'm good. Coulda used a few more minutes with the
fanged healer, but it's after sunrise." He looked out the window at the drenching rain before he started up the stairs. I
followed, taking in his back. In the human world he would
have needed stitches. Maybe a lot of stitches. In the ranger
world and the world of vamps, not so much. "What?" he
said to me, as if he could tell I was staring at his wounds.

"Ed missed some. You need an urgent care center."

"Whyn't you just put pressure on it all and tape me up.
Ed can heal me tonight. It'll be more expedient than a
trip to urgent care."

Expedient was Eli's word, used whenever I wanted
him to get medical care. Home remedies were more *expedient* than drugs. Pressure and butterfly bandages were
more *expedient* than stitches. "Dumb man," I said.

Eli shrugged, which made him bleed faster, and led
the way to his bathroom.

I pulled the covers over my head, hearing rain scudding
against the windows. Not thinking. Not feeling. But I
rolled back and lifted the boxing gloves off the bedpost,
snuggling with them under the covers. Breathing deeply
of Onorio scent. Wishing I could tell Bruiser about the
sweat house and the revelations of my past. Wishing he
was here with me, holding me.

Dreams dragged me under.

Bruiser texted me after one p.m. with the words, *Lunch?
My place? Not cooking but got goodies. Will send a car.*
Subtext: he'll send a car instead of worrying that I'd walk

and confront a killer again. The shooter (if there had been one aiming for him, or me, or both of us, the last time I took a walk) was still missing. The lemon-smelling one. Right.

I texted back, *Send car in 15.* I'd had nowhere near enough sleep, but the five-plus hours would have to do. Besides, I needed to tell him about Nicolle's attack and see what Alex had on Clan Des Citrons. I hung the boxing gloves back on the bedpost and crawled out of bed.

I threw on jeans and boots and a leather jacket. It was almost cool enough in NOLA for my traditional winter wear. I kept weapons to a minimum—a couple of stakes, a short-bladed silver-plated knife in my boot, and a single-holster shoulder harness with an old but trusty H&K. Left my hair down. I was ready ten minutes before the car was due and so I woke up Alex, who was asleep on the couch. "Update."

Alex made a noise that could have come from a seventy-year-old woman as he sat up and woke his electronics. "I got more vid of the car that picked up Dominique at HQ. One was a security cam shot of the car."

I felt something settle heavily in my midsection, right above my vaunted gut.

"And?" I asked softly.

"Brive-la-Gaillarde, France, is the hunting territory of the Blood Master of Clan Des Citrons. Her name is Julietta Tempeste. And she came to the U.S. on a tourist visa two months ago. She was sucking face with Dominique in the getaway car."

"Last known address?" I asked.

"Charleston, South Carolina. But I tracked one of her credit cards to a Hampton Inn off I-10, four days ago. She checked out. Probably in town now."

"Probably sent people ahead to gather up any dissatisfied local fangheads."

"I've put a ping on her credit card use. If she shows up I'll let you know and get as much of the video of her entourage as possible, with IDs and dossiers. But I got more."

"Go on."

"There was another face in the SUV."

"Crowded."

"Right. And the face was someone you fought before. Bancym M'lareil."

I'd staked Cym, but she had gotten away. I should have found her again and taken her head. Hindsight and all that. Regret was a bitch. "I'm betting Dominique took her off the battlefield when I killed Shoffru and healed her. Then they swore to the lemon heads."

"Probably working with the enemy from the very beginning," Alex said.

"Thanks, Kid. Bodat?" I nudged him awake where he snored in a chair. "Either shower or you can move the desk to the back porch."

"I bathed yesterday!"

"Day before, dude," Alex said.

Bodat sighed and headed for the stairs.

"Hey, Kid," I said. Alex turned his head to me again. "You done good." Alex grinned with pride and tilted his head at me in a gesture that was pure Eli.

It was still raining when I got to Bruiser's third-floor apartment. I knocked before opening the door and toeing out of the Lucchese boots I had pulled on against the rain. The music was turned down low, something bluesy and jazzy all at once and the place smelled heavenly. Bruiser smelled even better when he opened his arms and I exhaled against his chest, sorta melting into him. I was tall, too skinny, but solid muscle and stronger than most men, thanks to my skinwalker abilities. But Bruiser was bigger and taller and though I was capable of taking care of myself, he always made me feel safer. And there was something about a man in a soft flannel shirt and worn-out jeans that hyped up the comfort level for me.

"Are you well, love?"

"I'm just ducky. And you smell fabulous."

I felt his mouth curl up against the side of my head. "I have smoked salmon, butternut squash soup made with white wine, three flavors of goat cheese, and bruschetta."

"Sorry. What? I zoned out after smoked salmon."

He chuckled and took my hand, leading me to the kitchen and the tall white leather stools that fronted the island. It was cool today and Bruiser had kept the tall French doors closed on the temps and the rain so it was cozy in the apartment. He poured me a glass of white wine, ladled steaming butternut squash soup into big soup bowls, and set one in front of me. He was doing the three-course-meal thing. Probably as the only way to get me to eat anything more than the meat.

Tears filled my eyes. I blinked them away, but not before he saw them, or smelled them.

"Jane?" Alarm in his tone.

But I held up my hand and shook my head. "I'm good. Just sleep deprived and tired and . . . and I feel so . . . grateful? Happy?" I reached over and took his hands, squeezing them as I bowed my head, saying a silent thanks. Wordlessly, I listed the ways my life was better, richer, happier. Tears scalded down my face as I silently prayed.

When I stopped, he said softly, "And I am eternally thankful for Jane Yellowrock in my life. Amen."

I lifted my eyes to his and was startled to see tears pooled there, mirroring my own. Except I was all salty and snotty and splotched, I was sure, and he was still gorgeous.

"There was a time when I believed that I was nothing in life without the Mithrans, without my position with Leo. That without his blood I'd be useless and lacking in value of any sort. And then I met you, a woman with enough power to stand against him, tall and strong and vibrant. Without being dependent on drinking blood." He kissed my knuckles, released one hand, and lifted his glass in a toast. "You give me courage to be Onorio. To Jane Yellowrock."

"And to us," I toasted back and drank. And said, "Holy crap, this is good!" I sipped again. "I actually like this one. It's really, really good! It's—" I had no wine-type words to describe it.

"Buttery," Bruiser said. "You always like buttery whites. It's excellent with the soup."

I sopped my face with the cloth napkin and spooned

some soup into my mouth. I wasn't fond of squash, but this stuff was different. "Apples. It has apples in it. And something green and sweet. And chicken stock."

"Anise," Bruiser said. He was trying to share with me his own appreciation of wine and fine food. "It's from the anise, or fennel, plant."

I placed the cloth in my lap, slung my loose hair out of the way, and sat like the lady one of the housemothers had tried to make of me. "I like it."

We ate. And ate. And when the soup was gone and the wine bottle was empty and the salmon was picked down to the bones, Bruiser took a warm towel and wiped my hands clean. The towel smelled of oranges and so did his mouth when he kissed me and led me to the couch. "Sit. We need to talk and work for a bit."

"Yada yada."

He sat beside me and pulled a soft fuzzy blanket over us. "Yada," he agreed. "But I can rub your feet while we chat."

"You are the best boyfriend ever."

He took my feet and gently squeezed them. "You first."

I started with the easy stuff, telling him about Aya and Aggie One Feather, the usual debrief stuff. "But there's something else. The Kid tracked Julietta Tempeste. She came to the U.S. on a tourist visa two months ago. Alex is trying to track her."

"Clan Des Citrons. Does Leo know?" he asked.

"I texted him an update."

His fingers worked the kinks out of my feet as he thought it through. Bruiser frowned, the lines on either side of his nose pulling down. Those lines had become deeper with worry and with the problems that piled up against us.

His frown softened. "My turn." He told me stuff I didn't half listen to. "Leo got a letter in the mail from the Carusos."

"The old funeral home directors, the ones who created revenants and the revenant concoction?"

"Yes. The letter was held by their attorneys here in

New Orleans, and mailed when it became clear that Titus Flavius Vespasianus would come ashore. They acted against Leo for decades and left under duress because Laurie's daughter was being held by Titus. They deliberately left that bottle of Titus's secret revenant potion in their fridge for Leo to find."

"Deliberately? Are we supposed to fall for that?"

"The lawyer agreed to be bled and read by Leo. He believes it to be true. Leo wants us to save the entire Caruso family if possible, if he wins the Sangre Duello."

"Easy peasy. Not."

Bruiser smiled slightly. "Katie is in Atlanta. She invaded the lairs of a dozen Mithrans and ash-staked them in their sleep, disabling them. Then she dragged them to a room filled with silver-plated scion prisons. She'll start her own negotiations tonight."

"Katie did that in the *daytime*?" I enunciated the last word. "Because, vampires."

"Katie slept in the blood of eight clans. She will be the strongest Mithran in the Americas for quite some time."

"Meaning that if she wanted Leo's position she could have it."

"Indeed." He kneaded harder into the arch of my foot.

I might have moaned. "You have very talented fingers."

"I do. And I'll take you to bed and prove it soon." His fingers pressed and rolled and crept and knuckled up my calf to a sensitive spot in the middle of my calf.

"Oh . . . Holy moly."

"Meanwhile, Lawrence is recuperating." When I got an eyelid to open and looked blank, he said, "Lawrence Hefner. Leo's valet? Injured in the were attack, trying to save Leo?"

I nodded, closing my eyes. Lack of sleep was catching up to me. "He hates being called Larry."

"He has protested being in bed with Gee DiMercy, most vociferously. Leo found it necessary to promise to skin Gee alive if he so much as tried anything of a sexual nature with Lawrence."

Gee would still try something. Something innocuous.

Just to give Larry a hard time. I smiled and stretched to give Bruiser access to the tendon on the outside of my other foot.

"Leo told me about the potential three islands for the duel," I said, "but what happens if the negotiations with Titus end up with us all in international waters, on a boat, instead of on land? Wouldn't that leave NOLA open for a coup d'état?"

"Not if Edmund is left onshore."

My breathing almost stopped at that. Edmund. Leo's heir. One of the top vamp fighters in the United States. "That's why Leo made Edmund his official heir. To protect New Orleans," I said.

"And you the Dark Queen," Bruiser said quietly, his fingers stopping, to simply hold my feet. "Between the two of you, with your ability to timewalk, you could protect the city and her people."

"He's planning to leave me ashore if an island isn't chosen. Son of a gun. I didn't know," I said, just as softly, touching my belly and the faint pain there. Indigestion maybe. "I didn't understand that move on the chessboard. Making me DQ wasn't because he's selfish. It was because he's . . ." I stopped. No way was I going to say Leo Pellissier was a good man. "A good king."

"Yes. He is." There was something soft and sad in his tone, as if he wished Leo had been a better man too.

"But if Titus knows all this about Ed and me, that we could hold the city, then . . ." I opened both eyes and said, "Then what?"

"Then he won't push to have the fight in the water, but on land, land that Leo owns or at least has some appearance of owning. Titus will want to kill you, Edmund, and Leo at the Duello."

I closed my eyes again, letting the ramifications run through me.

Long pleasurable minutes later, Bruiser said, "Leo has scrapped your idea of having all his people go naked at the opening ceremonies of the Sangre Duello to shock and dismay the EVs."

"Thank God." I grinned evilly. "Too cold?"

"Precisely. Though he did profess sadness at not being able to see you naked in your half-fighting form."

I opened one eye again and glared. "This is the stink-eye. Keep it up and I'll give you the stink-eye with both eyes."

"I consider myself warned." His brown eyes melted me inside. Along with his very, so very talented hands. "The lab has sent a preliminary report of the contents and DNA from the bottle of mixed blood found in the Caruso Family Funeral Services. They have detected the blood of five major players and perhaps a dozen lesser players, all very old and powerful Mithrans, mixed with traces of chemicals, a long list of them. And unlike the usual putrefaction and decomposition of Mithran blood, these chemicals keep it stable for a long period. Months. Perhaps years."

I opened my other eye, so I could see him with both, this time in concern. "Is it drinkable? Can humans or vamps drink it to be turned?"

"No. But it stops necrosis of flesh, is bactericidal, and speeds healing dramatically."

"The U.S. military PTBs would give their accumulated right testicles for that formula. Eli told me so."

The laughter in Bruiser's eyes went deeper, as if he was envisioning a pile of right private parts and a long line of pained military brass. He said, "As would any pharmaceutical company, any foreign power, any billionaire who wants to live forever without becoming bound to a vampire."

I almost said, *That sucks*, but it would have been funny and funny didn't fit here.

"They have managed to reverse engineer the formula," he said. "Leo has personally completed preliminary testing. It works."

"Mmm. And if Leo can reproduce it in quantity, he will have the single most financially lucrative and medically important pharmaceutical product to hit the health profession since penicillin."

"Indeed."

Which would give Leo almost unlimited financial revenues, until the patent ran out or someone else reverse engineered it. Right. And Leo would be in terrible danger from outside and inside forces because such a product and such an economic stranglehold would change every financial market in the world. And Leo would have all that power. I sighed. Leo, king of the world.

"Enough talk." Bruiser put my feet on the sofa, then stood and picked me up. And carried me to his bed. Enough talk indeed.

CHAPTER 13

After I Spill Some Blood and Kill Some People

Some hours later, as we lay cuddled in blankets with pillows stuffed around and behind us, I said, "So Leo isn't going to do the whole naked bit. But isn't there something else he can do to discombobulate the EuroVamps? Something . . . I don't know, American, all muscle cars and *Grease*-style hairdos?"

Bruiser stiffened, rolled over on top of me, and kissed me hard. "You are not only beautiful but you are bloody brilliant. That, my dear girl, is a lovely thought." On elbows and knees he rolled from the bed, grabbed his clothes, and was gone before I could think twice. To the empty walls, I said, "Onorios can move almost as fast as fangheads." I narrowed my eyes at the ceiling. "And I don't have a car. Dang it."

But . . . Bruiser called me beautiful. Wow.

I pulled the covers close and fell asleep.

I napped for an hour longer and then rolled out of bed feeling pretty dang wonderful. Good enough to check e-mails, answer texts, and return voice mails. And do

some research on Julietta Tempeste, head of Clan Des
Citrons. There wasn't much except that Julietta and her
predecessors as clan Blood Master had loved lemons—
lemon tea, lemon preserves, and drinking from humans
who had eaten large amounts of lemons.

I had a blitzkrieg moment. Were lemons grown in
Louisiana? And if so, where?

I did an online search and discovered that there were
three nurseries and two lemon groves within driving distance of NOLA. One of them had a large B&B, called
Lemon Grove Farm and B&B. I dressed, making calls
and getting Alex to research each of the places, with an
emphasis on the bed-and-breakfast.

By the time I got home, Alex had broken through the
security system on the B&B and found evidence that
vamps had taken over the place. In stored footage from
motion detectors, we saw two unmoving bodies on the
floor in the kitchen. People were walking past the living
room security camera in total unconcern. There was one
very clear image of Dominique. Another that looked like
Cym. And we had a name on the owners. The Stephenses,
family of five and a dog.

"When were these acquired by the surveil?" I asked.

Alex, his head bent over his screens, said, "Last one
was last night, nine twenty-seven p.m. Then, it looks like
they dismantled the system. All cameras are currently
offline. I have images of people—most of them human,
not vamps—beating the cameras with household tools. A
broom. A tire iron. Other stuff. They got every single
camera. But they forgot to wipe the memory."

I made more calls and got a team together. Within an
hour, an armed party of Derek's best and I were on the
way south and east in a caravan of armored vans. Eli and
I took up the entire bench seat behind the driver, our gear
in gobags on the floor at our feet, comms units hooked up
and tied into the main system at the house, where Alex
monitored progress at the B&B and rallied PsyLED to
meet us there.

Over my cell, which was hooked into our comms system, he said to Ayatas, "I don't give a flaming pink fla-

mingo if you're busy. My sister and brother are on the way
there with an armed team to do your job."

I was speed-loading an extra mag with silver-lead
rounds when the words *flaming pink flamingo* came over
the system and I laughed silently. Eli gave a quirked
smile, amusement and pride in his eyes.

"PsyLED is lead on this, not Jane," Ayatas said, his
irritation clear. "You inform *my* sister that she and her
team are to stay off-site until we get there."

"There are dead humans in the still shot I sent you,"
Alex said, his tone inflexible and hard and so very adult,
"and this is taking place in Leo's territory, so forgive me
if I correct you. Leo has authorized his Enforcer to proceed with 'all haste.' His words. I've contacted the state
police and passed the information along to the governor's
office. Per the MOC, PsyLED is welcome to take part in
the rescue operation, but the Enforcer to the Master of
the City of New Orleans will not be waiting to engage the
enemy." And I heard a click.

"Did you just hang up on FireWind?" Eli asked.

"Yeah," Alex said, the word staticky. "You got a problem with that, my brother?"

"Not at all. Just seeking clarification. Our ETA to the
B&B is twelve." Eli pushed his mic away.

The van swayed and bumped and thumped its way
along the road, which hadn't seen much in the way of re-
paving since Katrina. The potholes had potholes. Air blew
into the cab as we weaponed up and went over the online
visuals, which were from older satellite pics. Wrassler had
a drone ready to launch overhead to acquire on-site visuals
of the house and grounds and provide us with more visuals
than the ones currently available to us.

Except for me, the entry party were all former military
and were equipped with mechanical breaching tools and
devices, prepared with varied and dynamic techniques to
be used based on what we found on the grounds and inside the house. They were armed with shotguns loaded
with silver fléchette rounds, flashbangs, and vamp-killers,
among other, less lethal weapons. Thanks to the fact that
the house was a B&B, we had excellent intel from the

online photos, including photos of the basement with its high-placed windows. Basements were rare in South Louisiana, rare enough to make Alex take a good look at the existing pics.

A mile out, we pulled over. Into my earbuds, Alex said calmly, "The house was built in the 1880s, about twenty feet higher than most in the southern part of the state. It was built on an old Indian mound."

"Burial mound?" a voice asked.

"No," Alex said. "The local tribal peoples from as long as two thousand years ago built mounds to live on. Lots of reasons why, but the likelihood of the Mississippi and the Atchafalaya and other rivers to flood was probably the reason. No ghosts," he added.

The man who had asked chuckled as if it had been a joke. But he sounded relieved.

I heard the soft whirr of the drone when it took off and checked the video monitor on my helmet. Wrassler said, "Drone visuals on your monitors. Vehicle tracks all through the yard and on the grass. Only one car in the drive. There are no vehicles present with vamp-tinted windows."

That was bad. It meant the likelihood of vamps being on-site had just dropped drastically.

"Taking a chance and dropping the drone down to get a closer look," he said.

I had seen sites where vamps had lived and eaten and killed and departed. This had all the markers, from the stuffed mailbox to the tire tracks through the lawn to the unused and dirty children's swing set out back.

"Move out," Eli said, his voice grim. We were out of the van and jogging through the underbrush, down the road, moving out in a fan and into our assigned positions. I followed Eli up the mound into the winter-dormant foliage that covered a low wall near the carport. I could still smell jasmine. The team began to call in with their op names and positions acquired. One voice added, "Meyer lemon trees fruit year-round. These should be producing and they've been stripped of fruit—all fruit, not just the ripe ones. Recently."

I took a breath, mouth open, drawing in air over my

tongue and through my nose with a soft *scree* of sound. I covered my mic and said to Eli, "Death. Several days old. Multiple people. I don't smell . . . I don't smell, or hear, activity."

He covered his mic and said, "Copy that. Didn't know you could smell activity."

I shrugged. It wasn't something I could explain. It fell under a category of weird, like people who could walk into a house and tell if anyone had been there recently. Movement of air currents. Presence or absence of faint sounds or echoes. Whatever.

Eli said, "Tracks in the yard are hours old. I think they bugged out."

"And left the bodies," I said.

We were both right. By the time PsyLED got there, we had called the coroner and left the house to the five human corpses and the dead dog. I didn't want to think about what Des Citrons had done to the people in the B&B. But I knew this. I'd kill them when I found them.

I sent a text to Alex. *Make sure this was a random kill site. No attachment to Leo or any clan.*

He sent back, *Roger that.* The kid was growing up.

Five hours after I leaped out of bed to go to war with Des Citrons, Shemmy dropped me off at home. Eli had reached the house an hour before and I envied him the hot shower he had undoubtedly taken, as I entered the house, hearing the sound of hammers and a skill saw from the third floor, and men talking from the living room. Neither group heard me, so I stopped in the shadows of the door to eavesdrop.

Edmund said, "Titus agreed to the location, and proposed the first-round combatants. His people and Leo's are close to deciding on a time to begin. Thank you," he interjected as if he'd been given a glass of wine or a really good cookie. "Leo dispatched Derek Lee and an initial security crew, his entire housekeeping crew, and the combined and motley gangs of tattooed and disreputable-looking carpenters, electricians, and plumbers to the accepted house."

"Security is Jane's and Yellowrock Securities' job," Alex said. "Why weren't we sent?"

"Derek is taking a scouting team," Ed said. "Jane is too important in the search for Des Citrons to waste her talents watching carpenters ripping into walls and floors."

"But if Jane's there she'll make sure we have indoor plumbing. And hot showers," the Kid said.

"Showers. We don' need no stinkin' showers," Bodat said.

"Forgive my saying so," Edmund said, "but that is incorrect. You both need showers, quite desperately. What did Jane used to call you?"

"Number two? When she called my bro number one?"

"She called you shit? Dude."

"Bodat. Shut up," Alex said, sounding tired.

"What? What'd I say?"

"Stinky," Eli said, his voice with that Zen modulation it acquired when he was cleaning his weapons. "Which we'll call you again if you don't go up right now and shower. Both of you."

"Jeez. You people," Bodat said.

"Upstairs," Alex interrupted. "Let's get cleaned up and you packed. Your bus leaves for the last inhabitable room in the toe of the state in half an hour. If you're not in place we can't set up cell or satellite, and Wi-Fi on the island."

I stepped back, into my bedroom doorway.

"But what'd I say?" Bodat complained as they passed me without seeing me in the shadows.

"Things will be more primitive than usual," Edmund said. "I've seen the house, though that was over sixty years ago. Old-fashioned bathrooms and only two of them. No central heating or air-conditioning. The bedrooms without windows are limited so Mithrans will be sleeping several to a room. Humans will have only three or four rooms to choose from, mostly bunk-bed-style sleeping areas, if I recall. Ancient furniture."

Eli said, "George thinks we'll leave for the island fast

and the Duello will start in less than two days." When Edmund said nothing, Eli asked, too casually, "Have you seen the proposed list of elimination rounds?"

Edmund didn't answer.

"That bad?" he asked.

"Everyone wants to fight Jane. Every single one of the Europeans," Edmund said at last. "From Titus's sous chef to his primo."

I heard soft clicks and snaps as Eli worked, growing more noisy than usual. Edmund's admission had disturbed him. "Show me."

I had seen the list. I wanted to blow off steam. I slipped into my room and changed into exercise gear: tight, Lycra-based running pants and a padded sports bra. Bare feet. I walked into the living room and pointed at Eli. "Spar. Now." Then at Edmund. "And when I wipe the floor with him, it'll be your turn."

Edmund's lips lifted faintly. "As my mistress desires."

I didn't even bother to fuss about the mistress comment. I turned on my toes and raced up the stairs, across the construction mess, into the bedroom with the sparring mats. And faced away from the door, toward the windows. I let my body loosen. I breathed. Let my mind stop. Relaxed until a white haze filled my brain and body, not silent, but a place, a state of mind, an existence without sight, texture, or sound. An absence of sensation.

Then I let it bleed back into me. A rubberized mat covered the wood floor. I let my soles feel the mat, the cushioned perception of weight, of gravity. I smelled the chemicals that composed the mat. Heard water come on in the showers. And I heard Eli enter the room, so silent a waking cat wouldn't have heard him. The air moved. Smelling of Eli.

I ducked, dropped. Opened my eyes. Captured my balance on one foot and both fists. Swung the other leg out and around. Missed him.

Took a blow to my rib cage that sent me into the wall. I laughed. It sounded not quite right. I launched myself at him. Took a blow to my abdomen. Block block block. Strike strike. Blow. Block. Pain woke me up. My fists tightened. My crouch deepened a quarter inch. And I attacked. *Fastfastfast*. Beast chuffed through my throat.

Eli's heel came at my throat.

Killing strike. Knowing I would dodge. Because I was faster than Eli. Always had been.

Time . . . stopped.

And then . . .

I was standing in the room, eyes closed. Back to the door. And I smelled Eli.

I dropped and rolled, shouting, "Edmund!"

He was instantly in the doorway, the little pop of sound that announced a vamp moving fast. My eyes were wide. Eli, in attack position, was staring at me. I slammed my spine to the wall and foot-crawled hard, to stand against it.

"Jane?" Eli said. "What?"

"Time did something. I already had a fight with you. And now we're starting over. Something's wrong." A spike of pain lanced through my head. And I remembered time doing something weird with Leo recently. Tears welled over and fell from my eyes. Scoured down my cheeks. Though whether from what was happening or from the memories of the tortured bodies of the Stephens family at the B&B I didn't know. My skull spiked with pain and I wanted to hurl. I put one hand to my head and one to my belly, which felt hard and tight. "Something's very, very wrong."

"I'll make tea, my mistress," Edmund said. "Eli. Come with me, please."

Eli looked like he didn't want to go, but he followed Edmund. They left me there, alone in the spare bedroom with the fighting mats. The stench of rubber. And a body that hurt. As if I'd been beaten.

In the kitchen Edmund was preparing a fast cuppa chai in the Bunn coffeemaker. Eli was sitting at the table. I pulled an afghan off the couch and wrapped it around me, ignoring that it smelled of Bodat and pizza. I was cold.

I watched them. They seemed fine.

I sat at my usual place. No one said anything.

Upstairs, one shower went off. I hadn't heard it come on in this timeline.

Ed placed the mug of spiced tea in front of me. The cup was one with a saying on it. I DON'T NEED ANGER MANAGEMENT. I JUST NEED PEOPLE TO STOP PISSING ME OFF. The tea had a thick layer of frothed cream on top. My tears, which had stopped, gathered again, at the kindness. I wrapped my icy fingers around the mug and lifted it from the table. Sipped. The frothed cream made it perfect. The tea and cream were delicious and quickly helped my belly pain to ease. Ed put two Tylenol on the table and I took them without argument.

"Jane," Edmund said, when my mug was half-empty, "tell us what happened."

I gave them a blow-by-block-by-blow description of what I had experienced. They said nothing. I sipped. They looked at each other. Something about the exchange hit me as wrong, but I couldn't place it.

"Did Beast do the time change?" Edmund asked. "Your eyes were glowing gold when I got to the sparring room."

"B—" I turned my thoughts inward. Beast stared at me a moment, turned away, and padded, *pawpawpaw*, into the darkness of our minds. "Maybe," I whispered, thinking. Remembering. Especially remembering the last big fight between EuroVamps and our side, in a warehouse where a weather witch had been forced to create storms and to collect arcenciels for their timewalking magic. What if . . . what if it wasn't just me who had messed up time? What if it had been Beast too? And the witch Adan. And . . . the arcenciel trapped in the anode of crystals that same night.

That possibility hit me like a Mack truck. What if it had been all of us, in tiny little changes back along our shared timeline? And the pain in my head and belly might be contributing to it too, my messed-up genetics switching on and off and . . . changing things around me. We might all be screwed six ways from Sunday.

Edmund brought coffee to the table and poured me a second hot cup of tea. I heard the whirring sound of the new stirring device in the background, before he added a froth of cream to my cup. I was a long way from Cool Whip.

Hammers and buzzes of saws from the third floor grew loud and a sound like a stack of lumber dropped from a height shook the house. Eli's body twitched and I could tell he wanted to check on the men upstairs, but he drank his coffee instead, his eyes on me.

"Remember the fight in the warehouse?" I said after I drank through the cream. "Adan Bouvier was in a magical cage, working storm magic, blood-starved, pretty much insane. There was an arcenciel trapped in the crystal. Cerulean. Adan was using her to alter time. Beast . . . my Beast seems able to twist time too. I wasn't doing anything with time and yet I kept losing moments. Odd little things that I didn't notice immediately but that added up to me being uncertain about the sequence of events."

"That happens in battle," Eli said. "Especially after you've been in a few firefights. You lose some things. Memories will skip from event to event like a stone on still water. Others are so detailed and brilliant and sharp they play out for you like you're going through it all over again."

"Like you're experiencing it again?" I asked.

"In a way. For me it's always clearly a memory. But it can be intense and comprehensive and meticulous in detail."

"Since the warehouse fight, I've noticed small bits of time stuttering. Or two events that happened in different ways. But they both feel real." I sipped some more.

"I have called Soul, my mistress," Edmund said, bowing his head. "She and Gee will be here soon."

My fingers clenched on the warm mug. "Why?" Though I knew the answer.

"Because they and Brute are the only other time-walkers we know."

As if they knew that Ed had told me they were coming, as if they'd waited for the words to be spoken, a knock sounded on the front door. Ed let them in, murmured words of greeting and explanation. "They don't know about Beast," Eli said, his voice so low I could barely hear him. "You want me to stay while you talk? If not, I'll give you priva—"

"Stay," I said. My voice sounded a little pleading, which should have ticked me off, but didn't.

He nodded. Looked up as our guests entered the kitchen. Soul sat to my left, her billowy clothing shades of misty gray that darkened into purple near her feet. Gee, looking taller, more muscular, took a seat at the foot of the table, his hair longer and blacker. The changes were an easy adjustment for his glamour. He said, "The little goddess is evolving."

"Am I?"

"We hunted together. You flew in the form of my friend."

I had taken the form of Anzu and flown into the far north with Gee DiMercy. We had hunted were-creatures who had killed humans. "Sabina said it would be okay, but . . . skinwalker tradition teaches us that if we take the form of a sentient being, that's the first step into darkness. Am I evolving into *u'tlun'ta*? Is that what this time-changing thing is?"

"*U'tlun'ta* do not evolve. You did not take the form of a living body. You did not eat the body while it was alive so that you might also take the memories and the dreams and the hopes. That is what *u'tlun'ta* does to take the path into darkness," Soul said, which was more than I had ever been told or figured out on my own. "You did not make of her a victim. That is not why time is slipping."

Slipping. That, or timewalkers were playing with time all around me. Or . . . using me as a focus to affect their own changes on the future, if that was even possible. "Then why is time slipping?"

"Some physicists suggest that our universe is one of an ever-growing stack of universes," Gee said, "a new one created each time we make even the smallest choice."

I stared at my cup. "Right. So I'm slipping into a different universe?"

"I don't think so," Gee said. "I think you are reinventing this one in small, personal moments."

"Unconsciously," Soul said. "It can be done by accident. And it is very, very dangerous."

By accident. That sucked.

I thought about that. About all the things that had happened to me since I came to New Orleans and went to work for Leo. I had changed. Maybe too much. Maybe so much that I was trying to undo some of the changes, subconsciously, by accident, or, *crap*, what if it was happening even in my sleep? No. No way. I slowed my breathing, forced calm into me. Edmund appeared and placed a cup of tea in front of Soul and a cup of spiced coffee at Gee's elbow. "You're not their servant," I snapped. "You're the heir to the Master of the City."

"I am also hospitable to guests, my mistress." There was censure in his tone. Mild but there.

I blew out a breath that was too aggravated to be a sigh and drained my mug. "Sorry." I set the ceramic mug on the table with a small thump. "You're right."

Ed replaced my mug with a fresh one. Chai. Frothed cream on top. I was an ass. "Thank you, Edmund," I said in my best Bethel Christian Children's Home manners. "The tea is delicious." Ed didn't reply. I said, "Soul, if my DNA started forming new strands, would that make it possible that I'd slip into timewalking without intent, even unconscious intent?"

The room was very still. Upstairs, two men were arguing over a measurement. One of them called the other a shithead. I'd have to say something. We didn't cuss in this house. But I didn't get up. I stared at my mug instead.

"How has your DNA changed?" Soul whispered.

"It's got an extra strand. Maybe two."

"I see," Soul said. "Timewalkers from this world often have peculiar genetics. Some have fallen into time-slipping."

"What happened to them?"

"I've known only a few. Two vanished. One died of very fast-acting malignancies. The others lived long lives and died happy, surrounded by friends and family."

The last part sounded like a lie, but it also sounded good, so I let it stand. "How did they survive?"

"They learned self-control. They learned to be happy in spite of illness, pain, war, pestilence, and death."

"Drink your tea, my mistress," Ed said softly.

I drank my tea. Self-control. That was something my housemothers had tried to pound into me, growing up. "Is there a class I can take?" I asked, a small smile trying to find my lips. "Maybe an online course? I'm kinda busy right now, but I'm highly motivated and ready to learn."

Soul smiled with me. "This has happened only when you are fighting? In danger? When others you love are in danger?"

"This time, Eli kicked just as I stood. His foot was coming for my throat. Killing strike. He hadn't pulled the kick yet and it was about to impact." Eli's eyes tightened, a minuscule move as if a single nerve twitched. To him I said, "Yes. I was going to avoid the kick. But my brain said otherwise." To Soul, I said, "So far as I've noticed, it's battle, when I think I'm about to be injured. Muscle memory takes over. I'm fighting. Then things are different. Little things, but—" I stopped again, remembering when Ayatas shot me. Beast had stopped time then. I frowned, wondering how much she contributed to time-slippage. Could anything be considered insignificant when it came to stopping time?

"You must not lose focus," Soul said. "When fighting, you must remain rooted to the Earth, your center of gravity aligned with the Earth's. You must fight with the concentration of meditation."

"Zen," Eli said. "The Zen of warfare. The knowledge that battle is taking place around you. That you are in the middle of it. But without leaving the inviolability of your own concentration." Eli read books on war and fighting. Strategy and tactics. The mind-set of the warrior.

"You think that'll work?"

"I've known a few guys in my life who could do that. They're all dead."

"Did they live a long life and die happy, surrounded by friends and family?" I asked.

"Sure."

A lie. Lots of lies floating in the air. "Thank you for coming," I said to Soul and Gee. "I appreciate the effort, the time, and the wisdom you shared with me." And that was pure Tsalagi. Way better than the housemothers' prattle.

They said their good-byes and left, Edmund letting them into the night and shutting the door.

"Let's spar," Eli said. "You can practice meditating and I'll practice hurting you."

"That sounds like a good idea, except that I'm so full of tea I'd slosh." But I was thinking that I didn't have time to learn a whole new way to fight in time for the bloody battles.

"Go pee and meet me in the workout room. And this time you'll know I don't mean to hurt you. You'll keep that uppermost in your mind. You have to be able to control this before the firefight." He meant the Sangre Duello. Eli got up and left, his feet silent on the stairs.

Edmund came to the table. He stood beside me, placing his hand on my shoulder.

"The Sangre Duello will soon be over. For good or ill, all our lives will change. And you can rest. Take a . . . What is the American word? Retreat? A strategic withdrawal? You can ride Bitsa into your mountains and heal."

"That's a good idea." I had taken a break once, when Bitsa was being built. I'd nearly been beheaded and was so close to death that it took a long time to get well. I'd hunted and slept and eaten a lot of game. Shifted as often as I needed to continue healing.

"You haven't ridden Bitsa since you came back with her," Edmund said. "Why?"

"Bitsa is for freedom," I said before I thought. "I'm tied here, until the Sangre Duello is done. It's the only way I can protect the people I love."

"Your little witches. Your godchildren. Children who would be killed or taken and turned by Titus Flavius Vespasianus, Emperor of the Mithrans and renowned hater of homosexuals, Jews, people of color, and witches."

"Well. That's great to know. Yeah. So, thank you for that insight. A retreat is a great idea. After I spill some blood and kill some people. But for now, I'll go spar with Eli and find my center. My Zen moment." If I sounded a little sarcastic, really, who could blame me?

* * *

At midnight I was standing under an icy shower, trying to
let the cold water beat the bruises out of my muscles.
Fighting while in Zen meditation was painful. Not letting
time slip wasn't as hard as I expected, but it did require
total concentration, concentration that left instinctive
fighting moves all to muscle memory and Beast. In some
ways that was better than my usual sparring methods; in
other ways it was not up to my usual speed and skill level.
I had jammed knuckles and purple bruises along my rib
cage. My knee was wobbly. I needed to shift to Beast and
heal, but there wasn't time. Time. Ha-ha. If I got the
chance to shift I'd take it, but it didn't look likely. Mean-
time it was Gatorade, hot tea, ice packs, and the cold water of a bruise-fighting shower.

I heard banging on my door, and knew the boys
wouldn't bother me unless it was an emergency. I threw
on a robe and opened it to see the Kid standing there. He
said, "We got a problem. The Stephens family at the
B&B? The one Des Citrons drank down? They were the
blood-servants of Laurie Caruso."

I frowned at him, trying to put that together with logic
and sense.

"The clan didn't end up there by accident or just because they owned some lemon trees," he said. "I'm betting they were looking for the bottle of blood the Carusos
left behind."

"The bottle Leo's had for long enough to get it reverse
engineered," I breathed. "How many other blood-servants
did the Carusos leave?"

"One family in Marigny, the Chiswells, husband and
wife and two kids. House is near the corner of Frenchmen
Street and Dauphine. I've sent the GPS to our cells."

I pushed the door closed and dressed fast in my red
leathers, with enough weapons to fight off a platoon of
vamps. I opened my door to see Eli racing down the
stairs. Followed him into the street and into the SUV. He
handed me a comms set and I put it on, fastening my

silver-plated titanium gorget around my neck. "Intel on the place? Backup?"

"Nothing." He roared the vehicle the wrong way down the street. "The Tequila boys are off doing Leo's initial security work. No answer on Ayatas's or Rick's cell. We could twiddle our thumbs and wait."

"No."

"Then we're on our own."

I sent a text and got an immediate reply. "No, we aren't. We have Jodi from NOPD, and SWAT."

"Hooahh."

It had been a while since Eli had used the old Army term, meaning, "Good," and "Let's do this," and a dozen other things. I figured it was a good omen.

Eli slowed and I took video of the place. The Chiswells' home was a brick Creole town house with arched windows at ground level, rectangular windows on the second floor, and arched windows on the third. Nonfunctional shutters were painted a deep emerald green and the front door was painted a paler shade of the same color. Iron balconies were on both upper floors and an iron gate enclosed the front porch. The roof was steeply pitched, with side gables and multiple dormers. Lots of plants were out front and on every balcony. A wall surrounded a tropical garden in back, though I didn't smell lemons. I did smell blood, not much, but fresh.

My cell rang. I accepted the call. "Jodi."

"You sure about this?"

"I smell blood. We don't have time to negotiate. We need to do this now."

"What do you mean you smell—Oh. Right," she grumbled. "ETA is four. Smell's not enough to be considered exigent circumstances or threat to public safety. Pull down Dauphine, park, and stay put. We're waiting on a paper." She meant a warrant to enter the house. And that might take a long time.

"Right." I ended the call.

Eli pulled over into a parking spot and we got out. "Four minutes is enough time for a recon. Your nose and my infrared and low-light and we'll know where everyone is," he said.

I pulled on Beast's night vision and the world turned silver-gray tinted with greens and charcoal. "Windows are closed, drapes closed. Let's do a walk-by. Let me see if I can pinpoint the blood." Immediately I wrapped one arm around Eli's waist, as if we were out for a stroll.

Eli tapped his mic as we came abreast of the front door. "Cameras on front porch."

"I'm in the system," Alex said. "They came in the front. Fast and violent. Four vamps and three humans. System went offline, but again they didn't wipe the history."

"The blood I smell is at the front of the house," I said as we rounded the corner and slipped down the narrow ease-way between the Chiswells' and the house next door. From above us, I heard a scream, full of terror. A child's voice. I remembered the bodies at the bed-and-breakfast. I stopped. Eli stopped, his eyes scanning everywhere. The scream came again, terrified. In pain. "Third floor," I said, following the sound up. "Back of the house."

"Over the fence in back."

"Copy that," I said, and tapped my mic. "Call Jodi. Tell her we have vamps in the house and children in distress on the third floor. We're considering that exigent circumstances. Going over the wall and in at the back. Tell her to hit the house at the front, ASAP."

"Okay." The mic went silent. Then he said, "Jodi is pissed, but they're parked three houses down on Frenchmen. They'll enter in two."

Eli checked his watch. "Your Beast has senses I don't. You take point." Pulling on Beast's strength, I raced to the fence and leaped. I caught myself with Beast's grace and peeked over the top before I slipped over, into the leaves of an elephant ear plant. I managed to break several of the huge leaves. Eli landed beside me and broke some more.

There were four cars in the small lot. Eli said, "Dried mud and grass on the bumper. Centipede, just like the Stephens place." He moved toward the back door and a security light came on. We ducked back into the foliage just as the door opened. A vamp stuck his head out, spotted a cat on a windshield, cursed, and shut the door. We didn't hear a lock turn. But I did smell a lot of blood.

Kits, Beast growled.

"We're going in now," I said into the mic. To Eli I added, "Stay behind me. I heal better than you do."

Eli said nothing, but he raced up the stairs and turned the knob. The door opened. I rushed in and stopped, my back to the wall. Into his mic Eli muttered, "Back door was unlocked. A child is screaming. Repeat. We have breached the back. Wall directly ahead, stairs to the right."

The entry was a well-lighted mudroom. The vamp who had stuck his head outside was close. I could smell him. We needed him to be quiet. We needed him out of action. We also needed him alive to question. I pointed to my eyes and then at the doorway to the left, telling Eli I was taking a look. I drew a fourteen-inch vamp-killer and advanced on the opening.

Three feet from me, the vamp walked around the corner. His eyes met mine. Bled black; his fangs snapped down. He vamped out. He started to shout. I raised the vamp-killer and shoved straight forward, my feet automatically moving into La Destreza. The point of the blade entered his throat and cut through. Blood shot over me. The vamp dropped. The blade, hanging in the spinal processes in back, dragged my hand down.

I waggled the blade and pulled it loose, stuck an ash stake into his belly. But I didn't take his head. *If* he survived, he might give us intel.

Eli pointed up the narrow stairs, probably servants' stairs way back when. He raced up. Taking point. Stupid man. I followed. We were on the second-floor landing, staring up the stairs to the third floor, when I heard a squeak on the front porch.

I ran faster, passing Eli. At the top of the stairs I followed the scent of blood and pointed to a room with the door open. Light spilled into the hallway. We raced inside. On the floor just inside the room was an adult male, his throat cut, the blood already stopped. Three people sat on the bed staring at him. Silent. Horrified. The back window was open. I raced to it and looked out.

The front door blew in with a crash. "NOPD! Freeze! Put down your weapons."

I caught a glimpse of a body clearing the back fence in a single bound. Vamp. I dove out the window. "Jane!" Eli shouted. I dropped and landed on a car, caving in the roof but breaking my fall. I took off after the vamp, over the wall. I was halfway down the street when I heard a car start back at the house. It bashed through the gate and pulled away at speed. In the other direction, the running vamp was gone. "Crap. Crap, crap, crap, damn it, *crap.*" That wasn't nearly strong enough. I had to go back inside and deal with a dead father. A traumatized family. I really needed to learn how to cuss properly.

I went in through the back door, noted that the vamp I'd staked was gone, relinquished my weapon to the SWAT OIC, and went on upstairs. The woman was holding her children and weeping; the children were wailing. Jodi was trying to calm them. SWAT officers were everywhere. I stood in the corner and listened until Jodi managed to calm the woman enough to ask questions. Only one answer was important to me.

"They kept asking us for the bottle. But Laurie left it for Leo Pellissier, in a place where his people would find it."

"Why?" I asked, wondering if she'd give me confirmation about the contents of the letter Leo had received. "Trying to cover their bases?"

"No." The woman looked up. Despite the blood on her face and the panicked children in her arms, she had dignity and poise that made me embarrassed for what I'd just said. "Laurie hoped Leo would figure it out and then rescue them. They didn't change sides willingly. The emperor has held her daughter prisoner for decades. She's on that damned boat in the gulf." She smelled of the truth.

Beast thought at me, *Kits are afraid. Jane should change to Beast so Beast can comfort them.*

Not this time. Beast's killing claws and teeth would frighten them.

Beast has big killing teeth, she agreed.

I turned and went down the stairs. Outside. And away from the fear and horror and the stench of blood and death. Texted Alex what had happened. We had lost our only lead into the lemon clan.

We had been home less than an hour when my cell sang out with the ringtone Alex had programmed for Leo, "Night of the Vampire" by Roky Erickson. I turned off the shower water, wrapped in a bath sheet that covered me from neck to knees, as if Leo could see me over the cell (which had never been set up with FaceTime just because of moments like this), and answered the call on the line about slipping in blood. It seemed appropriate. I said, "How may the Enforcer and the mistress of Clan Yellowrock assist the Master of the City?"

"Pack your bag," Leo ordered. "You and the Youngers are needed at the house on Spitfire Island. All has been done that can be done without you. It is time to finalize security measures." The call ended. I heard a cell ring upstairs, Leo calling the boys. He left little to chance these days.

I set the cell aside, facedown, and twisted my hair, letting the rinse water drain down the shower. I dressed in jeans and layers—a warm silk-knit tee, a tunic sweater, and a short denim jacket. Wool socks. A pair of iridescent green snakeskin Lucchese boots. It was warm for winter, but it was still winter.

I got out my larger gobag and a pack of plastic zip bags. I tossed in a gallon bag of toiletries, a quart bag full of makeup, mostly different kinds of red lipstick, but mascara and other stuff too. I packed a gallon bag of silver stakes, another gallon bag of ash wood stakes. One pair of dancing shoes. My most comfy combat boots. A hanging bag of dress clothes and the red and white leathers. Since I didn't know the sleeping arrangements, I rolled up two pairs of sweats and put them in a plastic bag with undies and socks. T-shirts. An extra pair of jeans. Flops.

I stood at the foot of the bed and studied the bag. It was nearly full. I had come to New Orleans with less than this.

From the top of the closet I pulled all the magical trinkets and magical weapons and stuffed them into the bag, including the Glob and *le breloque*, the gold laurel-leaf crown that had probably helped me become the Dark Queen. I added the robe that hung on the back of my bathroom door. I almost never used it, but the sleeping arrangements sounded like summer camp. I added my pillow. I had become addicted to high-quality pillows, mattresses, and linens. My life was out of control.

The gobag was too full of magic and undies for weapons, so I started a pile to the side. When I had stripped my room of everything that went bang, I sat on the gobag and got it zipped shut, but it was a near thing. I nearly stabbed myself with the stakes in a place that was totally inappropriate for traditional staking. I was still sitting on the bag when Eli's scent swept under the door and he knocked. "Come in."

He opened the door. "Orders from Leo."

"I got them too. Ruined the end of a perfectly good shower."

Eli studied the bag under my backside. "You got weapons in that?"

I could have told him about the magical stuff and the stakes, but when Eli asked that question, he meant things that go bang. "No."

"Ammo?"

"No."

"Fighting leathers?"

I narrowed my eyes at him. "In the hanging bag."

He frowned hard. "Do not tell me you packed girly stuff in that."

"I did. I totally did. And I'm not ashamed." Much. I let the teasing drift away. "Something I need to say. You are my brother. My second. You are the one I depend on most when my life is on the line."

Eli's eyes didn't move from me, but I knew he had spotted the printed papers on my bedside table. "You've been studying the Vampira Carta and the Sangre Duello."

"Not as much as I should have. But there's this thing called La Danza de los Maestros de Sangre."

"Dance of the Blood Masters." A grin split Eli's face. Not a happy grin. A bloodthirsty grin. The grin of a man who had just seen a move on the vamp chessboard that he had missed until now. "Babe." His grin went wider. "Leo's a sneaky bastard."

"He assures me he was conceived on the legal side of the sheets. That was an important thing back then. But yeah. Loopholes are a good thing. And Leo was thinking ahead. Way ahead."

"He couldn't blood-bind you, and you could use witch amulets like a pro, so he promoted you."

I gave a minuscule nod.

"And because he promoted you to Blood Master of your own clan, and to Dark Queen status, you can claim the dance."

La Danza de los Maestros de Sangre was a specific way of fighting between Blood Masters. It was magic and weapons and no-holds-barred fighting—claws and teeth, guns and blades, silver stakes—like mixed martial arts and sword fighting and magic all at once. All together. I nodded.

"But you still packed like a girl?"

"I did. Makeup and a scrap of lace formal and everything. So he won't expect La Danza de los Maestros de Sangre from me."

Eli's face went stiff and unyielding. "You'll mess with time in La Danza."

I nodded.

"You'll get a headache. Stomachache."

"That just means I'll have to kill him and get back in time fast."

Eli's scowl went deeper, drawing down the lines on his mouth. I had won. And we now had four secret weapons in the Sangre Duello. Me in half-form, me as Clan Yellowrock Blood Master, me as Dark Queen, and La Danza.

"Eli," I said softly. "Having the Sangre Duello on an island no one knows about means that any vamps who want to chase us down and interfere will have a harder time. And Uncle Sam's ICE and other enforcement agencies will also have a harder time. Win-win."

"Still doesn't outweigh the dangers of you time-walking." He walked away.

He had a point.

A moment later he reappeared in my doorway with his weapons gobag that was already half-full. "Don't forget extra ammo for the Benelli."

CHAPTER 14

Then You Date Her

The Gulf of Mexico raced beneath us, black water and whitecaps and the occasional boat lights below, stars and a clouded moon above. Wind and prop noise were muffled through the earphones as Grégoire's Vietnam-era Bell Huey blasted through the night, the pilot making excellent time.

Hate flying, Beast thought at me. *Hate helo-copters. Hate bird wings. Will bite Leo for making Beast go on helo-copter.*

Yeah, yeah, yeah. Just give me warning. I want to enjoy that.

Will tell Jane. But will bite Leo. Hate earthquake.

I thought about that one and realized she was referring to the intense vibration of the helo. It was pretty awful. *Okay by me, but wait until after the Sangre Duello. I need Leo alive. Or undead. Whatever.*

Beast is best ambush hunter. Best ambush fighter. Beast is best at everything. Why does Jane want Leo alive? To mate?

No. Leo is like a big-cat on the African plains, I thought as the helo rumbled into my veins and nerves, making my body quiver. *He has smarts and claws and big teeth. He's a good fighter. A really good leader. He's a good ambush hunter. We need him.*

Like male African lion in pride? Big-cat to fight off other cats? Big-cat to keep kits alive?

Yes.

Ambush hunter. Leo caught Jane and drank from her. Leo won. Leo beat Jane.

The memory of Leo trying to bind me slammed through me. I gripped the safety handle by my head. My mouth went dry. *Yes.*

Leo is good ambush hunter. Leo beat Jane. Beast beat Leo. Leo will keep kits of Asad and Nantale alive?

I had forgotten about that, about the kits. *Leo and I will.*

Leo and we will keep kits alive. Many more than five fights. We will kill many more than five vampires and their humans to save kits. And Beast will drink the blood of her enemies.

Five was as high as Beast could count. *Beast. No drinking blood.*

Beast didn't reply.

Beast. No drinking blood, vampire or human.

The cat padded away from me, showing me her back, a sign of insult. *Dang cat.*

The helo shuddered hard and banked. Alex, sitting beside me, gagged. The Kid looked green and sweaty in the dull lights. I handed him one of the specially made puke bags. He took it with shaking fingers.

Spitfire Island was a spit of land with a house that didn't seem to be on any map. It was hidden behind and to the west of Last Island on the barrier islands, and it was a lot bigger than I expected, for a name that had *spit* and *fire* in it. I had been expecting an island small enough to spit across or one small enough to raze with a single campfire. Instead, in the landing lights of the helo, I saw low-growing, wind-twisted trees, sawgrass waving in the rotor wash, and palmetto palms. Birds flew into the night in fear or guarded nests beneath the trees. What looked like an alligator—usually a freshwater critter—slid into the salty water of the Gulf of Mexico. And I saw the house.

Holy crap. The house.

I had envisioned a cottage with four bedrooms. I saw a green-painted three-story house perched on dozens of massive poles driven into the sandy land, with a staircase that rose twelve or fifteen feet from sand to a front porch. There were working metal shutters painted dark green lashed back to reveal white-painted windows that were open to the night air, with light blasting into the night. The house—mansion—had a simple hip roof atop the third floor with some kind of metal grating over it that was tied into the ground with long metal rods. Solar panels were built into the mesh, and I wondered if it would power all the lights glaring into the night.

There was no grass on the grounds, but the sand was pristine and sparkled in the landing lights of Leo's helicopter. Low trees caught the bobbling landing lights, twisted scrub, and sword plants, which seemed appropriate. And there were people everywhere, three with flashes directing the helo to the sandy landing zone, marked out by shells in lines. No independent landing lights. No protection against the erratic winds, the helo taking the buffeting back and forth as it descended.

The touchdown was jarring and Alex fell out onto the sand, throwing up everything in his stomach, which was mostly pizza and garlic and cheese. I did better than expected, especially considering Beast's catty annoyance. I might get seasick, but I did okay on the sashaying winds for the short flight. My stomach warned it would not be so sanguine on a longer flight. I stepped onto the sand, Eli beside me. We helped Alex to his feet and I slung the heavy gobags over a shoulder as we raced to the men and women waiting at the edge of the flashlights that illuminated everything in bright flickers of still life.

I recognized none of the construction types, who had stopped work to oversee our landing, some pointing. Some had beer bellies and were wearing boots and dirty layers. One grizzled woman stood scratching her stomach, a hard hat in her other hand. One guy looked like he'd stepped off a magazine cover—tall, dark, and handsome, with a carefully groomed scruff, a mustache, and jeans that rode low on his hips. I could see him in a tweed jacket, teaching on a university campus. Four looked like bodybuilders, all muscles and shape and form. One of them was a woman and she had shoulders to die for, like a power lifter, muscles you could still use. Her hair was pulled back in a tail.

Derek and some of his guys stood between the landing site and the house. Beast took over for a moment and, before I could stop her, she tossed my gobag at Derek. He caught it by instinct. Irritation flashed through his eyes. Beast chuffed. I could see the gold of my/our eyes reflected in Derek's. I had a feeling that my co-Enforcer disliked my Beast as much as he did me. I grinned at him, showing too many all-too-human teeth, and said, "Thanks."

He tossed it over his shoulder and then took my weapons bag and Eli's two bags too. Dude had been drinking vamp blood, and a lot of it, to be so strong. There was a time when Leo's other Enforcer would have hidden his extra-strong, vamp-blood-enhanced physique. Not now. And then I remembered the list of fights and wondered how many Derek was lined up for. He led the way up the steps and out of the wind and prop noise, his feet light, unhindered by the extra weight. Yeah. He had been drinking lots of vamp blood. As much as his humanish system could process. Not that I blamed him. He wouldn't heal as fast as I would, if he took a lethal wound. He'd be much more likely to die. Like Eli.

Even with skinwalker healing, which was faster than normal even if I didn't shift, I was still sore from my beating. Having someone else carry my gear was helpful, though I'd never tell Derek that. We followed Derek and I felt Beast prowl through my brain and out through my nerves, edgy, uneasy, spitting in frustration. *Want to kill vampires. Want to eat vampires. Want to drink vampire blood.*

As I took the stairway to the front porch entry, the construction types behind me offloaded supplies while people who were headed back to shore for the rest of the night

climbed aboard. The roar changed and the helo took off
again. I could feel the wood stairs strain beneath the
weight of the men and women following me.

Between the open risers, I spotted summer ocean gear
lashed to the pilings beneath the house, lit by security
lights. Behind chain-link fencing attached to the pilings
were brand-new lounges, kayaks, paddles, paddleboards,
a midsized johnboat with a new-looking motor. All the
stuff needed for a long weekend in the sun. In the center
beneath the house was an open space where the workers
had piled supplies, slung hammocks, and set up a table
for meals.

To the side of the summer stuff were boxes and crates
piled on wood pallets. Near the unopened boxes was a
pile of flattened cardboard and shaped foam packing material, plastic straps, and the glint of staples. At the back
was wallboard, enough two-by-fours and two-by-sixes to
build another mansion, strips of unpainted molding,
stacks of five-gallon buckets, and various other construction materials. We climbed the steps.

The porch on the first floor was screened and appeared
to wrap around the entire house. It had its own roof system, plank floors, and hammocks, tables, and lounge
chairs were scattered around.

Inside, the smells of salt water, sawdust, glue, beer, cigarette smoke, and paint were heavy on the air, though the
windows were all open and the salty gulf wind blew
through. I stepped to the side of the entrance and propped
Alex against the wall. Eli looked around and his nose
crinkled just a bit. The workers crowded in behind us.

I raised my hands to my mouth and shouted, "People!
Heads up! Gather in the entry!" I wished I had a mega-
phone. The acoustics were horrible.

The bodybuilder woman stepped in front of me and
cupped her hands around her mouth. In the better light I
could see she wore no makeup, but heavy sunscreen had
caked in the folds of her ears. She was sweaty and tanned
and had highlighted brown hair. "Yo! Yellowrock is here.
Getchur asses to first floor!" Her words echoed off the

walls and ceiling and my eyebrows went up high. She had lungs and a gift for projection.

She stuck out a hand. "I'm Bambi. They call me Mike, for Microphone. And because I hate the dead deer/pole dancer image of Bambi."

"I can see why."

"The guys all been wanting to meet you. Some of them think you need a good beer. Others think they have a chance to get you in the sack." She ran a loose strand of hair behind her ear and her brown eyes took me in from toes to bun. "I told them you date the former primo. Showed them a pic of him on my cell. In a tux. Dude is hot."

"Oh," I said, not quite sure how to handle her spiel.

"They backed off. But if you happen to have the bad taste to dump the man, swing him my way. I just broke up with my boyfriend."

"Uhhh."

Without waiting for my answer she moved to the side and squatted down.

"Babe," Eli said. "Close your mouth."

"My boyfriend just got hit on."

"She's forthright," he said, with that micro smile that meant he was teasing me. "That makes her interesting."

"Then you date her."

Eli looked at Bambi/Mike, speculation in his eyes. He hadn't been with anyone since he and Syl had stopped calling. He'd be happier if he and a willing female partnered up for a night. Or more. "Hmmm," he said.

I glanced back at Bambi and then at Eli and gave her a thumb up, concealed at my side. Bambi checked Eli out and I could practically feel the sexual tension in the air when their eyes met. I had a feeling my second would be spending the night with a girl named Mike.

On the heels of that thought the front room and entry filled with workers from the upper stories and the rest from outside. Voices and work boots against wood floors filled the room, along with the stink of testosterone and Italian food. No one seemed inclined to be quiet. So I stepped out into the middle of the room and stood, feet

braced shoulder width apart, and hands at my sides. Eli
and Alex stepped behind and beside me, one to either
side. It was like having a support team. Not that I needed
a team, but it would speed things along faster than having
to prove to the men that I was worth listening to. If I had
to break bones to get their attention, that might slow up
the work on the house.

Bambi/Mike shouted, "Shut up!" And then she added
some colorful language about how their mothers were all
sluts and whores and their daddies dated werewolves.
There was general laughter, but they all quieted and
turned to me. I leaned down an inch or two and whispered in Alex's ear. "Full background on her."

"Soon as Bodat and I get the hardware in place to get
online. We don't even know if this cobbled-together system will work or not, yet."

I wondered if Bambi wanted a job with the MOC,
or even with Clan Yellowrock. Which was a very weird
thought.

"I'm Jane Yellowrock." I looked from man to man to
woman. "We have a little over thirty-six hours to get this
place ready for vamps and their humans. Vamps start arriving just after dusk night after next. That means all construction, plumbing, and electrical finished, electronics
and security installed, painting, touch-ups, and punch list
completed, all in thirty hours. That'll give the next crew
six hours to clean and stage it."

"Lady, you got no idea what goes into a job like this."
The speaker stepped forward, and it was the young, good-
looking man from the landing site. He had charisma and
charm to balance his looks, and from the heads nodding
around us, it was clear he was some kind of leader, official
or otherwise. "You're not familiar with the ins and outs
of a construction site." He gestured with a hand as if to
show me that the house was a construction site. "Most
women have no idea." He gave me his best, most charming smile, one with condescension in it. He wanted me to
know my place.

I felt Eli tense at my side, a meager increase in the
tightness of his muscles. I studied the pretty boy, with his

model-perfect teeth, his careful scruff, his clean, matching layers and plaid overshirt, and his citrusy cologne.

Citrusy . . . An electric shock shot through me.

Pretty Boy went on. "It's physically and mentally demanding. Making impossible deadlines sounds great on TV shows, but reality is a different matter." Condescension deep enough to drown in.

"Sounds like you know what you're talking about," I said. "You a foreman?"

"Yeah. Marco." He pointed to his chest. "Madderson Construction. We're in charge of the project."

"Who's your number two person?"

Pretty Boy pointed to a short, lean, graying, clean-shaven man with deep sunbaked wrinkles. Veins crawled over his lower arms beneath the cuffs of his rolled-up sleeves. This guy's clothes were dusty, wrinkled, and sweat stained, though I had a feeling they had been clean when he started his workday. I walked close to Pretty Boy and breathed in his scent. Lemons . . .

"Alex," I said softly, "what is Marco's last name?"

"Agrios."

A name I had heard recently, somewhere. It came to me. Agrios had run with the Zips, the local gang who had helped in the attack at the jewelry shop. A name that Andromeda was going to ask around about, ask her brother who ran with the Razors. And maybe she had. And maybe she had died because of that. The shock in my system intensified, fueled by anger.

"He smells like lemons," I said.

"His background check was stellar," Alex said. "Except . . ." The word held a tone of disgust and self-loathing. "Except that Agrios means Citrus. Titus was thumbing his nose at us. My Spanish is pretty sucky so I didn't catch it." Des Citrons had an inside man. And we hadn't caught him. I wanted to hit something. I was pretty sure my Beast had risen inside me and that my eyes were glowing. A lot of thoughts raced through Marco's eyes, his body tensed and his scent vacillated. Uncertainty, worry, and a flash of joy. We hadn't said the words Des Citrons. We hadn't said anything about the emperor. His scent stabilized, the smell of a man who was about to bluff.

"Derek," I said.

"Yes, Enforcer," Derek drawled. I looked his way to see that he was enjoying all this. I got the feeling that he'd had a run-in with Pretty Boy already. "Help our pessimistic friend pack and see he makes it back to shore. He's fired."

The smell of dismay and hostility filled the air. The workers might not like Marco, but they liked a woman coming in and taking over even less. Alex and Eli stepped out, shoulders back. An unspoken threat.

"For what cause?" Marco asked, his hands fisting. He stepped into my face. "You don't have the authority to fire me, lady."

I didn't bother to respond to his claim. I couldn't put a human in restraints just because he smelled like lemons. But I could get him off the island and to a vamp who could drink the answers out of him. "Derek. He needs to be bled and read." The words were oblique, telling Derek that Marco might be an enemy blood-servant, and more dangerous than a human.

Understanding filled Derek's face. "My pleasure, Enforcer," he said. Derek and two of his men descended on Pretty Boy, who had turned a lovely and satisfying shade of red. There followed a scuffle and some cussing and the vision of Derek and his security pals half carrying the man out the front door. The smell of antagonism from the construction workers had deepened. They looked twitchy, apprehensive at the loss of the pack leader and the rearrangement of their previous social order. I had picked the infiltrator out of the lineup and made my own impression all at once, and not a good one. Go, me. Finishing the house still hung in the balance. I could turn the crews to me, or I could ruin everything. I usually ruined things.

"That man stank of lemons. Anyone notice that?"

"So what?" a man asked. He was beer-bellied and wearing a sweat-stained T-shirt.

I said, "Lemme guess. He was new to the firm. Been with you for less than two months. He just walked in one day and took over, with the acceptance of the powers that be, and yet he knew next to nothing about construction. Am I right?"

The guy rubbed his scruffy chin and hunched his shoulders, thinking. "Okay. So?"

"The enemies of the Master of the City stink of lemons. Marco was a blood-servant. I don't know how he wormed his way into Madderson Construction, but I'm guessing it was by coercion."

The guy blinked as if he had missed something, and then cursed softly.

"Anyone else want to go home?" I asked.

No one responded.

"Fine. You"—I pointed to the number two man—"ever been a foreman on a construction site?"

"Most of my life," he said, not watching the inelegant removal of Pretty Boy.

"Name?"

"Renny Coozer."

"Renny, you're now the official Madderson foreman for this project. I'll personally handle any fallout from the owner."

Renny nodded once. A man of few words. I liked that.

"I'll continue what I came to say." I scanned the men and women. They turned from the door and looked at Renny. Then at me. There were some unhappy expressions still, but there was also comprehension and a few of the people looked delighted. Riding on top of the uneasy, unhappy stench there was something else. Respect, maybe?

Beast/Jane. We are alpha.

So far, I thought back. *Let's see if money will make that more than a passing fancy.*

"I know I'm the newcomer here. And what I know about construction can be written on the head of a pin in longhand. But I know hard work. You're already on overtime," I said to the crews. "As of now, you're on bonus time. You get this house finished in thirty hours, according to the plan Renny lays out, and you will each make ten percent of your yearly base salary. In cash. To be paid

by the MOC." The unhappy stench on the air cleared up
fast, eyes tightened, smiles started, and I could see them
each calculating how much money they stood to make.
"You get to police each other," I continued. "If word
comes to Derek Lee that someone's slacking and letting
other people do their work, with the plan to cash in on the
bonus anyway, that person will be shipped back to shore.
I expect you to work hard, work steady, work together,
and take breaks and sleep time as needed. I don't intend
anyone to crash and burn.

"I want the foremen of each crew to meet with Renny,
Eli Younger, and Derek, when he gets back, to give them
an idea of what needs to be done and in what order. This
project, the approval of the MOC, as well as cash bonuses, are all on your shoulders."

I turned to the side. "Mike. I'd like a tour of the house.
Alex, come with. See what you need to get this place
rigged for security and satellite cells or remote Internet
or cameras or whatever it is needs doing."

The house was in better shape than we feared and worse
shape than we hoped. The pylons driven into the sand
continued up through the house, which should have made
the space feel cut up and small, but the poles had been
wrapped in fancy woodwork and allowed an open floor-
plan. The first story was all party space, with a restaurant-
quality white kitchen and brushed steel appliances that
had clearly been updated in the last couple of years. Alex
ran a hand along the white and gray countertops and said,
"Carrara," with reverence, so that had to mean they were
top of the line. Interesting. Leo may not have been here,
but his people had kept up the investment.

There was a dining table that would seat twenty in a
pinch, three seating areas, and a library full of moldering
books. Except for the kitchen and the big table, all the
furniture was old and decrepit, but the staging crew was
supposed to bring replacements. The ceilings were a little
over standard height and looked like old pressed tin, the
ancient Hunter Fan Company fans still worked, and the
floors might have been cypress under the layer of con-

struction dirt. The walls were cream or eggshell throughout the lower floor and the wood moldings were stark
white.

"Windows?" I asked Mike, to see how well she communicated. Or how well she read my mind. Either way.

"All new three years ago. Shutters all new. They look
antique, but they're electronic hurricane shutters and
slide into recesses in the walls. Benefit of keeping out
hurricane winds is that they're also lightproof. So vamps
are safe by day," she said casually. When I didn't reply she
added, "Unless someone hits a wrong switch and the
shutters open. But there's a twenty-second delay and an
alarm built into the system, so theoretically any light-
sensitive person could get to shelter."

I made a small sound of doubtful agreement and she
went on.

"Sleeping area is on the second story and there are
decorative fire escapes built into the outer walls." Without waiting for us, Mike headed up the wide stairway,
located beside the kitchen, in front of the entry.

To Alex I said, "Cameras and electronics look possible?"

"Not a piece of cake, but . . . we can get something."
He needed to get more than something. He needed to get
a system set up that would allow for the Sangre Duello to
be uploaded to pay-per-view on the Internet.

I made another small sound as we reached the second
floor. It was constructed with a central walled-up, contained area, encircled by a wide hallway, and long narrow
bedrooms around the outside. It was set up like insert-
able boxes, a small central space, a wider open ring, and
more box. I figured the central area was for vamp sleeping and the outside rooms were for humans. As I had
been informed, there were four bedrooms for humans,
two on the front of the house, facing the ocean, and one
on each side. Along the back was an even more narrow
room, one that appeared to have been a very recently enclosed porch, not much more than eight feet wide along
the back wall. In the hallway there was an ice chest, several sawhorse tables, six mesh folding chairs, a fifty-

gallon garbage can full of trash and flies, and cola bottles everywhere.

The walls on this level hadn't been freshly painted, and the color scheme was less than pleasant with clashing tropical colors and ugly murals. Alex said, "This might have been painted by grade school kids," and he was right. This floor also stank of mold, even with the windows open to the night air.

Walls and wallboard were missing between some rooms, temporary studs visible where one bath had been enlarged and added onto. I didn't ask where the water came from or where the plumbing drained to. I didn't really want to know. But the baths were mostly raw pipes. Two men came up beside me and one said, "I'm Jake. Master cabinetmaker. Time constraints mean nothing is custom, but ready-made cabinets were delivered today. I'll get them in and leveled as fast as I can. The wood floor system is uneven and there's not a single wall or floor or ceiling that's plumb in this place, but I'll get them done." Jake pointed at the African American man beside him. The name stenciled on his shirt was Trevis. "Trevis has the plumbing complete except for tying to faucets and drains. Fixtures are under the first floor on the sand."

Trevis nodded at me, silent.

I remembered the boxes and stacked crates downstairs. "Lot of things a large group of vamps and humans can do without, Trevis. Plumbing isn't one."

Mike said, "Renny suggested we put in fighting mats on the sand under the first floor. We could add a shower outside since drains wouldn't be needed."

They knew the Sangre Duello was going to involve fighting and blood and were thinking ahead. Alex grunted. Eli frowned.

Trevis added, "They fight down there, the sand makes cleanup easier between bouts. The shower would keep some of the bloody mess out of the house, could be used to wash off blood, sweat, and gore outside rather than track it inside up the stairs."

The idea was brilliant. "And?" I asked.

"And Marco said no," Jake said.

"You want the fighting area and shower under the house?" Trevis asked me.

"I think it's nifty. Is it possible to get an outdoor shower installed and still hit our timeline?"

"Can do," Trevis said and trotted off, calling for Renny.

As he left, five men and the stocky woman I had seen earlier strode up the stairs. They carried hammers, hefty tape measures, skill saws, and an air of determination. In seconds they were banging permanent studs in place beside the temporary ones, hanging wallboard, and discussing ways to finish the walls without the finishing compound drying, which took three days in dry air. I knew finishing compound. It was the stuff that went under, above, and around wallboard tape to keep the seams from cracking. I'd seen Eli use it on the various house repairs. I'd been rough on the formerly freebie house.

I looked at Mike and dipped my chin in approval at the crew.

"Money talks," she said.

"I hope so." Especially since I hadn't cleared the expense with Leo's accountant, Raisin. My promise would be a smack to the Mithran coffers. "Let's see the vamp sleeping quarters."

The central area was separated into four tiny, square rooms, all opening into a foyer of sorts. There were two official doors and an escape hatch out through a hidey-hole that led to a long drop to the sand, like a dumbwaiter chute. No windows. Extra-thick walls. I smelled old blood when Mike lifted the escape hatch. Some vamp had dropped through it in the distant past, badly wounded. Two electricians carrying toolboxes and ladders came in behind us and started work.

"The center rooms were already in place and the walls soundproofed when the full crew got here," Mike said, "finished some time ago and ready for color. Soon as the last of the new bathroom walls are in place we'll blow the paint on. We have enough equipment to blow the entire house in about three hours. And if we run out of solar power, we have generators. Paint will dry well enough in eight hours for the electricians to put up the lighting fixtures, and your staging team can work around the wetter spots. You can get the painters to stick around to touch up as needed."

Mike was good, answering my questions before I asked. She led us back into the hallway, squatted, and indicated the unpainted wallboard. "Finishing compound won't cure in time. It'll look okay for a day or two, but in the wet air, it'll mold if we don't come back and strip the tape, recompound the walls, and repaint, but this is the best we can do." She looked up at me, speculation in her eyes. I couldn't place her expression. Beast raised her head, sniffed, and sat up, vaguely interested, but not telling me why. When I didn't say anything, she asked, "You don't talk much, do you?"

"Not really." I pointed at the stairs up. "Let's see the third floor."

The third floor was one huge space, empty of workers, with gigantic wood pillars that held up the roof system and passed straight through the house, deep into the sand below. The room was vaulted with weathered gray-toned tongue-and-groove boards and big, slow-turning, copper fans, green with verdigris. There were hidden lights in the unpainted rafters and beams that cast quirky shadows. The walls were pale, maybe once painted white. The floor was cedar planks inlaid with darker wood in three places, each in the shape of La Destreza fighting rings. Not modern fighting rings, but octagonal fighting rings like I had seen in books. All the windows were open to the night air, and there were a lot of windows. For the first time I considered the kind of views that every window and the wraparound porch would have by day. Spectacular. I wondered how the house had survived hurricanes and floods. It was amazing.

"I love this room," Mike said, turning in a circle, as if seeing all the views. She was balanced, rooted, her stance bringing Beast to the surface, turning my attention to the woman. Something about her movements. A dancer? Ice skater? "I could live here forever," she said.

"I can see why," Alex said, looking at me. "Dibs?"

I chuckled and shook my head. "No. You can't claim this room."

"I can imagine painting in this room," Mike said, her voice almost dreamy. "Canvases there and there"—she pointed—"to take advantage of the light. It's amazing by day. Soft and ethereal."

Despite the claw hammer and oversized tape measure on her belt, Bambi was an artist at heart, and better educated than her rant at the construction workers had indicated. Sadly, the room she was admiring wasn't for artists or canvases; it was for fighting.

"Could be used for an artist's atelier," she said. "Could be a sleeping loft. There are heavy-duty steel screws in rings in all the supports, for backdrop cloths or to hang hammocks."

The breeze shifted. I caught the scent of lemons, coming through the windows. Three stories up.

CHAPTER 15

Jane Was Sick from Walking through Time

Beast moved. *Fastfastfast.* Grabbed Alex left-handed and spun-tossed him out of harm's way. He was still in the air when an object flew through the window. I/we leaped. Beast and Jane in perfect concert. Caught it. Let it swing me around and in the same motion, threw it out a different window. Heard odd popping sounds. Identified the device only after it left my/our hand. Hand grenade. Just outside the window, it exploded. Debris peppered inside the room.

My hand went numb. *Spelled?* I thought. Alex landed, rolled down the stairs. Shouting. More popping. Gunfire. Bambi/Mike dropped to the floor for cover.

I/we rushed window the grenade came through. Soared out the opening, into the night. And saw Marco dropping toward the roof of the porch below.

Beast is fast. She took over. Twisted in the air, away from the light in the window.

Marco landed on the tin roof. Turned, fast as a blood-servant. A blur in the darkness. He raised a weapon. Fired at the window we'd just left.

Beast landed beside him. Fisted hand. Hit Marco on jaw. Uppercut. All weight and might behind single blow.

Marco snapped back. Fell from roof. To land on sand below. *Beast is best hunter!*

I/we whipped back. Caught edge of porch roofing. Metal and wood. Extended claws. Caught weight. Swung inside to porch, landing on railing. Man standing there squeaked. Everyone was down on floor. Taking cover.

Thanks, I thought to Beast as she gave me back my body.

I jumped the final distance to the sand and knelt beside the limp form of Marco. He was breathing. I grabbed his arm and rolled him over. Knee at his back. I tried to trap his arms, but my hand didn't work.

I heard the individual, particular percussion of Eli's feet on the steps, flat-out run, three stairs at a time. Smelled Eli. A nine-mil and handful of zip strips entered my field of vision.

"Can't," I breathed. Holding up my hand and arm.

Marco came back to consciousness and shook himself like a dog. Started fighting again, or trying to. Eli took over and strapped Marco's wrists together. Not as easy to do as it sounded, with a screaming, punching, crazy blood-servant, one with broken legs from his fall, beneath him. One-handed, I banged his head on the ground, maybe harder than was necessary, to subdue him. Eli strapped his ankles together above his boots with heavy-duty zip strips.

When he was restrained, I removed Marco's weapons. Everything. Down to the silver stake strapped to his calf.

I sat on Marco, breathing hard. Lip dripping. Blood all over my casual clothes, dang it. "How did he get free? How did he get up to the third floor?"

"My fault," Derek said, stumbling out of the darkness, the stink of his blood on the air. "I thought we had him contained at the LZ. Son of a bitch got free. Pulled a move I haven't seen since the military, and faster than shit. Hit me over the head. My guys are down too. Alive, but out." He sat down hard on the sand, as if he was dizzy. Blood dripped from his nose and the back of his head, and curdled into his collar. With my good hand, I pulled him forward and inspected the wound. "Ow," he said, jerking away, only to grab his head again, the stink of his nausea acrid on the air.

"Concussion," I said. A human would have needed stitches and a dark room and concussion protocol. Derek had been drinking powerful vamp blood. He'd likely be fine.

He said, "There are fire escape ladders built in beneath some of the windows. He must have used those. I'll make sure they come out first thing in the morning." He cursed, held his head a moment, and lifted a hand to the house and the workers congregated on the porch. "We need lights in the LZ, now!"

In the distance, the sound of rotor blades cut the air. The helicopter was closing in on the unlit landing site. I felt more than saw people rushing out to the landing area. Lights came on. A generator roared, concealing the sound of the helo. Bright lights sliced the night, illuminating the landing site. LZ. Landing zone. Right.

"Alex. You okay?" Eli called.

"Jane broke my tablets," Alex said from the front door. "And maybe my nose."

Eli glanced up at his brother. "No, she didn't."

"No. But she could have," he said sulkily as he clunked down the stairs to us. "Jane wasn't playing nice when she threw me down the steps."

"Big-cats do not play nice," Beast said through my mouth, her voice growly.

Both Youngers went still as stone.

I swallowed Beast back. "Sorry. But my arm is broken. I grabbed the grenade he threw in the window and then I hit Marco with the same arm. I think the grenade was spelled." I held up my arm. My lower arm bent to one side then the other.

Eli looked it over. "Dang, Janie. Now, that's a broken arm. Comminuted fracture of both bones. Hey, you"— he pointed to a man on the porch—"go get my gobag." The guy took off. "I'll splint it," Eli said.

"As happy as I am to provide a medical lesson in orthopedics," I whispered beneath the sound of the helo and generator, breathless, "I'm about to pass out from the pain. I have to shift. I need privacy and I also need to check on Bambi/Mike."

"Soon as we stabilize that arm we can get you back to the third floor to shift, killing two birds. Broken hand too," he continued as he tucked my fingers into the waistband of my jeans to give it some support. "Stay put." Eli bowled Marco up into his arms and over his shoulder in a rolling/rising, all-in-one move I'd seen him do before. He pointed to my swollen hand. "I'll be right back to splint that. I mean it, Janie. Stay put." Eli carried the attacker toward the landing zone, Alex on his heels, carrying one of Eli's nine-mils.

"Stay put? I'm not your puppy dog." Eli was too far away to hear me.

Derek chuckled and then retched, throwing up onto the packed sand.

The smell nearly did me in. No way could I stay put. I jutted my chin to the retching Derek and said to a passing carpenter, "Bring him in. Put some ice on his head."

I cradled my arm and hand and crawled to my feet. I climbed the stairs to the porch, breathless, aching, passing the workers, trying not to hurl or pass out, as that would ruin my badass image. *Right.* I made my pained way up to the third floor, ready to shift into Beast and heal my broken arm, the big room last seen as I leaped out the window. Halfway up the last steps, the smell of blood met me.

"Eli!" I screamed. "To me!"

Bambi/Mike was on the floor, her blood in a wide pool. I knelt at her side. She was still breathing, but there couldn't be enough blood left in her to keep her alive for long.

Eli tore up the stairs, took in the scene at a glance, and began shouting orders. "Hold the helo. Get Leo on the helo's comms system. I need a med kit, now!" He went to work trying to stabilize Bambi/Mike with nothing except his bare hands, the stuff in his pockets, and pressure.

Alex repeated the orders, shouting. People boiled into the third-floor space.

A man landed beside Eli, placing an oversized red case on the floor and opening the latches with sharp snaps of metal and plastic. It was the T-shirted potbellied man from earlier, and he had a massive emergency kit. "I'm an EMT," he said, already tearing packages. "Cut her clothes open. Tampons." He handed Eli a handful of packages. "Leave the tail hanging out. Then Gelfoam. Don't put the foam inside. There may be intravascular compartments. We don't want to risk embolism."

Eli didn't bother to tell the guy he had field medical training and had used the products before to stop bleeding on the battlefield. He just ripped Bambi's clothes and found three entrance holes, on her torso, lower abdomen, and left arm. He stuck a tampon in each. Rolled her over and shoved three tampons in each exit hole on the back. Pulled open the Gelfoam pads and placed them over the wounds. Sanitary napkins followed. He wrapped them in place with heavy sticky tape. The other guy tied a tourniquet on her arm and started an IV. Fast. I had EMT training too and recognized Ringer's lactate, a plasma expander. It wouldn't replace blood, but it would slow shock. Outside, the helo landed.

I settled to the floor. My pain unnoticed. Watching.

"Call for a medical chopper?" the potbellied guy asked. "They carry blood."

"No time. Let's get her to the helo. You can call it in on the way. You're going with her."

Two workers placed a door on the floor as backboard and they loaded Bambi/Mike onto it. Someone tossed a sleeping bag at them and they tucked it around the pale-as-death woman. And then I realized she was awake. Silent. Her eyes on Eli.

"I gotcha, Mike," he said. "You're gonna be fine."

"Dying," she whispered.

"No way. Leo himself will meet you onshore. His blood will heal you. I guarantee it. All you have to do is stay alive to the mainland. Got it?"

"That's all?"

"That's all. Piece a cake. Let's get her to the LZ, boys," he said.

Together they lifted the door and carried her down. And I was alone. I heard them race down and down and down the stairs and outside. Heard the helo's rotors speed up.

Alone, I lay flat on the old flooring and cradled my arm. I tried to sink into the Gray Between, but it wasn't happening. So much for anything Zen in my life. *Beast. I need help.*

Beast pressed down on my pain receptors and sent something like endorphins into my bloodstream, muting the pain. I'd never get all my clothes off. I'd have to shift clothed and I'd ruin the boots. What had I been thinking when I pulled them on? Boots at the beach?

I heard footsteps clattering back up the stairs, Eli being deliberately noisy, but stopping before his head rose above floor level. "You still human?"

"Sadly yes."

"You need help getting your clothes loose?" he asked.

"Boots?" I asked.

Eli came all the way up and knelt at my side, studying my injuries. He had washed his hands, but he still had blood smears on his wrists. He shifted position and eased my boots off one by one, without shaking me and my broken bones. "I'm not a good second," he said, as he removed the stakes and the knives in my boot sheaths and set them to the side.

I tried to smile. "You're a great second. I could have just shifted, but I'd have ruined the boots. I like this pair."

"You're rough on the girly stuff. You're rough on fighting leathers. I can't think of a single piece of clothing you're not rough on."

"Lucchese boots," I said promptly, waggling my toes at him.

Eli huffed in amusement. "Can you move your arm? Let me get to your waistband?" I supported and lifted the broken arm and hand. Methodically, he loosened my clothes. He said, "You can shift and your legs will slip out of the pants, but the shirt and jacket are pretty thick."

"Cut 'em off me. I'll try not to weep at the loss of my wardrobe."

Gruffly, sarcasm in the tone, he said, "Good. I hate it

when you whine." Eli slid his arms around my back and shoulders and sat me upright. I gagged with the pain. He pulled a blade that looked sharp enough to shave with. "Good arm first." He cut up the sleeves of the uninjured arm and across to the neck opening, though he left the lapel in place. He eased the jacket and shirt off the shoulder and peeled it toward my back. He started at the lapel on the injured side and cut through to the shoulder, before he pulled all the slashed cloth forward and created a modified sling with the cut clothes, placing them under my broken arm as support. He secured the messy sling with knots and zip ties.

"Ingenious," I said. I was glad I'd worn ugly, heavy sports underwear for the weather.

"Of course."

"You unhappy that you and Mike won't be hooking up?"

"Oh, we'll be hooking up, just not the way I planned. Though I may wait a bit. Hospital dates are awkward."

I tried to grin at his small joke and winced.

"I heard you on the helo's comms system. Brief me."

"Leo's pissed. He's on the way to the mainland LZ. He has two helos shuttling now. Someone will read Marco tonight. Leo will heal Bambi. Del is sending an armed team to check on the CEO of Madderson Construction—armed in case they were colluding or are in trouble. HQ is taking no chances." Eli stood and walked back to the stairs, his feet silent on the old floors. Partway down, he stopped and his voice floated back into the vaulted room. "Edmund's on the way too." I hurt too much to respond. "Babe. Alex says you threw him down the stairs, out of harm's way. He's pissed at not getting in on the fight." I said nothing. Softer, Eli added, "Thanks for protecting him."

"My pleasure. Scoot."

He went on down the stairs. And once again I sought the Gray Between. It was cool there, the lights silvery gray with darker gray motes shooting through. My own magics, the ones now moving in a star pattern inside me, expanded.

The shift started. Pain slammed through my arm.

Claws ripping my skin. Nails being driven into my broken bones. *Painpainpain* . . .

Woke up tangled in Jane clothes. Pants and inside pants and cut shirt and stupid tight inside shirt. Stupid human clothes. Scratched off cloth tied around front leg. Claws tangled in cloth. Snarled. Ripped off pants and inside pants. But could not get off inside shirt. Shirt Jane called jog and bra. Was stuck. Growled. Calling Eli. Eli did not come. Growled louder. Eli did not come.

Whistled kit call. *Eli! Eli! Eli!*

Eli did not come. Eli did not know kit call. Screamed kit call. *Eli! Eli! Eli!*

Eli called, "Jane? Beast?" Sounded afraid.

Eli should be afraid. Beast is best hunter. But Eli would laugh human laugh at sight of Beast in Jane bra. Growled softer. Thought about jumping out of window. Was hungry. Wanted to hunt fish in curling water, what Jane called gulf water. Water did not run one way like river water, but rolled everywhere, and to land. Was strange. But. Wanted bra off. Was too tight on Beast chest. Did not know why Jane wanted to wear bra. Growled again, uncertain.

"You planning on eating me if I come up? I have a raw steak."

Beast's ear tabs perked up. *Eli has dead cow?*

Beast padded to stairs, *pawpawpaw*. Smelled blood of dead cow on air. Warm meat. Stuck head around stair wall and saw Eli, sitting on stair with plate and small slab of meat. Alex sat on bottom stair with white-man gun and tablets, working. Guarding Beast's den. *Good kits. Good guard.*

Humans with hammers made loud noises. Hurt Beast's ears. Loud scream of saw hurt too. Snarled, showing killing teeth.

Eli went stiff. "Jane?"

Am Beast! Am not Jane!

"Beast? Okay. Beast. What's wrong? Is it your arm? Didn't it heal right?" Eli smelled of worry like mother big-cat to kits. "Can I look?"

Snarled again, but backed away. Eli would laugh. Beast would swipe him with paw, claws sheathed, and knock him down. And then eat steak.

"Oh." Eli stood on floor, looking at Beast. Did not smell human laughter. Did not hear human laughter. Did not see human laughter on Eli face. Eli had warrior face on. No expression. Was good face. Eli set plate of raw meat on floor and pulled steel claw. "Want me to cut off the bra?"

Beast snarled harder. But Eli did not laugh. Beast padded closer. Sat, front legs straight, head high. Mouth open. Panting softly. Killing teeth showing through open mouth.

Eli stepped close, steel claw sharp. Eli put knees on floor. Started cutting through bra. "I'm sorry. I should have thought to cut the bra. My bad."

Turned head and looked at Eli. Dark skin was shining. Black clothes were good for night hunting. Should take Eli hunting one night. Eli sawed. Bra came loose and Eli peeled bra down Beast legs. Bra was dead. Jane should kill bras.

Beast padded around Eli to plate and tore into food. Lay on wood floor and pulled cow part between cat feet and claws and ripped and chewed and swallowed. Was cow with water-blood, the way humans like meat, instead of fresh meat with thick blood. But was good. Beast finished cow meat and licked water-blood off of plate and off of paws, tongue cleaning pelt. Jane said Beast tongue was like paper made of sand. Beast had never seen paper made of sand.

Eli was sitting, watching. Beast butted Eli with head. Eli fell over. Beast chuffed with laughter. Beast rubbed head and jaw over Eli head. Made Eli smell like cow and like Beast. Was good smell. Eli made blowing sounds. "I'd say thanks for the love, but since there isn't a shower on the island yet, maybe not."

Beast chuffed. Trotted to open window. Stood with front paws on ledge and looked out. Moon was high. Not one-day moon. Not pregnant moon, big with young. But bright enough to see beach and water that curled like

Beast's tongue. Looked back at Eli. Chuffed. Looked out at night. Back at Eli. Eli did not move. *Stupid Eli.* Looked out and back and chuffed.

Eli's face scrunched. "You want me to go with you?"

Beast made small sound of pleasure, like when kits first walk. Leaped out window and down. Landed with thump on porch roof. Looked back up. Eli was at window.

"Gimme a minute. I'll be right there."

Beast made happy sound again. Stupid humans did not understand different chuffs but understood other sounds. Beast leaped to ground, paws stretching out and landing in deep sand, front paws first, then back paws. Padded through shadows to beach. Smelled salt. Dead fish. Salty water. Could see far up both sides from house. Beast liked beach. Sat and waited for Eli. Could see many small fish in edge of water, near small dock. Could see bird floating on water, sleeping. More birds under low trees onshore. Bigger fish in deeper water? Looked at house. Eli was racing down steps into night.

"Jane?"

Chuffed. *Am Beast. Not Jane. Eli is stupid kit.* But Eli was kit for Beast to take care of. Did not know if Eli could swim. Beast did not like water, but Beast could swim. Could catch fishes.

"Oh. Hey, cat. Water looks good and cold. I'm for a dip if you are."

Beast chuffed. *Yes. Cat. Beast. Not Jane.* Eli pulled off outside clothes and raced into water, two legs splashing loud. Made sound like owl, like *hoooo*, at cold water. He dived. Started swimming with head in water. Looking for fishes! But scaring off fishes with arms in air, splashing down onto water. Beast padded into water that curled and rolled and curled again and went nowhere. Slid deep, spread paw pads and swam into water after Eli. Water was cold. Felt good on Beast coat.

Eli dove deep to catch fishes and missed. He came up out of water with many splashes. "That's either freezing or refreshing," he shouted.

Beast was close by. Eli did not need to shout. Fishes were all gone. Eli was noisy kit. Would not eat fish today.

Beast snorted through nose and licked jaw and muzzle.
Eli splashed water at Beast and laughed. Beast chuffed.
Silly kit. Swam to Eli and put paw on shoulder. Pushed
down. Eli went under. Made laughing noises under water
and swam away. Came up on Beast's other side. Splashed
Beast again. Dove. Eli was playing with Beast!

Played for long time with Eli, splashing and ducking
and dunking. Then swam to shore and shook water from
pelt. Eli was cold. Left Beast lying onshore to put on human clothes. And to watch new helo-copter-bird that was
landing. "I gotta take care of business, Beast. Talk to you
later." Eli went to nesting spot for metal bird.

Beast crept, belly to sand, *pawpawpaw,* to sleeping
birds beneath trees. Gathered paws close. And leaped!
Grabbed two birds in paws. Feathers flew. Birds squawked
death sounds. Other birds flew, screaming warnings,
"Danger! Danger! Beast is here!"

Beast bit through necks of birds. Carried dead birds to
edge of water to eat. Beast was best ambush hunter.

Sun had made sky brighter, and helo had flown away
again, when Eli came back with clothes for Jane. Eli
placed clothes under bushes, on soft sand. Beast wanted
to make Jane wake up under bushes with spiky leaves.
But Eli looked at Beast and said, "No playing games with
Jane. She was hurting when she shifted." Beast looked
away. Eli was not cat. Eli was not good fish-hunter. Eli
made splashes when he swam and scared off fishes. But
Beast would do what Eli wanted. Sometimes Eli was kit.
Sometimes Eli was littermate. Humans were confusing.

Beast stretched on sand and thought about Jane.
Looked into snake at center of all Earth creatures. Jane's
snake was tangled like ball of yarn that housecats played
with. Jane was sick from walking through time. Jane
would die soon if Jane's heart-snake did not heal. Beast
would think on this. Beast closed eyes and let Jane become Jane.

I came to facing the sun, lying on sand, a chilly breeze
blowing in off the water. I shivered. Except for the cold,

my waking place was, for once, comfy instead of on prickly pine needles or lying in mud or staring into the maw of a hungry alligator. Beast's sense of humor was peculiar sometimes. I figured I hadn't been Beast long, since I hadn't been awake inside her body. Or Beast had been doing something catty and evil that she didn't want me to know about, and so kept me asleep. It was a peculiar part of our relationship that she could keep me unaware of her activities when we were in cat form, but I had almost no control over her when in human form. I figured it was because of the decades we spent as cat, Beast in total charge of us, when I first accidentally did black magic and stole her body and soul. I shoved my hair out of the way in a sleek shush of sound, rolled to my knees, and brushed sand off me, checking out my arm and hand for bone placement. They looked okay, healed nicely. Pain all gone.

Someone had left a pile of neatly folded clothes on a towel. Thoughtful. Eli for sure. I dressed in sweatpants and shirt and slid my feet into flops, folded the towel, and slung my hair back. Trudged to the house. I passed yawning men and women, some carrying hard hats, some not, all looking tired, all carrying travel mugs and slurping down coffee as if it was the nectar of life. I smelled bacon and eggs and maple syrup and honey and grape jelly and I found myself racing up the stairs and into the house.

Eli held up a platter full of food and indicated a sofa with a low table in front of it. I hated to sit on the moldy sofa, but I wanted the food. I sat and dug in. And it was delicious. A platter of bacon, a dozen eggs, and a stack of pancakes later, I sat back and accepted a mug of tea from Eli. He was watching me with amused affection.

"What?"

"Beast and I went swimming last night."

"Beast hates the water."

"She played 'dunk the human' with me. She swims pretty good."

"Hmmm." A playful Beast was a rarity. Or maybe she was cat-spiteful only with me. "Okeydokey, then. Where is Alex?"

"Busy with his tablets, talking to Bodat on the mainland. They have communications, if only between the two of them."

I nodded. "Update."

"Painting will begin around ten on the third floor, soon as they can get the place tented to keep the overspray off the beams and rafters and floor. Second-level bathrooms are being tiled from floor to ceiling and the fixtures will go in this afternoon. Shower on the lower level will be ready by dark and the workers have drawn straws for the order of testing out all three showers."

I leaned back on the smelly sofa and stretched out my legs, crossed my feet at the ankles. I'd eaten so much my belly looked like I'd hidden a soccer ball under my shirt. I patted it. And burped softly. "Who's the cook?"

"Leo sent us Deon last night."

"Deon? As in Katie's Deon? As in wears spangles and glitter and way better makeup than I do?"

Eli's lips twitched as he sat on a wooden rocker across from me. "He's managed to proposition every other man on the job site. Some of them are uncomfortable, but since he's feeding them they aren't griping. Much."

"Okay. But if any of them try to hurt Deon there'll be hell to pay."

"Noted and already passed along. The walls on the second level that are ready for paint will be sprayed this afternoon in an eggshell color. The ones that have to be redone later due to insufficient curing time for the joint compound will be sprayed in a medium charcoal shade to minimize obvious wet and to make them easy to find when the fighting is over."

"Good thinking."

"We have about half of the cameras in place. Alex and two hardware specialists are creating a satellite and Wi-Fi network across the island that will be linked to George's boat. Or to a satellite. They're arguing. Don't ask me details. I didn't understand one word in three."

"Don't worry. And spare me the technical stuff."

"A barge with supplies and carrying furniture to replace the old shabby stuff is on the way. George's boat will arrive this afternoon late and will be anchored off-shore, with a johnboat ferry."

I said nothing and Eli grinned. And waited. I scowled. "Fine. I'll ask. Is Bruiser coming ashore then?"

"Yes, Bruiser is coming ashore then."

"What about Marco?"

"One of Leo's people drank him down. Julietta Tempeste sent him and his Blood Master to the home of the CEO of Madderson Construction. The next day Marco was hired. Old man Madderson, whose construction company has done business with Leo for fifty years or more, is upset that he let Leo down, and also horrified that a vamp had access to his mind and will to that extent."

"Bambi/Mike?"

Eli's lips twisted down, just a fraction of a fraction, and I knew it wasn't good news. "She didn't make it. They were doing CPR on her when the helo landed. Leo turned her, according to her wishes in her sign-on papers."

I looked away. If she survived the devoveo, the years of madness that a vamp went through after being turned, Bambi would wake up two or ten or twenty years from now, with a savage desire to drink down every human she saw. "Okay. What do I do?"

"Rest. Sleep as much as you can. Starting tonight we go on fanghead hours. As soon as the upstairs paint is dry enough, we work out. Practice swords," he added when I looked puzzled. "You're gonna Zen. I'm gonna beat your ass."

"You can try."

We fought and practiced and fought again all day, making plans to keep ourselves alive. We ate great food and lounged on the porch, we mounted cameras and tested them, and we even managed to nap. If there hadn't been the Sangre Duello and our deaths hanging over us, it would have been fantastic.

Night breezes were blowing in through the open windows, carrying out the stench of paint and floor cleaners and other toxic stuff. I was stretched out on a leather uphol-

stered bench, faceup, staring at the tongue-and-groove
ceiling. My arms were out to allow my chest to move more
freely as I was trying to remember how to breathe and I
tried to suck in air to keep from asphyxiating. The padded
wooden practice swords I had used to defend myself were
by my sides on the floor. Sweat had pooled under me and
ran off the leather seat to puddle beside them.

There were fifty of the benches, in ten different colors
of leather, placed all around the third-floor walls. They
had been offloaded from the barge as part of the staging
furnishings. They were hard and stiff, but I might have to
sleep here because I might never be able to move again.
My hands and feet were tingling. I was pretty sure I was
dying.

Eli fell to a bench beside me, stinking of sweat, trying
to recover. Bruiser and the B-twins had worked us to exhaustion. My honeybunch moved to stand over us, sweating and blowing, trying to get his breath back. "You've
improved vastly. And fortunately," Bruiser said, "as challenged, you get to choose weapons."

"Also, your second or your primo or your Enforcer
may fight for you, and your primo is in great need of exercise," a bored voice said. "He also has the ambition,
and some say the skill, to best Grégoire as the finest
swordsman in the Americas." Edmund stepped from behind a roof support. "This," he said with a delighted grin,
"will be an epic battle."

I managed a grin too, and then concentrated on sur-
viving. Lying there, staring at the ceiling, I decided I
wasn't going to die. Not today. Not tomorrow. Not at this
Sangre Duello at all. I had to stay alive. For my friends.

I was sitting on the sand as the sun rose, watching clouds
roll in, dark and angry and filling up the horizon from the
distant water to the vault of the sky. The waves had
changed from soft and lapping to a high surf that sprayed
me with salt and wet down my clothes and my braid. I was
alone, resting, after studying the fight list, looking for
weaknesses in the opponents and their fighting styles. It

was what Beast called tracking, hunting prey, following spoor, finding tall limb over water. *Ambush!*

"It's Fight Club," I'd said to them all, "but with swords and knives. And we can cheat. Got it." Except that, even with discussing the fighting weaknesses of Titus's strongest vamps, I felt a creeping panic beneath my skin. I knew that people I loved were gonna die. People fighting challenges that were intended for me. And if Leo lost the final battle with Titus, and if I didn't win my own fights, the witches in the United States would take on the EVs. They might win, but they'd more likely be killed in a massive paranormal genocide. My godchildren would die. At some point the military would take on the vamps, but likely not in time to keep the vamps from coming ashore. I had tried not to think about this. Tried not to emote about this. But the Sangre Duello was dire. This was the final battle against the EVs. The biggest, baddest uglies on the face of the earth, landing to kill us.

So I'd stomped off, to sit on the sand and stare at the dawn storm rolling in. In twelve hours the vamps would be here. Leo and his people first. Then Titus. And whatever vamps would try to kill us all.

Maybe at first my Enforcer, Gee DiMercy, or my primo, Edmund Hartley, would take my matches and defeat my enemies. And like the coward I am, I'd let them. And maybe they would win for a match or two or seven. But eventually, at some match with an older, better fighter, they would lose. One, or the other, or both, would be maimed or die. Because I let them fight for me. Eli had tried to explain rank to me. Had tried to tell me I wasn't a grunt anymore, not frontline troops. The pep talk hadn't helped.

Because after the best of the sword fighters were down, Eli would try to fight for me. He was looking forward to it, to facing battle again. So I'd disable him to keep him back. And then, while he cursed me for taking him out, I'd fight. And because we had worked our way up the lists, this would be the best fighter of them all.

Beast is best hunter. Beast is best ambush hunter.

I stared at the coming storm as the sky went darker

instead of lighter with the dawn. Rain splattered on me and dimpled the sand. And Beast sent me a vision of tall branches and soaring rock faces, wet with rain, trees lashed by wind.

Beast whispered inside me, *Half-form teeth and fangs and claws. And Beast will drink the blood of her enemies and eat their hearts. Beast is big-cat. Beast will rip out throats of her enemies.*

And lead me further down the path of blood and death, I thought. *Because I can't figure out how to get off that path or how to change direction.*

Or maybe the angel Hayyel will pop in and save me.

Right. Sure. Not.

Beast chuffed with amusement.

"Jane," Alex shouted from the house. "See if you have a cell signal. If so, call someone onshore and see if you get through."

I rolled over and dialed the number of Gee DiMercy. The call went through. And I gave my Enforcer directions, instructions, and, when he argued, orders. I'd developed the belief that Titus would betray the agreements whether he won or lost. And I had an idea how to defeat that.

CHAPTER 16

A Mad Witch Is Never a Good Witch

The outdoor shower worked, the bathers' privacy assured by clapboard walls and a twisting cattle-path-style entrance. There were small and medium palm varieties planted around it and around the house as landscaping. Lounge chairs were on the sand at one beach so vamps and humans could watch the moon rise. More chairs at another so humans could watch the sun rise. And chairs at a third for sunset watching. On such a small island, most of the beaches were in line of sight from each other.

The island looked pretty. More importantly, we now had six fighting rings, three on the third floor and three under the house on the hard-packed sand. These were laid out with river rock, brought in on the tugs and half buried in the sand. Lights had been mounted. Outdoor bouts had sounded like a lark to the vamps who were already on-site, and they did look pretty spiffy, though fighting on sand, even hard sand like that beneath the house, was tricky. The construction types had earned their bonuses.

The house was staged. The furniture was in place: sofas, chairs, tables, lamps, beds. A lot of beds, mostly bunks, but a few kings, and queen bunk beds for the vamps. A pool table that had to weigh half a ton. Food, wine, and alcohol had been ferried over. There were rugs tastefully placed and art hung on the newly painted walls. Linens had been brought in. The housekeeping staff had made up the beds, put towels and washcloths and soaps and hotel-sized toiletries in the bathrooms. There were even flowers all over, live ferns and leafy things. Plus the cut flowers all over the kitchen in crystal vases.

The entire island was gorgeous. The house was stunning.

Since four p.m., the two helos and two chartered boats had been taking the construction types back to shore and bringing in our people. The last helo carrying humans and construction equipment was taking off with a rotor roar and lights flashing against a cerise sky as dusk knocked on the horizon. The next helo would begin the transfer of vamps.

Soon, the house and the entire island would be packed. Even with the construction crew gone, there would be too many people, creatures, beings, their scents all mingled and mangled and jarring, merging into an overwhelming pong, though the constant breezes and perpetual gulf rains would blow and wash a lot of it away. The noise of helos and voices and stomping feet and complaining already hurt my ears. Everyone was rushing around getting settled, storing gear. It was a morass of conflicting stinks and sounds and color.

Part of me loved the excitement, looked forward to the fights. I figured that part of me was nutso. The rest of me wanted to hitch a ride back to NOLA. It crossed my mind that I could maybe swim back if I only had a dolphin bone or maybe even a shark tooth. But . . .

We had been given notice of the beginning of the Sangre Duello. Just a few hours away, at ten p.m., Titus, his first round of fighters, his security, and his blood-servants would all be ashore. There would be no preliminaries, as at a parley. No long titles or jibber jabber. No semipolite or stiletto-sharp discussions. There would be two hours for the seconds to approve of the final arrangements of the first bouts, for the weapons of the first round to be chosen and inspected, and for the fighting rings to be assigned. Titus and his minions would be fed a meal and then led up the stairs to the third floor, settled on benches, and given time to armor up and warm up as needed.

At midnight tonight the first bout would begin.

I was not ready, but my gear was all here, including the things I'd told Gee DiMercy to pack and ship. Leo had approved my idea to defeat a betrayal by Titus by involving Ayatas and Rick, though not on the island as PsyLED had wanted. Maybe I was learning how to sneak around and strategize in overlapping layers like the vamps. Or like Beast. Thanks to my one phone call, my final plans were in play.

I was on my knees beside the bunk bed I'd chosen when I heard a familiar *tap-tap-tapping* of heels on wood floors, climbing stairs. I dropped to my butt, my back to the door. "No," I whispered. But the familiar cadence was still climbing, followed by a *thump-thump-thumping* I couldn't place. I scooted around to the door and spotted Molly, my BFF, taking the last step to the second floor, her red hair already springing into tight curls with the salty moisture. She was dragging a large bag, what I'd heard her refer to as a portmanteau. The bag opened into two parts, and had been designed half for clothes and half for magical trinkets. By the way it thumped on the steps, I knew she had packed heavy on the magical crap.

Molly was not supposed to be here. She was not to have been told the time and date of the Sangre Duello. I'd left orders. Another head appeared over the half wall of the steps as the person attached climbed behind her. This one was familiar as well, with straight long red hair, and pointy nose as seen from the side. Molly's niece. Shiloh. Technically, as her clan master, my scion.

"My room is one of the windowless rooms. Yours is there." Shiloh's hand pointed toward my room. "And we haven't told—Oops."

"Yeah," I said, standing in a single twisting motion that unfolded my legs and pushed me upright, hands free.

"My scions, who swore to me. You didn't tell me that either of you would be here. And after I expressly forbade it."

Molly's eyes flashed and I knew I had screwed up. Molly had never liked being told what to do. "Your Enforcer and your primo countermanded your orders," she said, her words precise. "As did the leader of the witch coven of New Orleans, Lachish Dutillet. Adan Bouvier was not the only witch on that boat with the emperor, not the only one in captivity. You need magical protection from attack from the gulf."

I stared at her with horror. I hadn't told her about Adan, about what had been done to him. I'd tried to protect her from the awful truth of what Titus's vamps did to witches.

"Humph," Molly said, asperity in the tone. "Yes. I heard about him, from Lachish, Adan the vampire weather witch. She heard about him from someone else." Her tone said she should have heard about Adan Bouvier from me. She was right. I dropped my eyes. "Jane. You need the witches to keep you safe while you fight. We need Leo's vampires and the rest of Clan Yellowrock to keep the witches safe and alive. Leo dies and we are all royally screwed."

My face must have given something away because Molly dragged her portmanteau across the hallway to me, her eyes boring into mine, her voice rising as she continued to speak. "You think the witches don't know what will happen to us, to our families and our children, if Titus wins this stupid"—she shouted—"foolish"—she shouted louder—"blood challenge?"

I backed into my room, toward the open window. Toward escape. Molly followed, into the too-small room. The heavy, two-door case had little wheels that squeaked and bumped over every uneven place in the floor. Molly was wearing a deep, dark, bloodred winter dress with a little black jacket and black heels. Red wasn't usually Moll's color, but this looked powerful on her. And she was wearing a pearl necklace and carrying, in her other hand, a small rosemary plant. "Look at me," Molly demanded.

Molly is predator, Beast thought, admiration in her words.

Molly is angry, I thought back. *And a mad witch is never a good witch.*

"Jane!"

I looked her in the eyes. "I'm here not because you need me," she said. "I know you can take care of yourself. I'm here because my people need me."

"You're pregnant," I blurted out.

Kits, Beast murmured.

"I noticed," she said, pronouncing all the syllables like cutting blades and hissing snakes. "I'll be behind the scenes, not up front. Not out in the middle of any witch-magic battle that might take place. My job is to monitor for interfering magical activity and warn the others. Lachish and Shiloh and Ailis are here to fight. And Soul is here, somewhere, to help in case they have another timewalker, to spot any interference of that nature and stop it. I'll be under a *hedge of thorns,* the newest one B—" She stopped. She had almost said Big Evan, who wasn't out of the closet yet. "That I could make. *Hedge of thorns 3.0.* With other modified, portable *hedges* and inverted *hedges* available to me, all defensive, as stipulated in the Sangre Duello rules, what precious few that there are. I'll be the safest person on this island. But you need us all to make sure the EVs don't cheat and use witch magic to attack."

Cheating wasn't allowed outside of the fighting rings. Cheating with magic was not allowed anywhere near a Sangre Duello except La Danza. Cheating with weapons and tactics inside a ring and within a bout was a different matter entirely. I was betting all I had, and all I was, on an inside weapon cheat. But Moll was right. The Sangre Duello did need magical monitoring. And in case of magical attack, we'd need someone who could deflect a spell of offense until we could deal with it.

But . . . Molly. There were things I hadn't told her. *Crap.*

My best friend in the world leaned into me and I felt magics on my skin as she initiated a spell of silence to cover up her words. She whispered so softly a fanghead couldn't have heard it. "And my special magics will save the day if all else is lost."

Her special magics. Her death magics. Magics that would drain every bit of death and undeath for miles around. I stepped around her and walked out, past people in the hallway.

Behind me, Molly claimed the bunk bed beneath mine. "She'll be okay," Molly said to someone in the hallway.

But I wouldn't. Not if something happened to Moll. What in blue blazes was Big Evan thinking by letting his pregnant wife out of his sight?

I passed through people and vamps coming up the stairs. Dozens of people. I wanted to head outside, but I had a job to do. This one last job. Keep Leo safe, to keep Molly safe. So instead of running away, I walked around the second level, checking out the arrangements, thinking about cheats for inside the fighting rings.

Leo and his scions were sharing one of the tiny central rooms. Koun, Gee, Tex, and Edmund—my vamps—were in a second room. The third room had bunks for Dacy Mooney, Ming Zoya of Mearkanis, and Ming Zhane of Glass. In the fourth room was Sabina Delgado y Aguilera and Shiloh Everhart Stone. I had tried to keep Shiloh off island. She was my responsibility, not that Shiloh seemed to think so. The placement of the vamps had been carefully thought out, the weakest vamp under the protection of the outclan priestess.

In the outer ring of rooms were the humans and Leo's and my human staff, divided by gender. In one of the larger rooms were Lee, Leo's assistant Scrappy, and four blood donors: Tia, Ipsita, Christie, and Maryanne, who was Edmund's human lover and blood-servant. Maryanne hadn't been around much since Edmund became my primo, but I'd always found her to be a levelheaded and serene woman.

In the second room set aside for nonvamp females were Lachish Dutillet, the head of the witch coven of NOLA, and Bliss—aka Ailis Rogan, a witch in training. Lachish glared at me when she saw me in the doorway.

She didn't like me much. Didn't hate me, but didn't like me, despite the fact that I had killed the vamps that had killed her own daughter. She thought I was a trouble-maker and a meddler. Not that I blamed her. I'd been called both since I walked out of the woods at an apparent age twelve, naked, carrying the scars of bullet wounds and a gold nugget. Mostly I deserved the rep. Bunking with the two witches was Soul. The arcenciel was present not in her official PsyLED capacity but as the unofficial leader of the rainbow dragons that Titus's goons had tried to capture and enslave. Lachish turned her back to me and said to Soul, "It's a *wyrd* spell, one that breaks crystals from the inside. But to test it you'd have to be inside a crystal spell."

"No," Soul said. "That will not happen."

I didn't know if Titus's people and any witches on board could scent or identify what Soul was. I didn't know how safe she might be. But then, if Leo lost the last bout, none of us were safe.

Lachish extended a folded paper. "You are a stubborn woman. Here is the spell, the *wyrd* and the directions to break a crystal. If you get caught, try it. If it needed to be refined and you didn't let us experiment, then it's on you." Lachish was an irritating but succinct woman.

I slipped away before Soul replied. I'd known I wouldn't have a room to myself. I'd known I'd be bunking with others, at least with Del, Brenda Rezk, and Ro Moore, Katie's Enforcer. Brenda was a security specialist assigned to Atlanta and Ro was a cage fighter and mixed martial arts specialist. Ro had nearly died in a recent fight at HQ. No way was she up to full fighting form yet and I resented Leo for bringing them both. Molly would be the fifth roommate. I hoped being pregnant didn't make her snore or have to pee all day long. I could kick the others into silence; not so much Molly. We were wall-to-wall bunks with one empty. I figured someone would fill the empty bunk bed eventually.

I checked in on the third, smallest bedroom. Neatly stacked against the narrow wall space, floor to ceiling, were suitcases belonging to Bruiser, Brian, and Brandon.

The Onorios were bunking together in a space almost big enough for one small bed. It was . . . cozy. Right. Cozy. Claustrophobic. Cramped. I looked over the luggage and didn't see weapons cases. That answered one question. The Onorios would not be fighting. They were to be judges and referees, not fighters. I wasn't happy about some of our best fighters relegated to the sidelines, but the negotiations had been intense. Leo wouldn't have given up them as fighters without good reason. Leo had arranged to remove three of Titus's foremost fighters in return, and gained the home court advantage referees. But if I was injured I knew that Bruiser would kick the referee title to the four winds and protect me. Bruiser would hate himself if he reneged on a vow to act as observer and judge. Another reason to stay alive and healthy. I eased away and shut the door behind me.

The big back room had been set aside for the rest of the blood-servants' bunk beds and this room was a madhouse, the location for most of the cursing, shouting, and thumps. They'd be sleeping in shifts and some of them would have to switch out bunks, but no one would have to sleep on the floor. Eli, Alex, Troll, and Wrassler were on the far end of the room. Derek and his security men were positioned near the door: Angel Tit, Chi-Chi, Tequila Sunrise, T. Sweaty Bollock, T. Jolly Green Giant, P. Shooter. Three of the Vodka boys. Deon, acting as chief cook and bottle washer for us all, had a curtained lower bunk for himself. Twelve male blood-servants, who were also the house-keeping crew and the medical team, would be sharing three sets of bunk beds, switching out cots to sleep in shifts. Pretty much, the long narrow room was wall-to-wall bunks. By day and night the air here would carry the roar of snores and the massed stink of sweat, bad breath, BO, and dirty clothes.

As satisfied as I could be with the current accommodations, I wove between people and down the stairs. The main room was perfect, but too full of people, most lounging on the sofas, cells or tablets in hand, checking the new Wi-Fi connection. It was too slow. Lots of complaints. I left through the back door, crossed the screened

porch, where more people lounged on new outdoor furniture or in hammocks, and outside. The smell of were-
creature hit me.

The werewolves were sleeping outside, under the
house, on the sand or in hammocks, unless a major tide
brought in high water, in which case they'd be sleeping on
the third floor when it wasn't in use for duels. The weres
included Brute, the entire wolf pack camera team, and
two grindylows.

Werewolves are ugly.

I stepped down the narrow stairs. They were older
than the wider front stairs, and squeaked with each step.
Yes. I can see how you might think so. Wolves and dogs.

*Werewolves are not pack turned. Werewolves are loyal
to Leo.*

I slowed. *And how do you know that?*

*Beast can smell stink of betrayal on weres. Beast does
not smell stink of betrayal on wolves.*

Would have been nice to know that, I thought, with a
lot more snark than I planned.

Beast chuffed. *Beast is still learning to use good nose
from ugly dog. New stinks are hard to learn.* Beast padded away from me, into the depths of my mind. No cops
were here in any official capacity.

I moved away from the house and into the relative
quiet of the dark. I found a wind- and storm-beaten tree
to rest against and sat on the low limb, looking out over
the ocean. I didn't see U.S. Navy ships. Maybe Leo had
found a way to keep them off the shore, though they had
to know that warm bodies were here because the defensive *hedges* were not yet in place. The military had satellites and the ability to track heat signatures. In a few
hours, here on this one island, would be the greatest ac-
cumulation of powerful Mithrans in the world. If the military had the ability to scan through a *hedge of thorns*
thrown up by Lachish and the other witches, the possibility of a missile mishap existed, one that accidentally decimated an island and a house that had never appeared on
maps . . . The opportunity was there. The military could
track all the boats and the helos arriving and departing.

Military satellites would see what civilians couldn't.
Would they take the chance that Leo would win and the
peaceful status quo would be maintained? Or would Uncle Sam wipe us all out? I was becoming a paranoid conspiracy theorist.

The cynical part of me said the government would
dither and yammer and yada yada for days, at which point
the Sangre Duello would be over, for better or worse. The
really cynical part said they would blow us to kingdom
come. It started to rain, an icy deluge that chilled me to
my bones. "Great."

I was back at my little limb, dancing shoes ground into
the storm-wet sand, silk-clad butt resting on the wind-
scoured bark, as the helo landed, its rotors chopping the
night. These would be the last deliveries. The NOLA
vamps were now all on Spitfire Island. Staff raced to un-
load luggage from the helicopter. A few raindrops splatted down for a moment, big splashy things that left star
patterns in the sand.

I watched from the shadows as Leo stepped from the
helicopter, a black shadow in the night, his hair flying in
the rotor wash. He was dressed for travel in black jeans
and a black sport coat with a white shirt, more casual
than I ever remembered seeing him. He was walking to
the house and the line of waiting blood-servants when he
stopped. Swiveled his head in that unhuman way they
have, his nostrils fluttering. And his eyes settled on me in
the dark.

Abruptly, he changed course and came to me, stepping gracefully on the sand. He stood staring down at me,
the scent of ink and papyrus and black pepper whirling
on the prop wash, Leo's scent. His power spun after it,
spiky and intense, like flaming velvet. The wind shifted,
carrying away the helo noise, enough to talk. "My Jane.
You sit in the dark. Do you grieve when no death has yet
occurred?"

"People I love will die in the next night or two. People
you love."

"War is always hard. Death is inevitable, even for Mithrans."

"I love how you comfort me."

Leo laughed, that wonderful laugh the powerful ones use, that sends shivers down your spine and makes magic dance on the air. "There is no comfort in war, my Jane. Nor in death. I would not attempt to comfort one who faces battle. There are only platitudes in words."

Maybe I was still human enough to want platitudes? But I didn't say it.

"The corset style suits you well," he said.

I reached up and touched the décolletage of the scarlet corset-styled top, designed by Madame Melisende, Modiste du les Mithrans. The golden lace was made from silk thread, as soft as heaven. My breasts were hefted high, making it look like I had a lot more in the boob department than I did and my doubled gorgets were propped on mounded flesh. My black skirt was a fighting formal, designed for dancing and weapons and battle, but on first glance looked soft and feminine.

My combat boots, the red leathers, a brand-new undergarment, and the white, buttery-soft-as-pigskin motojacket fighting leathers were spread on the bunk, ready for the right moment to change. The leathers were backed with Dyneema fabric and hard plasticized armor between the layers. They were lined with silk and there were defensive anti-spells woven into the entire thing. Both sets of leathers were adjustable, so that if I shifted into halfform, they would shift with me, stretching where I expanded and contracting where I shrank. But I wasn't wearing the leathers. Instead, I was dressed in sexyformal garb, weapons chafing my exposed flesh.

The helo lifted away before I spoke, the artificial wind whipping the low branches and throwing sand. As it flew away, I heard the approach of the other helo. It was a staggered landing pattern, so the staff didn't have to reassemble every few minutes, and it had been going on all evening. But Leo's was supposed to be the last one. A surprise for us all? Someone unannounced? Someone to throw the entire Sangre Duello into total discord? Sure. Why not? Sometimes I thought Leo was more cat than I was. I deliberately didn't ask about it. I said, instead, "I like the white leathers. They're different. But this will make a confusing impact."

"True. And when you fight, you will be the only snowflake among us."

Snowflake. He was baiting me. Again I didn't reply.

"Though perhaps a well-knapped white-quartz blade might be a better analogy."

The helo's lights danced across the sand.

"I know why you are so sad, my Jane," he said unexpectedly. "Fear rides a red horse, its coat the color of blood, the color of battle and of loss. Fear is the greatest enemy."

I frowned as the new helo circled, the lights touching everywhere. "I can't fight like everyone wants me to," I said at last. "Falling into that Zen meditation that Eli talks about is hit-or-miss. And when I hit I just slice people up." Like Callan. "And when I don't fight in Zen, I lose bits of time."

"You may not have to fight at all. Nor might I. But if fight you must, then fight as you dance," he said, his eyes piercing through the dark, his hair already curling in the wet air, "and as your cat hunts. You have balance and muscle memory and claws and teeth. You have deep perception of how an enemy moves and breathes, in the same way you sense how a dance partner moves and breathes, and what steps he may make next. I have seen you take in an opponent and gauge his or her frailties and weaknesses and strengths in the space between heartbeats. You have timing and stealth and joy in movement. All these things are yours by training and nature, my Dark Queen. Incorporate what you can, but do not try to change now. Fight your way. No European will expect such a thing." He held out a hand. "Come. Let us greet the last arrival."

"If it's a suckhead, I hope he can bunk with you. We're out of room."

"I fully expect at least one of them to lair with me."

Hmmm. My mind cataloged the missing vamps as I put my hand into his and let him lead me to the line of waiting staff. The helo finally landed. And Katie stepped onto the sand.

I watched as she leaped from the helo and threw herself into Leo's arms and our hands were pulled apart. I turned and looked out over the water, to see bow and stern lights juddering up and down the waves. It was the first small boat ferrying the Europeans' food sources ashore. Blood-servants. Humanish people who had been drinking on the oldest vamps still undead, who had been around long enough to have seen more than one century roll around. Blood-meals who wanted my people dead. People I might have to kill in order to stay alive long enough to see this blood duel through. I turned away from the helo and the beach and moved across the storm-wet sand to the house.

At the bottom of the steps I spotted Molly, Ailis, and Lachish. They were putting the final touches on the circle that surrounded the house, the new fire pit, and the traps built in here and there, the circles dug by hand with small shovels for the *hedge of thorns 3.0*. Their laughter was ripped by the wind, sending tatters of sound along the shore. The three witches had prepared other defenses on the island, things they hadn't told me about for two reasons—because they weren't sure how well they would work over salt water, and because Molly was afraid I'd depend on something that was iffy at best. They had three or four dependable defensive workings ready; the others were less reliable. They had one offensive working at their disposal, but using it went against everything they stood for. They'd use it only as a means of last resort, and again, they weren't talking to me about it. My job was hardwired and Wi-Fi security, fighting, killing, not witchy stuff.

But . . . there were things I hadn't told Molly. Things like the fact that I might have a brother. Things like Cym had been in New Orleans. But then I hadn't expected to have to tell her things until we were face-to-face over a nice cup of tea in her kitchen after all this was over. Molly wasn't supposed to be here. I stepped down to her and Moll raised a hand, offering me a smile. It withered when I didn't smile back. She frowned and demanded, "What?"

"Couple things. First, I'm afraid that Bancym M'lareil may be on the island, or may make her way here."

Molly might have paled slightly. Cym and Jack Shoffru had access to a lot of black magic and they had tried to control Molly's death magic. Cym had kidnapped Molly. Hurt Molly. Hurt her horribly. "Son of a witch on a switch," she swore. "When were you going to tell me that?"

"Ummm. Never? You weren't supposed to be here."

Molly's eyes flashed with fire and I almost turned tail and ran as she stalked up to me. Beast, her attention captured by the predatory posture, stared out at her. *Molly is predator.*

Yeah. And scary.

"You were protecting me?"

"Pretty much." I shrugged uncomfortably. "With you both on the island, you will be one of her prime targets. All she has to do is control your death magics, point them at Leo, and poof, Titus has everything he wants. Or take out Leo and Titus and then she and Dominique would be in charge."

Molly reached up and gripped my chin, turning my face down to hers. Softly, she said, "You helped me learn to control my magic. If Cym comes near me, I'll drain her."

"But you don't have your familiar with you." Meaning that her control would be less than optimal.

Beast took over and spoke through my mouth. "Beast will be Molly's familiar if Molly-predator needs cat. Beast is best big-cat."

Molly stared into my/our eyes. "Fine. But don't keep things from me, big-cat. Understand?"

"The I/we of Jane and Beast understand."

Molly's expression went accusing, fingers tightening on my chin painfully. "Don't think I didn't notice what you did there. Promise me you will not keep things from me. Promise me."

I blew out a breath. "I promise. Beast promises."

"Good enough. What else?"

"I might have a brother who's nearly as old as me, a skinwalker. He works for PsyLED."

Moll's mouth opened and closed. "Well," she said at last. "That sounds like a good story for when we're winding down from this crazy party. If I wasn't preggo, I might even have to send Big Evan off with the kids and open a bottle of wine." She squinted slightly at me. "You and this brother okay?"

"I think so. Or we're getting that way."

"Good. I want to meet him." Moll went back to work.

My chin hurt where she had pinched it. "Yeah. Moll's scary."

I climbed to the porch. Alex was crouched there with his camera gear and Eli's night combat gear, cataloging each blood-servant on the ferryboat and taking stills with the low-light and infrared cameras. Behind him was a camera man—camera werewolf—with a shoulder-mounted camera. It was Scout, a werewolf I hadn't gotten to know yet, with a green grindy on his shoulder. She snarled at me, looking stressed out with so many humans—potential victims of werewolf rage—around.

Scout focused in on the sight of the beach and through his earbud, I could hear Champ talking, giving the color or the overview or whatever you called it, in his pristine British accent. The leader of the werewolves was in a closet we had set aside for the production room/security room, and it was pretty much wall-to-wall screens from every wall-mounted and shoulder-mounted camera on the island. There wasn't enough bandwidth to allow all of us comms equipment, but the island was so small we could likely hear a good scream from end to end.

Every flaw, every flub, every wound and death, every single thing that happened for the next two nights, would be filmed and sent out live in the pay-per-view agreed upon between Leo and the werewolves and Titus. Lot of money riding on the pay-per-view, the gambling, and maybe documentaries after.

I blinked the salt and grit out of my eyes and walked through the house, feeling tiredness in every muscle of my body, an ache in my middle that called for antacids.

Bandit and Rocky were in the kitchen tasting things and making suggestions to Deon. Ro and Brenda, Katie's retinue, were bent over a schematic of security equipment, offering suggestions. The stink of vamp and werewolves and sex and blood and adrenaline were all mixed together in a gagworthy stench. The house and the spit of land were too small for us all.

Only hours until midnight. Our side could have used some sleep.

I don't know what Titus or his retinue were expecting when they came ashore and walked toward the steps leading to the house. Applause? Bowing and scraping? Tugging on our forelocks?—which meant pulling the hair at the front of our heads. Surely he had expected fighting armor. What he saw as he approached was Eli and me standing at parade rest, not wearing leathers, but fully weaponed up with dual longswords, things that go bang, and two vials of holy water each. At my waist, I was wearing my sheathed Mughal Empire, watered-steel dagger, my gift from Bruiser. We looked like a walking advert for overlapping time periods. A take-no-prisoners duo from multiple eras, me in a nineteenth-century-style corset top and formal skirt, but wearing weapons, Eli in jeans and a muscle shirt, with even more weapons. With bare feet. Eli and I also had our battle faces on. A bizarre unwelcoming committee of two. We'd been standing in place for nearly an hour in the moonlight, as the EVs kept us waiting. Playing games already.

The extended waiting period was being filmed by Scooter in the rushes and sea oats of a sand dune. It was a terribly boring job. So far.

Titus was a small man by today's standards, not quite five feet, seven inches tall in his dress shoes and black tux. He was clean shaven, his eyes a teddy-bear brown, deceptively nonthreatening, and his hair was worn in a modern style, not the old-fashioned one in the portraits I had seen.

His power swept before him. It hit me, a burst of icy intensity, shattering across my flesh in a shotgun blast of energy that charred and froze at the same time. It would have brought me to my knees had I not been expecting it. In Beast-sight, it flashed on the foundation of the *hedge of thorns* in the sand.

I was reminded of Leo's power the one time I had been standing close to him when he was about to lose control or else he was funneling all the power of all the vamps in his vicinity. One or the other. Or both. It had been the opening moments of a feeding frenzy, something I had no desire to ever see.

Titus's power was like that but more. An exhibition. A demonstration. A painful shower of smoldering barbs that iced where they touched. I took a slow breath. Eli's eyes narrowed at his own discomfort.

Titus turned his head to scan the house. A gold chain glinted at his neck, dropping inside his collar. Gold on his fingers. At his wrists. A beach wind and the house lights caught his curls. I wanted to giggle but kept it in for fear it would sound like, well, like a titter of fear.

We stayed put as the group approached, blocking the bottom of the stairs. Staring them all down. Staring down Titus's Enforcer, a hulking female Viking vampire named Glacie, though I suspected she had originally been a Gertruda or a Hilda. Staring down Titus's primo, Taviano, one of the human warriors who had challenged me. Him I looked over and then ignored as they got close enough for them to see us clearly. Our blocking the way was a pointed insult. Taviano put both hands on his swords as if ready to cut his way through once they reached us. We still didn't move.

The man who claimed to rule all the fangheads in the world was forced to come to a complete halt in front of us. Because this was Sangre Duello. Courtesy and vamp etiquette were distant rules that could be twisted and bent to intimidate or bewilder. Titus looked us over, giving the boob flesh a pointed and condemning glance. But his attitude declared that Eli and I were beneath his notice. We still didn't move.

Just before Taviano and his boss could react to the insult that the blocked stairs represented, Eli and I swiveled on our heels and stepped to the sides. From above us, Leo boomed, "Titus! Come on up, dude. We have beer." I slid my eyes to Leo. He was standing there in the same jeans he'd been wearing when he landed, a brown bottle in one hand. And he was barefoot. Just like the Fifties Americana I had suggested.

Katie was by his side, wearing a billowy dress and flops and an expression that tried hard to appear excited, despite her role as inelegant, unsophisticated, and vaguely vulgar. "We have an entire . . . keg . . . of beer."

I was sure Katie hadn't had a beer in centuries. The whole sentence sounded strange in her usually sophisticated mouth.

Titus's face went paler than vamp-normal. His mouth opened. His eyes went human wide, not vamped-out wide. And his power stuttered and fell. "Beer?" Titus repeated. And then he barked a torrent of French and what might have been Italian to Taviano. Shock and anger in the tone. Insult. Confusion.

"Come on up!" Leo shouted again. And the MOC and his heir turned and walked away from Titus, Katie's flops flapping against the wood porch. The three cameras caught every word and gesture. If I survived the night I'd have to watch this someday. The MOC and Katie had succeeded in gaining the initial emotional upper hand. Point one to Leo.

And then I caught a whiff of lemons and a glimpse of the woman closest to Titus. Julietta Tempeste, Blood Master of Clan Des Citrons. Behind her was Dominique.

Beast leaped to the front of my brain. *Enemy,* she thought at me.

Yeah. Enemies. All of them. I stared at Julietta and when she looked up, I grinned at her, showing too many teeth, my eyes glowing gold. She faltered. And I laughed, my voice a low growl.

At the sound, the Europeans tightened around Titus, a group of men close to him, and the semicircle of women behind. The emperor stepped through the residue of *hedge of thorns 3.0,* his individual power signature sparking in Beast's vision as a dotted line of energies.

And then something happened. I wasn't sure what. Just something different. Unexpected. Magic raked across me, familiar, gray and black with motes of red. The magics in my middle reacted, speeding up in the Vitruvian pattern of the star within me. And then it was gone and I wasn't sure what had happened, except that Titus had done . . . something. And then . . . that thought slipped away.

The front room was full of casually dressed humans, reading, speaking into their cells, thumbs flying as they sent texts. Two guys were stretched out on the rug on their stomachs, a spirited game of checkers between them. Not the dignified game of chess enjoyed by most older vamps, but gauche American games. Beer bottles were everywhere. The first two rows of a pyramid of beer cans had been built at the base of a window.

Deon shouted from the kitchen, his island enunciation like honey and whiskey, "Titus, honey, come and get you'self a corn dog. We got us three kind of mustard to Dip. It. In!" Deon demonstrated dipping a corn dog into a small container of Grey Poupon and biting off the end. It was a decidedly sexual act, Deon at his most amazing, putting on a show, the kind he had performed at Katie's Ladies when he chose to participate in the evening entertainment. Chewing, he pranced out from behind the Carrara marble–topped island while waving the emperor and his peeps over. The chef was dressed in feathers, spangles, and rhinestones from head to toe, an outfit that looked like the love child of Bollywood and Brazilian Rio Carnival.

I thought Titus—the homophobe that history had never gotten right—might stumble.

In Rome, sexuality and sexual expression had been far more open and varied than in modern times, but Titus had never participated, more pope than playboy. Judging from his expression, the emperor was still a straight, conservative man.

"Grab your corn dog and beer and come on up, hoss." Tex stood at the bottom of the next flight of stairs, Brute beside him. The white werewolf was staring at Titus, panting, salivating, as if he might want a little taste. "We got us some fightin' to do."

Deon held out a carnival treat on a stick. Daring Titus.

Titus reached to accept the corn dog and Taviano stepped between them. Deon smacked the dog down onto a paper plate on the island and put both hands to his hips. "Sugar, if I wanted to poison the kink-ly sort, I'd do it in Earl Grey tea, not in a corn dog. That would be downright sacrilegious." Deon picked up the paper plate and slapped it against Taviano's chest. "Now you take that food and you eat it." Ziggy slid a hand around the stunned primo to whack a bottle of beer into Titus's hands.

Titus's secundo leaned in and whispered something in that foreign, Italian, Frenchy talk to the king, then led him up the stairs. Deon grinned evilly. He'd been having fun. From behind me Ziggy said, "Honey, if I'd known you were going to play I'd have put on Queen Bitch and helped. That looked like fun."

"It was," Deon said, "what that old dude deserved."

Titus's shoulders went back and he stepped up the stairs, straight toward the lens of a camera and into the view of the world. Leo, with a faintly pleased smile on his face, followed. Katie winked at me as they passed. Winked. At me.

Point two to Leo. And to Shakespeare. Leo's opening salvo had been stolen from Petruchio, his own Kate by his side. I grinned suddenly, showing a lot of teeth. I couldn't have been prouder. This was the stolen theme from *Taming of the Shrew*. Ro and Brenda, wearing jeans and sweatshirts, followed Katie and Leo. And then the rest of the NOLA retinue.

This little show was surely my fault from way back when. Go, me.

CHAPTER 17

Stuck His Nose into My Crotch

We were standing on the third floor, the windows open to the cool night breeze, the corroded fans turning overhead. The air smelled of salt, smoke, and vamp, a weird mixture of herbs and blood and sex, poorly hidden beneath the wonderful aroma of food.

On the table set aside for heavy hors d'oeuvres were more corn dogs; a slow cooker full of beanie weenies with Louisiana hot sauce; pigs in a blanket; and three plates of deviled eggs, each a bit different, and one made with that green horseradish-like stuff they use in sushi. There were two kinds of slaw, one made with ginger and soy, and lots of fixin's, including pickled okra, pickled beet, pickled pickles, and corn on the cob. Buns. And a massive, monstrous bowl of boudin, big enough to bathe in, sitting atop a platter of crackers. On the platter beside it there was a whole barbecued pig and at least ten bottles of various kinds of hot sauce, from all over the South, including two featuring the Carolina Reaper, the hottest pepper in the world, created by PuckerButt, in South Carolina. I picked up the bottles to see I DARE YOU STUPIT and REAPER RACHA

SAUCE. It might have been my imagination, but my hands
tingled from the peppers, even through the glass. If the
table didn't catch on fire from the sauces, it might die
from the weight of the food. Pretty sure I heard it groan-
ing as I stepped away.

The bar had been set up near the back of the room.
There were five huge buckets full of ice and beer bottles,
the aluminum leaking condensation onto newspapers
placed on the floor. No colas. No water. No juice. No fancy
wines.

On a table beside the bar was a churn of homemade
ice cream, double chocolate brownies, and the fixings for
s'mores to take outside to the fire pit, which was blowing
on the wind and smoking up the joint. To my right, I
heard the werewolf pack leader/commentator describing
the food as "regular ol' American picnic in the moonlight." Champ had a way with words.

"Deon," I muttered, "you are a-mazing. A Wonder-
Chef. You need your own cape."

"Only if I can get a magic wand too," Deon said from
behind me. "Oh, wait." He put a finger to his lips. "I have
a magic wand." He gamboled away, his buttocks bouncing.

"I may have to stab out my eyes," Eli whispered.

I gestured with my head to the emperor. He was eating
a corn dog. On international paid TV. On his plate was a
wasabi deviled egg. And a mound of boudin. A squirt of
hot sauce was curled atop it. I had a moment to wonder if
that was the PuckerButt sauce and if the fanghead king
would go up in flames if he ate some. I could wish.

Vamps didn't eat human food often. I had a feeling
Titus wasn't prepared for modern spices, and that Deon
had prepared for that lack of familiarity with as much
care as he had prepared his costume and attitude to irri-
tate a homophobe. Titus scraped a mess of boudin onto a
cracker and took a bite. There was a funny sound, a sort
of an inhale/groan/gasp.

A dozen of the king's humans surrounded him, hiding
him from view. Leo saw it and slipped to the side, giving
someone a tiny finger wave, his index finger lifting and
falling. A warning. My eyes followed the MOC for a mo-

ment as he stepped behind the dessert table and picked
up something. The tips of his swords appeared below the
table, one on each side, mostly out of sight. The film crew
stepped back.

The EV emperor's humans were all traditionally gorgeous. The males all wore tuxedoes; the women were
dressed in conservative black dresses, hems to the floor.
Yeah. Titus was still hung up on sexual expression, life-
styles, and activities. Leo knew Titus's sexual proclivities.
Of course he did. And Leo, with Deon, had set all this up,
maybe months ago, as part of whatever other strategies
he had percolating in his multilevel, long-view, three-D-
chess-game-of-politics, devious mind.

A wave scent of humanish blood washed through the
room and out on the salty wind. The magic in the fighting
chamber changed. Leo, weapons still out of sight, began
to slowly vamp out. Katie, in her sundress, appeared at
Leo's side, her bastard sword in a two-hand grip. Edmund appeared beside me, close enough for me to hear
the soft pop of displaced air. Gee stepped to my other
side. I could smell Eli somewhere close but didn't turn to
look.

His humans backed away from Titus, then the vamps,
forming groups, females and males. The emperor stood
there, cold and unamused, his mouth burned red at the
corners where he had bitten into the PuckerButt sauce
and it had scalded him. He was armed with two swords,
just like Leo. "You parley with your ruler without respect," he said in stilted English. At the words, all his
vamps drew their blades.

I tried to figure out why, and realized Titus was using
treaty-making wording, not Sangre Duello terminology.

Brandon—wearing a tux, unlike the rest of us—
stepped forward. Calmly he said, "There has been no
parley called. Parley was made null and void when the
scions of Titus Flavius Vespasianus, Emperor of the European Mithrans, came ashore, on the territory of Leo
Pellissier, without legal writ from the Master of the City
of New Orleans and the Greater Southeast, in violation
of immigration laws of the United States of America.

Said scions acted without proper honor and outside of the Vampira Carta in leading attack on the scions and humans of New Orleans."

My eyebrows went up. That was a mouthful of legal mumbo jumbo.

Brandon finished with, "There is no treating. There is no parley. This is Sangre Duello." Brandon stepped back.

"You play silly games," Titus said to Leo. He lifted his arms high, the steel edges of his longswords glinting in the overhead light, the silver plating on the rest of the blades flashing. He was wearing armor imbued with so much magic that it glowed in Beast-sight. "You have challenged the emperor of the Mithrans and the Naturaleza. *En garde.*"

Our vamps darted in. Our humans scrambled away.

Leo, still in jeans, moved around the table, blades bared, his two besties at his sides. Katie vamped out. Grégoire moved with a dancer's grace, lending balletic beauty to the three of them. The expression on Leo's face said he was ready to fight, the agreements as to the order of duels be damned. His swords started to spin. Grégoire's blue eyes narrowed. The three looked deadly. But Titus's people spread out. Blocking the stairs. Others faced our humans, ready to engage, a barroom brawl to the death. More weapons were readied on both sides. The EVs had been looking for an opportunity to attack and end it all quickly.

The filming continued, and the camera crew were speaking to one another through their short-range headsets. One tripped. Hit the floor with an echoing thump. Titus whirled on him, sword up.

What did Titus benefit by pushing this to the finish right now? And then a tingle of magic brushed across my skin. Was Titus wearing an amulet treated with a mind spell? I didn't know and couldn't take a chance.

I drew on Beast's scream and shouted, "Hold!" Everything went still as the word echoed in the rafters. Leo blinked, his face startled, though he didn't looked ticked off at me so that was good. But I had no idea what to do now that I had their attention, a skinny girl, holding a ceremonial sword that would be useless in any real battle. Flying by the seat of my pants. Again. But at least the ratcheting up of aggression had stopped. "I demand . . ." The word came to me only a beat too late. "Redress. This human"—I spoke the word as if it were an insult, and pointed my Mughal blade at Titus's primo—"little Tavi, has challenged the Enforcer of the Master of the City of New Orleans. I have accepted his challenge and I will not be denied." All my weapons sheathed except the curved Mughal blade, I advanced on Taviano.

My Enforcer stepped between us. "This challenge by this human child is mine to take, my mistress," Gee said, enunciating like an actor in a pre-sound-system play. At his statement, the camera wolfman rolled out of the way, to his feet, and out of danger. Gee drew his swords. "I would not have you sully your blade with the weak, watered-down blood of this human creature."

Beast chuffed. *Sully. Is good word. But humans like meat with watered-down blood.*

"Sully? You dare!" Taviano ground out, swords bare, advancing on Gee and me.

"Enough!" The word shook the rafters and made the overhead fans sway. Sabina elbowed a vamp and two humans aside as if they weighed nothing and stepped between us, her magic hot and frozen all at once, making the space we occupied seem too small, too tight, airless. The place fell so quiet that I could hear her white, starched clothing swish. Her hands were hidden in the skirt's copious pockets. "The outclan priestess signed the final agreements. Thus I am both final witness and judge." Sabina pulled her gloved hands from her pockets. In one was a seven-inch-long sliver of wood, sharp as a stake on one end and worn smooth on the other. The energies in the room went sideways: hot/cold/smoky/sour, with magical glints of pale gold and motes of fearful black. The stench of the undead increased, the sickeningly sweet smell of funeral flowers and dried herbs and lemons.

The weapon Sabina held up was a big sliver of the Blood Cross, the historical, cursed, magical origination element of the vamps. This one was smaller than the

cross-shaped section that had charred the priestess's hand
to the bone, but was still larger than any other piece I had
seen. Where had she gotten it? I'd once peeked into her
hiding place, inside the sepulcher where she might—or
might not—sleep by day. I hadn't seen this one. And I had
kinda ruined the tiny one she had loaned me when it had
been absorbed into the Glob. Sabina held the holy-cursed
wood over her head and people backed away, leaving only
the main challengers, the TV crew, and Sabina in the center of the room.

"Vespasianus," she said. "So speaks the outclan priestess. You raised weapons against the titular challenger out
of order. Pellissier, you raised weapons as well, though in
what might have been defense. The primary contenders
will both take places on either side of the room. You will
not speak unless I give you leave." Her hawk-sharp gaze
pierced the room's occupants, and I had a flash memory
of my high school librarian, a stern-faced woman who
had carried a ruler to smack tables with, if not students'
hands. "Your people will separate and sit. Vespasianus's
people there." She pointed to her left. "Pellissier's people
there." She pointed to her right.

No one moved. Sabina dropped her hand and pointed
the splinter of the Blood Cross at Titus Flavius Vespasianus, holding it like a wand in a *Harry Potter* movie.
"Now!"

Titus's people moved back, human feet sliding on the
floor, vamp feet silent. As they shifted position, so did
Leo's people until there was a twenty-foot space between
them. Then thirty. The fighting rings were exposed where
there had been only people before. Titus sat on a bench,
looking regal but stymied. So did Leo, looking ticked off.

"All combatants in the first three rounds will dress in
fighting armor and return," Sabina said. "I allow you five
minutes, no more. Go."

People dashed down the stairs or popped out of sight.
No one remaining on the third floor moved, the vamps
doing that still-as-marble thing, common among the undead. Only the humans and weres and I breathed. I
slipped down the stairs last to dress in the white armor.

About halfway down the stairs I realized the corset was tied in back. Fortunately, Deon joined me and unlaced the corset top, helping me into my fighting clothes. I turned on Beast-speed and the costume change, as Deon called it, took only two minutes. In a little over four minutes we all began to return to the third floor. I hoped that wearing the girly clothing, and now the white leathers, made people think I had no fighting skills. First impressions and all that.

At exactly five minutes, Sabina turned her head in one of those bizarre, squicky motions that was more lizard than human and looked around the room. "You," she said, pointing at Shiloh and drawing a piece of paper from a pocket in her robes. "You will read the order of trials and announce the combatants. The first will begin now." Sabina sat down on a bench, her skirts scratchy in the quiet.

Shiloh slid between vamps and humans. Her face was too calm for this summons to be unexpected. Shiloh, part witch, part vamp, had been planning stuff with the vamp priestess. This shouldn't have been a surprise. The position of outclan priestess had always been held by a witch or shaman turned vamp, and Shiloh fit the bill perfectly if she turned down a place in Clan Yellowrock. Dang. Something else I'd need to address if I lived through this.

Shiloh took the paper and unfolded it. "First challenge," she said, "is from Concetta Gallo to Jane Yellowrock. Challenger and challenged, approach the central ring." I started to walk in, but Gee beat me to it. "I accept the challenge for the Enforcer of Leo Pellissier, Master of the City of New Orleans."

"And by what right do you accept the challenge?" Sabina asked.

A happy-sly look on his face, Gee DiMercy, the misericord of the New Orleans vamps, said, "I am the Enforcer of Clan Yellowrock."

"Clan—" Titus shot to his feet. "This is an outrage! No human can be a Blood Master."

Sabina stared at him. For a moment nothing happened. The emperor had been told not to speak by an outclan priestess. Kings were important. If they rallied their people they could kill a priestess true-dead. One-on-one, priestesses were more powerful. Titus went quiet, drawing his dignity around him like a cloak. He bent his head slightly in a royal nod.

Sabina said, "Do you wish to address a point of order? If so you may speak."

"Yes. I contest the concept of a non-Mithran as Blood Master of a clan."

Dressed in fighting armor, Edmund stepped next to Gee. To Sabina he said, "Permission to speak to this point of order."

Without taking her eyes from Titus, Sabina nodded.

Edmund said, "I am Edmund Hartley, a master Mithran, formerly Blood Master of Clan Laurent—my clan, given by covenant to Bettina, now master of Clan Laurent."

Wait. Covenant? "What covenant?" I demanded.

Edmund continued speaking. "I am also heir to the Master of the City of New Orleans and heir of Clan Pellissier. I speak as one of power. Only days ago, Jane Yellowrock completed a blood-binding upon me, a master Mithran, making me, according to the Vampira Carta, her primo."

Every single vamp on the far side of the room inhaled in shock. Good thing the windows were open or there'd be no air left for the humans. For myself, I'd forgotten to breathe.

I hadn't wanted to claim Edmund. It had been the only way to save his life.

Ed said, "Such a binding gives Yellowrock the right to be appointed as a clan master. Jane Yellowrock is now master of Clan Yellowrock. And I am now her primo."

Coldly, Titus said, "A master Mithran, heir of massive territory, in the position of servant? No. This is absurd. I will not allow it."

"The outclan priestess allows it," Sabina said, her words cutting. Titus started to speak again, but Sabina went on. "To the challenged is the choice of weapons."

Gee said, "Dual swords. No shields. Smaller blades as desired."

"To first blood or to the death?" Sabina asked the combatants.

Someone at the back of the room answered, "Blood."

"Blades and first blood. Begin." Everyone stepped back except Gee, wearing metallic painted plasticized armor, and Concetta Gallo. The tiny woman, shaved headed, olive skinned, looked fourteen, though she was over two hundred. Her armor was silver-green and shiny, and she was a master swordswoman.

The combatants crossed swords, gave half bows, and from somewhere a single bell-tone sounded, echoing in the ceiling. They attacked. Blades clashing, glinting, flashing, they advanced and withdrew. Danced the Spanish Circle around the octagonal fighting ring. Gee cut, a controlled transfer of weight and balance, so smooth it looked as if nothing had happened. A deep cut sliced the woman's face, bisecting her cheek from ear to nose. Instantly it bled in a drench, as all head wounds do, the flesh already swelling and drooping, to expose bloody teeth through the wound. They both stepped back, off the ring, but not as if they wanted to, and not as if they trusted the other to abide by rules of first blood. The bout had lasted all of five seconds. Maybe just four.

One of the film crew cursed softly, presumably at the speed.

Fast, Beast said, inside me, entranced. *Want to fight fast with steel claws.*

Brandon said, "Results of this duel are acceptable to the Onorios."

Sabina said, "Next rounds, apace, now that Pellissier has drawn first blood." She looked to Shiloh. "Call the next three bouts, which shall take place, as Americans say it, back-to-back."

"No," Titus said, adding what sounded like, *"Es una locura."* Then in English he added, "This is mayhem. Unacceptable."

We waited while someone explained to Titus that the phrase meant the bouts would follow one after the other, not with the fighters standing back-to-back while battling.

Titus shook his head and rattled off more foreign words, before adding, "Following this farce, it will be a privilege to teach the Americans their place and restore proper order, decorum, and protocol to these neglected shores." As insults went that was a good one. I wondered if Titus had crib notes in his hand. Wisely I didn't ask that question.

Leo narrowed his eyes, but he didn't speak either. That might have had something to do with the film crew or with Bruiser's hand on his shoulder, holding the MOC in his seat. Or playacting. Leo had planned for this night for, maybe, centuries.

Shiloh said, "Nibolio Mancini challenges Jane Yellowrock. Simon Costa challenges Jane Yellowrock. Lanbros Alafouzos challenges Eli Younger."

My heart took a dive. Lanbros was a three-hundred-year-old vamp. He was a killer through and through. Eli was dead. I started forward, but someone held me back. The irony of Leo and me both being held back wasn't lost on me. I snarled and jerked my arm free, but waited.

Gee said, "The honor of facing Nibolio Mancini is mine."

Sounding like a bored roué, Edmund said, "I shall die of the tedium, but the *honor* of facing Simon Costa shall be mine." The way he said *honor* let me know that Edmund and Simon didn't like each other much.

"My name is properly pronounced *See-MOH-neh*," the man said to Edmund, "as you are well aware. And though it is a dishonor to fight a former slave, I accept the humiliation of this bout, out of great regard for my master and emperor."

I was watching Edmund's undead face. Yeah. He'd been a slave. And though his expression gave nothing away, that history was still a hard pill to swallow.

A voice from the stairs said, "The honor of facing Lanbros Alafouzos is mine." I spotted Koun ascending to the third floor. He wore no armor and was mostly naked, wearing only a loincloth, his body tattooed with blue and black dye in what was said to be Celtic symbols. "I am the chief strategist of Clan Yellowrock," he said, as a cameraman stepped around him, getting the full three-sixty, front and back. "No one may gainsay me."

Koun stepped up to me and dropped to one knee. So quietly no vamp on the far side of the room could have heard it, Koun said, "I yield unto you all my honor."

Faster than my eyes could follow, Koun leaped from his crouch, going high, over the heads of those still standing, to land in front of Sabina, one knee on the floor, both hands touching the floor for balance, his blond head bent. "Mother bless me, for I have sinned."

Sabina touched Koun's head. "You have done well, my son. You are the only warrior to remember the old ways. Not even our once-emperor has been so proper."

Titus snarled.

Sabina finished, "My blessing upon you, Koun of the Celts and of Clan Yellowrock."

And then I remembered a rare codicil of the Vampira Carta that dealt with Sangre Duello. All the fighters were supposed to do homage to the clan Blood Master for whom they fought, and then to any outclan present. No others. No one in their right mind insulted an outclan priestess, yet Titus's warriors had forgotten. So had Leo's and mine, thanks most likely to the fact that weapons had been drawn out of order. Points against both sides.

Quickly Gee and Edmund bowed to me and to Sabina, followed by Titus's people to their leader and then to the priestess. Sabina pointed to the octagonals inlaid in the floor and directed the three groups to take their places. "Gee DiMercy. Weapons?"

"Single sword," Gee said, sounding bored. "Left hand only." I figured it was the Mithran equivalent of "I'll beat you with one hand tied behind my back." Except that cheating was allowed, so hidden weapons might be used too.

Sabina asked, "Nibolio Mancini. First blood or death?"

Nibolio was a swarthy, hairy man with a full beard like some Renaissance peddler or fruit seller. "To fight one-handed is cowardly. First blood. This weakling does not deserve to die at my hand."

Sabina said, "Edmund Hartley. Weapons?"

"Two swords," Ed said. "No shield."

Sabina asked, "Simon Costa. First blood or death?"

Simon was a Renaissance angel with eyes as blue as the sea on a postcard. "Death."

My heart stopped beating, but Sabina went on. "Koun. Weapons?"

"Double-headed axes. Blades of steel."

"Lanbros Alafouzos?" Sabina asked. "To death or blood?"

"I withdraw. I do not fight with the garden tools of the pagan and the barbarian."

"Yellowrock and Koun," Sabina said, "challenge from Alafouzos is withdrawn and his name stricken from the Sangre Duello. Death match is to be held downstairs, on the sand rings. Go now and await me." Simon and Ed took the stairs silently.

Koun stepped to me, people making way for his broad nakedness, a glint in his eyes that said he had chosen the weapons knowing that Lanbros would back out. None of the camera crew was nearby, so I murmured to him, "Chief strategist of Clan Yellowrock," I said. "Nice title."

Koun agreed with a tilt of his head and murmured, "Battlefield promotion, my master. Self-awarded." He took his place behind me, next to Eli. The clean bell-tone sounded, and I caught a glimpse of a female I didn't know, holding a polished triangle bell and a metal beater. She was strawberry blond and short with cool green eyes. And she was missing three fingers of her left hand in what looked like a permanent injury, perhaps one from before she was turned.

Behind the bell ringer and to the side were most of our nonfighting humans, lined up on benches. Eating popcorn and drinking beer. Titus looked that way and his lip curled. More *Taming of the Shrew*. Go, humans. Titus's nonfighting humans were on the far side of the bell ringer, still dressed in formal wear and looking uncomfortable in the sticky winter ocean breeze.

Nibolio Mancini and Gee engaged, left-handed, swords clanking in the first clash. In the next second Gee cut off Nibolio's beard and through his throat. Springy beard hair and blood flew everywhere. Nibolio dropped to his knees. Another vamp dashed in to drag him off the octagonal. For a vamp, it wasn't a lethal wound, but he wouldn't be fighting anytime soon. Gee strolled off. This one had been a two-second duel.

"Did you get the shot?" a tiny British voice asked.

"Got it. Golden," Bear, the hairy camera wolf, answered.

"Downstairs," Sabina said. She popped down, as did a larger number of vamps. Humans raced down the stairs. I leaped out the window, landed on the metal roof. Only to push off and land on the sand below, balanced on the fingers of one hand and my toes. I pulled on Beast's speed, my heart in my throat. Rushed to the rock-bounded fighting circles.

The bell chimed again. I thought I might vomit.

Edmund and *See-MOH-neh* both attacked at once. The cage of death that was La Destreza was sketched in the air between them, glistening steel that caught the low lights, cut-cut-cut, too fast to see. Blood splattered. Edmund bleeding from a cut above the eye. *Holy crap*. To the death. "No," I whispered, the word drawn out.

Something was wrong with Edmund. He was moving slow. I'd seen him fight and this wasn't right. He looked almost clumsy. Koun leaned in and murmured to me, "Strategy, my master. Strategy. Do not fear."

I didn't look away from the fight. Edmund took another cut, this one to his forearm. Simon laughed, looking like blond boy playing a game, not vamp dueling to the death. Their swords whipped and whirled in a complex cage of death. Moving so quick they were blurs. Cut, cut, lunge, cut, too fast to see, even with Beast-sight.

I shoved my hands into my jacket pockets. My left fist hit something, opened, and encircled it. I had to wonder how the Glob got into my pocket. The Glob was one of my collection of magical trinkets and, its name notwithstanding, it was a powerful *objet de magie*. It was composed of the small sliver of the Blood Cross that I had ruined for use by anyone but me, part of the iron spike of Golgotha, and the blood diamond, all melded into one. The diamond had started out as an amulet crowded with the power of sacrificed witch children, only a few of whom I had been able to rescue. The Glob was magic that had claimed me. Magic that had been fashioned by and activated by my blood and the energy of a witch's lightning curse. The Glob heated in my hand, a searing spurt of electric energy, quickly gone. And then I realized that the Glob might have found its way into my pocket without help. Magical objects as powerful as the Glob sometimes had a will of their own.

Ed took another cut. Stumbled. Dropped to one knee. Bent his head. Bowed his back. And sliced with a backhanded cut into the outer side of Simon's right knee. He followed it up by blocking two strikes and then delivering a backhanded cut to Simon's side. So hard, so smooth, so perfectly delivered that it appeared to slice through the flesh and stop only when it reached the vamp's spine. Simon of the funky pronunciation toppled, dropping his swords. Edmund shifted his body to the side, an expression of shock on his face. As if he hadn't expected to kill his opponent. Playing to the cameras? Or hiding what he could do from the EVs?

Simon landed. He was nearly in two pieces. Blood pulsed everywhere in a wide spray, puddled beneath his body, soaked into the sand, the air redolent with his vamp smell—wild roses and moss. Edmund struggled to his feet. He took the vamp's head. It took three cuts, wielding the sword like an ax, ungainly, awkward. Not my primo's usual grace and beauty with a sword, not in any way at all. But the head of the beautiful blond angel rolled to the side. The sand soaked up more blood. The night breeze swept through beneath the house, salty, clean, fresh. The fighting arena was utterly silent for a space of time that lasted for a dozen of my speeding heartbeats.

This was the first death. Sent out on camera to the entire world, those who loved blood sports would be whooping it up at home. Watching instant replays. Our people stood, staring. Titus's undead and their blood-dinners stood. The smell of uncertainty coiled in the air, a descant of scent beneath the melody of fanghead blood.

And the stillness ended. Moving like fish in a school, Titus's people rushed in, gathering the head and body.

Brandon stepped from the group of Onorios who were acting as judges along with Sabina. Brandon seemed to be the spokesperson. He said, "Results of this duel are acceptable to the Onorios."

Sabina said, "Next duel in fifteen minutes."

I tried to catch Bruiser's eye, but he didn't turn my way, bending his head to the B-twins as the three talked. Some vamps left the fighting area, to walk under the stars on the beaches. Ed came to me, limping. "You scared me," I said.

"My heart is both saddened and full of joy," he said. "Saddened that I frightened my mistress. Full of joy that my mistress cares."

"Uh-huh. Keep it up, Eddie Boy."

I started to turn and caught Titus's eyes on me. In them, I could read multiple emotions: avarice, curiosity, hatred, a cold fury that let me know how much he had liked the blond angel Simon. And how much he blamed me for the vamp's death. And the fact that he had seen me leap what amounted to four stories in two bounds. *Good.* I put my thoughts into my eyes. *Chew on that, Your Magisterial Ass. Stuff you saw on the stolen video? It's all true. And I'm coming for you.*

I gave him a toothy grin and put all that into my body language as I strolled into the darkness. The shadow of a camera wolf was beside mine, and I knew my leaps were now part of the permanent record of the Sangre Duello. So was the death of Simon. And the vision of Titus watching me. The camera wolf fell away, finding something better to shoot than me in the dark.

Once I was beyond the house and prying ears, I had myself a silent bout of anger, pounding the sand. My hand—the one that had healed around the magical thingy when it was created—was furiously squeezing the Glob as I hammered it on the earth. For long seconds, I couldn't force myself to stop or to let go. It hurt my hand. I got sand in my eyes. But I felt better after my temper tantrum.

*   *   *

On both floors, the next rounds began.

Leo's side was winning.

Ro Moore chose wrestling as her weapon and defeated her opponent according to standard wrestling rules. Gee took on two vamps at one time and killed them both on the sand. There was enough blood and gore to make the wolves dance in glee. The pay-per-view numbers had started smaller than anticipated, but they had now out-paced expectations and were growing rapidly.

Brenda Rezk took on a Vespasianus security guy, and the finish was two simultaneous cuts. The cut to her arm was a surface wound, while the other guy was carted away needing major vamp blood to heal. She lost on time, but won on wounds delivered.

After that things went sour.

Maryanne, Edmund's lover and blood-servant, died at the hand of a woman named Cupid, her head rolling across the sandy rings. Edmund went still as death, except for the human tears that spilled down his face as she fell. His tears tore into me like claws into raw meat.

The bout bell rang upstairs. I hugged him and left him to his grief.

"Results of this duel are acceptable to the Onorios," Brandon said behind me. And for the first time since I met the Onorio twins, I wanted to slap them, slap all three of them.

In the next match, which was supposed to end with first blood, Titus's swordswoman cheated at *en garde* and Gee took a hidden steel blade into his belly and out his back, followed by a Z-shaped move that carved his in-nards into Zorro-inspired spaghetti. Anzus were lethally allergic to steel and couldn't heal themselves on Earth. Gee didn't die, but only because his organs were not human-sited, but Anzu-sited. And because Leo fed him from his own wrist. My Enforcer was out for the night. Likely for the rest of the Sangre Duello. The cheater won. Cheating was smiled upon in the Sangre Duello.

Edmund took the ring, facing off with two blades to first blood, against a vamp who called himself Jeedalayn, which was supposed to be Somali for the verb "to whip." Jeedalayn had little to no dossier beyond his presumed age. My primo stood there in blue armor facing a six-hundred-year-old vamp. Something in Jeedalayn's stance caused my heart to flutter. It may have stopped. I had a very, very bad feeling. The bell sounded, the tone a clear pure note of death.

Jeedalayn slithered. Swords so fast they sang on the air. In half a second, Ed took two cuts. Blood flew. His opponent stepped back, honoring first blood. But my primo's left hand was nearly severed at the wrist, bloody, splintered, and cut bone exposed, his hand hanging by tendons. His right thumb was equally nearly amputated.

Bile boiled into my throat at the sight. Someone again held me back as Leo's clan members rushed to provide assistance and clean up the blood spatter. Two blood-servants bundled my primo into sheets and carried him down the stairs. I followed, the scent/taste of his blood and pain heavy on the air. My feet felt strange on the stairs, as if they didn't quite touch down. As if I might slide off and into another dimension. And I still held the Glob. It was so cold, it was like clutching an ice cube.

Behind me I heard Brandon say, "Results of this duel are acceptable to the Onorios."

I managed to not whirl back and coldcock him.

In Edmund's shared cubicle in the center rooms, the vamps and humans placed my primo on a bed. My primo. Someone I should have protected. A woman said, "I have him. Del, get the bottle."

"Right here, Mama. I'm ready."

A half-familiar smell hit the air: blood and chemicals. I blinked, to focus on Dacy Mooney, kneeling on the mattress beside Edmund, his right hand in her left. The heir of Clan Shaddock said, "Ed, honey, we're gonna coat your thumb with the blood remedy. This will hurt."

"They say it feels as if one is being immolated."

"I wouldn't know. You can tell me."

Dacy upended a small glass vial over Ed's severed thumb and a thick, syrupy drop formed on the end of its rubber spout.

I recognized the scent of the blood remedy. Leo's Texas biomedical lab indeed had reverse engineered the revenant potion left by the vamp funeral director when the Caruso blood-family skipped town, to back the EVs. But instead of creating it to make revenants, Leo had made his version for healing. The MOC was a dangerous creature, but sometimes he was also a pretty cool dude.

I still wondered at the oddity of the Carusos leaving their bottle, and at the letter Leo had received claiming they had betrayed him only to save Laurie Caruso's daughter. It could be insurance, a bid for protection should Titus lose. Carusos playing the long game, maybe.

Dacy dribbled the drop on Ed's severed thumb and pressed the thumb back in place. Ed screamed. He continued screaming as Dacy and six other vamps held him down so Del could apply the blood mixture to the ends of his amputated hand. Del's blond head bent over my primo, her fighting leathers the color of her eyes. Ed screamed, his ululation so high-pitched that I went deaf and had to step from the room. Yeah. That was the reason. Not my own cowardice at seeing a man I cared for injured and in agony for trying to protect me.

Shiloh walked down the stairs toward me, followed by a line of men and women. "Leo wants you to follow this one," she said, her long straight red hair swinging. Except for hers, I had never seen straight red hair. Red hair was always curly. Stupid thoughts. Stupid duel. I hated this. These mind games and blood and death.

"Why do I need to follow you?" I asked, my lips feeling numb. Edmund was being tortured. I could hear his screams through the soundproofed door. I placed a hand on the door, as if I could ease his pain through the steel.

"Your two best fighters are down and out," Shiloh said. "Koun is slated to fight seconds after this bout, so he can't fight this one."

"She's trying to tell you that I accepted my own duel,"

Eli said. He descended the last four steps and stopped beside me.

The acid in my stomach boiled. "Why?" I whispered.

Shiloh said, "Challenger is Lucrezia Borgia. Eli Younger chose weapons."

"I picked matching German Sig Sauer P320s," Eli said.

"*Naturellement*, I contested such barbarism," the female vamp behind him said. "However, the priestess has denied my disputation."

I recognized the woman. Hers was one of the histories I'd studied in preparation for the EVs' visit, a VIV, very important vamp. She shouldn't have been on the roster until later tonight at the worst. Tomorrow at best. And Gee or Ed should have been fighting her. Not Eli. I followed Shiloh down the stairs, not sure why we were going down and not up. My brain was wrapped in cotton. Ed was screaming. I could still hear him.

Shiloh said, "Lucrezia Borgia chose death."

My boots halted on the stairs. I came to a stop, my mind flashing with useless information. Lucrezia was the illegitimate child of a pope and his mistress, in the early 1500s, and had become an assassin for Titus. She was a master at hundreds of weapons. Her dossier said that she practiced all night every night, with blades and firearms. I was so cold at the thought that my head started buzzing and nausea boiled in my gut. The P320 was a brand-new modular weapon, a serialized gun. It could be modified to shoot nine-millimeter loads, altered quickly to fire .357 Sig, .40 S&W, or even .45 ACP—automatic Colt pistol.

No matter how good vamps were, there were always weapons old vamps hadn't fired, because they figured the ones they were most familiar with were the best. This was sometimes true, sometimes not. There was a chance, a small chance, Lucrezia had never fired this modular and wouldn't have the muscle memory to make her a perfect shot. I started my feet moving again, down. Down to the death rings.

Eli was standing on the front porch, moonlight brightening the world around him, making his black leathers seem darker, as if he himself were a pathway into the underworld. I set my eyes on him, but he didn't look back, though he surely had to feel the weight of my gaze. He led the way down the steps.

We were halfway down to the beach when Shiloh said to me, "The duel is at forty paces, twenty each, approximately one hundred feet, depending on stride. Since it's with firearms, it's all very methodical and according to protocol covered in codicils other than the Sangre Duello."

I walked away from Shiloh, across the sand, following Eli. He was breathing slowly. The pulse in his neck was equally slow. Zen. Warrior face on. But he smelled—strangely—of excitement and joy. On the beach, the gulf's waves curled on the sand. Lightning split and danced in the distant sky, a storm so far away it looked as if the clouds and water were one. With Beast-sight I studied the building cloud. Not magic lightning. Just one of the ubiquitous storms on gulf water. Thunder rolled in with the waves, long and low. The tide was high, making the beach a narrow strip. The wind was cold, and I shivered as it needled its way through my clothes.

Eli bent to his second. That second couldn't be me, so Tex had accepted that position, and they spoke in voices I might have heard had I tried. Brute trotted across the sand to me and stuck his nose into my crotch.

I batted him away. "Stop that."

He chuffed with laughter and sat close beside me. A moment later he leaned his entire body against me, from calf to hip, in what was clearly an attempt to comfort me. I could feel his panting breaths and his body heat through the leather uniform and I realized how cold I was. Probably shocky. Because I couldn't help my people. And Eli was facing a warrior who had been fighting and shooting for centuries.

I scratched Brute's head between his ears. "Dang werewolf."

He chuffed in agreement.

Lucrezia was a pretty woman with golden hair and blue-green eyes. She looked way younger than her stated age when turned, and I figured she had been changed a decade or so prior to her reported death and her human self had been replaced with another woman. It was likely that replacement human was the woman recorded by history as having gained a huge amount of weight while supposedly grieving a dead husband, and died young.

Brute's head on my leg, I stood to the side and watched the combatants, standing back-to-back. Snatches of instructions came to me on the wind. Eli and Lucrezia shook hands. Tex shook Lucrezia's second's hand, a human who had been fed on and had been sipping vamp blood for over two hundred years. She was currently known as Whimsical Lou. Stupid name, but that was what the second called herself. Whimsical Lou, No Last Name. The seconds walked out to the positions where their firsts would likely stand, and waited. Eli and Lucrezia stood back-to-back.

The moonlight was a long streak across the choppy water, ahead of the storm. I heard a distant bell-tone and Eli and Lucrezia strode away from one another, Shiloh counting off the paces. On his last pace, Eli stepped quickly to the side. They turned and fired, but Eli was a foot to the side of where he should have been. Lucrezia's shot missed. Eli's hit her chest, just left of midcenter. She screamed in that sound of a vamp dying, though it was all drama queen.

They had used standard ammo so the shot would fly true over the distance. She'd live.

I laughed in relief, the sound billowing on the wind and out to sea. The smell of Lucrezia's blood sharp on the air.

Eli had survived and won his bout. Except that this was supposed to be to the death. He strode toward the downed vamp.

And then time broke in slow motion.

Time in battle is subjective, thick and viscous like taffy. An avalanche of images.

Brute snarled.

Beast leaped into the forefront of my brain, screaming challenge.

In agonizing, protracted fragments of time, Lucrezia's

second, Whimsical Lou, took two long steps into the dueling space, drew a long-barreled handgun. Aimed. Fired.

The round hit Eli. Midcenter. I could see it as it pierced his leather jacket.

Beast screamed. I/we leaped, raced down the sand. Grew claws with my right hand. Drew a blade with my left. The blade took the Whimsical second through the right eye. The claws tore out her throat. All while in midair. She fell. Rolled into the low waves, dark in the moonlight. A shot rang in the night, taking Lou in the chest. Tex, holding his six-shooter, fired again. Lucrezia fell. Tex stood over her. Firing until the chamber was empty. Time snapped back.

I rose from the landing crouch and sprinted to Eli, my combat boots crunching, throwing sand. Eli wasn't moving, lying on the shore, facedown, head to the side. One arm twisted, outstretched in the slight surf, clear salty bubbles pooling in his palm. My body was so cold it felt like a shard of iceberg. Tears filled my lids and clung there as if holding on to the rims of frozen cliff faces.

I heard Shiloh ask calmly, "Have the deceased signed papers to be turned?"

Bruiser's voice, sounding cool and distant, said, "Lucrezia is true-dead, as is Whimsical Lou. The judges await status of Eli Younger."

I knelt, rolled Eli over, placed a hand on his chest, and . . . felt a heartbeat. Didn't smell blood. I leaned in and sniffed, a long cat-*scree* of sound, pulling in air over my tongue. No blood. I pressed down on his chest, feeling the kind of armor Uncle Sam's men wore to war, not just armor against blades, but against bullets. My tears spilled onto his face. I put my mouth at his ear and hissed, "If you're not dead, I may kill you for scaring me to death."

"Sorry, Babe." The words were a breath against my cheek, his lips scarcely moving. "Just remembering how to breathe."

I thought I might pass out from the relief that rammed through me. I shouted to the wind, "He's alive. Eli will not be turned."

"Never wanted to drink blood," he gasped.

"Are you hit?" I whispered back, asking if the round penetrated the armor.

"Not," he whispered, the sound creaking with tight breath. I dropped my head to his, forehead to forehead. "But I'm going to kill Lucrezia Borgia."

"My mistress. Lucrezia Borgia is true-dead," Tex said. "I took her conniving, snake-belly-low life and her head."

"Good. I think she broke my rib," Eli said. "Sucker hurts."

I rolled Eli up into my arms. He grunted with pain, tightening up to protect the hurt rib. "Babe," he wheezed. "Next time? We've got a backboard."

"Oh. Right. Sorry." I tucked his head against my shoulder and carried him up the stairs and into the house as if he was the most valuable thing in the universe.

"Results of this duel are acceptable to the Onorios."

CHAPTER 18

Rainbow-Colored Baby Bunnies and Lollipops

The body of Lucrezia Borgia disappeared, probably back to the EVs' ship in deeper water. I spared a single thought that the Carusos might be aboard, forced into making the dead into revenants. But I just, flat-out, didn't care.

Instead, after I deposited Eli in the vamps' sleeping lair for a hit of Tex's healing vamp blood, Sabina called me to the third floor. She stood in the center of the middle fighting octagonal and said, "The challenges to Jane Yellowrock have been met, all but one. This latest is for dominance over Clan Yellowrock, and that by Dominique Quessaire, formerly of Clan Arceneau, now secundo heir of Clan Des Citrons."

Beast growled.

I snarled. *Dominance duel. Holy crap.* Time again did that battlefield slowdown, where everything happened in overlays of understanding and images. Dominique moved up the stairs and through the scions and blood-servants like a snake through tall grass. I put my hands in my pockets, slouched as if irked by inconsequentials, and looked the challenger over with jaded eyes.

Dominique stank of lemons and fresh human blood. She was dressed in fighting leathers dyed the color of her blond hair, which she wore long and down. On her neck was a necklace of small gray moonstones the same shade as her pale eyes. On the necklace was a pendant, a ruby wired with gold.

I pulled on Beast's sight and saw the tracery of old, faint magics in the moonstones, empty of power now, but once likely used by a moon witch. The ruby, however, was something more powerful. Intense red motes flashed through it, motes that seemed to call to my own magics. I felt a pull in my midsection, as if I'd swallowed a bag of iron filings, as if a magnet drew on them. Pain slithered through my belly. I almost stepped back. I'd seen a ruby like that before. In fact, I had a ruby like it in my box of magical trinkets.

And if there were two of them, what did they do?

What could they do together? *Ahhh.* Dominique might know or guess that I had the other ruby.

I had been challenged by Dominique Quessaire. Dominique was a traitor. She had waited to try for my head until after I had something she wanted—my clan and my people. My ruby? Had she been looking for it in Leo's office when she beat holes in the wall? And Adrianna—her lover whom I had finally killed true-dead— had been after *le breloque*, the crown of the Dark Queen, when I took her head. Dominique wanted the most important *objets de magie*. Dominique had visions of grandeur.

She had seen me fight, knew what I could do. She was good with two swords, even better with one. Better than me by far with any weapon.

My mind circled back to Adan. Adan had been playing with time. The last moments of the battle that had freed Adan flashed through my memory. There was something there, something important about using magic. Time slapped back to full speed.

"As the last member of the inner circle of Clan Yellowrock able to wield a weapon, I accept for my master," Koun said. He was standing behind me and I had no idea when he had appeared there. "Weapons," he said, "one sword, one battle-ax, no armor."

"I will fight the Blood Master of Clan Yellowrock and no other," Dominique said. Her tone and her stance were insolent and there was a trace of something in her light eyes that said she expected to win by cheating. "First blood."

"Challenge accepted. One blade each, no longer than fourteen inches. Claws and talons," I said. And then I smiled, letting my lips expose my teeth slowly in threat. Beast peered through my eyes. "Jewelry is acceptable."

Dominique blinked, realizing that I knew about the ruby, knew she was going to cheat with magic against the most important rule in Sangre Duello and dominance fights. And that I didn't care.

"Here and now," Dominique said.

I gave her a jut of my head and drew on Beast energies. Everyone cleared the floor space and I moved to Eli. My partner and second was holding a Desert Eagle .50-caliber handgun at his thigh. He holstered it with a tiny click. "You sure about this?" he asked.

"Yeah. I'm sure." Because I had remembered the thing I had learned when Adan was in a cage, harnessing the timewalking magic of an arcenciel. Stealing her magic. If I could feel the pull of Dominique's ruby, then I could use its power. And the motes of power in my middle said I could take all its magic for myself. I was becoming the Dark Queen in truth.

"What blade?" he asked.

"The Mughal blade."

Eli paused in helping me prepare for this fight. "Why?"

"Because the myth that came with it said that the blade has magic in it. It will deflect or lessen the mortal blow of any enemy. Whoever owns the blade can't die in battle."

Eli shook his head, not happy with my answer. He preferred weapons that blew things up.

I glanced around, noting where everyone was. Ro Moore was standing in front of a window that had once been a fire escape. Her gaze went from the fighting rings to the roof below and back, watching for anyone who might want to interrupt the proceedings with a hand grenade. I hadn't even considered that possibility. I was getting lax. Good thing I had trained smart people. I nodded to her. She nodded toward the windows at the back of the room with a faint smile.

I looked there and saw Brenda Rezk guarding that possible access. Yeah. Smart people. Go, me.

I was ready. *Beast?* I thought. *I need some claws. Just claws.*

Jane needs killing teeth and power of half-form.

Not this time. Just claws.

My fingers went knobby and hard and I gasped. The tips burned as if I'd stuck them into red-hot coals. Beast's retractile claws re-formed at the tips, ten killing claws. My fingertips oozed blood and I licked it off. *Ouch,* I thought at her.

Deep inside, she said, *Five and five killing claws.* She sniffed at me, and turned away.

I stepped into the fighting ring and closed my eyes, breathing in Eli's Zen and my skinwalker meditation. Letting my body relax and tense all at once, just as if I was going to shift into a difficult form. The bell sounded. My eyes opened and Dominique attacked, shouting, *"Ralentissez!"*

A thin line of power shot from her necklace. A slow-down spell, hidden in the ruby and released with a *wyrd*. Time slowed down. The five pointed energies in my middle reached out and wrapped around the line of magic. Altered it. Pulled it in.

Incorporated the *wyrd* and the energies into my own.

A silvered vamp-killer stabbed at me.

I bent around the blade in a dance move. Stepped into her reach. Clawed her face with one hand, slicing deeply into her waist with the Mughal blade. I yanked on the blade, cutting into her.

Dominique screamed, that piercing vamp ululation that said she was dying. Her eyes flashed scarlet. Her fangs schnicked down. She ripped away, tearing my blade from her flesh. She disappeared with a tiny pop of sound.

Toward the window where Brenda Rezk stood guard. Dominique landed, ripped at Brenda. Tearing out her throat. Dived through the window. Landed on the roof below with a loud, hollow thump. Brenda fell, her blood a pulsing spray, her head at an awful angle. Titus's second caught Brenda's body. Eased her to the floor. It was too late. There was not enough left to save.

Koun leaped after the traitor. Paused in the window. His gaze tracked Dominique, his body and tattoos catching the lights in strange blue and black shadows on pale skin. He watched her run, his head following her progress around and toward the water at the front of the house. A moment later, he tilted his head to me and said, "In spite of the angel of death, all is well, my master."

No one else had moved.

Sabina said, "Magic was used by Dominique Quessaire. Her penalty is true-death."

I stilled. I had used magic too.

Sabina went on. "Magic was used by Jane Yellowrock, though only in self-defense, and after Dominique's attack. The outclan priestess rules this an acceptable use. No penalty to Yellowrock." Part of me wilted, but I didn't let it show on the outside.

Softly, Grégoire said to someone, "Bring Dominique back to me. Her true-death is mine."

I thought, *If he hadn't brought her back when her throat was ripped out we wouldn't be in this mess now.* Grégoire and Leo had been hunting for the clan who had allied with her. They had taken a gamble that Brenda had paid for with her life.

Bodies moved; vamps and humans departed. I watched as Brenda was carted down the stairs. Dead. Killed for spite, not as part of the Duello. Killed for not a damn thing. The cleanup crew started on the blood. People went in search of dinner and beer. I dropped to a bench and mourned the blood-servant.

We'd made a mistake. We needed more toilets. Even vamps had to pee, it seemed, and either eating corn dogs and drinking beer made them pee more, or they had trouble getting out of their fighting leathers, or they were just being pains in the backside. The lines to the bathrooms were ten people long, ninety percent of them female. Most males were outside finding a likely tree. I chose to do my business outside. At which point I discovered how freaking hard it was to get out of the new leathers. The uniform was comfortable in every way, except for a female needing to answer the call of nature. When I finally got my business done, my leathers in place, and my weapons holstered, sheathed, and hidden, I was frustrated and ready to hit something. I headed to the circle of *hedge of thorns*, my BFF, and the murderer, Dominique.

Molly was stretched out on a lounge chair, under a blanket or three to keep out the cold wind, her baby bump hidden by the swathing. Dominique was standing on the sand, in an inverted *hedge of thorns*, fists bunched, frothing at the mouth, screaming obscenities, I assumed, from her expression, though I couldn't hear her.

"How'd you turn down the volume?" I asked.

Molly laughed, a sad but ladylike laugh I'd never master. "Lachish's family uses it on the farm to keep the sound of tractors and farm equipment to a minimum. It's a noise version of a *confuto* working, and I'm totally stealing it and setting it on myself, so I can sleep in on Saturdays and Big Evan has to get up with the children."

I squatted beside her lounge chair. "That's evil."

"I'm a death witch. What did you expect?"

"Rainbow-colored baby bunnies and lollipops?"

Molly spluttered with laughter. "People who dye baby bunnies should be shot."

"I'll tweet that to my congressman for inclusion in next year's bills. Has Grégoire been to see her?"

"Yes. He condemned her to death by facing the sun. He'll have her chained in silver at sunrise." She hesitated. "Are you sure? Burning to death . . . Witches were burned at the stake. I've read the accounts. Family accounts. Firsthand . . ." Her voice trailed away.

I touched her shoulder, not knowing how to comfort

her. "She killed Brenda Rezk. She used magic in a dominance duel during the Sangre Duello. She was a traitor.
But I'm not sure of anything. Not anymore."

"Except that we love each other?"

I nodded slowly, feeling all the tension slide from my
shoulders, down my spine, out my feet, and into the sand
beneath me. "Except that. And that fangheads are evil,
no matter whose side they're on."

"True." She tilted her head at me, her red curls flying
in the wind off the gulf. "I know you stayed in New Orleans to keep us safe."

The tension shot back into me.

Molly held out her little finger. "Friends forever. Pin-
kie swear?"

I hooked my little finger into hers. "Best friends forever."

Moll pulled her finger from mine and her hand under
the blankets. "Quit worrying about me, Big Cat. I'm
warm and safe."

"Even though Titus did something with magic when he
crossed over the *hedge* and onto the property? I just remembered."

Molly frowned. She hadn't noticed that. *Crap.*

"Even though Dominique is wearing a ruby exactly
like one I own?" I asked. "And hers might be full of dark
magic?"

"Even that. Do you want the evil ruby?" At my expression she said, "Sorry. The ruby isn't technically evil. It
doesn't contain a curse and the working in it was used up
and can't be renewed." I didn't tell her that I had absorbed the working. I trusted Molly completely. But . . .
maybe not about Dark Queen magics and what my five-
pointed-star magics could do. "It won't hurt you," she
said. "I can freeze her for thirty seconds and open a passageway into the *hedge*."

I watched Dominique from my vantage point, crouch-
ing on the sand. I said, "If you can do that, sure."

Molly squirmed higher on her lounge chair and pulled
a hand from the covers. "You'll have thirty seconds."
Louder, she called, "Lachish? Jane wants something on
Dominique."

The older woman appeared from the darkness, look-ing grumpy. "Of course she does. Jane always wants something."

It felt like being slapped in the face. "Have I done something wrong?" I asked.

"No," Lachish said. But her tone said otherwise.

Molly said, "Lachish. Jane's trying to save us."

"We could just incinerate the entire house and be done with it. It might be worth the punishment."

Or Molly could just use her death magics and drain the life and undeath of everyone here. The words and the thought sent a cold shock through me. I looked at the house. The most powerful vamps in the world were all in one place. "You do that," I said, my voice reasonable, un-emotional, a false calm, "and there will be a power strug-gle in the vampire world like nothing we've ever seen on the face of the earth."

Lachish blew out a breath and turned her Creole-dark eyes to me. "Think I don't know that? Leo is the lesser of two evils. If Leo loses and Titus wins, all bets are off."

I looked at Molly. A death witch. Draining the vamps to death would kill her baby and probably drive her in-sane and expose what she was to the entire world, but . . . Molly could do it. It was likely that the coven leader of NOLA could do that same thing in a different way. This was why the witches were really here and I didn't know whether to be happy at the extra layer of protection for the U.S. humans or terrified.

Lachish stood next to Molly's chair. They both pointed the fingers of their right hands to the *hedge*, and Lachish said, "Dominique, *confuto. Hedge, concesso.*"

Dominique went utterly still, her mouth open and her face frozen in a mask of vamped-out fury. The *hedge of thorns* appeared as a thin, uneven film of light, like a layer of plastic.

"*Resigno,*" Lachish said. A small thin opening ap-peared from the top of the *hedge* to the ground. "Go."

I raced to the spell of confining, studying it as I moved. Mentally counting off the thirty seconds, I stopped in front of the *hedge* and examined the gem. There was no active reason to take it. But my gut, the magics coursing through my middle, said it was mine. I reached into the *hedge's* opening and grabbed the moonstone necklace. Gave it a strong yank and the clasp broke. I slid it from Dominique's neck. Stepped back, the magical gem dangling. And caught a vision of an emblem embroidered into Dominique's undershirt. A lizard eating its tail. Jack Shoffru's emblem. I looked around, hoping to see something that might be the anomaly that was Cym's magic. There was nothing.

Moments later the *hedge of thorns* snapped shut, its energies began to move again, visible in Beast-sight, and Dominique started raving. She saw what I had in my hands and fell utterly still for a moment. Then she threw her entire body at the *hedge*. Again. And again. Not that it did her any good.

I examined the necklace, its central gem and its energies. The ruby's magic had changed in the scant moments I'd held it. Instead of zipping all over the place in vaguely round patterns, as they had when resting against Dominique's undead flesh, the energies had begun to angle in and out. They formed a star pattern, like the pentagram of my energies. The ruby seemed to have the ability to evolve to suit the person who held it or wore it against her skin. It was a battery for power.

Beast thought at me. *Like meat. Dangerous prey meat. Eat meat of stone. Beast can be big, best ambush hunter.*

It was a boost to existing magic, and it made me feel pretty good. Calmer. Stronger. Which meant there would surely be a backlash at some point, that other shoe dropping, because nothing in magic is without cost. It might also be a mood booster, because I felt more hopeful than I had only a moment past, the weight on my shoulders still heavy, but not full of terror.

Feeling better even though nothing in my life was really improved, I went back to Molly's chair and knelt on one knee on the sand. Lachish had already moved away, into the dark again. I kissed her cheek and said, "I love you, Molly Meagan Everhart Trueblood."

"I love you too, Jane Doe Yellowrock. Now go kill bad things." She shooed me away.

"Yes, ma'am." Standing, I walked toward the house, shoving aside the small niggling thought that Molly could be passively drinking down all the death on Spitfire Island, just like a moon witch in full-moonlight absorbing lunar magic power. Could be growing stronger and more deadly death by death. *No. Not Molly.* Not pregnant with a witch child that might die from the death.

Enough of this crap. I can't suspect everyone I love.

I strode back into the beach mansion and into my shared room. I knelt, pulled my luggage out from under the bunk bed, and rattled around in the bags and suitcases until I found the box of magical trinkets. I left a mess of unfolded clothes, dirty clothes, and toiletries on the floor and I didn't care.

The ruby was in the box, and I lifted it out, a smoothed crystal of stone, smaller than my distant memory, smaller than the ruby that Dominique had worn. This stone was zipping with scarlet motes of magical power too, racing in a round pattern. I yanked the clasp off the new ruby and let the moonstones clatter from the wire into the bottom of the box, catching the ruby in my other palm. I scrounged around some more and found the necklace I had bought when I first came to New Orleans, one I had worn dancing, and bent the focal stone free from its wire wrapping. Pressed the wires around the rubies to hold them in place on the chain so they were encased together. I hooked it around my neck, centered them close to the gold nugget I always wore, and made sure it all could be seen easily. I made my way to the third floor, straightening my back, firming my face and my steps.

I was partway up when I heard Sabina speak. "Emperor Vespasianus's weapons master, Salvatrice Bianchi, challenges Pellissier's Adelaide Mooney to a death match. Are both present?"

I raced the rest of the way to the third floor.

Sal and Del stepped forward. Sal was a behemoth of a woman, broad and tall and muscular, her two feet of hair braided into a long column and wrapped in leather at her back, the hair-sheath reminiscent of a binding on a horse's tail. Her fighting leathers were old and scored and torn. Del was dressed in golden leathers smeared with the blood of previous opponents, matches I hadn't witnessed. I'd seen Del in a skirmish and sparring, but never in combat.

The bell chimed. My heart lurched.

Del dashed forward, her swords circling, cut, cut, cut, cut. Blood flowed, steel clashed. Del's opponent dropped to one knee, bleeding from two head wounds, a hank of scalp and hair on the floor. I started to shout encouragement. But Salvatrice dropped her left sword. Before it landed, she pulled a small blade. Stabbed up. Into Del's body. Catching her at the unprotected spot where thigh armor met abdominal armor plate. Sal's sword clanged to the floor.

Del made a small sound of surprise, like, "Oh." She stumbled.

Salvatrice rose to her feet, stepping closer to Del. Drawing the blade up Del's side, along the protective plate, through her body. Scarlet pumped over Salvatrice's hand, to her elbow. Splatted hard on the wood outside of the octagonal. Salvatrice twisted the blade to the side and across, a move that cut through bowel, kidneys, liver. And descending aorta.

I could hear the sound of things inside of Del tearing, separating. "Oh," she said again. Del fell, her knees and hips going limp. She landed on the wood floor, Salvatrice falling with her, in a languid motion. Removing the blade with an upward twist.

Sal stood, her blade dripping.

Brian said, "Results of this duel are acceptable to the Onorios."

How could they be acceptable?

"This round to Titus Flavius Vespasianus," Sabina said, as if unperturbed at the death. "Has Leo's primo signed papers to be turned?"

Dacy raced forward, her face blanched whiter than the moon through the windows. "I will not lose my daughter.

I decide for her." Dacy dropped to the floor, an ungainly motion for a vamp, and ripped her own lower arms lengthwise, to increase bleeding. Placed one wrist to her daughter's mouth, the other deep inside Del's body. But Del didn't drink. Didn't swallow. After two long minutes, Dacy rose to her feet and turned her back on Del, bloody tears streaking her face. She said, "Take Adelaide to my bed." And the heir of Clan Shaddock walked down the stairs as her people rushed to wrap Del's body in bloody sheets and carry her down.

I was certain I wasn't breathing. Certain that my heart wasn't beating. Del was my friend. Had been my friend. Del was dead. Or could Leo's healing blood potion save her? How good was it?

Sabina said, "Aloisio Esposito, tercero of the Europeans, has challenged Pellissier's secundo heir, Grégoire. The bout will begin in five minutes, to allow time for blood removal. This will be the last bout of night one of the Sangre Duello."

I knew about Aloisio. This was going to be bad.

I slid unnoticed into the shadow of one of the wood-beam roof supports. I reached up and gripped the two rubies and the gold nugget together. My other hand went into a pocket to grip the Glob, though I didn't remember putting it away. I prayed a wordless prayer, begging. Did God really hear the ones who fell away? I had personally fouled a baptismal pool full of holy water. Would he hear the prayer of someone with so much blood on her hands? Surely it was God that had sent Hayyel to me. Unless the angel was hanging around my life to exact heavenly justice on me at some predetermined point. I didn't know, and I feared that my faith had grown thin and worn and was full of holes.

We stood on the sand.

Aloisio Esposito, tercero to Titus, or, as some vamps called it, troisième, was third in line to the crown of the Europeans, the current Master of the Cities of Madrid, Barcelona, Lisbon, Marrakesh, Casablanca, and the Balearic Islands—basically Spain, Portugal, and Mo-

rocco. He'd been fighting for centuries, had a head count
of more than a thousand names—humans and vamps—
and he was nearly as old as his emperor. Aloisio was not
a pretty vamp; his face was scarred by pre-turning sword
cuts and his back was rumored to be marked by the scars
of whip lashings. But he had vibrant, caramel-colored
eyes and he was tall and slender as a reed, with well-
defined shoulders and a tapering back. He walked like a
racehorse, with a long, rangy stride and a slight bounce in
his step. Aloisio Esposito had not lost a first-blood bout
in centuries. He hadn't lost a death match in, well, ever.

Sabina did not announce anything or ask about weapons. She said nothing as they approached the central octagonal.

Grégoire and Aloisio were both wearing black, their
matte fighting leathers new and well armored. The death
bell rang, the note pure and clean and deadly.

The attacks were so fast I could hardly see the movement of the blades, glistening in the dim glow of the
lights mounted above us. They clanged, clanked, shushed
as blade slid upon blade. Blood flew in scarlet drops.
Grégoire's hair was stained scarlet. Aloisio's neck was
bleeding. Just above it, his earlobe was nicked and missing a wedge. Step, step, step, feet silent in this dance of
death.

Weapons a blur.

I wasn't breathing. The Glob flashed with a blistering
heat.

In the same instant there was movement in my periph-
eral vision. Flashing.

I dropped. The blade thunked into the pillar above
me, right where my eyes had been. Perched on my toes, I
whirled. No one was there. Looked back to the duel. It
was even bloodier. Splatters flying in the air. Splatters on
the sand. One landed on my face, cold vamp blood.

I grunted, my eyes still whipping around the space,
away from the duel, which was in its seventh second,
searching for anyone who looked wrong, who wasn't
watching the fight with enough attention, or with too
much attention. No one looked out of place or guilty. My

eyes slid to the side, refusing to focus. And I realized someone was beneath an obfuscation spell. Bancym M'lareil? I pulled on Beast-sight and the rubies heated in my hand. I saw the form of the woman on the far side of the sand, hidden beneath the witch working. Now that I knew where to look, she was slender and muscular, arms akimbo, swords at her sides. I let go of the rubies and she vanished from sight. Had Dominique been using the ruby to keep track of Cym? Yeah. Made sense. Fast thoughts. Fast as the blades.

I glanced at the duel. Eleven seconds.

Our witches were farther back on the sand, not close enough to help. This one had gotten inside the *hedge of thorns*. Had to be in the moments when the *hedge* was dropped so we could come and go. She had walked over the outline of the *hedge of thorns* without Molly seeing her, which meant she had come in with Titus, her witch energies absorbed among the vamps.

A thump sounded. My eyes flew to the battle. Grégoire was on his back. Aloisio stood over him. My heart fell through the sand beneath me.

CHAPTER 19

It's Poisoned

Grégoire rolled away, swift as thought. Aloisio bent over. His guts spilled out onto the floor in a bloody, reeking, gagworthy slither. Black and scarlet, like eels and raw meat. Aloisio dropped to his knees. Grégoire rose and whipped his sword in an arc. Aloisio's head rolled to the side.

Grégoire bowed to Sabina. He was a bloody mess but still standing, his enemy's intestines in a coil around his ankles.

"Golden," the camera wolf muttered.

"Results of this duel are acceptable to the Onorios," Brandon said, his voice emotionless. But I could see the strain on his face. He had sworn to Grégoire. The twins loved Blondie. This had been the hardest one he had watched, knowing that if his master died, he could not avenge the true-death.

I stood and pulled the knife from the wooden support. It was the length of my hand and fingers from tip of blade to tip of hilt. It was old and not well cared for, dried blood in the crevices. I sniffed it and caught the stench of humans and vamps and magic. Death spells in it? I looked around but couldn't spot the witch anywhere. I regripped the rubies. Nothing. She had moved.

Sabina clapped her hands three times and said, "The Sangre Duello will recommence one hour after dusk. For now there are food and beverages here and below for the humans. The Mithrans who wish to sup before sleep or before departing must hurry. Dawn is nigh."

Grégoire, stepping gracefully out of the intestines, walked off the octagonal and toward the stairs to the beach mansion. His footprints were bloody and as he passed me, I realized I was smelling his blood. A lot of his blood. I swept an arm under his and supported him to Leo's room. The MOC followed me and there was a lot of harried French, staccato orders, too fast for me to pick out words. I eased Grégoire onto the bed and Leo fell on his friend, tearing his own flesh to heal him. The bottle of healing blood potion was on the mattress beside Leo's knee. It was nearly empty. I had no idea if there was another bottle or not.

Grégoire met my eyes with his blue ones and said, "My people have bound Dominique in silver and placed her on the sand for the dawn. You will not save her this death by taking her head."

"I won't save her." I moved away and went looking for the witch.

I didn't find the witch, but I told Lachish what I had seen and she was searching the house and grounds with a version of a find-it spell. Molly was in bed, grumpy but resting, only because I picked her up and carried her inside, to bed, and set a guard over her. She could get up to pee. She could have food and fluids delivered. That was it.

Dawn was breaking and the screams of Dominique could be heard across the island and far out to sea probably. I'd never heard such horrible screams. But I didn't go look. And I didn't shut my ears to the sounds of wails. I found the courage to check on our own dead and wounded. Del was on Dacy's bed with her mother, one of the Robere Onorios, and three humans, her naked body cradled against Sabina, the outclan priestess doing some witchy shamanistic thing over her that looked vaguely familiar and totally scary. Sabina's eyes were closed and she was speaking in a language I didn't recognize.

Del wasn't undead. She wasn't alive either, not breathing, no heartbeat, her body gray and mottled all over, rigor mortis setting in. Her fingernails and toenails were perfect, a blaze of scarlet. All I could think was that she had gone for a mani-pedi without me. And that thought brought tears to my eyes. I pulled off the chain with the two rubies and carried them to Sabina, holding them out. Saying nothing. The gems dangling, twirling. They were batteries. Maybe they'd help Del.

The twirling slowed. Stopped. Without opening her eyes, Sabina reached out, taking the gems. They sparked and the motes within took on a different formation. "They will be returned," Sabina said, her voice a monotone.

I shrugged helplessly and backed out of Dacy's room to look in on Grégoire. Leo had him on the bed with a dozen humans. It was a big naked mess of blood and sex. Ditto on the backing away.

Edmund was cuddled between Gee and Katie and three humans, asleep, Ed's arm in an inflatable cast, his thumb wrapped in gauze and supported by shaped metal strips. They were all naked. Something else I didn't need to see. I shut that door and went to feed my face. I was starving. Deon had changed into short-shorts tight enough to fit a small child and his wife-beater T-shirt was stretched across his torso, sequined in rainbow hues with a unicorn on the front.

I stole a serving platter and loaded it up with enough bacon and eggs to stuff a great white shark, took a place alone at the long dining table, grabbed some utensils from a basket of knives, forks, and spoons all standing upright, and started eating. A brown arm and hand reached around me and placed a teapot and an empty mug beside the platter. Eli took the chair beside me, holding a tiny cup of espresso. I gave him the stink-eye at his lack of food. I knew what that meant. He'd eat mine.

He stole a piece of bacon. Ate it. I said nothing. He stole another one. Ate it too. Then a third. Around the slice of bacon he said, "They couldn't turn Del."

I stared away from the food and out the windows at the pink sunrise, my appetite temporarily throttled. Tears gathered in my eyes and then dried. They were trying to make her an Onorio. Very few survived that transition, and the ones who did were never really the same after. The transformation was mental, emotional, spiritual, and physical. I liked the changes in Bruiser. A lot. But that didn't mean that Del, if she lived as Onorio, would like herself.

Eli took another piece of bacon. "You're letting me steal your food," he said.

"It's poisoned. I'm letting you get your comeuppance."

"So we'll die together?"

Del wasn't dead. Not yet. Maybe she could be saved. I ate a few forkfuls of eggs, forcing them down, thinking. "Okay. Not poisoned."

"I love you too, Babe."

I frowned. Deon brought me a plate of pancakes with butter on top and syrup that drizzled down the sides. Protein and pancakes. Heaven on earth. "I might have to marry you," I said to Deon.

"You and me? Oh! Let's include Ziggy. We'd make beautiful brides! A threesome walking down the aisle together."

He sashayed off.

Eli shook his head, bemused. "You do know how much you've changed my life, don't you? And you're the smallest part of the weird that my life has become."

"Weird is fun. Keeps you on your toes." Weird might keep Del alive.

He stole another piece of bacon. I turned the platter to make it easier for him to eat from. Eli smiled. Took a knife and fork from the upright basket and started eating. "Beast okay with me eating from your plate?" he asked.

"Beast thinks of you as her kit. I'm surprised she didn't take the fork and feed you."

Eli burst out laughing.

*   *   *

Five minutes before the Europeans landed for the night,
I was in my whites again. Edmund had insisted on directing my dressing, and because he was in so much pain that
he had woken before sunset, I let him—though I put on
my own undies, a white uni, and my boots all by myself.
He worked with Deon and Ziggy in the rest of the dressing experiment, including a gold turtleneck under doubled gorgets, Queen Bitch's makeup (too much and all of
it glittery, I was sure, though I hadn't seen myself yet),
and weapons (lots of them). Edmund, working mostly
one-handed, had braided my hair into a fighting queue
with a crown of stakes. I wore the Mughal blade in its
scarlet-velvet-covered scabbard, two long swords, and
blades all over me.

"I'll clank as I walk," I complained.

Ed gave me a look that disagreed. "You will be perfect."

"No. You will be magnificent," Ziggy said earnestly.
"And though QB will be dreadfully jealous to have competition, after seeing you, I may create a JY ensemble for
the next drag queen competition. I'll show a lot more
breast, of course."

"Of course," I said.

"And my pants will be a G-string under leather chaps."

Ziggy was currently wearing crinkled gray linen pants
and a gray hoodie out of some slick slubby material like
flax. Unisex clothes. Lots of makeup. Blinged-out flip-
flops. I shook my head. He kissed me on the cheek. "I'll
look stunning, Legs. I promise I'll do you proud." He
held up a mirror to me. I looked like a different woman.

Ziggy had applied golden and sapphire shimmer to my
lids, a sparkly gold eyeliner over Cleopatra-style black
liner, mascara that made my lashes look a mile long. A
dusting of golden shimmery cheek color, red lipstick, and
the pièce de résistance, lines back from my eyes and
cheeks like whiskers, drawn in shimmery gold. I didn't
have the heart to tell him that none of it would matter
when I fought. "Thank you. I look amazing."

"Of course you do, honey chile. Everything I do is amazing."

I didn't go in for the first two rounds, instead sitting with the Kid and Champ in the production/security room, studying the low-light and infrared cameras for evidence of a witch. The two rubies had been returned by Sabina when she woke, returned without comment. I hadn't asked if Del lived or died. I was too chicken. But I'd placed the rubies onto the chain at my neck and they had realigned to my magics the moment I held them. Batteries. Maybe boosters too. We didn't spot a witch under an obfuscation spell, but what we did see was grim.

Katie stood in the center octagonal ring on the sand, her bastard sword held in a backhand stance. She wasn't the Katherine I met when I first came to New Orleans, a confused, olden-day vamp lost in the modern world, nor was she the Katie who had risen nearly insane from a box of blood. This Katie was vibrant, steady, her power shooting throughout the room, so electric that Titus himself winced in surprise. So strong that I could feel it in the cramped room below.

Katie said, "I accept the challenge of Postumus, who seeks the head of my love and my master, Leo Pellissier."

"Who is Postumus?" I asked, not remembering the name in the long list of combatants.

In a dead voice, Alex said, "Marcus Cassianius Latinius Postumus. Founder of the Gaelic Empire in 260 or so."

He would be old. Skilled. Devious. My heart tightened in my chest.

The bell dinged. A bearded vamp stepped forward, muscular, short, a powerful barrel of a man.

Four seconds later, Katie was down, her foot nearly severed, her throat sliced from ear to ear, and a stake in her chest. Her opponent was dead, both arms severed and his head across the room, but Katie was in bad shape. She was carried up the stairs in a dripping bloody sheet. Leo's people won the first match, but with Katie down and out, we may have lost the Sangre Duello.

"You okay?" I asked the Kid.

"I'm finer than fine," Alex answered, eyes on his cameras, his kinky hair sticking to his sweaty face. It was hot in the closet, with all the equipment running and no AC. "Or as good as I can be without energy drinks, mainlining espresso and Clif bars." I said nothing. As Sabina talked to Titus and Leo, their voices coming through the windows and not the system, Alex said, "You let Eli fight."

"Your brother didn't leave me a choice. He said yes."

"You coulda coldcocked him and carried him from the line of fire."

I nodded slowly, knowing that Alex could see me from the corner of his eye. "I could have. I didn't."

"You wanna tell me why?"

"Eli wanted that fight. He chose a good weapon. Something she wasn't likely to have fired. I had read the dossier on the woman."

"Not an acceptable reason." He turned his head and met my eyes, his brownish ones darker in the night. "You. Let him. Fight." It was an accusation, the words widely spaced and venomous.

"He misses it, misses the adrenaline rush, the heightened senses. You know it. I know it. I thought this was a good choice. The safest choice."

"That asshole coulda shot him in the head, not the chest. Eli coulda not worn a vest. My brother could be dead."

"I know. I screwed up. I'm sorry."

Alex nodded, a minuscule gesture much like one Eli would make. "Don't let it happen again, Janie."

I smiled, my lips stretching for the first time since Eli was shot, knowing that I had no control over Eli's actions at all, but not wanting to say that to Alex. "I'll do my best." I tapped one of the screens. "Soul. On the outer edges of the island. What's she doing?"

"Walking the periphery of the island. She's been doing it since the EVs came ashore."

"Okay." I wasn't sure what Soul was doing or planning, but there wasn't much I could do to stop her.

"Anomaly." He stabbed a different screen. "There."

A slender shimmer moved up the stairs to the second floor and proceeded to the third floor.

Alex said, "Go."

I pulled on Beast's stealth, gripped the rubies, and raced after the Cym-shaped shimmer.

A camera wolf caught my movement and followed.

The smell of magic hit the air, faint but harsh as tar—a curse being cast. As the scent blazed out, I could see Cym, standing on the landing at the third floor, glistening beneath the obfuscation spell, which she couldn't hold strong while casting a curse. I was ten feet from her and at least six feet below her. She raised her arms. The prickle of magic blazed out. There wasn't time.

Time . . . I could—

Beast took over. Shoved up with my back legs. I leaped. In midair, I/we drew a fourteen-inch vamp-killer from a sheath at my calf. Spun that arm back, winding up. And took her through the neck, near her head. I landed fourteen feet beyond her, in front of Sabina. A bloody blade in my hand. My mind thought, *Thank you, Beast*. She hadn't let me bubble time. I started to stand upright. Stopped. Unable to move.

A dozen swords were at my throat. Carefully, I set the blade on the floor. "Intruder," I whispered. And sucked in breaths I hadn't taken while I leaped through the air.

"Golden. Absolutely, fucking golden," the camera wolfman said.

Cym's death had broken her spell. Her body, blood, and partially attached head were visible. Her lemon scent filled the room, drifting from her body and blood. The wolf moved the camera along her body and up to her head. Cym was dressed vaguely as a pirate, with embroidered vest, a white shirt with full sleeves, thigh-high boots, tight pants, and gaudy, mismatched jewelry. "Sorry 'bout the language, Champ," the camera wolf added, not sounding at all apologetic, "but that was fuc—fricking fabulous."

"She was under an obfuscation spell," I said. "Witchcraft in the Sangre Duello is disallowed." Only in La Danza could it be used.

"She wasn't dueling. You killed her?" Titus asked. "For using a spell? Isn't that what witches do?"

With a vamp-killer I turned her head to expose her fangs. "Witch. Also a Mithran. Also a member of Clan Des Citrons, who are sworn to Titus Flavius Vespasianus." With the tip of the blade I snagged Cym's fancy white shirt and pulled it from the vest. On the front was the emblem of a lizard eating its tail.

Titus looked momentarily nonplussed that I knew all this. Then he got over it. "One acting on her own. Or a traitor to my cause."

"She threw this at me last night." I held up two fingers to show I didn't have a weapon and slowly inserted them into a throwing knife sheath. I removed the knife and extended it, hilt first, to Leo.

Leo, no weapons drawn, hands clasped behind his back, walked slowly to me and sniffed along its length. "Magic and the mixed blood of humans and Mithrans. A blade improperly cared for. Or coated with a death curse." He accepted the blade in one palm, holding it so the light fell on it. "Steel, double-sided blades, set in an olive wood hilt." Leo's eyes drifted to Titus. "For Christmas in the year 1702, you gave me a set of throwing knives made from olive wood."

"You were my servant," Titus said dismissively. "I gave similar sets of blades to everyone in my retinue. There were hundreds of you. I decimated an entire olive grove to accommodate the wood needed."

Without taking his gaze from the emperor, Leo said, "She attacked you yesterday, my Enforcer. Who was she attacking this time?"

I thought back to the wild leap in the air. The direction of Cym's barely seen arms. The people on the other side of her. "She wasn't throwing a blade. She was casting a curse. I believe it was directed at Sabina, the outclan priestess."

Leo's eyebrow quirked up, just the one. "Indeed?"

That's what it looked like. I didn't say that. I said, with certainty, "Yes."

Beast is best hunter. Beast will eat witch head.

Beast will not.

Beast hungers.

"Who sent her?" Titus asked.

"You. Me. A third party who wishes to rule," Leo said. "Any of a hundred names come to mind, including Clan Des Citrons, who killed cattle on my hunting lands before joining with you."

"They were on your lands?" Titus made a *tsk-tsk* sound. "I would never allow an unsworn Mithran onto my lands. I control my lands and my cattle better than that."

Leo chuckled, that silky sound that coated the flesh of all prey, a laugh full of power and conquest. "They are on your boat, sleeping with you and yours. After being on my lands. How did they get from the house where they killed, to your ship?" Leo's laughter sang in the rafters. "They are there. Safe. You must ask yourself, what did I offer them to turn on you?"

Titus flinched, just the tiniest bit. So did I. Had Leo helped the clan to get away and to Titus? Had he turned them? Had he let those people die and then helped the killers get free? No. I'd have heard. Alex would have heard. Leo was sowing discord among Titus and all his people. Probably. "My Enforcer. Do you know how she came to this island?"

I moved to the window and called down, "Lachish! We need you up here." To the EVs I said, "Lachish Dutillet cast the ward around this house."

Lachish stepped up the last step, walked over to the body, and silently studied it. She had to have been waiting to be called. When I killed the vamp/witch she probably felt the energies and headed up the stairs. She turned to the room and put her shoulders back. Speaking to Titus, she said, "Each time the Europeans have come ashore, there has been an anomaly at the ward. There is no proof, but, there is the anomaly. And we have recorded the timing with electronic security."

Sabina said, "Points against the Europeans for trying to disable or kill a judge. The next such infraction will result in severe penalty. True-death is not ruled out."

Titus said, "You cannot bring me to true-death."

Sabina pulled her gloved hands out of her starched

skirts. In one hand was a spear of wood. "I can and I will."

Titus took a step back before he could catch himself.

He pursed his lips, then nodded once, regally. "Your ruling is accepted."

He looked at Leo and some unheard communication seemed to take place. Leo and Titus stepped silently across the wood floors, both wearing fighting leathers tonight, both moving gracefully, as if they danced a gavotte in some drafty old palace. Both with hands clasped behind their backs.

"Do you recognize her?" Leo asked.

"I do not. You?"

Liar, liar, royal pantaloons on fire.

"Yes. She is Bancym M'lareil, once sworn to Jack Shoffru. He tried to take my lands and ended up as a pile of ash."

Titus looked ever so slightly impressed. "I wondered what had happened to that old pirate. I suppose you should take her head," he said.

"Since she hid among your retinue to come ashore, I relinquish the honor to you. Such humiliation should be avenged."

Titus's eyes went narrow as he realized he had been both insulted and gifted with the task of taking the head of his sworn scion. But he drew his sword and took Cym's head. Cleaned the blade on her clothes.

"Well done, my Enforcer," Leo said. To the emperor he said, "Shall we return to the festivities?"

"Of a certainty."

Festivities? Fangheads celebrated the weirdest things.

Titus added, "Though you have few in leadership positions with which to continue. Do you abdicate New Orleans and the territories you administer?"

"I do not. Do you abdicate the territories of Western Europe?"

"Tedious as it may seem, I do not."

"Then let us cut to the chase," Leo said. "It is an American phrase meaning that we should cease all this meaningless bloodshed. I suggest that we, you and I, duel tonight."

"We alone?" Titus asked, sounding surprised. The two circled back to the witch's dead body and then meandered toward Sabina, who waited patiently at the head of the room. "But your Enforcer has yet to duel."

Enforcer. Glacie was next on the list. Glacie, the hulking woman vamp. I had actually seen video of her fighting. She was deadly. And . . . Leo was trying to keep me safe. Why?

Dark Queen . . . That.

"We alone. On the sand, much like the death match between Kyros and Nicanor," Leo said. "It was a thing of beauty, and the mastership of all of Greece was granted into the talons and fangs of Kyros."

"It was a splendorous bout," Titus agreed, standing beside Leo, the two now looking out the nearest window, standing with much the same posture, feet shoulder-width apart, hands clasped behind their backs. "The view of the water here is magnificent. I suggest we engage there, on the beach sand, beneath the moon and stars."

"Shall we toast to this?"

"Oh ho!" Titus slapped Leo's back in what looked like camaraderie. "I have heard that you retain the services of a human from the Orient, one who tastes of hazelnuts? Is this so?"

"Ah," Leo said. "Chin Ho. He is actually Grégoire's, but he is here. His name means Precious and Goodness. He is from the land now known as Korea, and is most beautiful to look upon, as he is to taste. He is about fifty years old and is aging well, like a fine wine. I would be honored to have your opinion," Leo said, all civility and elegance.

"I have a lovely woman I would share with you," Titus said.

I took off before I barfed. They were talking about humans as if they were liquor and slaves. Ticked me off. I left the third floor and took the stairs to the ground, under the house. The fighting rings here had absorbed the blood, and the blood itself had been diluted with water from the shower. In spots, the sand was the pale pinkish color of watery blood.

What was a Dark Queen even supposed to do in this situation?

Jane will fly by cloth over haunches.

Seat of my pants.

Yes. Jane/Beast will know what to do when Jane must do it.

This is ridiculous. Stupid.

This is fighting for territory. Beast has fought for territory before. And has eaten big-cat who challenged for hunting grounds.

That does not make me feel better.

Beast is best ambush hunter.

Still stupid. Stupid Sangre Duello. Stupid fangheads. Stupid Leo.

Then again, I thought, war between countries where millions of young human men and women died while their leaders sat in safety behind the lines was even more stupid and ridiculous. Plans were made and discarded, cities were taken and lost, and people died for nothing. Still. This sucked. I went back upstairs and raided Deon's commercial fridge, taking a heaping tureen of roasted pig meat and a single fork to the front porch. I set it on a table and dropped onto a lounge chair, putting my booted feet up. And ate.

Bruiser took the chair beside me. He was holding two glasses of wine. "I'm not certain of the proper wine for whole smoked pork, but decided on an Australian Cabernet-Shiraz and a Chilean Merlot. Which do you prefer?" He held out both glasses.

"Shouldn't you be off doing Onorio stuff?"

"If I have to do another Onorio task I think I shall go raving mad. I need to be with you." He still held out the glasses.

I remembered that the Merlot had sucked all the moisture out of my mouth. "I'll have the Shiraz. Unless you have a Boone's Farm Fuzzy Navel. That reminds me of Creamsicle, and I'd kill for a Creamsicle right now." The words were out of my mouth before I could stop them. "Not really," I amended. "Not kill."

"I know what you meant, my love. And no, I kept the

Boone's Farm for our celebration when we are safely back home."

I shoveled in meat. Drank the Shiraz. It was okay. Bruiser seemed to like the Merlot. "I thought there was supposed to be only beer on the island. Nothing the Euro-Vamps would approve of."

"Officially. I brought a few bottles of my own. May I?" he asked, gesturing with the wineglass at my tureen.

I offered him my fork. He waved it away and took some of the pulled pork in his fingers and ate. My heart melted. And melted again when he licked his fingers and took another portion. *This*. This was why I loved him. Bruiser was powerful, elegant, and rich, but there was nothing pretentious about him.

I set aside my fork and we both ate with our fingers and drank wine, watching the night's distant storm on the ocean, lightning flickering through the clouds and down to the crashing sea, miles away. But growing closer. The breeze picked up. Stunted trees danced in the wind, leaves flying away with the approaching squall.

Bruiser asked casually, "Is it a magical storm? Like something that Adan created?"

"No," I said. "Just a nightly gulf storm. Mother Nature getting in the last word." I let a pause fill the space between us, as the gulf splashed and the wind soughed. I took Bruiser's hand and his fingers wrapped around mine. We sat that way for some time.

We were still sitting when the tramp of feet alerted us. I set aside the huge bowl and leaned over Bruiser. Kissed him gently. He tasted of pork and fancy wine. And love.

Battle wasn't made for quiet moments or relaxing. It was made for the kind of focus that narrowed down to life and death and survival. This break from that intensity and emphasis and single-minded concentration was probably stupid. But I felt the tension flow out of me at the touch of his lips. I breathed into his mouth, and he smiled, his lips moving against mine. And it was exactly the short, peaceful break I had craved without realizing it. I pulled away slightly. "Thank you. I needed that."

"As did I."

I tilted my head, thinking about the way I had just re-laxed. "Did you just share your Onorio magic with me?"

"It's proscribed. I would never do such a thing in the midst of a Sangre Duello."

My honeybunch just lied to me. It was so sweet I wanted to cry. Instead I said, "If—When Titus loses, that ship can just sail away."

Bruiser's lips pulled up slightly, though the smile never reached his eyes. "So it seems." His tone said that he knew or guessed that Leo—or I—had that eventuality covered. "However, there are any number of treacherous strategies that the passengers on the ship might attempt. And you have made certain that most of them will not succeed."

That meant that Bruiser knew about the plan I had put in place with my one cell phone call from the island. Interesting. Gee had spilled the beans. Or Alex had been listening in when I made my call and told my sweetcheeks. Or . . . something. "Okay," I said just as softly, thinking about all the people on that ship. "Okay."

We stood twenty feet from the surf on the flat sand. A long, undulating wave train rolled in, over and over, off the gulf. The storm was coming ashore, thunder a constant, disorganized, booming echo, lightning striking down in blasts of light that illuminated the tossing sea, rain in heavy sheets, visible in the flashing bursts. The wind picked up, carrying with it the ozone of lightning and the faint scent of dead fish on the otherwise clean and salty air.

It wasn't a magical storm. I knew how to recognize those. But . . . lightning. And Brute was here, which suggested that Hayyel, the wolf's angel, had eyes on the proceedings. Soul in dragon form zipped through the storm clouds, in human sight looking like cloud-to-cloud lightning; in Beast-sight a light dragon, filling herself with power. I didn't know why, but the vision made me itchy, worried, anxious. Soul could see and alter the future when she wanted. I knew that. She knew the possible outcomes of this final duel. I shivered in the cold wind. There was something circular and cyclical about this fight beneath this storm. As if it encapsulated everything that had happened since I arrived in New Orleans.

Leo took to the beach, carrying one longsword and a small sword shaped like a Gurkha kukri, the blade roughly twelve inches long and slightly curved. Titus was similarly armed, but with straight blades. Both wore armor. Leo's hair was back in a bun that secured it from whipping in the wind.

Bruiser touched my shoulder and went to stand with Brandon and Brian, the Onorios all in one place. The outclan priestess stood across from them. They had been in that configuration all through the Sangre Duello. Arbiters and judges.

Leo's people stood closest to the house. Titus's people were on the water side of the imaginary ring. The scent of lemons was faint but present, riding atop the smell of salt and vamp. The moon still shone overhead, days away still from the full phase, scudding clouds obscuring her light from time to time, casting shadows on the white sand. I took the Glob in hand and stuck it in my pocket, holding it. A good-luck talisman. Its magic shocked my hand, magic captured from the lightning storm that had made it.

I held the rubies and the gold nugget I never took off in my other fist against my chest. I was armed. Heavily armed. But my arms and ability wouldn't decide this fight. They were useless.

The combatants tapped their sword tips to the sand, though I hadn't seen that before. Maybe a remnant from the Greek fight they had both relished.

The bell toned.

Leo struck. Titus blocked with his short blade. It wasn't the elegance of La Destreza. It was something else. Something cruder, older, battlefield coarse. The swords clanked and clanged. Thunder rumbled. Lightning struck the water out at sea. The moonlight flicked beneath rushing clouds. A storm wave crashed on the shore, foamed up around us all. We spectators danced back, away.

Not Leo and Titus. Feet in the rising surf, they fought.

Cut, cut, cut, stab, block, block. Cut, cut. Rain shattered down and stopped. Wind gusted and fell still. All in the space of a dozen heartbeats.

Both combatants were bleeding, the blood black in the moonlight. My hands tightened on the stones, the Glob in one hand, the nugget and rubies in the other. Leo was injured. Titus was favoring his left leg. Titus dropped to one knee. Sprang away. Leo was winning. Hope, deadly foolish hope, sprang up in me. Rain pelted down, fat, heavy drops that marked the sand like stars. Beast peered out through my eyes, watching everything. Spotting something out in the surf, something dark and silvered, standing there. Vamps from the ship, waiting to attack. Smelling of lemons.

Lightning hit the water, far off, but close enough to feel electricity in the air, heated as angel wings along my body. Fear of lightning quivered along my nerves, unresolved. The strike illuminated an image of Leo, his arm whipping forward, one knee forward, back leg outstretched. Steel sword high and swooping. Killing strike.

But Titus stepped to the side. Faster than vamps can move. He was simply . . . not there.

I felt the magic within me shiver and sing. The magic that formed a five-pointed star, a near perfect harmony of time and place and purpose. It pulled and twisted. Time thickened, a turgid, icy weight in the air. The Gray Between opened, a slice in reality, dove gray energies with black motes of darkest power.

I stepped outside of time. The noise of the surf and storm deepened, basso thrum.

Titus was on the outside of the sword strike. His longsword back. Titus had . . . timewalked.

So had I, though not by choice. He had pulled me out of normal time with him, but he hadn't noticed me. His attention was intent on Leo. Raindrops glistened, hanging in the air. A thousand possibilities, caught in the storm. Beast growled. Reached out a paw.

Time snapped back. Normal. Crashing loud.

Titus lunged forward. Straight and true. The blade taking Leo high on his chest.

Lightning touched down. Blinding, dazzling. Only feet away. Magic captured in the Glob reached for the energy in the brilliant bolt. Sucked it inside, to fuel its own might. Power exploded in the air. Sizzled through the sand. The Glob broiled, roasting my palm, and Glob magic flashed out and absorbed it, faster than the lightning could die away. Rain blasted down, drenching, scarring the sand.

I was soaked through with the possibilities of the future. Half-blinded.

But I could see enough.

Leo staggered back, into the surf. Off balance, about to drop to one knee.

Titus's sword swung forward, the weight and torque of his entire body behind it.

The blade cut into Leo's neck. Blood spraying into the rain.

Leo's head flew into the air.

His body fell.

Rain shattered onto the earth.

Leo died.

Leo . . . died.

Rain sliced me. Slashed my face. Sluiced down my leather jacket. The future and the past in every drop, icy from the fall through the heavens. I screamed.

CHAPTER 20

Shoulda, Coulda, Woulda

Suddenly I was in my room, digging around in the box of trinkets. Pulling out the bone fragment I needed. I didn't remember getting here. Timewalking. Didn't care.

Beast? Fighting form.

Beast is ambush hunter, she thought at me. Using my hands, she grabbed a second box from under the bed, a box of bones and teeth. Shoved my hand inside. The Gray Between ripped across me, tore its way along my spine.

My bones snapped and popped. My belly wrenched and flipped as nausea bent me double before it vanished. Pain shot through me, twisting the length of my skeleton, stretching my muscles, broadening shoulder joints, re-forming hips and pelvis, twanging in my jaw as my teeth grew. I tasted blood as the tissue and bone in my mouth and jaw tried to accommodate the transformation and the new fangs.

And . . . I took on mass.

The rubies on my necklace shattered. Bloodred crystals melted and disappeared. I threw back my head and screamed Beast's challenge, the sound roaring through the house and out the windows to the assembled vamps on the beach. In ten seconds I drew back my shoulders. I was half-form, my pawed feet stretching out the sides of the specially made combat boots, my jaw full of teeth designed to tear meat. My eyes glowed golden. But I was more. I was bigger. I was—

Beast is sabertooth lion. Beast is big.

The rubies. You—

Beast took mass from rubies. Took snake in heart of all creatures from bones. Took Glob magic. Gave magic to Jane. Beast is best ambush hunter.

I/we slid *le breloque* onto one arm. Took the Glob into my fist. Pulled the Mughal blade. I stepped back into normal time. My belly crunched, my head ached, but I shoved the pain away.

I leaped through the window and landed on the porch roof. Roaring my challenge. My body lit by lightning that flashed from the ordinary, natural lightning storm. The vamps on the beach turned to me, looking up, as rain and lightning slashed down. The vamps rushing from the surf stopped, waiting. I shoved the crown they all wanted onto my head. My voice a deeper octave, I screamed, to be heard over the storm, my voice a roar not heard on the Earth in millennia. My voice a basso reverberation, I shouted, "The Dark Queen challenges Titus Flavius Vespasianus for control of the Americas and of Europe. The Dark Queen demands La Danza de los Maestros de Sangre!"

Titus's eyes went wide and he stepped back into the surging waves. Lightning hit the water and the shore, a two-pronged strike. Titus vamped out, his jaw unhinging and sliding back into place. This was the first time I'd seen him in fanged form. Five-inch fangs, as long as the priestess's fangs, thick at the base and serrated. Top and bottom. Titus had dog fangs. And three-inch talons.

Beast fangs are bigger.

"By what right do you challenge?" Brandon called out.

"By the right of the Dark Queen and by the death of Leo Pellissier. A death not dealt by the sword used by Titus Flavius Vespasianus, but by witch magic. Vespasianus cheated with witch magic, outside of the protocol

of Sangre Duello. Ask the witches." I pointed with the
Mughal blade to Molly and Lachish, who stood together
beneath a *hedge of thorns* that glowed like the sunrise.
"Ask the arcenciel who watches this Duello." I pointed to
the clouds. "Only within La Danza de los Maestros de
Sangre may magic be used in battle. This challenge is legal and it is mine!"

Titus must have known he was shit-out-of-luck, because he shouted back, "I accept!" He shook his long and
short swords at the sky. "The weapons we carry! And the
weapon of time! The blood of my enemy still on my
blade."

"Here and now!" I shouted back, my voice low, a growl
of fury. "And in time! *Prepararse para la muerte.*" I threw
myself forward, leaped from the roof, and dropped toward the sand. Landed before him, my half-form knees
bending, taking the fall. I slammed *le breloque* onto my
head. It clamped down on me as if sealing itself to me.

"Unto true-death!" Titus screamed.

The death bell rang. Battlefield time-sense took over.

Titus's longsword descended. He threw a smaller blade
at me. In Beast-sight, I saw it spinning, flipping. I stepped
aside.

Beast clawed again through the Gray Between. Time
slowed. Slowed. The consistency of frozen taffy. Time
stopped. Pain speared me through my right eye. Nausea
rose in a vile rush that twisted my guts. The storm was
heavy, rain suspended like crystal bullets striking down.
It was hard to breathe. And dangerous to move. If I
looked at the rain, I would see moments of time, might
change moments of time. But if I didn't look directly at
the drops . . . I focused away from the rain. The time-
droplets moved back, out of my way, leaving regular raindrops close to me.

Carefully, making sure I didn't move quickly enough
to accidentally alter time in any of the time-drops, I
ducked beneath the sword strike.

Beast is best ambush hunter. Beast reached out for a
droplet of rain. In it was the immediate past. The image
of Titus's sword striking Leo's neck.

I stopped her. Thinking. Trying to see what might happen if we took that small part of time. The droplet beyond it was an image of Titus's people attacking the Onorios. The droplet beyond that was an image of his people attacking the witches, a sword thrust through Molly's belly, killing her and her daughter. Lachish dead in the rain, magical implements on the sand. Ailis dead. Koun and Tex dead. The droplet beyond that showed a bomb landing on the beach, another on the beach house. Titus's ship exploding. Everyone dead. And worse beyond that. A pathway running with blood.

Every time-drop near the death of Leo showed only destruction and devastation. If I went back in time and saved Leo, far worse would happen. I studied the drops. Praying for that one, looking for that one, single drop that might show me another path. But . . . every drop, each and every one, displayed the beginnings of a war between the Europeans and the American vamps. Further back were images of humans drained and dead in the streets. Humans hanging from streetlights in the French Quarter. Bombs dropping on New Orleans. Soldiers and tanks in the streets. Vamps at war with the United States.

Eli and Alex dead on the floor of our home.

Edmund lying back-to-back with Gee, both dead, beheaded.

All because I saved Leo. The pain in my head grew worse. I fought to keep my gorge down, swallowing the sickness there.

Heart aching, I said aloud, "We've messed up too much as it is. We can't fix this by timewalking."

Beast is best ambush hunter. Beast can save Leo.

No. We'll screw up things. Mess up people's lives. If we save Leo, that will change something that may have been supposed to happen. No.

Beast/Jane screamed, the sound lost in the vibration of thunder. And then Titus moved. He stepped into the time bubble with me. His sword swinging down. I caught it on the curved Mughal blade and stepped close, ramming up. Hit him in the jaw with an uppercut. The Glob sliced his chin and busted his lips. It sucked his power

away. A sudden scalding burst of might I felt in my paw/
fist.

Titus threw back his head and screamed. I tossed the
Glob high, where it left the bubble of time, hanging in
the air, and, Beast-fast, pulled a vamp-killer. Thrust with
the vamp-killer, through his chin and up into his skull.
Ripped out the knife, twisting. Titus shivered, shook,
seizing as if the lightning had hit him. I slung back the
arm and took Titus's head.

I pushed the headless body out of the bubble of time,
leaving him half falling and headless.

Speared his head from out of time on the Mughal
blade. Pulled it to me. Sheathed the vamp-killer. With a
claw, I lifted the thin chain that still rested on the emper-
or's chest. Inside was a tiny quartz crystal with a minia-
ture arcenciel inside. She was purple and gold and
shimmering with fury. This explained why Soul had stuck
around. One last arcenciel caught in crystal, a slave to a
vamp who wanted to rule time. I tucked the crystal into
my pocket. Reached for the Glob.

Carrying the head and my weapons, I left Titus's body
standing headless in the stationary raindrops. And I padded on my massive paws away from the fight. Into the
storm, under the low trees. I dropped the head and fell
beside it. I cried until my guts hurt. Until my body felt
broken and scoured and bleeding.

Time still stopped, I pulled the crystal and said to the
trapped dragon, "I can't trust you not to bite me. So I'm
going to make sure you're freed when I'm not nearby." I
placed the crystal on a shell and left it there, in normal
time. I picked up another shell and held it directly above
the crystal. And dropped it. The shell fell from twisted
time and hung suspended above the arcenciel. The moment it hit, the slave to time would be free. But Leo . . .
Leo would still be dead.

I moved away from her, carrying the weapons and the
head of the emperor. A strange amalgamation of odors
were caught on the heavy, salty wind—Leo's paper-and-
ink-scented blood, a strong fragrance of fresh-cut lem-

ons, and surf-wet werewolves. I looked out into the gulf
to see the forms, unmoving, caught in time as they rushed
ashore through the dark. Clan Des Citrons. Wet rogue
werewolves were behind them, and two grindylows were
closing in from the water and the storm-drenched beach.

I looked to the side. Eli was closing in. Firing. Caught
in a sprint, angling into a safe line of fire. Derek raced
beside him. Leo's vampires rushed to attack, swords and
bare-handed. Dacy Mooney, Del's mother, was in the
lead, her sword arching back to take a Des Citrons vamp's
head. The smell/sight/sound of Molly's earth magic, red,
blue, vibrant, tearing into the night. The sight of the Bighorn Pack, one dropping his camera, racing to the battle.
Overhead, three arcenciels were in real time, dropping
from the clouds, glistening in the night.

And then there were Aya and Rick, rising from the
water, Benelli shotguns at the shoulder. One had fired,
the low, hollow thrum of shotguns, the shot hanging in
the air. Slightly farther back, two Navy SEALs were rising out of the water, picking off the emperor's vamps and
humans. When time returned, the wolves would howl.
The vampires would scream. The stench of silver fléchette
rounds tearing through flesh, and the reek of poisoned
blood, would taint the air.

My not-so-secret last-ditch defense to protect our people and to keep the military from accidentally taking us
all out. Because of my phone call, Gee had made sure
that Ayatas FireWind and all the might he could call
upon were a presence in the dark, in case Titus pulled a
fast one and his people attacked. All of Leo's merged
paranormals were here, fighting together. Finally. But too
late to save the Master of the City.

I should be out there. I needed to be there. I tensed to
move. Pain slashed through me. I fell to the sand, hands
and knees catching me. Gasping. Pain like a thousand
snakes in my gut, biting me all at once. I screamed. Boneless, I landed on the sand.

Beast padded into the forefront of my brain. She
pressed down on me, sending me to sleep.

*   *   *

Beast looked inside at Jane's snake. The snake that was at the heart of all beings was twisted, knotted, frayed. It had four strands, not the two strands it was supposed to have. It was broken, like the body of prey that raced away and fell off a ledge into a deep place.

Beast looked into Jane's belly. There were dark places there. Sickness. Growing fast. Jane was dying. But . . . Beast was best ambush hunter.

Beast found own form and shed mass into sand on beach. Stepped into form of *Puma concolor*, mountain lion. Shifted. Beast's snake in heart of all things was healthy. Was strong.

Time returned, storm throwing cold rain and lightning to ground. Arcenciels dove to earth. Trapped arcenciel leaped for sky. Rain beat into pelt. Lightning flashed, hitting water. *Hate storms. Hate rain.*

Struggled out of Jane clothes. Shook pelt. Did not help. Rain still fell, cold and wet. Beast looked out at storm. At dark forms fighting in curling water. Eli and Derek and Tequila boys, fighting. Rick and Ayatas firing on vampires arising from water. Other humans with them. Hunters Jane called military. Smelled lemons and silver and blood. Smelled human blood and vampire blood. Smelled much death. Bruiser stood on sand, watching fighting. Seeing Leo body. Tears leaked down his face.

Bruiser shed tears for friend.

Fighting slowed. Tequila boys carried bodies to shore. Vampire bodies smelling of Titus and of lemons. More fighting on ship out in curling water. Derek had sent Bruiser's boat to attack emperor's boat. Was good Enforcer. Derek did not need Jane now.

Beast hungered. Considered head of dog-fanged king of vampires. Was like alpha lion of strongest pride of African lions. Was tasty? Beast *pawpawpaw* to head. Licked at neck. Was tasty. Strong blood. Beast extended claws. Pulled head to body. Lay belly to sand. Ate mouth and face of vampire. Ripped off jaw from alpha of vampire pride. Was strong blood. Strong flesh.

Would stay Beast for one day or five. Would be good to hunt for fish in water and kill birds nesting onshore. Crunched into skull. King of vampire brain was tasty.

Much later, after sun rose and its warmth stole territory from winter night, Beast looked up. Eli was watching. Leaning against tree, arms crossed to hide claws. Human sign of peace. Beast chuffed. Licked lips. Batted parts of skull to Eli. Crown of skull whirled in sand. Stopped. Beast panted. Waited.

"Leo's in a box of blood. His head is still attached, but not by much. Probably not enough to save him."

Beast growled. *No. Leo head was gone. Flying. Eli is stupid kit. Leo is dead.*

Eli said, "And worse, an arcenciel appeared out of nowhere and bit him. Arcenciel bites are psychotropic and psychotoxic. It might be months before we know if he survives and if he's sane."

Beast took a soft, slow breath, understanding. Arcenciel Jane set free hadn't bitten us. Arcenciel changed time. Arcenciel bit Leo body.

Eli kept talking. "The Vodka boys set up a distraction with George's boat and a SEAL team boarded Titus's ship. Freed the captives—the Carusos, two witches who had been using a form of Cym's obfuscation charm to hide the ship from the military, an Onorio who hung in chains. Turned all the others over to Edmund."

Beast licked own jaw and muzzle free of blood. Tasted good on tongue.

"While Soul fought her own kind and then tried to save Leo, Derek and I took the fight to the water. Rick and Ayatas and a small group of SEALs caught Clan Des Citrons and the rest of Titus's fangheads trying to get ashore. For once you didn't just fly by the seat of your pants, Babe. You did good setting that up officially. Ayatas had the ear of the FBI, CIA. You figured he had the ear of the other government services and military too."

A tone of satisfaction entered his voice. "The fangheads didn't make it ashore."

Beast chuffed. *Jane is sneaky.* Made sound of kit call, high-pitched and sweet.

Eli kept talking. "Edmund already took over the reins
of the U.S. territory. Leo did well to make Ed his heir.
He's making peace with everyone, whether they want it or
not." Eli smiled slightly. "He's good at this. He's spoken to
the press, to the governor, and to members of Congress on
the phone. He's making plans to go to Europe and take
over there, in your name, and he's taking Grégoire with
him to take over those holdings at the same time. He appointed Alesha Fonteneau to run NOLA until he gets
back. Once things are settled, he wants you to go to the
European court and take over as the Dark Queen."

Beast shook head in human way, side to side, trying to
think like Jane. *Leo head is not gone? Saw Leo head fly
into air.* Thought about arcenciel in crystal. About Soul
hiding on island. Timewalkers. Better timewalkers than
Jane.

Eli smiled tiny smile. "Molly's okay. So is her baby.
You staying here for a while?"

Beast nodded once. Stupid human move.

"There's food in the house. Call when you want to
come home."

Home. To Jane den. With Eli and Alex. With Jane sick
and dying. Beast snorted softly. Eli walked away.

I woke up under the low tree. Human shaped. Naked.
The sun was a scarlet wash of color in the west. There was
a bag that looked waterproof hanging in the limbs of the
tree just above me. I reached up and touched it. The bag
was dry. The sand beneath me was dry. The air was cold
and damp, blustery, but the sky was bright, the cerulean
blue of sunset with a single star and a sliver of moon half-
hidden in distant clouds. The island felt empty. The house
had no lights. Everywhere was dark, silent. Deserted.

I was alone.

I rolled carefully to my feet and untied the bag. Found
inside a pair of jeans wrapped around undies and a bra,
three T-shirts for layering, and a warm jacket. Running
shoes beneath them with a pair of wool socks stuffed into
the toes. On the bottom was a vamp-killer and *le breloque*. And the Glob. Memories came hard and fast. Del

dying. Katie in danger of dying. So many others. My memory of Leo's head flying. Flying. Flying. Over and over. And time bending, bubbling, twisting. Changing reality. Changing every moment of the possible present.

I blinked the images away, only to see them again, on the back of my lids. I had a feeling I would see them forever. Yet, atop that was the memory of Eli telling Beast that Leo might still live. That he was poisoned by an arcenciel bite. Things not in my timeline. I shivered hard in the cold wind. Studied *le breloque*.

I had killed the emperor. I was now the Dark Queen of the vamps. De facto ruler of the fangheads. "This sucks," I said to the empty beach.

I pulled on my clothes. Braided my hair in a sloppy braid. I picked up the crown, slid it over one arm, took the vamp-killer and the Glob, and trudged to the house. There were no lounge chairs dotting the shore. No fire pit. No people.

The island was silent. I was marooned on a deserted island? That would be a kicker, if I was stranded here. So much for being the Queen of the Suckheads.

I climbed the steps to the house and found the front door unlocked. I kicked the sand off my shoes and went inside.

The windows were shuttered closed, leaving the house dark inside. The furniture was cocooned under white sheets. The house sounded big and hollow and empty. It even smelled empty.

"Beast? How long did you keep me asleep?" My voice echoed in the empty rooms.

We grieved, she thought at me. Which was sort of an answer.

My stomach growled. I made my way to the kitchen. Opened the refrigerator. The light inside came on, proving that the solar panels on the roof three stories above were still working. Which meant plumbing. A shower would be nice. The shelves inside the refrigerator were full of food and beer and wine. Boone's Farm Fuzzy Navel. I chuckled and pulled the note off the bottle in front.

It read simply, *I love you. Come home.*

Bruiser was fine. That was good. I stuffed the note in my bra next to my heart. I removed the bottle and opened it. Drank it down. It tasted fantastic. Beyond fantastic. I opened another, wishing for once that I could get roaring drunk. Skinwalker metabolism wasn't agreeable to a good roaring drunk.

Brains are better, Beast thought at me.

"Gack," I said aloud, my stomach rumbling.

Pig is good, though.

I opened the freezer. The pig had been fully pulled and placed in zippered, gallon-sized plastic bags. Five of them, frozen hard. I stuck one under the kitchen faucet and let water run over it until it was soft enough to remove the meat from the plastic and then nuked the gallon of meat until it was hot. While it thawed and heated, I checked the food in the fridge, knowing the smell would tell me how long I had been alone on the island. The beanie weenies didn't smell perfect, but I pulled them out and stuck them in the microwave when the pork was hot. Dumped the pig into the soup tureen on the kitchen island. That was when I spotted the card on the Carrara marble. Heavy card stock, folded over, red writing on white paper. It was the red of one of my lipsticks. Bloodred. Not so favorite anymore.

The note was arranged like an upside-down pyramid. It read:

Chère, I done left you rest of that pig you like so much.
The Kid done left you a satellite phone. Eat.
Call home. We come get you.
Deon.

I spotted the phone on the island too. Didn't pick it up.

While the beans heated, I carried the tureen around, snacking, and made a quick tour of the house. Someone had stripped the wet wallboard tape from the walls, reapplied fresh. There was no luggage left. No sign of blood on the floors.

When the microwave dinged I brought the bottle of Boone's Farm and the food to the front porch and sat down in the dark. Night had fallen fully. The surf sounded lazy and languid and soothing.

I ate and drank. Watching the tide roll in.

When my belly was full, I put the leftovers in the fridge and took a hot shower. The house was cold, but someone had left an electric blanket on the bed I had used, along with a set of sheets and my luggage. The blanket smelled like Molly. Eli had said that she was okay too. I pulled on sweats and the wool socks that had come with the shoes and wrapped myself in the blanket. I fell on my bunk and let sleep pull me under.

I woke at dawn. Ate pig. Drank wine. I was halfway through the bottle when I saw a flash of a head flying through the air. Leo's head. Memory. Intense as reality. Stark, electric. I blinked. Sobbed once, hard and harsh and dry. Eyes burning. Leo was in a blood box. He might not be true-dead. Or not exactly true-dead.

A second image slammed into me. Titus's head in my hand, then dropping to the sand.

I'd killed him. It was what I did. I killed people. Beings. Sentient creatures. But I should have killed Titus the moment he walked up to the house on the beach, surrounded by his people. I should have drawn the Mughal blade and taken his head right then. Shoulda, coulda, woulda.

Hadn't.

I finished the bottle. There were more. Bruiser had left me twelve, an entire case. The wine sat heavy on my stomach. Queasy. So I drank more.

My second morning on the island in Jane form, I crawled from bed and walked naked down to the beach to swim. The air was warmer, eighties, but the water was cold when I dove in and swam deep. Halfway hoping I'd be eaten by a shark. I wasn't that lucky.

When exhaustion claimed me, I crawled up the shore and lay in the sun on the sand. Naked. Alone. When the sun threatened to burn even my golden-toned skin, I rinsed off in the outside shower and went in search of something other than pig. I found a baked fish in the freezer, next to a plastic container that was marked with the words RICE PUDDIN'. I microwaved them both. Ate the entire fish—which had Deon's touch on it, lemon and herbs—and the whole container of rice pudding, which tasted like coconut and rice and dates and cranberries. They shouldn't have tasted good together, but they did.

I drank another bottle of wine, deciding that I'd drink a bottle per day from now on, to mark off the days as human. But I didn't feel so well. And I was tired. Grief could make a person tired. Right? Right.

Days passed. A helo flew over once and I waved it off. It left. I was okay. I just needed privacy. But instead of feeling better, I was feeling worse. A lot worse. After the last bottle of wine, I knew it was time to call for extraction. I'd been walking on the beach at sunset, the empty bottle in my hand, swinging. I'd tried singing. Quit when my own ears protested. I was a mile along the beach, heading back to the house, when the sickening feeling hit me, a wrenching nausea that tossed me to my knees, retching. I vomited up everything I'd eaten for dinner, hard and nasty. Onto the sand.

It was full of blood.

I used to throw up blood when I bubbled time, but it had been days. Weeks.

"Beast? What's happening?"

Jane is sick. Jane may be dying.

Relief zipped through me like lightning. I wouldn't have to keep on. I thought about being sick. *It's the snake in the center of all things, isn't it?*

Jane is broken. Jane has darkness growing in her. Beast sent me a vision of my insides.

I have cancer, I thought, wonderingly.

Jane is dying. Jane has broken time. And time has broken Jane.

Well. How 'bout that.

The helo landed on the beach two hours after dawn.

I climbed on and accepted the ear protectors. Put them on and strapped myself in. Gave the pilot a thumb up and settled back to not enjoy the ride. I was weak and nauseous. Pretended to be fine. Eli met me at the landing site, took one look at my face, and grasped the bag I carried. Led the way to the armored SUV. Headed to HQ, which was where I told him to go. We rode in silence, his battle face on, giving nothing away. Midway there he said, "Babe."

"Don't," I said. "Please don't."

He nodded and threaded through traffic. Parked in front of HQ.

"I'll be just a minute," I said.

"I'll wait for you." The way he said it held overtones of, *I'll wait for you forever, no matter what.* I didn't reply to the tone. I didn't have forever. I opened the bag that had been waiting for me on the backseat and removed the small weapon. Stuck it in my waistband at my spine. Just in case. Picked up the vamp-killer and strapped it to my thigh. Stuck the Glob in a pocket. Also just in case. I shut the door.

HQ looked the same as I climbed the steps. The outer doors opened. The inner doors opened. The smell inside was different. No blood. No sex. No scent of fading funeral flowers or parchment. There were vamps here, sleeping, but not in great numbers and not the ones from before. Instead there was a long line of humans waiting. Wrassler limped toward me, his hands out, a welcoming smile on his face. I held up my hand to stop him. "Not now," I said softly.

Wrassler's face fell and he gave me a truncated nod before stepping back in line. No one frisked me. No one said anything about the weapons on my person. Everything was different.

Silently, I took the elevator to the basements, all the way to sub-five. I was armed with a fourteen-inch silver-plated-steel vamp-killer with a crosshatched handle, the Glob in my pocket, and a small .32 pistol loaded with silver-lead rounds. I didn't need anything else for this.

The doors opened. The lighting was low. Brute was sitting at the feet of the Son of Darkness. One of them, anyway. Joses looked pretty good for a heartless lump of vamp-meat. Stinkier. Hairier. Brute had been biting him enough. Joses was halfway to being a werewolf-vamp bag of bones.

"Hiya, Brute."

He panted at me, his white coat catching the low lights with an almost ethereal glow.

"Leo's in a box of blood. He isn't in charge anymore." I pulled the vamp-killer. Dropped the bag. "Okay with you if I finish this?"

Brute chuffed. Tilted his head, tongue lolling. He looked at Joses, his eyes staring at the vamp's wrists and ankles, where he hung, suspended on the wall. Brute chuffed what might have been a warning. Looked at me. Turned his massive head back to Joses and whined, a single plaintive note.

I walked past the white werewolf and positioned myself.

"You will not." The words grated out, harsh as stone on stone.

I looked at Joses. He was looking back at me. Eyes focused, black pupils in yellow orbs. Sane-ish. As sane as the old ones ever got. Talking. Giving orders.

"Say again?"

"You will not. I live. Forever."

"Yeah?" I reared back, the vamp-killer in a two-hand stance. Joses's shackles snapped. Shattered. Fell away. He surged off the wall, spider-fast, pushing, bowing, springing, leaping in explosive force. Right at me. Beneath the vamp-killer blade.

Time slowed into a battlefield intensity. I saw/smelled/ felt/heard the pop of displaced air. Vamp speed on meth, a rupture in reality. And he grabbed me. Claws sinking deep. Inside the vamp-killer's reach. Beast shoved into me, claws bursting from my fingertips, fangs ripping through my jaw.

Too late. Too late.

The Son of Darkness opened his mouth. Unhinged his jaw. I reared back, my claws piercing him. Shoving him away.

Foolish kit. Not defense. Must attack, Beast thought.

A werewolf roared. I jerked to the side. Not far enough. The SOD's five-inch fangs sank deep. But there was no pain. He was healed enough to have vamp saliva. *Analgesic,* I thought. His magic shot into me. Struck at my core, at the five-pointed magic that resided there. My

mind flickered on and off. All I could think was . . .
How . . . ? And then even that was gone.

Joses sucked deeply at my torn shoulder. Moved his
head to my throat. My blood felt heated and languid. My
muscles softened. My joints relaxed. My arms came up
around him.

Suddenly I was in my soul home. Lying on the damp,
cool gray stone. Staring up at the ceiling, domed overhead. Hayyel's wings fluttered where they rested, draped
down the walls.

Beast appeared over me, her golden eyes glowing. She
lay atop me, her cat warmth soothing. And then she slid
into me, falling through my soul, to the place where we
were one. And I was back in the basement. Things were
happening around me. Roars. The ground was shaking.
People were screaming.

Beast lifted my hand away from Joses. Slid it into my
pocket. Curled my fingers around the Glob. Beast eased
my hand out of the twisted cloth and raised my fist. She
pressed it into the wound on Joses's shoulder where my/
our claws had pierced him. Into his blood. The Glob that
held a shard of the Blood Cross and part of the spike of
Golgotha woke. Blazing hot. Attacked. Sudden as a
pouncing mountain lion. It gripped Joses's magic. Tore it
free. Joses stopped. Frozen.

The memories of Joses Santana opened. And I fell
into the sensation and person of Joses—Yosace, Bar-
Ioudas. I saw, I felt, I knew . . . *knew* . . . the moment the
two Sons of Darkness killed their sister and spilled her
blood onto the pile of bloody wood. Onto their father's
dead body. Chanted as she died. Chanted and spoke
wyrds so ancient, even Yosace didn't know the meaning.

Knew the moment the betrayer opened his eyes. Took
his first breath. And attacked.

Knew the feel of Ioudas Issachar's fangs buried in Joses's own throat.

Knew the moment the sons finally trapped their father
and chopped him into bits with a stolen Roman sword.

Knew the moment they walked the streets of Jerusalem and tasted the first kiss of blood.

Knew when they killed. Killed again. Innocent blood, so full of life.

Then hiding. Always hiding. Always running. Always going back and back and back again to the pile of bloody broken wood, the pile of the Blood Cross, that had given them this undeath.

Fleeing the Christians who sought to kill them.

Escaping the hell that the Romans brought upon the rebellious city. Taking the ones with whom they had shared their gift of undeath.

Reaching safety. Settling in Rome. Later in France. And later still in Spain. Traveling the world, from Africa to the steppes of what is now Russia and China. Drinking from the Khan who would change the world. Giving Genghis power and success in return for servitude and safety and enough humans to satisfy them. For centuries. Hundreds. Thousands. The power behind the conquest of the world. Then back to Europe. And—

The memories stopped. I returned to myself.

The Glob was so hot in my palm that I could smell the flesh there scorching. I blinked. Holding the Glob in his blood, I pressed the Son of Darkness away from me. Hands gripped his head and pulled back. Other fingers gripped his jaw and pulled down. I smelled Eli. He hadn't stayed in the SUV. Of course he hadn't.

The fangs of the Son of Darkness slid from the lower curve of my neck.

Beast rolled me over and to my feet. People backed away fast. I picked up the vamp-killer I had dropped when I embraced the SOD. I raised the blade and swept it down.

And took the head of the Son of Darkness, Joses Santana, Yosace Bar-Ioudas, the son of Judas Iscariot. There was almost no blood. The body quivered. Shook. The fingers clenched and opened. I held up the head. Its eyes blinked. Focused on me. "Huh," I said.

The lips moved, though there was no sound. "I live," Santana's head said.

I considered that.

Beast thought at me, *Vampire head is tasty.*

I did not want to know how she knew this. I looked over my shoulder. "Brute? You hungry?"

The werewolf stood and padded to me. Sniffed at the head of the creator of the vamps. Brute chuffed. Santana's mouth opened in horror, a silent scream. I tossed the head up into the air like a basketball. Brute leaped. Caught it in his fangs.

"When you're done"—I indicated the pulsing body on the floor—"be sure to clean up any mess." Brute chuffed again, muted through the hair of his dinner. "We don't want anything left to regrow." Brute nodded and dropped the head to his paws.

I looked around at the humans who stared at me in fear and horror. As if I was a monster. Which I was. All except Eli, who looked vaguely amused. To the others, I said, "Go back upstairs. Leave the wolf to his dinner. When he's done, burn the bones and scatter the ashes." They turned and fled.

I walked to the elevator and the doors closed behind Eli and me. My last glimpse of the SOD was Brute eating all the soft tissue of the face, in preparation to ripping off the jaw and eating the brains. I had been with Beast when she ate skulls and brains. I knew how it was done. Messy but effective. She sent me an image of Titus's head as she ate it. *Gack.* The elevator rose to the foyer, the two of us silent, me trying to decide what I needed to do next.

There was the undying heart in the hands of the NOLA witch coven. Wherever that was. I figured I could leave that to Eli.

I left the way I came in, but this time there was only Wrassler waiting. I stopped and shook his hand. He hugged me. I hugged back. Silent. Tears in his eyes. I stepped back and asked, "Del?"

Wrassler shook his head. "Her mother took her back to the mountains. She was buried there, in the family plot."

I blinked away the tears. "Jodi? Did she ever say yes?"

Wrassler beamed. "We're planning a June wedding."

"Congratulations!" I hugged him hard. Holding him close, so I couldn't see his face, I asked, "Leo?"

"Buried in the Pellissier mausoleum, beneath the new moon, with the blood of his enemies poured upon him, with the potion of blood he created from the Caruso vial. Buried with all honors and glory due to his name." Wrassler stopped, breathed in slowly. "He didn't rise with the full moon."

My heart clenched. But . . . Leo had given part of himself to me when I tasted his blood. I wondered what would happen if . . . I reached out with my mind, with my skinwalker magic, calling to him. *Leo? Are you there?*

But there was nothing. No answer. Not even a hint of a whisper of a breath of undeath. I shook my head and left HQ, Eli on my heels.

I heard the lock clack closed as I got into the car. Laid back my head.

Eli drove me to my freebie house. My house. My first home ever. I had the deed. I owned it outright. A fierce sense of possession washed over me. Then it rolled away like the surf on the island. I got out of the SUV and went inside. Alex rushed up and hugged me. I hugged him back, as if memorizing the way he felt against me, all bone and muscle and inches taller than when we first met. Eli gestured to him and the Kid stepped back.

"We'll catch up after dinner," Alex said. "I'm in the middle of security for your new clan home." I nodded and he stepped away.

Dropping off my gear, I walked around the house looking things over. Eli stood in the middle of the living room, watching, waiting. He said nothing, as I noticed the missing wall and the exposed fireplace. I could smell paint and fresh building materials.

I'd asked him once to see if he could find and restore the original fireplaces. This was my answer. While I hid on the island, he had found one, uncovered it, and repaired it, with a ceramic surround, a bronze facing, and a heavy Victorian-style mantel carved with curlicues and fleurs-de-lis. Beautifully restored. It was on the small wall between living room and kitchen. I'd never have thought about a fireplace there. I checked out the kitchen to see that we now had a copper farmhouse sink and commercial fridge, things Eli had been wanting. I checked out the laundry, which was unchanged, and followed him up the stairs. He had refinished the bathrooms, with sleek quartz countertops and new fixtures and fancy tile. My partner had been busy. I smiled at him to show I liked it.

A smile lit up his face and he led me up the new narrow staircase to the third floor.

It was amazing. The central space was vaulted and wood floored. The bedrooms in back—office spaces to make the housing and insurance companies happy—were finished. The bathroom was a tiny cubicle done up in marble and antique ceramic tiles.

I finally spoke. "This is gorgeous."

Eli nodded, his face full of compassion. "Babe."

I held up my hand and shook my head.

"But—"

I shook my head again. "Edmund?" I asked. Ed. Leo's heir. The vamp primo of the Dark Queen. Complicated. Just the way Leo wanted it.

"In Paris," Eli said. "As your emissary. Setting up a cabinet, establishing your power, sending out edicts in your name."

"Good. It'll be easy for him to step in when I abdicate." I walked away and down the stairs. Behind me I heard Eli talking on his cell, his tone frustrated.

I spent the day in my bedroom, moving money around, writing e-mails and letters—on real paper with a pen. Predominantly my abdication as emperor of the EuroVamps, dated to the coming full moon. Eddie Boy could have it. Sending texts. Appointing people to positions of power. Choosing two vamps as temporary heirs to the European Mithrans—Grégoire as heir, and Katherine as second heir. Seemed simple enough. If they didn't abdicate. Granting Ming of Glass status as Master of the City of Knoxville. Granting Lincoln Shaddock Master of the City of Asheville. This made sure Amy Lynn Brown was safe, in Clan Shaddock, protected by her now-powerful Blood Master. Trying to figure out how to ensure that Leo's newest werelion cub fosters were safe, but not sure how to do that. I ended up leaving that for Edmund to determine.

I also appointed the Youngers as coheirs of Clan Yellowrock. Gave them money and power to protect Molly and
Big Evan and my godchildren.

Kitssss, Beast whispered before falling silent again.
All Beast's kitssss. She had been oddly uncommunicative
since I returned to my human form. I didn't know what
her relative silence meant, but she wasn't missing; she was
still there inside with me, so I was okay with her silence.

Rereading the will I had signed months ago, a will that
left trusts for my godchildren, for Molly and Evan, for the
Youngers. Leaving everything else to the heirs of Clan
Yellowrock. I wasn't sure the office of Dark Queen could
be passed on, but if it could, it would go to the entire
NOLA witch coven. I left Bruiser all my magical items
and Bitsa—the things that held me here and gave me
power, and the one thing that spoke to me of freedom, my
panhead bastard Harley.

I sent a letter of intent to the B-twins, the Robere
brothers, who were the lawyers of the NOLA vamps, to
sue Raymond Micheika, the leader of all the weres on
earth (and especially the leader of the African weres, the
most politically powerful group). In the letter I accused
Raymond of treachery against Americans, on American
soil. I told the Roberes to proceed with legal papers in my
name, with any charges and grievances they could think
of, and asked them to send a copy of the paperwork to
whatever legal department in the U.S. government would
be most effective at keeping Raymond off U.S. soil. I
signed it, *the Dark Queen of the Mithrans and the Blood
Master of Clan Yellowrock of New Orleans.* I even signed
papers for the house that had once been Rousseau Clan
Home. It was big enough to be the Clan Home of Clan
Yellowrock, the official clan residence, and it was actually
two full-sized homes in one, perfect for clan business.
And it had a pool. I toured a few more houses online
while I was at it, and bought two more. Money wasn't a
problem. Not now. Not ever again. I talked to Bruiser on
the phone, loving the sound of his voice, loving the fact
that he loved me. His last words were, "Ed took the Lear-

jet, so I'm flying commercial. I'll be back from New York on the red-eye. Don't wait up. I'll crawl in beside you."

"I won't wait up," I promised.

I checked the news for the last weeks to discover that there had been a number of grisly deaths on the full moon—homeless men slashed to death with knives, throats slit. The grindys had been at work, killing people bitten by the rogue wolves, the new, fledgling werewolves the rogue pack had created. The news of the insane serial killer had hit the airwaves like a tsunami and then disappeared when the killings stopped. If the dead had been wealthy, the press would still be going nuts over it, but since they were poor and largely unidentified, the press had drifted quickly to other stories. *Typical*, I thought cynically. As well as I could tell, the rogue pack were all dead too. I wasn't sure why the grindys didn't kill all the werewolves and be done with it rather than letting the Bighorn pack survive and thrive. Maybe it was the fact that they had a leader and they didn't spread the were-taint. Maybe something else.

While I worked I packed. Quietly. Surreptitiously. Weeding through the things I now owned. Finding that I ended up with just enough to fit in Bitsa's saddlebags, which, oddly enough, was mostly just the clothes, boots, and weapons I used to travel with and a few of the smaller magical trinkets I wanted to keep.

An hour before dusk, I walked out of my room and through the house, hearing Alex in the shower, smelling roast in the oven. I eased outside. I was weaponed up. Dressed for the road and the cold weather. Riding leathers. Boots. I walked across the side porch.

Ed's fancy car was gone, just like so many things. I loaded Bitsa's saddlebags. Opened the wrought-iron side gate with its fleur-de-lis scrollwork at the top. Straddled my bike. Sat there, staring out through the gate.

"You not gonna say anything?" I asked.

Laconically, Eli said, "Figured that was your job, since you're the one running away from us."

I looked back. My partner was sitting in one of the

rusted metal chairs we had picked up in a junk place somewhere, the kind with a frame made of a single length of metal pipe, and that rocked back and forth as the metal gave and returned to normal. But he wasn't rocking. He was dressed in jeans and a zipped jacket. Boots. He looked good. Best brother I might ever have.

"I'll be back." *Liar, liar, pants on fire. I'll be dead*, I thought to myself. Didn't say it aloud. "I need some time."

He nodded, that minuscule motion that was all Eli. He stood. "You'll need these." He stepped off the porch and walked to me. In his hand were two small white boxes. I opened the first one to see the medicine bag that had once belonged to my father. Symbol of the life I had lost, the violence I had found. "Ayatas says you should open it."

Instead, I closed the box and Eli gave me the other one. In the bottom of the box was a stack of business cards. New. The logo at the top was of a crown stabbed through with two stakes. Below that were two lines.

JANE YELLOWROCK.

HAVE STAKES, WILL TRAVEL.

I smiled slightly and tucked a card into my jacket pocket. The boxes, I shoved into the saddlebag on top of my ammo and stakes. I tilted my head up at him. "I love you."

"I love you too, Babe."

"Tell Alex—" I stopped.

"I'll tell him," Eli said softly.

I rose up and dropped my weight down, kicking Bitsa to life. She spluttered for a while, so I pulled on my helmet. Adjusted the fit of the Benelli M4 so it didn't pinch my butt. Looked up at Eli. His eyes were intense, calm, so . . . alive. I smiled. He smiled—a real smile full of joy, of family.

I gave Bitsa some gas. Pulled along the two-rut drive and out onto the street. Gave her some more gas. And took off for I-59. And the road to home.

EPILOGUE

I stopped several times for gas, for fluids. No food. I couldn't keep anything down. I was getting sick fast. The cancer Beast had told me about was taking over. I could feel hard knots in my abdomen. I just hoped I'd get back to Appalachia in time to shift into her, so she could return to her beloved mountains. I wasn't sure we'd ever be able to be Jane again, but Beast could take care of herself.

It was well after midnight when I stopped at a Hampton Inn and Suites off of 459, the loop around Birmingham, my butt tired, my body cold and weary. I paid for a room and took a long hot shower. Dressed in sweats. Climbed into bed. Couldn't sleep. Belly hurting. The pain was kicking in.

At three forty-two I heard the rotors of a helicopter, distinctive, familiar. I lay in the dark, tears in my eyes. I hadn't wanted this. Hadn't wanted to make anyone else hurt. But I'd paid with a credit card. Of course I had. All along the route—Cokes, coffee, gas. Hadn't even thought about it. And there was the Kid. Probably mad as hell, cussing, probably drinking energy drinks as he traced my passage north.

The knock sounded at my door. I got up. Stopped to look at myself in the mirror. I looked like crap. Well, I was dying. So there was that.

I opened the door.

Bruiser was leaning against the doorjamb. Dressed the way I'd first seen him the very first time in New Orleans. Dark slacks. Dress boots. Crisp shirt. Dark jacket. "Hiya," I said.

Bruiser stared at me, as if memorizing my eyes, my mouth. But when he spoke, his voice was without inflection. "Soul visited. She says you're sick. She says you smell like cancer."

I took a slow breath. Watching him. "I'm dying. I'm guessing I have a few days. Two weeks at the most."

"You're heading back to the mountains. To the estate you bought today. Yesterday," he amended, his face giving nothing away. "You intend to shift to Beast and let her live out her natural life span."

"Pretty much."

"And you didn't think to share that with any of the people who love you?"

"I'd thought about it. A lot." But I'd been alone most of my life. I had figured to end it that way. Not knowing what else to say, I shrugged.

Bruiser moved into the room. I let him. Shut the door. Crossed my arms over my chest, knowing I looked defensive. Not able to care.

Bruiser sat on the end of my bed, feet planted, legs splayed, hands clasped loosely between them. He looked at me. Silence and time and a weird sensation of space built between us, though neither of us moved. "Do you want to die?" he asked. When I didn't answer, he said, "If you want to die, I'll get on Grégoire's Bell Huey and leave you to your business. But if you want to live, we have options. Well, one option."

I frowned at him. "I'm not doing chemo. My RNA and DNA are screwed up. I've seen how fast this stuff is growing. How aggressive it is. And I have a feeling chemo might kill what's left of the healthy cells faster than the cancer." The cancer was growing in a star-shaped pattern. The Vitruvian Man pattern of my magic. I pressed my middle, feeling the lower points of the star. *Magic cancer. Go, me.*

"Chemo isn't on the list."

"Onorio magic?"

"Onorio magic kills and tames. My magic can't heal. Not you. Not anyone."

I frowned harder. "So what's your plan?"

He shook his head. "Do you want to live or not?"

Tears spilled over. I nodded, the motion jerky. "Yes."

"With me?"

I nodded again.

Bruiser's smile appeared, so full of relief and joy that tears prickled at my lids. Gently he said, "Come live with me, and be my love, / And we will some new pleasures prove, / Of golden sands, and crystal brooks, / With silken lines, and silver hooks." When I frowned harder he laughed and shook his head. Got up and opened the door.

Outside, leaning against the wall opposite, stood Ayatas FireWind. His hair was loose, a silken wave, his body relaxed. "May I enter your house, *e-igido*?"

I nodded. He entered and stood before me, his feet spread, his body rooted. "Where is the box Eli gave you before you left New Orleans? The box with our father's medicine pouch in it."

I lifted the box from the dresser and gave it to him. I wouldn't need it anymore. Dead people didn't need mementoes of the past. They were, themselves, mementoes of the past.

"Do you remember the note that said there was something in it if you ever needed it?" Aya asked.

I nodded.

"Did Eli Younger not tell you to open the pouch?"

I nodded. "I didn't."

"And do you remember the story I told about the soldier you stabbed on the Trail of Tears?"

I nodded again.

"*Uni Lisi* instructed me not to tell you this unless you

needed to know, or if you asked. You didn't ask. I would have told you had I known you were sick." I watched my brother, his face calm, inscrutable as an Elder of the Tsalagi. "When you stabbed the soldier, he hit you very hard. Enough to break bone. To cause you to bleed great amounts of blood." He opened the box and removed the medicine bag, handling it so carefully that the dry-rotted edges didn't even dust away. "*Uni Lisi* put this in your father's medicine bag that day."

Gently he pulled out a leaf-wrapped something, the leaf cracking and falling to the floor, desiccated into nothing. Inside was a short length of broken bone and three teeth, a canine, an incisor, and one molar. Whole and complete. Child's teeth. I blinked. The memory came back to me, a vision of a fist rising to my face. Fast. Powerful. Violent. The sensation of pain exploding through me. A bone-breaking agony that tore through my jaw as the memory forced its way to the surface. My breathing sped up. Then the memory fell away, leaving a place of darkness where it had been only a moment before, bright and vivid. I didn't speak, staring at the small bit of bone and teeth.

"When you attacked the white man on the Trail of Tears, he hit you," Aya said. "He knocked out your teeth. Broke out part of your jaw. *Uni Lisi* gathered it up and kept it, even after she forced you into the bobcat and sent you into the snow." His golden eyes glinted at me. "They're your teeth. It's the only way she could think to convince you who you are. Who I am. She said that you'd remember. That you'd know."

I remembered, but . . . I also knew the depths of revenge and treachery. Uncertainly I asked, "You're sure? It's mine?"

"That is what the Keeper of the Secrets of the Skin-walkers said."

I accepted the small, fractured length of bone and teeth, holding it on my outstretched hand. Holding a memento of the before times. A piece of myself.

Bruiser asked, "Do you think there might be enough genetic material?"

When I didn't answer, Bruiser said, "Can you use the genes in these teeth to shift into a healed you?"

I considered them. "I don't know. I'd likely be five years old. *If* there was enough viable genetic material to find a pattern."

"Maybe. Or maybe you can merge the DNA with your own. Clean yours up."

I looked at Bruiser. And let a small smile onto my face.

"Will you try?" he asked. "I have searched for you all of my life. I don't want to lose you now."

"Yes," I said softly. "I'll try."

Relief flashed across his face, like the sun peeking between storm clouds, and quickly gone. "Good. Will you marry me? The Roberes will write up a binding prenuptial agreement to protect your holdings and your status as Dark Queen."

My throat hurt, but I managed wryly, "It's immoral, and against the law, even in Alabama, to marry a five-year-old child."

"If you shift into a child, then I'll wait until you grow up. I'll wait as long as it takes."

Aya closed my fingers over the bone and teeth. "I can't promise anything," I said. "But I'll try to heal my body."

"And you'll marry me?"

"I will. But not until we see if this thing works," I said. Bruiser's face fell. I tucked the teeth and bone back into the medicine bag. Closed it up in the white box.

"So what now?" I asked them. "I'm heading to the mountains, to Robbinsville, North Carolina. I'd planned to shift there and let my Beast wander the mountains." And maybe track down *Uni Lisi*, Sixmankiller, the evil woman who had set me on this blood path, and kill her. Didn't say that.

"We have a Bell Huey waiting in the parking lot," Bruiser said. "Room enough for us three. And the bikes. Mine is in there already, waiting for Bitsa. You can get to the mountains in style. And fast."

I nodded, thinking, feeling the paper of the white box in my fingers, the hope inside.

Hate helo-copter, Beast said.

I know, I thought back. *But Beast is best hunter. Beast can hunt for a way for me to live.*

She thought back at me, *The I/we of Beast is not prey. We can find a trail through dense brush that is Jane's sickness. We can defeat timewalking death.*

Yeah. We are. We can. We can do this.

"Okay," I said. "Let's make this happen."

Read on for an excerpt of the first book
in Faith Hunter's Soulwood series,

BLOOD OF THE EARTH

Available now in paperback!

Edgy and not sure why, I carried the basket of laundry off the back porch. I hung my T-shirts and overalls on the front line of my old-fashioned solar clothes dryer, two long skirts on the outer line, and what my mama called my intimate attire on the line between, where no one could see them from the driveway. I didn't want another visit by Brother Ephraim or Elder Ebenezer about my wanton ways. Or even another courting attempt from Joshua Purdy. Or worse, a visit from Ernest Jackson Jr., the preacher. So far I'd kept him out of my house, but there would come a time when he'd bring help and try to force his way in. It was getting tiresome having to chase churchmen off my land at the business end of a shotgun, and at some point God's Cloud of Glory Church would bring enough reinforcements that I couldn't stand against them. It was a battle I was preparing for, one I knew I'd likely lose, but I would go down fighting, one way or another.

The breeze freshened, sending my wet skirts rippling as if alive on the line where they hung. Red, gold, and brown leaves skittered across the three acres of newly cut grass. Branches overhead cracked, clacked, and groaned with the wind, leaves rustling as if whispering some dread tiding. The chill fall air had been perfect for birdsong; squirrels had been racing up and down the trees, stealing nuts and hiding them for the coming winter. I'd seen a big black bear this morning chewing on acorns halfway up the hill.

Standing in the cool breeze, I studied my woods, listening, feeling, tasting the unease that had prickled at my flesh for the last few months, ever since Jane Yellowrock had come visiting and turned my life upside down. She was the one responsible for the recent repeated visits by the churchmen. The Cherokee vampire hunter was the one who had brought all the changes, even if it hadn't been intentional. She had come hunting a missing vampire, and because she was good at her job—maybe the best ever—she had succeeded. She had also managed to save over a hundred children from God's Cloud.

Maybe it had been worth it all—helping all the children—but I was the one paying the price, not her. She was long gone and I was alone in the fight for my life. Even the woods knew things were different.

Sunlight dappled the earth; cabbages, gourds, pumpkins, and winter squash were bursting with color in the garden. A muscadine vine running up the nearest tree, tangling in the branches, was dropping the last of the ripe fruit. I smelled my wood fire on the air and hints of that apple-crisp chill that meant a change of seasons, the sliding toward a hard, cold autumn. I tilted my head, listening to the wind, smelling the breeze, feeling the forest through the soles of my bare feet. There was no one on my property except the wild critters—creatures who belonged on Soulwood land—and nothing else that I could sense. But the hundred fifty acres of woods bordering the flatland around the house, up the steep hill and down into the gorge, had been whispering all day. Something was not right.

In the distance, I heard a crow call a warning, sharp with distress. The squirrels ducked into hiding, suddenly invisible. The feral cat I had been feeding darted under the shrubs, her black head and multicolored body fading into the shadows. The trees murmured restlessly.

I didn't know what it meant, but I listened anyway. I always listened to my woods, and the gnawing, whispering sense of danger, injury, and damage was like sandpaper abrading my skin, making me jumpy, disturbing my sleep, even if I didn't know what it was.

I reached out to it, to the woods, reached with my mind, with my magic. Silently, I asked it, *What? What is it?*

There was no answer. There never was. But as if the forest knew that it had my attention, the wind died and the whispering leaves fell still. I caught my breath at the strange hush, not even daring to blink. But nothing happened. No sound, no movement. After an uncomfortable length of time, I lifted the empty wash basket and stepped away from the clotheslines, turning and turning, my feet on the cool grass, my gaze cast up and inward, but I could sense no direct threat despite the chill bumps rising on my skin. *What?* I asked. An eerie fear grew in me, racing up my spine like spiders with sharp tiny feet. Something was coming. Something that reminded me of Jane, but subtly different. Something was coming that might hurt me. Again. My woods knew.

From down the hill I heard the sound of a vehicle climbing the mountain's narrow, single-lane, rutted road. It wasn't the clang of Ebenezer's rattletrap Ford truck, or the steady drone of Joshua's newer Toyota long bed. It wasn't the high-pitched motor of a hunter's all-terrain vehicle. It was a car, straining up the twisty Deer Creek mountain.

My house was the last one, just below the crest of the hill. The wind whooshed down again, icy and cutting, a downdraft that bowed the trees. They swayed in the wind, branches scrubbing. Sighing. Muttering, too low to hear.

It could be a customer making the drive to Soulwood for my teas or veggies or herbal mixes. Or it could be some kind of conflict. The woods said it was the latter. I trusted my woods.

I raced back inside my cabin, dropping the empty bas-

ket, placing John's old single-shot bolt-action shotgun
near the refrigerator under a pile of folded blankets. His
lever-action carbine .30–30 Winchester went near the
front window. I shoved the small Smith & Wesson .32 into
the bib of my coveralls, hoping I didn't shoot myself if I
had to draw it fast. I picked up the double-barrel break-
action shotgun and checked the ammo. Both barrels held
three-inch shells. The contact area of the latch was worn
and needed to be replaced, but at close range I wasn't
going to miss. I might dislocate my shoulder, but if I hit
them, the trespassers would be a while in healing too.

I debated for a second on switching out the standard
shot shells for salt or birdshot, but the woods' disharmony
seemed to be growing, a particular and abrasive itch
under my skin. I snapped the gun closed and pulled back
my long hair into an elastic to keep it out of my way.

Peeking out the blinds, I saw a four-door sedan coming to a stop beside John's old Chevy C10 truck. Two people inside, a man and a woman.

Strangers, I thought. Not from God's Cloud of Glory,
the church I'd grown up in. Not a local vehicle. And no
dogs anymore to check them out for me with noses and
senses humans no longer had. Just three small graves at
the edge of the woods and a month of grief buried with
them.

A man stepped out of the driver's side, black haired,
dark eyed. Maybe Cherokee or Creek if he was a mountain native, though his features didn't seem tribal. I'd
never seen a Frenchman or a Spaniard, so maybe one of
those Mediterranean countries. He was tall, maybe six
feet, but not dressed like a farmer. More citified, in black
pants, starched shirt, tie, and jacket. He had a cell phone
in his pocket, sticking out just a little. Western boots, old
and well cared for. There was something about the way he
moved, feline and graceful. Not a farmer or a God's
Cloud preacher. Not enough bulk for the first one, not
enough righteous determination in his expression or
bearing for the other. But something said he wasn't a customer here to buy my herbal teas or fresh vegetables.

He opened the passenger door for the other occupant

and a woman stepped out. Petite, with black skin and wildly curly, long black hair. Her clothes billowed in the cool breeze and she put her face into the wind as if sniffing. Like the man, her movements were nimble, like a dancer's, and somehow feral, as if she had never been tamed, though I couldn't have said why I got that impression.

Around the house, my woods moaned in the sharp wind, branches clattering like old bones, anxious, but I could see nothing about the couple that would say danger. They looked like any other city folk who might come looking for Soulwood Farm, and yet . . . not. Different. As they approached the house, they passed the tall length of flagpole in the middle of the raised beds of the front yard and started up the seven steps to the porch. And then I realized why they moved and felt all wrong. There was a weapon bulge at the man's shoulder, beneath his jacket. In a single smooth motion, I braced the bolt-action shotgun against my shoulder, rammed open the door, and pointed the business end of the gun at the trespassers.

"Whaddya want?" I demanded, drawing on my childhood God's Cloud dialect. They came to a halt at the third step, too close for me to miss, too far away for them to disarm me safely. The man raised his hands like he was asking for peace, but the little woman hissed. She drew back her lips in a snarl and growled at me. I knew cats. This was a cat. A cat in human form—a werecat of some kind. A devil, according to the Church. I trained the barrel on her, midcenter, just like John had showed me the first time he'd put the gun in my hands. As I aimed, I took a single step so my back was against the doorjamb to keep me from getting bowled over or from breaking a shoulder when I fired.

"Paka, no," the man said. The words were gentle, the touch to her arm tender. I had never seen a man touch a woman like that, and my hands jiggled the shotgun in surprise before I caught myself. The woman's snarl subsided and she leaned into the man, just like one of my cats might. His arm went around her, and he smoothed her hair back, watching me as I watched them. Alert, taking in everything about me and my home, the man lifted his nose in the air to sniff the scents of my land, his delicate nasal folds widening and contracting. Alien. So alien, these two.

"What do you want?" I asked again, this time with no Church accent, and with the grammar I'd learned from the city-folk customers at the vegetable stand and from reading my once-forbidden and much-loved library books.

"I'm Special Agent Rick LaFleur, with PsyLED, and this is Paka. Jane Yellowrock sent us to you, Ms. Ingram," the man said.

Of course this new problem was related to Jane. Nothing in my whole life had gone right since she darkened my door.